THE DOOMED CITY

THE DOOMED CITY

ARKADY AND BORIS
STRUGATSKY

Translated by Andrew Bromfield

CHICAGO
REVIEW
PRESS

Published by Chicago Review Press Incorporated
814 North Franklin Street
Chicago, IL 60610
ISBN 978-1-61373-596-1 (cloth)
ISBN 978-1-61374-993-7 (paperback) ·

This publication was effected under the auspices of the Mikhail Prokhorov Foundation TRANSCRIPT Programme to Support Translations of Russian Literature.

Library of Congress Cataloging-in-Publication Data
Names: Strugaëtìskiæi, Arkadiæi, 1925–1991, author. | Strugaëtìskiæi, Boris,
    1933–2012, author. | Bromfield, Andrew, translator.
Title: The doomed city / Arkady and Boris Strugatsky ; translated by Andrew
    Bromfield.
Other titles: Grad obrechennyæi. English
Description: Chicago: Published by Chicago Review Press Incorporated, 2016.
Identifiers: LCCN 2016009300 (print) | LCCN 2016010274 (ebook) | ISBN
    9781613735961 (hardback) | ISBN 9781613749937 (pbk.) | ISBN
    9781613749944 (PDF edition) | ISBN 9781613749968 (EPUB edition) |
    ISBN 9781613749951 (Kindle edition)
Classification: LCC PG3476.S78835 G7313 2016 (print) | LCC PG3476.S78835
    (ebook) | DDC 891.73/44—dc23
LC record available at http://lccn.loc.gov/2016009300

Typesetting: Nord Compo

Printed in the United States of America
5 4 3 2 1

CONTENTS

FOREWORD: THE EXPERIMENT

BY DMITRY GLUKHOVSKY

No Western science fiction writer, either American or European, has ever been as famous as the Strugatsky brothers were in the USSR. In the 1970s, whenever their latest book appeared, with an initial print run of only 500,000, only the truly fortunate were able to read it immediately. In 1979, Tarkovsky's film *Stalker*, based on the Strugatskys' *Roadside Picnic*, would finally win them recognition from the Soviet intelligentsia, and *The Enchanters* (1982), a screen adaptation of their story of magic *Monday Starts on Saturday*, would soon become an all-time audience favorite. But well before that, a long queue of relatives, friends, and work colleagues immediately formed for each one of those half-million books. Nobody found this daunting. We were used to having to stand in line and wait for the most valuable things. A month for a book, five years for a car, ten years for an apartment . . .

Of course, the difference was not merely in how many people knew the Strugatskys. The Strugatskys were known to the entire reading public of the Soviet Union, but there are also Western science fiction writers known to almost everyone.

The difference is in the attitude.

In the West, science fiction was always more the domain of dreamers. Science fiction literature filled a niche that it still fills to this day—a niche, moreover, that is growing narrower with every year that passes.

But in the USSR it became the absolutely genuine mainstream. The Communist Party and the government were implementing a grandiose project to remodel society, the state, the individual, and the entire world all at once—a project so fantastic that in comparison the most audacious of writers' fantasies seemed to be no more than a forecast of what was coming tomorrow. Standard Soviet science fiction—and the Strugatskys' early prose—transported us into the future promised by the ideologists: a future that was just and bright; a future in which communism had triumphed and peace had reigned on Earth for a long time already, Russian had become the language of international dialog, and all the dramatic events unfolded far out on the remote boundaries of the galaxy, to which earthlings carried progress and prosperity.

In the USSR the present day was always hard, but the deprivations seemed justified: all of us, as a country, were simply standing in line for a happy tomorrow. And science fiction writers showed us what was waiting for us there, at the radiant shop counter of destiny, in the communist paradise. They were obliged to show it: if you went up on tiptoe, you could see the front end of the queue. In the early 1960s, Khrushchev promised the advent of communism by 1980. Five years for a car, ten years for an apartment, twenty years for paradise . . . It turned out that we could get there simply by staying alive. In paradise, rationality and humanism would be triumphant. Everything there would be honest and just. In paradise, it was explained to us, absolutely everything would be free; society would take from each according to his abilities and give to each according to his needs. This was a plan that we were eager to believe in. And we tried to believe in it as much as we could.

The Strugatskys tried too. Having grown up in wartime Leningrad, they knew and remembered the price we had to pay for victory in the war, the price we paid for "the construction projects of the age," and the severity the shepherds were obliged to display if the flock they were driving along suddenly balked and refused to follow the trail to the Garden of Eden. But at the time it seemed that the end was simply too great and magnificent to ponder over the means.

In fact, any pondering could really only be done in the kitchen, among family and friends. And although in Khrushchev's and Brezhnev's time they didn't shoot people for their doubts, although the purges were condemned and the cult of Stalin's personality was debunked, the newspaper *Pravda* and Gosteleradio (the state television and radio service) were the only ones allowed to do the debunking, and then only precisely as far as was necessary within the limits of the clandestine infighting between the bulldogs of the Politburo.

Of course, *Pravda*, like the rest of the press, was not merely under the control of the state, it was the state's advance guard, its assault team. And so-called serious literature was another assault team of the same kind. The novels and stories that were published naturally performed precisely delineated political and social tasks: the heroic glorification of labor and military service, the depiction of everyday Soviet happiness, and the subtle interconnections between personal relations and relations of production. Everything else—from Daniil Kharms to Bulgakov, and from Pasternak to Solzhenitsyn, was not recognized as literature, as if it didn't even exist at all. Writers were not supposed to create but to serve. To color in the sketches dashed off by the Communist Party ideologists.

Science fiction, however, possessed greater freedom in this respect. After all, it wasn't about the present day and it wasn't about the Soviet Union. It didn't express any doubt that communism would triumph in the foreseeable future. It apparently didn't stick its nose into current business, but was always talking about something distant and abstract. So the demands made of it were different, gentler. But even so, there were demands: science fiction was no less subject to censorship than everything else that was published on paper.

Time passed, the country was still dawdling in the queue, and the shop counter selling happiness and justice was fading into the hazy future. Khrushchev, who had promised everyone communism within a lifetime, was toppled, and those who replaced him limited themselves to granting people the ownership of plots of land, each six hundred square meters, so that they could build dachas on them. Tomorrow refused to arrive; it kept on being postponed until the day after tomorrow, owing to technical difficulties. People started whispering uneasily in the queue. And as the leaders of the country grew old and relapsed into senility, the whispering grew louder. It was becoming clear that we were standing in the wrong queue. And the most frightening thing was that we might *always* have been standing in the wrong queue.

In the Strugatskys' work, too, the whispering became more and more audible through the fanfares of lines proclaiming the happy communist future on Earth. Certainly, everything on Earth was still hunky-dory and all for free, and everyone spoke Russian, but events taking place in the troubled outskirts of the galaxy sometimes suggested a different reading of the current editorial in *Pravda*.

In *The Doomed City*, everything apparently happens somewhere that isn't Earth, and not even on a different planet but in a special world—a hermetic world that is located outside time and space. Its characters have been plucked out of real life, but from various countries and various times in the twentieth century. Here we have a British colonel of World War I vintage, we have a German soldier who did his fighting in World War II, we have the "Soviet man" Andrei, coopted from the 1950s, and an American college professor from the 1960s. They all seem to speak the same language, but that language isn't Russian. Abducted from their own familiar earthly lives, times, and cultures, they have been transported to the City, where they have become the subjects of the Experiment, which has no beginning or end, while its goal and its meaning are kept secret from the participants, who are constantly subjected to various trials. No one, in fact, has any intention at all of keeping the subjects advised about the tests that are being carried out. The organizers of the Experiment look like ordinary people, just as officials of the Communist Party and case officers from the security services did—they smile just as gently and call for patience just as earnestly. And all the inhabitants of the City show patience.

The Doomed City was completed in 1972 but not published in full until sixteen years later, after the beginning of perestroika. It is surprising that it was published even then, because the allusion to the Soviet Union here is so transparent that there was reason to fear, not only for the Strugatskys but also for the censors who allowed the book to see print.

Never mind the fact that it is not only inhabitants of the former Russian Empire who are enlisted to the City, that there are foreigners there too. Never mind that the regime there changes, and in some ways this City also resembles the West—perhaps even more than it resembles the Soviet Union. Never mind that the Soviet Union also exists in this book in its own right, thereby testifying that it is not the City and the City is not it. All these defensive ruses are disavowed by the theme of the endless Experiment on living people.

The Strugatskys, in company with the entire country, were searching for an answer to the questions "What for?" "What do I need this for?" "What do they treat us like this for?" But as the final experimenters died out who might possibly have still remembered the purpose for which the Experiment had been undertaken, any hope of receiving an answer faded away. Our sacrifices and our deprivations could no longer buy us a ticket for admission to the Garden of Eden. At some point meaningful action had been transformed into eviscerated ritual, into a cargo cult; we were simply idly plodding around in circles. This queue had no beginning and no end. It was an ouroboros, with its own tail firmly grasped in its own teeth.

That is what I would have written about *The Doomed City*, my favorite book by the Strugatskys, a year ago.

But during that year, after several visits to their home city of St. Petersburg, I realized something. The City is not an abstraction. It is *this* city, Leningrad–Petrograd–St. Petersburg, built among the swamps, at record speed, on human bones, by decree of the czar, and destined to be the capital. It is this city, somber and dank, not designed for human inhabitation but obeying the order to gallantly stand and obstinately sparkle through the mist and the rust. It is this city—the "cradle of the revolution," the arena of the Bolshevik coup, the city that survived the interminable Nazi blockade, the city that the economical Germans cut off from supply lines but didn't storm, so that its inhabitants would all starve to death for themselves. But they survived and didn't surrender, although they were sometimes forced to eat each other, while the Soviet army was busy with more important business elsewhere. That wasn't the first experiment to be carried out on them, and it wasn't the last.

This was the discovery I made during the last year: the inhabitants of the thrice-renamed St. Petersburg had always called it what they still call it today—simply "the City." They love it desperately, and the more they have to suffer for it, the more they love it. The Strugatskys loved it, of course. But how do you honestly tell people about such a love?

In the West there is simply no need for the kind of science fiction that we had: you already have enough space without it to discuss the fate and fortunes of your own countries and your own peoples. "Serious" literature, for instance. Not to mention talk shows. But in a country where the main newspaper is called *Truth* precisely because it is crammed to overflowing with lies, there comes a point at which science fiction is transformed into a means for at least hinting at the true state of affairs. What people expected from the Strugatskys were genuine prophecies. The difference from the West was not only that millions of people stood in line for their books but also *what* those millions tried to find in the Strugatskys' novels. And what they found.

Because the Strugatskys' prophecies often came true. And weren't they the first who dared to state on paper that the City was doomed?

THE DOOMED CITY

Hastily the vicious pike
Called the small carp through his mike.
"Little carplings, how's your day?"
"Thanks, we're doing quite OK."

—Valentin Kataev, *Radiogiraffe*

. . . I know thy works, and thy labour, and
thy patience, and how thou canst not bear
them which are evil: and thou hast tried
them which say they are apostles, and are
not, and hast found them liars . . .

—The Revelation of Saint John
the Divine (The Apocalypse)

PART I

THE
GARBAGE
COLLECTOR

1

The trash cans were rusty and battered, and the lids had come loose, so there were scraps of newspaper poking up from under them and potato peels dangling down. They were like the bills of slovenly pelicans that are none too picky about their food. The cans looked way too heavy to lift, but in fact, working in tandem with Wang, it was a breeze to jerk a can like that up toward Donald's outstretched hands and set it on the edge of the truck's lowered sideboard. You just had to watch out for your fingers. And after that you could adjust your mittens and take a few breaths through your nose while Donald walked the can farther in on the back of the truck and left it there.

The damp chill of nighttime breathed in through the wide-open gates, and under the archway a naked, yellow lightbulb swayed on a wire that was furred with grime. In its light Wang's face looked like the face of a man with a chronic case of jaundice, but Donald's face was invisible in the shadow of his wide-brimmed cowboy hat. The chipped and peeling gray walls were furrowed by horizontal slashes and adorned with obscene, life-size depictions of women. Dark clumps of dusty cobwebs dangled from the vaulting, and standing beside the door of the caretaker's lodge was a disorderly crowd of the empty bottles and stewed-fruit jars that Wang collected, carefully sorted, and handed in for recycling . . .

When there was only one trash can left, Wang took a shovel and a broom and started sweeping up the trash left on the asphalt surface.

"Ah, stop scrabbling around, Wang," Donald exclaimed irritably. "You scrabble around that way every time. It's still not going get any cleaner, is it?"

3

"A caretaker should be a sweeper," Andrei remarked didactically, twirling the wrist of his right hand and focusing on his sensations: it seemed to him that he had slightly strained a tendon.

"They'll only make it all filthy again, won't they?" Donald said with loathing. "Before we've even turned around, they'll foul it up worse than before."

Wang tipped the trash into the last can, tamped it down with the shovel, and slammed the lid shut. "Now we can do it," he said, glancing around the arched passage. The entrance was clean now. Wang looked at Andrei and smiled. Then he looked up at Donald and said, "I'd just like to remind you—"

"Come on, come on!" Donald shouted impatiently.

One-two. Andrei and Wang lifted the can. Three-four. Donald caught the can, grunted, gasped, and lost his grip. The can lurched over and crashed down onto the asphalt on its side. Garbage flew out across ten meters as if it had been shot from a cannon. Actively disgorging as it went, the can clattered into the courtyard. The reverberating echo spiraled up to the black sky between the walls.

"God al-fucking-mighty and the Holy Spirit," said Andrei, who had barely managed to leap out of the way. "Damn your fumblefingers!"

"I just wanted to remind you," Wang said meekly, "that one handle's broken off this can."

He took the broom and shovel and set to work, and Donald squatted on the edge of the truck bed and lowered his hands between his knees. "Dammit . . ." he muttered in a dull voice. "Damned mean trick."

Something had clearly been wrong with him for the last few days, and on this night in particular. So Andrei didn't start telling him what he thought about professors and their ability to do real work. He went to get the can and then, when he got back to the truck, he took off his mittens and pulled out his cigarettes. The stench from the open can was unbearable, so he lit up quickly and only then offered Donald one. Donald shook his head without speaking. His mood needed a lift. Andrei flung the burned match into the can and said, "Once upon a time in a little town there lived two night-soil men—father and son. There weren't any sewers there, only pits full of slurry. And they scooped that shit out with a bucket and poured it into their barrel, and what's more, the father, as the more experienced specialist, went down into the pit, and the son handed the bucket down to him from above. Then one day the son lost his grip on the bucket and dumped it back on his old man. Well, his old man wiped himself down, looked up at him, and said bitterly, 'You're a total screwup, a real lunkhead. No good for anything. You'll be stuck up there your whole life.'"

He was expecting Donald to smile, at least. Donald was generally a cheerful individual, sociable—he never got downhearted. There was something of the combat-veteran-turned-student about him. But this time Donald only cleared his throat and said in a dull voice, "You can't shovel out all the cesspits."

And Wang, scrabbling beside the can, reacted in a way that was really strange. He suddenly asked in a curious voice, "So what does it cost where you're from?"

"What does what cost?" asked Andrei, puzzled.

"Shit. Is it expensive?"

Andrei chuckled uncertainly. "Well, how can I put it . . . It depends whose it is."

"So you've got different kinds there then?" Wang asked in amazement. "It's all the same where I'm from. So whose shit is most expensive where you're from?"

"Professors'," Andrei replied immediately. He simply couldn't resist it.

"Ah!" Wang tipped another shovel-load into the can and nodded. "I get it. But out in the country there weren't any professors, so we only had one price: five yuan a bucket. That's in Szechuan. But in Kiangsi, for instance, prices ran up to seven or even eight yuan a bucket."

Andrei finally realized this was serious. He suddenly felt an urge to ask if it was true that when a Chinaman was invited to dinner, he was obliged to crap on his host's vegetable plot afterward—but, of course, it felt too awkward to ask about that.

"Only how things are now where I'm from, I don't know," Wang continued. "I wasn't living out in the country at the end . . . But why is professors' shit more expensive where you're from?"

"I was joking," Andrei said guiltily. "No one even trades in that stuff where I'm from."

"Yes they do," said Donald. "You don't even know that, Andrei."

"And that's yet another thing you *do* know," Andrei snapped.

Only a month ago he would have launched into a furious argument with Donald. It annoyed him immensely that again and again the American kept telling them things about Russia that Andrei didn't even have a clue about. Back then, Andrei was sure that Donald was simply bluffing him or repeating Hearst's spiteful tittle-tattle: "Take that garbage from Hearst and shove it!" he used to yell, shrugging it all off. But then that jerk Izya Katzman had appeared, and Andrei stopped arguing; he just snarled back. God only knew where they'd picked it all up from. And he explained his own helplessness by the fact that he'd come here from the year 1951, and these two were from '67.

"You're a lucky man," Donald said suddenly, getting up and moving toward the trash cans beside the driver's cabin.

Andrei shrugged and, in an effort to rid himself of the bad taste left by this conversation, put on his mittens and started shoveling up the stinking trash, helping Wang. Well, so I don't know, he thought. It's a big deal, shit. And what do you know about integral equations? Or Hubble's constant, say? Everyone has something he doesn't know . . .

Wang was stuffing the final remains of the trash into the can when the neatly proportioned figure of police constable Kensi Ubukata appeared in the gateway from the street. "This way, please," he said over his shoulder to someone, and saluted Andrei with two fingers. "Greetings, garbage collectors!"

A girl stepped out of the darkness of the street into the circle of yellow light and stopped beside Kensi. She was very young, no more than about twenty, and really small, only up to the little policeman's shoulder. She was wearing a coarse sweater with an extremely wide neck and a short, tight skirt. Thick lipstick made her lips stand out vividly against her pale, boyish face, and her long blonde hair reached down to her shoulders.

"Don't be frightened," Kensi told her with a polite smile. "They're only our garbage collectors. Perfectly harmless in a sober state . . . Wang," he called. "This is Selma Nagel, a new girl. Orders are to put her in your building, in number 18. Is 18 free?"

Wang walked over to him, removing his mittens on the way. "Yes," he said. "It's been free for a long time. Hello, Selma Nagel. I'm the caretaker—my name's Wang. If you need anything, that's the door to the caretaker's lodge, you come here."

"Let me have the key," Kensi said, and saluted again. "Come on, I'll show you the way," he said to the girl.

"No need," she said wearily. "I'll find it myself."

"As you wish," Kensi said, and saluted again. "Here is your suitcase."

The girl took the suitcase from Kensi and the key from Wang, tossed her head, and set off across the asphalt, clattering her heels and walking straight at Andrei.

He stepped back to let her past. As she walked by, he caught a strong smell of perfume and some other kind of fragrance too. And he carried on gazing after her as she walked across the circle of yellow illumination. Her skirt was really short, just a bit longer than her sweater, her legs were bare and white—to Andrei they seemed to glow as she walked out from under the archway into the yard—and in that darkness all he could see were her white sweater and flickering white legs.

Then a door creaked, screeched, and crashed, and after that Andrei mechanically took out his cigarettes again and lit up, imagining those delicate white legs walking up the stairs, step by step . . . smooth calves, dimples under the knees, enough to drive you crazy . . . He saw her climbing higher and higher, floor after floor, and stopping in front of the door of apartment 18, directly opposite apartment 16 . . . *Dam-naa-tion*, I ought to change the bedsheets at least; I haven't changed them for three weeks, the pillowcase is as gray as a foot rag . . . But what was her face like? Well, I'll be damned, I don't remember anything about what her face looked like. All I remember are the legs.

He suddenly realized that no one was saying anything, not even the married man Wang, and at that moment Kensi started speaking. "I have a first cousin once removed, Colonel Maki. A former colonel of the former imperial army. At first he was Mr. Oshima's adjutant and he spent two years in Berlin. Then he was appointed our acting military attaché in Czechoslovakia, and he was there when the Germans entered Prague . . ."

Wang nodded to Andrei. They lifted the can with a jerk and successfully shunted it onto the back of the truck.

". . . And then," Kensi continued at a leisurely pace, lighting up a cigarette, "he fought for a while in China, somewhere in the south, I think it was, down Canton way. And then he commanded a division that landed on the Philippines, and he was one of the organizers of the famous 'march of death,' with five thousand American prisoners of war—sorry, Donald . . . And then he was sent to Manchuria and appointed head of the Sakhalin fortified region, where, as it happens, in order to preserve secrecy he herded eight thousand Chinese workers into a mine shaft and blew it up—sorry, Wang . . . And then he was taken prisoner by the Russians, and instead of hanging him or handing him over to the Chinese—which is the same thing—all they did was lock him up for ten years in a concentration camp . . ."

While Kensi was telling them all this, Andrei had time to clamber up onto the back of the truck, help Donald line up the cans there, raise the sideboard and secure it, jump back down onto the ground, and give Donald a cigarette, and now the three of them were standing in front of Kensi and listening to him:

Donald Cooper, long and stooped, in a faded boilersuit—a long face with folds beside the mouth and a sharp chin with a growth of sparse, gray stubble; and Wang, broad and stocky, almost neckless, in an old, neatly darned wadded jacket—a broad, brownish face, little snub nose, affable smile, dark eyes in the cracks of puffy eyelids—and Andrei was suddenly transfixed by a poignant joy at the thought that all these people from different countries, and even from different times, were all here together and all doing one thing of great importance, each at his own post.

"... Now he's an old man," Kensi concluded. "And he claims that the best women he ever knew were Russian women. Emigrants in Harbin." He stopped speaking, dropped his cigarette butt, and painstakingly ground it to dust with the sole of his gleaming ankle boot.

Andrei said, "What kind of Russian is she? 'Selma'—and 'Nagel' too?"

"Yes, she's Swedish," said Kensi. "But all the same. The story came to me by association."

"OK, let's go," Donald said, and climbed into the cabin.

"Listen, Kensi," said Andrei, taking hold of the cabin door. "Who were you before this?"

"An inspector at the foundry, and before that, minister of communal—"

"No, not here, back there."

"Aah, there? Back there I was literary editor for the journal *Hayakawa*."

Donald started the motor and the vintage truck began shaking and rattling, belching out thick clouds of blue smoke.

"Your right sidelight isn't working!" Kensi shouted.

"It hasn't worked in all the time we've been here," Andrei responded.

"Then get it fixed! If I see it again, I'll fine you!"

"They set you on to hound us ..."

"What? I can't hear!"

"I said, catch bandits, not drivers!" Andrei yelled, trying to shout over the clanging and clattering. "What's our sidelight to you? When are they going to send all you spongers packing?"

"Soon," Kensi said. "Any time now—it won't be more than a hundred years!"

Andrei threatened Kensi with his fist, waved good-bye to Wang, and plumped into the seat beside Donald. The truck jerked forward, scraping one side along the wall of the archway, trundled out onto Main Street, and made a sharp turn to the right.

Settling himself more comfortably, so that the spring protruding from the seat wasn't pricking his backside, Andrei cast a sideways glance at Donald, who was sitting up straight, with his left hand on the steering wheel and his right on the gearshift; his hat was pushed forward over his eyes, his pointed chin was thrust out, and he was driving at top speed. He always drove like that, "at the legal speed limit," never giving a thought to braking at the frequent potholes in the road, and at every one of those potholes the trash cans in the back bounced heavily, the rusted-through hood rattled, and no matter how hard Andrei tried to brace himself with his legs, he flew up in the air and fell back precisely onto the sharp point of that damned spring. Previously, however, all this had been accompanied by good-humored banter, but now Donald didn't say anything, his thin lips were tightly compressed, and he didn't look at Andrei at all, which made it seem like there was some kind of malicious premeditation in this routine jolting.

"What's wrong with you, Don?" Andrei asked eventually. "Got a toothache?"

Donald twitched one shoulder briefly and didn't answer.

"Really, you haven't been yourself these last few days. I can see it. Maybe I've unintentionally offended you somehow?"

"Drop it, Andrei," Donald said through his teeth. "Why does it have to be about you?"

And again Andrei fancied that he heard some kind of ill will, even something offensive or insulting, in these words: *How could a snotty kid like you offend me, a professor?* But then Donald spoke again.

"I meant it when I said you were lucky. You really are some-one to be envied. All this just kind of washes right over you. Or passes straight through you. But it runs over me like a steam-roller. I haven't got a single unbroken bone left in me."

"What are you talking about? I don't understand a thing."

Donald said nothing, screwing up his lips.

Andrei looked at him, glanced vacantly at the road ahead, squinted sideways at Donald again, scratched the back of his head, and said disconcertedly, "Word of honor, I don't understand a thing. Everything seems to be going fine—"

"That's why I envy you," Donald said harshly. "And that's enough about this. Just don't take any notice."

"So how am I supposed to do that?" said Andrei, seriously perturbed now. "How can I not take any notice? We're all here together . . . You, me, the guys . . . *friendship* is a big word, of course, too big . . . well then, simply *comrades* . . . I, for instance, would tell you if there was something . . . After all, no one's going to refuse to help, are they! Well, you tell me—if something happened to me and I asked you for help, would you refuse? You wouldn't, would you, honestly?"

Donald's hand lifted off the gearshift and patted Andrei gently on the shoulder. Andrei didn't say anything. His feelings were brimming over. Everything was fine again, everything was all right. Donald was all right. It was just a fit of the blues. A man can get the blues, can't he? It was simply that his pride had reared its head. After all, the man was a professor of sociology, and here he was down with the trash cans, and before that he was a loader. Of course, it was unpleasant and galling for him, especially since he had no one to take these grievances to—no one had forced him to come here, and it was embarrassing to complain . . . It was easily said: *Make a good job of anything you're given to do* . . . Well, all right. Enough of all this. He'd manage.

The old truck was already trundling along over diabase ren-dered slippery by settled mist, and the buildings on both sides had become lower and more dilapidated, and the lines of streetlamps running along the street had become dimmer and sparser. Ahead of them these lines merged into a blurred, hazy blob. There wasn't a single soul on the roadway or the sidewalks, and for some reason they didn't even come across any caretakers; only at the corner of Seventeenth Street, in front of a squat, dumpy hotel best known by its title of "the Bedbug Cage," was there a cart with a dejected horse, and someone sleeping in the cart, completely bundled up in tarpaulin. It was four o'clock in the morning, the time of the deepest sleep, and not a single window was glowing in the black facades.

A vehicle stuck its nose out of a gateway on the left, up ahead of them. Donald flashed his lights at it and hurtled past, and the vehicle, another garbage truck, pulled out onto the road and tried to overtake them, but it had picked the wrong guys for that. There was no way it could compete with Donald—its headlights glinted in through the rear window for a moment and then it dropped back, hopelessly outrun. They overtook another garbage truck in the Burnt Districts, and just in time, because the cobblestones started immediately after the Burnt Districts, and Donald was obliged to reduce speed anyway so the old rust bucket wouldn't fall apart.

Here they met trucks already going the other way, already empty—they were coming back from the dump, no longer in any hurry to get anywhere. Then a shadowy figure detached itself from a streetlamp and walked out into the road, and Andrei slipped his hand under the seat and pulled out a heavy tire iron, but it turned out to be a policeman, who asked them to give him a lift to Cabbage Lane. Neither Andrei nor Donald knew where that was, and then the policeman, a beefy guy with big jowls and tangled locks of light-colored hair sticking out from under his uniform cap, said he would show them the way.

He stood on the running board beside Andrei, holding on to the door frame, twisting his nose about discontendedly the whole way, as if he'd caught a smell of something, God only knew what—although he himself reeked of stale sweat, and

Andrei remembered that this part of the city had already been disconnected from the water main.

For a while they drove in silence, with the policeman whistling something from an operetta, and then, right out of the blue, he informed them that just today, at midnight, on the corner of Cabbage Lane and Second Left Street, they'd bumped off some poor devil and pulled out all his gold teeth.

"You're not doing your job," Andrei told him angrily. Cases like this infuriated him, and the policeman's tone of voice made Andrei feel like punching him in the neck: it was immediately obvious that he couldn't care less about the murder, or the victim, or the killer.

The policeman swung his broad face around quizzically and asked, "So you'll teach me how to do my job, will you?"

"Maybe it could be me," said Andrei.

The policeman screwed his eyes up ill-naturedly, whistled, and said, "Teachers, teachers! Whichever way you spit—teachers everywhere. He stands there and teaches. He's carting garbage already, but he's still teaching."

"I'm not trying to teach you—" Andrei began, raising his voice, but the policeman wouldn't let him speak.

"I'll get back to the station now," he informed them calmly, "and I'll call your garage, and tell them your right sidelight isn't working. His sidelight isn't working—got it?—and on top of that, he's teaching the police how to do their job. Pipsqueak."

Donald suddenly burst into dry, grating laughter.

The policeman gave a hoot of laughter too and said in a perfectly amicable voice, "It's just me for forty buildings, OK? And they forbid us to carry guns. What do you want from us? They'll start knifing you at home soon, never mind the back alleys."

"So what are you doing about it?" Andrei said, stunned. "You should protest, demand—"

"We have 'protested,'" the policeman echoed acidly. "We have 'demanded' . . .You're new here, are you? Hey, boss," he called to Donald. "Pull up. This is my stop."

He jumped down off the running board and, without look-ing back, waddled off toward a dark crack between the lopsided wooden houses, where a solitary streetlamp burned in the dis-tance, with a little knot of people standing under it.

"Honest to God, are they total idiots, or what?" Andrei said indignantly when the truck started moving again. "How can they do that—the city's full of riffraff, and the police are unarmed! It's absolutely crazy. Kensi's got a holster on his hip, what does he carry in it, cigarettes?"

"Sandwiches," said Donald. "'Due to an increase in the num-bers of cases of criminals attacking police officers in order to seize their weapons . . .' and so forth."

Andrei ruminated for a while, bracing himself like grim death with his feet to avoid being thrown up off the seat. It was almost the end of the cobblestones already.

"I think it's incredibly stupid," he said eventually. "How about you?"

"I think so too," Donald responded, lighting up awkwardly with one hand.

"And you talk about it so calmly?"

"I've done all my worrying," said Donald. "It's a very old directive; you weren't even here yet."

Andrei scratched the back of his head and frowned. Well, dammit, maybe there was some sense in this directive. When all was said and done, a solitary policeman really was tempting bait for those creeps. If they took away the guns, then of course they had to take them away from everyone. And, of course, the prob-lem wasn't that idiotic directive but the fact that there weren't very many police officers, and they didn't carry out very many raids—but they ought to set up one grand raid and sweep all this filth away at a single stroke! Get the local people involved. Me, for instance, I'd be happy to go . . . Donald would go, of course . . . I'll have to write to the mayor.

Then his thoughts suddenly took a new turn. "Listen, Don," he said. "You're a sociologist. Of course, I don't reckon sociology is any kind of science at all—I've told you that already—it's got absolutely no method. But, of course, you know a lot, a lot more than I do. So you explain to me where all this dross in our city comes from. How did they get here—the murderers, the rapists, the crooks? Didn't the Mentors realize who they were inviting here?"

"They realized, probably," Donald replied indifferently, shooting straight over a terrifying pit filled with black water without even pausing.

"But why then . . . ?"

"People aren't born thieves. They become thieves. And then, as everyone knows, 'How can we tell what the Experiment requires? The Experiment is the Experiment . . .'" Donald paused for a moment. "Soccer is soccer: a round ball, a square pitch, and may the best team win."

The streetlamps came to an end and the residential area of the city was left behind. Now the battered and broken road was flanked on both sides by abandoned ruins—the remnants of incongruous colonnades that had slumped into shoddy foundations; walls propped up by girders, with gaping holes instead of windows; tall grass; stacks of rotting timber; thickets of nettles and thistles; stunted little trees, half choked by creepers, standing among heaps of blackened bricks. And then up ahead a hazy glow appeared again. Donald turned to the right, carefully steered past an oncoming empty truck, spun his wheels for a while in deep ruts choked with mud, and finally braked to a halt a hair's breadth away from the red taillights of the last garbage truck in the line. He killed the engine and looked at his watch. It was about half past four.

"We'll be standing here for a good hour." Andrei said cheerfully. "Let's go and see who's up in front of us."

Another truck drove up from behind and stopped. "Go on your own," said Donald, leaning back in his seat and pulling the brim of his hat down over his face.

Then Andrei also leaned back, adjusted the spring underneath him, and lit a cigarette. Up ahead, unloading was proceeding at full tilt—trash can lids clattered, the tallyman's high voice shouted: ". . . eight . . . ten . . . ," a thousand-candle-power lamp under a flat tin plate swayed on its pole. Then suddenly voices from several different throats started yelling at once: "Where are you going? Fuck it!"; "Pull back!"; "You're the blind asshole here!"; "You looking for a smack in the mouth?" There were massive heaps of garbage, compacted into a dense mass, looming up on the left and the right, and a ghastly smell of rotten food wafted on the night breeze.

A familiar voice suddenly spoke right in his ear. "Cheers, shit shifters! How's the Great Experiment going?" It was Izya Katzman, life size and in person—disheveled, fat, grubby, and, as always, offensively cheerful. "Have you heard? There's a scheme for a final solution to the problem of crime. They're abolishing the police! To replace them they're going to let the crazies out on the streets at night. It's the end for the bandits and the hooligans—now only loonies will go outside at nighttime!"

"Cretinous," Andrei said frostily.

"Cretinous?" Izya stood on the running board and stuck his head into the cabin. "On the contrary! Most ingenious! No additional expenditure. Returning the insane to their permanent places of residence is the responsibility of the caretakers—"

"For which the caretakers are issued supplementary rations in the form of one liter of vodka," Andrei butted in, which sent Izya into inexplicable raptures: he started giggling, making strange, guttural sounds, spraying saliva, and washing his hands with air.

Donald suddenly swore in a hollow voice, swung open his door, jumped down, and disappeared into the darkness. Izya immediately stopped giggling and asked uneasily, "What's wrong with him?"

"I don't know," Andrei said morosely. "Probably you made him want to puke . . . But actually, he's been that way for a few days already."

"Really?" Izya looked over the top of the cabin in the direction that Donald had gone. "A shame. He's a good man. Only really badly maladapted."

"So who's well adapted?"

"I'm well adapted. You're well adapted. Wang's well adapted . . . Donald's been getting indignant with everything just lately: *Why do we have to stand in line to dump garbage? Why the hell is there a tallyman here? What's he tallying?*"

"Well, he's right to feel outraged," said Andrei. "It really is kind of cretinous."

"But you don't get all steamed up about it, do you?" Izya objected. "You realize perfectly well that the tallyman isn't his own master. They've put him there to tally, so he tallies. And since he can't keep up with his tallying, as you already know, a line forms. And a line . . . is a line . . ." Izya started gurgling and spraying again. "Of course, if Donald was in charge, he'd lay a good road here, with exit ramps for dumping garbage, and he'd transfer that great, muscly hulk of a tallyman to the police, to catch bandits. Or to the front line, to the farmers—"

"So?" Andrei asked impatiently

"What do you mean, 'So?' Donald isn't the boss, is he?"

"So why don't the bosses do it?"

"Why should they?" Izya exclaimed joyfully. "Think about it! Does the garbage get removed? It does. Does the amount removed get tallied? It does. Systematically? Oh yes. At the end of the month, a report will be presented: this month this many more cans of crap were removed than last month. The minister's happy, the mayor's happy, everyone's happy, and if Donald's not happy, well, no one forced him to come here—he's a volunteer!"

The truck in front of them belched out a cloud of blue smoke and moved forward about fifteen meters. Andrei hastily sat behind the wheel and glanced out. Donald was nowhere to be seen. Then he cautiously started up the engine and advanced raggedly for the same distance, with the engine cutting out three times on the way. Izya walked alongside, shying away in alarm when the truck started shuddering. Then he started telling Andrei some story about the Bible, but Andrei didn't really listen—he was soaking wet after all the strain he'd just been through.

Under the bright lamp they were still clanging garbage cans and the air was thick with obscenities. Something struck the roof of the cabin and bounced off, but Andrei took no notice. Oscar Heidemann walked up to them from behind, with his partner, a black man from Haiti, and asked for a cigarette. Almost invisible in the darkness, the Haitian, whose name was Silva, grinned with his white teeth.

Izya launched into a conversation with them, and for some reason he called Silva a "Tonton Macoute" and questioned Oscar about someone named Thor Heyerdahl. Silva pulled strange faces, made his fingers into eyeglasses, and pretended to fire a burst from an automatic rifle. Izya clutched at his stomach and pretended to be slain on the spot. Andrei didn't understand a thing, and apparently neither did Oscar; very soon it became clear that he'd been confusing Haiti with Tahiti.

Something skidded across the roof again, and suddenly a massive lump of agglutinated garbage smashed into the hood, shattering into pieces.

"Hey!" Oscar shouted into the darkness. "Stop that!"

Up ahead twenty throats started yelling again, and the intensity of the invective suddenly rose to a stratospheric level. Something was going on. Izya gave a plaintive squeal, clutched at his stomach, and doubled over—this time for real. Andrei opened the door and stuck his head out, and immediately took a hit on it from an empty tin can—it didn't hurt, but it was very insulting—while Silva ducked down and slipped into the darkness. Andrei gazed around, protecting his head and face.

He couldn't see anything. A hail of rusty cans, pieces of rotten wood, old bones, and even fragments of bricks was showering down from behind the heaps of garbage on the left. He heard a jangle of breaking glass. A wild bellow of outrage rose up over the column of trucks. "What are those bastards doing over there?" voices yelled, almost in chorus. Engines roared as they started up and headlamps flared. Some trucks started jerking fitfully backward and forward; evidently the drivers were trying to turn them so as to light up the crests of garbage from which whole bricks and empty bottles were now flying down. A few more men, huddled over like Silva, dashed into the darkness.

Andrei noticed in passing that Izya had crouched down beside the back of the truck with a tearstained face and was feeling at his stomach. Then Andrei ducked back into the cabin, grabbed the tire iron from under the seat, and leaped out again. Smash their heads in, the bastards! He could see about a dozen garbage collectors down on all fours, clinging on with their hands as they clambered up the slope in a frenzy. One of the drivers managed to set his truck crossways to the line after all, and the beams of his headlamps lit up a ragged ridge, bristling with fragments of old furniture, frizzy with old clothes and scraps of paper, and glittering with broken glass, and above the ridge the scoop bucket of an excavator, raised high in the air, stood out against the black sky. Something was moving on the scoop bucket, something large and gray, with a silvery sheen. Andrei froze, staring at it, and at that very moment a despairing howl rang out above the babble of voices.

"It's devils! Devils! Run for your life!"

Immediately men came pouring down the slope, tumbling over and over, on hands and knees, head over heels, raising clouds of dust, in a swirling vortex of torn clothes and tatters of paper. One man, clutching his head in his hands and pulling his elbows in tight to protect it, hurtled past Andrei, still squealing in panic, slipped in a rut, fell, got up again, and ran on, going flat out in the direction of the City. Another, breathing hoarsely, squeezed in between the radiator of Andrei's truck and the back of the one in front, got stuck there, snagged on something, and started straining to break free, also yelling in a strange voice. Suddenly it turned quieter, with only the engines growling, and then, as sharp as blows from a whiplash, came the crack of shots. Up there on the ridge, in the bluish light of the headlamps, Andrei saw a tall, lean man, standing with his back to the trucks and holding a pistol in both hands, firing again and again at something in the darkness behind the ridge.

He fired five or six times in the total silence, and then from
out of the darkness came the inhuman howling of a thousand
voices, a baleful, mournful caterwauling, as if twenty thousand March tomcats had all started wailing into megaphones
at the same time, and the lean man backed away, lost his foot-
ing, flapped his arms awkwardly, and slid down the slope on
his back. Andrei also shrank away in anticipation of something
absolutely appalling, and he saw the ridge abruptly stir into
motion.

Suddenly the ridge was swarming with unbelievable silvery-
gray, monstrously ugly ghosts, with thousands of blood-red, glittering eyes, and millions of damp fangs flashing in savage grins,
and a whole forest of impossibly long, shaggy arms waving in the
air. In the light of the headlamps, the dust rose up over them in
a dense wall, and a solid deluge of broken bricks, rocks, bottles,
and lumps of filth poured down on the column.

This was too much for Andrei. He ducked into the cabin,
huddled into the far corner, and held the tire iron out in front
of himself, frozen, as if this were a nightmare. He was totally
dazed, and when a dark body obscured the open door, he yelled
out, without even hearing his own voice, and started jabbing
the iron bar into the soft, terrifying thing that resisted and came
creeping toward him, and he kept on jabbing until Izya's plaintive
howl—"It's me, you idiot!"—brought him to his senses. And then
Izya climbed into the cabin, slammed the door behind him, and
announced in a surprisingly calm voice, "D'you know what they
are? They're monkeys. What bastards!"

Andrei didn't understand him at first, then he understood but
didn't believe him. "Is that right?" he said, stepping onto the running board and glancing around.

Right: they were monkeys. Very large, very hairy, very fierce
to look at, but not devils and not ghosts, only monkeys. Andrei
felt a hot flush of shame and relief, and at the same moment
something solid and heavy smashed into his ear so hard that he
smashed his other ear against the roof of the cabin.

"Everyone into the trucks!" an imperious voice roared somewhere up ahead. "Stop panicking! They're baboons! Nothing to be afraid of! Get in the trucks and reverse!"

There was sheer pandemonium in the column: mufflers popping, headlamps flaring up and going out, engines roaring unmercifully, clouds of gray-blue smoke swirling up toward the starless sky. A face flooded with something black and gleaming suddenly dove out of the darkness, hands seized Andrei by the shoulders, shook him like a puppy, and shoved him sideways into the cabin, and immediately the truck in front reversed and smashed into their radiator with a crunch, and the truck behind jerked forward and struck theirs like a tambourine, shifting the trash cans and setting them rattling, and Izya tugged on his shoulder and started hassling him: "Can you drive or can't you? Andrei? Can you?" From out of the bluish smoke came a bloodcurdling howl of despair: "They're killing me! Save me!" and the imperious voice kept roaring—"Stop panicking! The truck at the back, reverse! Move it!"—and from above, from the left, from the right, hard objects came raining down, clanking across the hood, smashing into the windscreen, and setting it jangling, and horns incessantly honked and hooted, and the abominable shrieking and howling kept getting louder and louder.

Izya suddenly said, "Well, I'll be going . . ." and, covering his head with his arms beforehand, he climbed out. He was almost run over by a truck hurtling in the direction of the City—Andrei caught a glimpse of the tallyman's contorted face among the trashcans. Then Izya disappeared, and Donald appeared without his hat, scraped and scuffed, all covered in mud, flung a pistol down on the seat, sat behind the steering wheel, started up the engine, stuck his head out of the cabin, and started reversing.

Apparently some kind of order had been established after all: the howls of panic faded away, engines roared in unison, and the entire column edged backward little by little. Even the hail of rocks and bottles seemed to have died down a little. The baboons jumped up and down and strutted about on the ridge of garbage but didn't come down—they just yelled from up there, with their dogs' mouths gaping, and derisively turned their buttocks, gleaming in the light of the headlamps, toward the column of trucks.

The truck bowled along faster and faster, spun its wheels again in a mud-filled pothole, shot out onto the road and swung around. Donald changed gears with a grating sound, stepped on the gas, slammed the door, and flung himself back in the seat. Ahead of them, skipping about in the gloom, were the red taillights of trucks headed for the City, going flat out.

We've broken free, Andrei thought in relief, and warily felt at his ear. It had swollen up and it was throbbing. Would you believe it—baboons! Where could baboons have come from? And such great, hefty ones . . . and so many of them! There had never been any baboons here . . . if you didn't count Izya Katzman, that is. And why precisely baboons? Why not tigers? He squirmed in his seat, and at that moment the truck jolted. Andrei went flying up and smashed back down onto something hard and unfamiliar. He stuck his hand under his backside, pulled out a pistol, and looked at it uncomprehendingly for a second. The pistol was small and black, with a short barrel and a ribbed handle. Then Donald suddenly said, "Careful. Give me that."

Andrei handed over the pistol and watched for a while as Donald squirmed around and stuck the gun in the back pocket of his boilersuit. Andrei suddenly broke out in a sweat. "So it was you up there . . . shooting?" he asked hoarsely.

Donald didn't answer. He blinked their single surviving headlamp as he overtook yet another truck. Several baboons darted through an intersection, right in front of their radiator, but Andrei wasn't interested in them.

"Where did you get a gun from, Don?"

Again Donald didn't answer; he just made a strange gesture with his hand—an attempt to pull a nonexistent hat down over his eyes.

"I'll tell you what, Don," Andrei said firmly. "We're going to City Hall right now. You're going to hand in the pistol and explain how you got hold of it."

"Don't talk nonsense," Donald responded, screwing up his face. "Why don't you just give me a cigarette instead?"

Andrei mechanically took out his pack. "It's not nonsense," he said. "I don't want to know anything. You kept it quiet—OK, it's your private business. And anyway, I trust you . . . But in the City only bandits have guns. I don't want to make anything of it, but basically, I don't understand you . . . basically, you've got to hand it in and explain everything. And don't go acting like it's all nonsense. I've seen the state you've been in just recently. Better go and tell them the whole story at once."

Donald turned his head for a second and looked into Andrei's face. It wasn't clear what that was in his eyes—maybe derision, maybe distress—but at that moment he seemed very old to Andrei, very infirm and somehow haggard.

Andrei felt embarrassed and perplexed, but he immediately pulled himself together and repeated firmly, "Hand it in and tell them everything. Everything!"

"Do you realize those monkeys are headed for the City?" Donald asked.

"So what?" said Andrei, bewildered.

"Yes indeed—so what?" said Donald, and burst into grisly laughter.

2

The monkeys were already in the City. They were dashing along the cornices of buildings, dangling from lampposts like bunches of grapes, dancing at intersections in macabre, shaggy hordes, clinging to windows, flinging cobblestones torn up out of the road, and pursuing frenzied people who had fled into the streets in nothing but their underwear.

Donald stopped the truck several times to let fugitives up onto the back; the trash cans had been flung off a long time ago. Once a deranged horse, harnessed to a wagon, dashed across in front of the truck, but now there was no one sleeping in the wagon, bundled up in tarpaulin, not any longer; squatting in it, swaying to and fro, waving its massive, long, hairy arms about and wailing stridently, was a huge, burly, silvery baboon. Andrei saw the wagon crash straight into a lamppost and the horse go hurtling on, trailing the snapped traces behind it, while the baboon flitted jauntily across onto the nearest drainpipe and disappeared up onto the roof.

The square in front of City Hall was a seething vortex of panic. Vehicles drove up and drove away, policemen ran around, disoriented people wandered around in their underwear, and at the entrance some men had pressed some official or other up against the wall and were shouting at him, demanding something or other, while he tried to fend them off by jabbing with his cane and swinging his briefcase.

"What an unholy mess," Donald said, and jumped out of the truck.

They ran into the building and immediately lost each other in a stupefying crowd of men in civilian clothing, men in police uniforms, and men in underclothes. The air was filled with the confused babble of innumerable voices, and the tobacco smoke made Andrei's eyes smart.

"You've got to understand! I can't, not like this—in nothing but my underpants!"

". . . open the arsenal immediately and hand out guns . . . Damn it all, at least hand out guns to the police!"

"Where's the chief of police? He was hanging around here just a moment ago . . ."

"My wife's still in there, can't you understand that? And my old mother-in-law!"

"Listen, it's no big deal. After all, monkeys are just monkeys . . ."

"Just imagine it, I wake up and there's someone sitting on the windowsill . . ."

"And where's the chief of police? Still snoring in the sack, is he, the fat-ass?"

"We had one streetlamp in our alley. They knocked it down."

"Kovalevsky! Room 20, quickly!"

"But surely you must agree that in just my underpants . . ."

"Who can drive? Drivers! Everyone out into the square, gather at the advertising column!"

"But where, damn it all, is the chief of police? Has he done a runner, the lousy bastard?"

"Right, listen up. You take some guys and get down to the foundry. Get those . . . you know, those rod things, for the park fencing . . . All of them, take them all! And get straight back here . . ."

"And I hammered that hairy face so hard, I broke my hand, I swear to God . . . And he yells, 'God almighty! What are you doing? It's me—Freddy!' Total darned bedlam . . ."

"But are air rifles any good?"

"Three trucks to seventy-second district! Seventy-third district—five trucks . . ."

"Kindly give instructions for the issue of supplementary kit. Only it has to be signed for, so they'll return it afterward!"

"Listen, have they really got tails? Or was I seeing things?"

Andrei was jostled, squeezed, and pressed up against the walls of the corridor, his feet were trampled black and blue, and he himself jostled people, squeezed through between them, and shouldered them aside. At first he looked for Donald, in order to be present as a witness for the defense at the confession and the handing-in of the gun, and then it hit home that the baboon invasion was obviously very serious business, if it had stirred up a hornet's nest like this, and he immediately regretted that he couldn't drive a truck, didn't know where the foundry with the mysterious rods was, and couldn't issue supplementary kit to anyone, and it seemed pretty much like he was no use to anyone here. He did at least attempt to inform people about what he had seen with his own eyes—maybe the information would prove useful—but some simply didn't listen to him and others interrupted as soon as he began and started telling their own stories.

He realized with a heavy heart that there were no familiar faces in this eddying whirlpool of uniforms and underpants—he only caught a brief glimpse of Silva with his head bandaged up in a bloody rag before the black man instantly disappeared—but in the meantime measures of some kind were clearly being taken, someone was organizing someone else and sending him somewhere, the voices were getting louder and louder, sounding more and more confident, the underpants started disappearing little by little while the number of uniforms noticeably increased, and the moment came when Andrei even fancied that he heard the measured tramping of boots and a marching song, but it turned that someone had simply dropped the movable safe and it had gone tumbling and crashing down the stairs until it got stuck in the doorway of the Department of Foodstuffs . . .

And then Andrei did spot a familiar face: a functionary, a former colleague of his from the accounts department of the Office of Weights and Measures. Elbowing his way through people coming the other way, he overtook the functionary, pressed him back against the wall and blurted out in a single breath that he, Andrei Voronin—"Remember, we used to work together?"—was a garbage operative now; "I can't find anyone, send me some-where to do something, you must need people, surely . . ." The functionary listened for a while, blinking crazily and making fee-ble, convulsive attempts to break free, then suddenly he pushed Andrei away, yelling, "Where can I send you? Can't you see I'm taking documents to be signed!"—and he took off down the cor-ridor, almost running.

Andrei made several more attempts to participate in orga-nized activity, but everyone rebuffed him or gave him the cold shoulder—everyone was in a terrible hurry; there was literally not a single person who was just standing there calmly and, say, drawing up a list of volunteers. With bitter resolve, Andrei started flinging open all the doors one after another, hoping to find someone or other in charge, someone who wasn't running around, who wasn't shouting and waving his arms about—even the most basic reasoning clearly indicated that somewhere around here there had to be something like a headquarters, a place from which all this feverish activity was being directed.

The first room was empty. In the second, one man in his underpants was shouting loudly into a telephone receiver and a second was cursing as he pulled on a regulation warehouse coat that was too tight. Protruding from under the coat was a pair of police breeches and ankle boots that had been patched over and over again, with no laces. Glancing into the third office, Andrei was lashed across the eyes by something pink with buttons and immediately recoiled, catching only a brief glimpse of a remark-ably corpulent frame, clearly female. But in the fourth office he discovered the Mentor.

He was sitting on the windowsill with his feet pulled up, hug-ging his knees and looking out through the window into the darkness illuminated by the scudding light of headlamps. When Andrei came in, the Mentor turned a benign, florid face toward him, jerked his eyebrows up slightly, as he always did, and smiled. And at the sight of that smile, Andrei immediately calmed down. His rancorous anger faded away, and suddenly it was clear that everything was bound to sort itself out in the end; everything would fall into place and basically turn out just fine.

"Just look," Andrei said, spreading his arms and smiling back. "It turns out that I'm no use to anyone. I can't drive, I don't know where the foundry is . . . I can't understand a thing in all this crazy uproar."

"Yes," the Mentor agreed sympathetically. "It's absolute mayhem." He lowered his feet off the windowsill, stuck his hands under his thighs, and dangled his legs, like a child. "Quite unseemly, really. Even shameful. Serious adults, most of them experienced . . . So they're not organized enough! Right, Andrei? So certain important matters have been allowed to slide. Inadequate preparedness, a lack of discipline . . . Well, and bureaucracy too, of course."

"Yes!" said Andrei. "Of course! You know what I've decided? I'm going to stop trying to find anyone, or trying to figure anything out, I'm just going to grab some kind of stick and go. I'll join a brigade. And if they won't take me, I'll go on my own. There are women left out there, after all . . . and children."

The Mentor nodded briefly at every word Andrei said. He wasn't smiling any longer; his expression was serious and sympathetic now.

"There's just one thing," said Andrei, pulling a wry face. "What to do about Donald?"

"Donald?" the Mentor echoed, raising his eyebrows. "Ah, Donald Cooper?" He laughed. "Of course, you think Donald Cooper must already have been arrested and repented of his sins . . . Nothing of the sort. At this precise moment Donald Cooper is organizing a brigade of volunteers to repel this brazen invasion, and of course he isn't any kind of gangster and he hasn't committed any crimes, and he got the gun on the black market in exchange for an old repeating watch. There's nothing to be done. He's spent his entire life with a gun in his pocket—he's used to it!"

"Well, of course!" said Andrei, feeling tremendously relieved. "It's obvious! I didn't really believe it myself, it's just that I thought . . . OK!" He swung around to leave, but stopped. "Tell me . . . if it's not a secret, of course . . . Tell me, what's all this for? Monkeys! Where have they come from? What are they supposed to prove?"

The Mentor sighed and slipped down off the windowsill. "There you go again, Andrei, asking me questions . . ."

"No! I understand everything, I do!" Andrei said with sincere feeling, pressing his hands to his heart. "I only . . ."

"Wait. There you go again, asking me questions to which I don't have answers. You must understand that at last: *I don't have answers!* The soil erosion under the buildings, remember that? The changing of water into bile . . . but then again, that was before your time . . . And now this—baboons . . . Remember, you used to keep quizzing me, asking how come—people of different nationalities, all speaking the same language and not even suspecting a thing. Remember how it astounded you, how perplexed you were, how you tried to prove to Kensi that he was speaking Russian, and Kensi tried to prove to you that you were speaking Japanese, remember? But now you've gotten used to it—those questions don't even occur to you any longer. It's one of the conditions of the Experiment. The Experiment is the Experiment, what else can I tell you?" He smiled. "Right, off you go, Andrei, off you go. Your place is out there. Action first and foremost. Each in his place, and each doing everything he can!"

And Andrei walked out—in fact, he didn't walk, he darted—into the corridor, which had completely emptied now, and skittered down the front steps into the square, where he immediately spotted a serious-looking crowd around a truck under a lamppost and merged into it without the slightest hesitation: someone thrust a heavy metal picket into his hand, and he felt armed, strong, and ready for decisive battle.

A short distance away someone—a very familiar voice!—was issuing stentorian commands to line up in a column three across, and Andrei, holding his picket on his shoulder, ran that way and found himself a place between a burly Latino wearing suspenders over a nightshirt and a skinny, flaxen-haired intellectual type in a rumpled suit, who was in a terribly nervous state—he kept taking off his eyeglasses, breathing on the lenses, wiping them with a handkerchief, sticking them back on his nose, and adjusting them with his thumb and forefinger.

It was a small brigade, only about thirty men. And the one giving the commands turned out to be Fritz Heiger, which was rather galling in a way, but on the other hand Andrei had to admit that in this situation Fritz Heiger, although he might be a random leftover from the Nazi defeat, had shown up in exactly the right place.

As befitted a former noncommissioned officer of the Wehrmacht, his manner of expressing himself was forthright, and listening to him was quite repugnant. *"Cov-errr ooff!"* he yelled loud enough for the whole square to hear, as if he were commanding a regiment on tactical exercises. "Hey, you there, in the flip-flops! Yes, you! Pull your belly in! And you, the one with your legs spread like a cow after she's been mounted! That applies to you too. Trail pikes! Not shoulder pikes, I said trail—you, the woman in suspenders! *Ten-shun!* Following me, forward . . . As you were! *For-ward maarch!"* They shuffled off raggedly.

Someone immediately stepped on Andrei's heel from behind; he stumbled, shoved the intellectual type with his shoulder, and the intellectual type, of course, dropped the glasses that he was wiping yet again. "Clumsy clod!" Andrei said to him, losing his temper.

"Be careful!" the intellectual type whined in a shrill voice.

"For God's sake!" Andrei helped him find his glasses, and when Fritz pounced on them, choking on his fury, Andrei told him to go to hell.

Andrei and the intellectual type, who kept thanking him non-stop as he stumbled along, caught up with the column and covered another twenty meters or so before they were all ordered to "board the trucks." However, there was only one vehicle, a special truck for transporting wet cement. When they got on board they could feel it squelching and slopping about under their feet. The man in flip-flops clambered ponderously back out over the side and announced in a high voice that he wasn't going anywhere on *that* truck. Fritz ordered him to get back onto the truck. The man protested in an even higher voice that he was wearing flip-flops and his feet were soaked. Fritz made mention of a pregnant swine. The man in the soaked flip-flops, not frightened in the least, protested that *he* certainly wasn't a swine, that a swine might possibly agree to ride in that filth—he offered his profound apologies to all who had agreed to ride in this pigsty, but . . . At this point the Latino clambered down off the back of the truck, spat disdainfully at Fritz's feet, stuck his thumbs under his suspenders, and strolled away at a leisurely pace.

Observing all this, Andrei experienced a certain malicious delight. Not that he approved of the actions of the man in flip-flops, let alone those of the Mexican—they had undeniably acted in an uncomradely manner and in general behaved like philistines—but it was extremely interesting to wait and see what our bruised and battered *Unterleutnant* would do now and how he would extricate himself from the situation that had arisen.

Andrei was obliged to admit that the bruised and battered Unterleutnant extricated himself with honor intact. Without saying a word, Fritz swung around on his heels, hopped up onto the running board beside the driver and commanded, "Let's go!" The truck set off, and at that very moment someone switched on the sun.

Struggling to stay on his feet, constantly clutching at the men next to him, Andrei watched with his neck twisted around as the crimson disk slowly kindled to a blaze at its usual spot. First the disk trembled, seeming to pulsate, growing brighter and brighter, turning orange, then yellow, then white, and then it went out for an instant and immediately flared up again at full power, so bright that it was impossible to look at.

The new day had begun. The impenetrably black, starless sky turned a hazy light blue—sultry, with a breath of wind as hot as if it were blowing out of a desert. On all sides the City seemed to appear out of nothing—bright, colorful, streaked with bluish shadows, huge and vast . . . Multiple stories heaped up on top of each other, buildings banked up above buildings, and not a single building was like any other, and the incandescent Yellow Wall could be seen, rising up and disappearing into the sky on the right, and on the left, in the openings above the roofs, an azure void appeared, as if the sea were over that way, and you instantly started feeling thirsty. Out of habit many of the men immediately looked at their watches. It was exactly eight o'clock.

They only drove for a short time. Apparently the monkey hordes hadn't reached this area yet—the streets were quiet and deserted, as always at this early hour. Here and there in the buildings windows were being flung open and still-sleepy people were stretching drowsily and watching the truck indifferently. Women in nightcaps hung mattresses out across windowsills; on one of the balconies a wiry old man diligently performed his morning exercises in striped underpants, with his beard fluttering. The flood of panic hadn't reached this far yet, but closer to the sixteenth district they started coming across the first fugitives—disheveled, not so much frightened as angry, some with bundles over their shoulders. When they caught sight of the truck, these people stopped, waved their arms, and shouted something. The truck roared as it turned onto Fourth Left Street, almost knocking down a very elderly couple pushing along a two-wheeled trolley with suitcases on it, and stopped. They all saw the baboons immediately.

The baboons were making themselves at home on Fourth Left Street, as if it were the jungle, or wherever it was they lived. With their tails curled into hooks, they shambled in slovenly crowds from sidewalk to sidewalk, bounded cheerfully along the cornices of buildings, swung from the lampposts, climbed up on advertising pillars and attentively searched themselves for lice, shouted to each other in booming voices, grimaced, fought, and made carefree, relaxed love. A gang of the silvery vandals was smashing up a food stall, two hooligans with tails were molesting a woman who was standing petrified in an entryway, white-faced with fear, and a shaggy-furred cutie, who had installed herself in a traffic controller's booth, stuck her tongue out flirtatiously at Andrei. The warm wind carried along the street clouds of dust, feathers from eiderdowns, sheets of paper, clumps of fur, and the already established odor of a menagerie.

Andrei looked at Fritz in bewilderment. With the air of a genuine battle commander, Heiger surveyed the field of imminent action through narrowed eyes. The driver shut off the engine, and the silence that ensued was filled with wild, absolutely nonurban sounds—roaring and mewing, a low, velvety whooping, burping, champing, grunting . . . At that moment the besieged woman started shrieking at the top of her voice, and Fritz went into action.

"Disembark!" he ordered. "Move it, move! Deploy in a line . . . Deploy in a line, I said, not a huddle! Forward! Beat them, drive them away! Don't jab at them, beat them! I don't want to see a single ugly brute left here! Beat them on the head and on the spine! Don't poke at them, beat them! Forward, move it! Don't stop, hey, you there!"

Andrei was one of the first to jump down. He didn't deploy into a line; instead he took a more comfortable grip on his iron bludgeon and went dashing straight to the aid of the woman. Catching sight of him, the long-tailed hooligans burst into peals of diabolical laughter and darted off down the street, hopping and skipping and wiggling their gleaming buttocks derisively. The woman carried on screeching with her eyes squeezed tightly shut and her hands clenched into fists, but she wasn't in danger anymore, and Andrei left her and set off toward the bandits who were ransacking the food stall.

They were powerful, seasoned veterans, especially one, with a tail as black as coal—he was sitting on a barrel, lowering his arm into it up to the shoulder, fishing out pickled cucumbers and champing on them with relish, every now and then spitting at his cronies, who were frantically ripping away the plywood wall of the stall. Noticing Andrei approaching, the black-tailed character stopped chewing and grinned balefully. Andrei didn't like the look of that grin at all, but retreat was impossible. He swung back his iron pole, yelled "Beat it!" and dashed forward.

The black-tailed character grinned even more malignly—he had fangs like a sperm whale—then skipped down lazily off the barrel, moved a few paces away, and started biting at something under his armpit. "Beat it, you pest!" Andrei yelled even louder, and swung the metal bar against the barrel. Then the black-tailed character darted off to the side and leaped in a single bound onto a second-floor cornice. Emboldened by his adversary's cowardice, Andrei darted over to the stall and smashed his iron pole against the wall. The wall split open and black-tail's friends scattered in all directions. The battlefield had been cleared and Andrei looked around.

Fritz's battle formations had disintegrated and the soldiers were wandering in confusion around the street, which was now empty, peering into entryways or stopping and throwing their heads back to look up at the baboons, who were spread out along the cornices on the facades of the buildings. In the distance the intellectual type was stomping along the street, whirling his pole above his head and raising clouds of dust as he pursued a lame monkey that was indolently trudging along just two paces ahead of him. There was no one to do battle with—even Fritz was at a loss. He stood there beside the truck, scowling and gnawing on his finger.

Quietening down again when they sensed that they were out of danger, the baboons went back to exchanging comments, scratching themselves, and making love. The most insolent of them moved lower, ranting unmistakable abuse, grimacing mockingly, and displaying their backsides insultingly. Andrei spotted black-tail again: he was already on the other side of the street, sitting on a lamppost and roaring with laughter. A small, swarthy-skinned man who looked like a Greek set off toward the lamppost with a menacing air. He took a swing and launched his iron pole up at black-tail with all his might. There was a clang and a clatter, broken glass came showering down, and black-tail jumped about a meter in the air in his surprise and almost fell, but adroitly grabbed hold with his tail, assumed his previous pose, and suddenly, arching his back, drenched the Greek with a stream of liquid fecal matter. Andrei felt the gorge rise in his throat, and he turned away. The defeat was absolute; it seemed impossible to come up with any kind of response.

Andrei walked over to Fritz and asked in a low voice, "Well, what are we going to do?"

"Fuck knows," Fritz said rancorously. "If only we had a flame-thrower . . ."

"Maybe we could bring some bricks?" asked a pimply young guy in overalls who had walked across to them. "I'm from the brick factory. We've got a truck; we could be there and back in half an hour."

"No," Fritz said categorically. "Bricks are no good. We'd break all the windows, and then they'd pelt us with our own bricks . . . No. What's needed here is some kind of pyrotechnics . . . Rockets, detonators . . . Ah, if I just had a dozen cylinders of phosgene gas!"

"Where would we get detonators in the City?" a scornful bass voice asked. "And as for phosgene, I think I'd rather have baboons . . ."

They began crowding around their commander. Only the swarthy-skinned Greek stayed away—he was washing himself off at a hydrant, spewing out infernal curses.

Andrei watched out of the corner of his eye as black-tail and his friends sneakily sidled over to the food stall again. Here and there in the windows of the buildings local inhabitants' faces, mostly women's, began appearing, pale from the terrors they had suffered or red with annoyance. "Well, don't just stand there!" they shouted angrily from the windows. "Send them packing, you men! Look, they're looting the food stall! Why are you just standing there like stuffed dummies? Hey you, the white-haired one! Give an order, can't you? Why are you just standing there like that? Good God, my children are crying! Do something so we can come out! Call yourselves men? Frightened of monkeys!" The men snarled sullenly and shamefacedly in reply.

"The fire brigade! We need to call the fire brigade!" insisted the scornful bass voice that preferred baboons to phosgene. "With ladders, and hoses . . ."

"Aw, come on, where would we find that many firemen?"

"The firemen are on Main Street."

"Maybe we should light up some torches? Maybe they'll be frightened by fire!"

"Dammit! Why the hell did they take away the policemen's guns? They need to reissue them!"

"Shouldn't we be getting back home, guys? When I think that my wife's there all alone right now . . ."

"Aw, now *you* come on. We all have wives. These women are someone's wives too."

"That's true, right enough . . ."

"Maybe we could get up on the roofs? From the roofs we could use something to . . . you know . . ."

"What are you going to reach them with, cretin? That stick of yours?"

"Oh, the lousy bastards!" the contemptuous bass suddenly bellowed in loathing. He got a running start, strained hard, and flung his metal pole at the long-suffering food stall: it pierced straight through the plywood wall. Black-tail's gang looked at it in surprise, paused for a moment, and then went back to devouring the cucumbers and potatoes. The women in the windows burst into derisive laughter.

"Well, anyway," someone said judiciously. "At least by being here, we keep *them* here, we constrain their actions, so to speak. That's something, at least. While we're here, they'll be afraid of moving farther into the City . . ."

Everyone gazed around and then suddenly started babbling, and the judicious individual was rapidly forced to pipe down.

First, it turned out that the baboons *were* moving farther into the City, notwithstanding the presence of said judicious individual. And second, even if the baboons had not been moving farther in, was this judicious individual planning to spend the night here? Live here? Sleep here? Crap and piss here?

At that moment they heard the lazy clip-clopping of hooves and the creaking of a cart; everyone looked up the street and fell silent. Approaching along the roadway at a leisurely pace was a two-horse cart. Sitting sideways on it, dozing with his legs dangling in their crude tarpaulin-fabric boots, was a large man in a faded, Russian-style army tunic and cotton breeches faded to match. The man's bowed head was crowned with a mop of light brown hair. He was holding the reins slackly in his huge brown hands. The horses—one chestnut, the other dapple gray—moved their feet lazily and also seemed to be dozing on the move.

"He's going to the market," someone said respectfully. "A farmer."

"Right, guys, the farmers have it easy with this—when will these bastards ever reach them . . . ?"

"Actually, when I imagine baboons in the crops . . ."

Feeling curious, Andrei took a closer look. He had never seen a farmer before in all the time he had spent in the City, although he had heard a lot about these people—supposedly they were dour folk and a bit on the wild and weird side. They lived far away in wild places, where they waged a harsh struggle against swamps and jungles, they only drove into the City to sell the produce from their farms, and unlike the City people, they never changed their profession.

As the cart slowly moved closer, the driver's lowered head trembled and from time to time, without waking up, he smacked his lips and jerked lightly on the reins. Suddenly the baboons, who had been in a relatively peaceable mood so far, flew into a state of extremely vicious agitation. Perhaps the horses annoyed them, or perhaps they had finally grown tired of the presence of outsiders on their street, but they suddenly started kicking up a ruckus and tearing around with their fangs glittering, and several of the most feisty scrambled up the drainpipes onto the roofs and started smashing the tiles up there.

One of the first pieces hit the driver of the cart right between his shoulder blades. The farmer started, straightened up, and looked around at his surroundings with his bloodshot eyes wide open. The first person he noticed was the intellectual type in glasses, who was returning from his futile pursuit, a solitary figure looming up behind the cart. Without saying a word, the farmer dropped the reins (the horses immediately stopped), jumped down off the cart, and darted toward his assailant, swinging back his arm as he went, but just then another piece of roof tile struck the intellectual type on the top of his head. He gasped, dropped his metal pole, and squatted down on his haunches, clutching his head in his hands. The farmer stopped, bewildered. Pieces of broken tile fell onto the road surface around him, shattering into orange crumbs.

"Brigade, take cover!" Fritz commanded valiantly, and darted toward the nearest entryway. Everyone scattered, dashing in all directions. Andrei huddled against the wall in the dead zone, watching curiously as the farmer gazed around himself in total bewilderment, clearly unable to fathom even a single little thing. His clouded gaze slid over the cornices and the drainpipes draped with raging baboons. He squeezed his eyes shut and shook his head, then opened his eyes wide again and exclaimed in a loud voice, "Hell's fucking bells!"

"Take cover," they shouted to him from all sides. "Hey, whiskers! Get over here! You'll catch one to the dome, you swampland simpleton!"

"What the hell's going on?" the farmer asked loudly, turning toward the intellectual type, who was crawling around on all fours, trying to find his glasses. "Who are all this lot here, can you tell me?"

"Monkeys, naturally," the intellectual type responded haughtily. "Surely you can see that for yourself, my man?"

"Well now, the things that go on round here," the dumb-founded farmer exclaimed, only now waking up completely. "You're always coming up with something or other . . ."

This son of the swamps was in a philosophical and well-disposed mood now. Having satisfied himself that the offense he had suffered could not really be regarded as such, he was simply rather flabbergasted by the sight of the shaggy hordes frisking along the cornices and clambering up the streetlamps. He merely shook his head reproachfully and scratched his beard. But at this point the intellectual type finally found his glasses, picked up his pole, and dashed lickety-split for cover, so the farmer was left in the middle of the roadway all on his lonesome—the only target, and a rather tempting one for the hairy snipers. The highly disadvantageous nature of this position was not slow in revealing itself. A dozen large shards crashed down, shattering at his feet, and smaller debris started drumming on his shaggy head and his shoulders.

"What the hell is all this?" the farmer roared. A new shard slammed into his forehead. The farmer stopped speaking and dashed lickety-split for his cart.

The cart was exactly opposite Andrei, and at first he thought the farmer would slump sideways onto it, send the whole damned shebang to blazes and race off to his swamps, as far away as possible from this dangerous place. But the man with the beard had no intention of sending the whole damned shebang to blazes. Muttering "You damn whores . . ." he started hastily unlashing the load on his cart with great dexterity. His broad back blocked Andrei's view of what he was doing there, but the women in the house opposite could see everything—they all suddenly started squealing at once, slammed their windows shut and disappeared from sight. Before Andrei could even blink, the hirsute farmer had squatted down on his haunches, and a thick gun barrel, gleaming with an oily shimmer, rose up above his head, pointing toward the roofs.

"As you were!" Fritz roared, and Andrei saw him dash out from somewhere on the right, moving toward the cart in huge bounds.

"Now, you bastards, you shits . . ." the bearded man muttered, performing some kind of intricate, extremely deft movements with his hands, to an accompaniment of slithering metallic clicks and jangling. Andrei tensed up in anticipation of thunder and flame, and the monkeys on the roof apparently sensed something too. They stopped hurling themselves about, hunkered down on their tails, and started twisting their dogs' heads to and fro, exchanging their comments on something in dry clicks.

But Fritz was already beside the cart. He grabbed the bearded man by the shoulder and repeated peremptorily, "As you were!"

"Hold on!" the bearded man muttered irascibly, jerking his shoulder. "Hold on, will you, just let me cut them down, the long-tailed bastards . . ."

"I gave you an order—as you were!" Fritz barked.

Then the bearded man turned his face toward Fritz and slowly stood up. "What's the problem?" he asked, drawling the words with immense contempt. He was the same height as Fritz, but noticeably broader then him across the shoulders and below the waist.

"Where did you get a gun?" Fritz asked abruptly. "Show me your papers!"

"Why, you little snot!" the bearded man said in baleful amazement. "He wants my papers! How do you like this, you white-haired louse?"

Fritz disregarded the obscene gesture. Still looking the bearded man straight in the eye, he barked loud enough for the whole street to hear: "Ruhmer! Voronin! Friese! Come here!"

Andrei was surprised to hear his own name, but he immediately pushed off from the wall and walked over to the cart, taking his time. From the other side, moving at a brisk jog, came sloping-shouldered Ruhmer—in the past he had been a professional boxer—and, running at full speed, one of Fritz's cronies, the small, skinny Otto Friese, a consumptive youth with large jug ears.

"Come on, come on . . ." the farmer kept muttering with an ominous leer as he observed all these preparations for combat.

"I urgently request once again that you present your papers," Fritz repeated with icy politeness.

"And you can stick your request up your backside," the bearded man responded indolently. He was looking mostly at Ruhmer now, and he had set his hand, as if by chance, on the handle of an impressive looking whip ingeniously woven out of rawhide.

"Guys, guys!" Andrei admonished them. "Listen, soldier, drop it, don't argue, we're from City Hall."

"Fuck your City Hall up the ass," the soldier replied, examining Ruhmer balefully from head to toe.

"Well, what's the problem here?" Ruhmer inquired in a quiet, very husky voice.

"You know perfectly well," Fritz said to the bearded man, "that guns are prohibited within city limits. Especially machine guns. If you have a permit, I request you to present it."

"And just who are you to go asking for my permit? Are you the police or something? Some kind of gestapo?"

"We are a voluntary self-defense brigade."

The bearded man smirked. "Well, defend yourselves then. If you're a self-defense brigade, who's stopping you?"

A regular full-tilt jawing session was brewing up. The brigade gradually gathered around the cart. Even some of the local male population crept out of entrances—some with fire tongs, some with pokers, and some with chair legs. They gazed inquisitively at the bearded man, at the ominous machine gun perched upright on the tarpaulin, at something rounded and glassy, glinting under the tarpaulin sheet. They sniffed—the farmer was enveloped in a distinctive atmosphere, compounded of the odors of sweat, garlic sausage, and strong liquor . . .

Andrei was surprised at the strange tenderness he felt as he examined the faded army tunic with the sweat stains under the armpits and a solitary, small bronze button (not even fastened) on the collar, the fore-and-aft cap with the mark left by a five-pointed star, tilted down over the right eyebrow in familiar fashion, the massive, tarpaulin-fabric, shit-crusher boots—the immense beard was probably the only thing that seemed out of place, that didn't fit the image . . . And then it occurred to him that for Fritz all this must evoke quite different associations and sensations. He looked at Fritz. The former Unterleutnant was standing erect, with his lips compressed into a thin line and his nose gathered into contemptuous creases, trying to freeze the bearded man with the glare of his steely gray, genuinely Aryan eyes.

"We're not required to have permits," the bearded man drawled in the meantime. "We're not required to do anything at all, except feed you spongers."

"All right, then," the bass voice boomed from the back rows. "But where's the machine gun from?"

"A machine gun—so what? It's the coupling of town and country, isn't it? A carboy of moonshine for you, a machine gun for me, all honest and aboveboard."

"Oh no," the bass voice boomed. "A machine gun, that's not just some sort of toy, not a threshing machine or something of the kind."

"It seems to me," the judicious individual commented, "that farmers are actually allowed to have guns!"

"No one's allowed to have guns!" Friese squeaked, and blushed violently.

"Well, that's stupid!" the judicious individual responded.

"Damn right it's stupid," said the bearded man. "I'd like to see you out in our swamps, at night, in the rutting season . . ."

"Whose rutting season?" the intellectual type asked with keen interest, pushing through into the front row in his glasses.

"The rutting season for them as needs to rut," the farmer answered him disdainfully.

"No, no, if you please . . ." the intellectual type said hastily. "I'm a biologist, you know, and I still can't—"

"Shut up," Fritz told him. "And as for you," he went on, turning to the man with the beard, "I suggest that you follow me. I
suggest it in order to avoid unnecessary bloodshed."

Their glances clashed. And would you believe it, somehow,
from some minute feature or other that only he could spot, the
man with the luxurious beard sensed who he was dealing with
here. His beard split apart in a malicious grin, and he pronounced
in a repulsive, obnoxiously thin little voice, "Milch und eggsen?
Hitler-kaput!" He wasn't in the least bit afraid of bloodshed,
unnecessary or any other kind.

It was as if Fritz had been punched on the chin. He flung
his head back, his pale face turned crimson, the knotted muscles
stood out on his cheeks. For a moment Andrei thought he was
about to fling himself at the bearded man, and Andrei even leaned
forward, ready to stand between them, but Fritz controlled himself. The blood drained back out of his face and he announced
drily, "That has nothing to do with the matter. Be so good as to
follow me."

"Oh, leave him alone, Heiger!" the bass voice said. "It's obvious he's a farmer, isn't it? When have you ever heard of anyone
hassling farmers?"

And everyone around started nodding and muttering that
yes, he was clearly a farmer, who would drive off and take the
machine gun with him—he really wasn't any kind of gangster
at all.

"We need to repel the baboons, and here we are playing
policemen," the judicious individual added.

That relieved the tension immediately. Everyone remembered
about the baboons, and the baboons turned out to be sauntering
around wherever they fancied again, behaving as if they were at
home in the jungle. It also turned out that the local population
had apparently gotten sick of waiting for decisive action from
the self-defense brigade. They had evidently decided that the self-
defense brigade wasn't going to do anything useful, and they'd
have to somehow make shift for themselves. And women carrying

pocketbooks, with their lips firmly clamped shut in no-nonsense
determination, were scurrying about on their morning errands,
many of them clutching sticks from brooms and mops to fend
off the most persistent of the monkeys. The shutters were taken
down off a shop window, and the stall-keeper walked around
his looted stall and groaned, scratching his back and clearly trying to figure something out. A line sprang up at the bus stop,
and the first bus—yes, there it was—appeared in the distance. In
contravention of a municipal council bylaw, it sounded its horn
loudly, scattering the baboons, who were not familiar with the
traffic regulations.

"Yes indeed, gentlemen," someone said. "Evidently we shall
have to come to terms with this as well. So we can all go home,
commander?"

Fritz glowered morosely at the street. "Well now," he said in
an ordinary human voice. "Home it is then."

He swung around, sticking his hands into his pockets, and
was the first to head toward the truck. The brigade straggled
after him. Men struck matches and lit up, and someone asked
what they could do about being late for work; it would be good
if they could get some kind of official note . . . The judicious
individual had an answer for that too: everyone would be late
for work today, so what point was there in notes? The jawing
session around the cart dispersed. The only ones left were Andrei
and the biologist in glasses, who had set himself the firm goal of
discovering exactly who it was that had a rutting season in the
swamps.

As he dismantled the machine gun and stashed it away again,
the bearded man condescendingly explained that the creatures
who had a rutting season in the swamps were redbacks, and the
redbacks, brother, were something like crocodiles. Had the biologist ever seen crocodiles? Right, then. Only covered in fur. This
red kind of fur, coarse and stiff. And when they were rutting,
brother, you'd best keep your distance. In the first place, they
were big brutes, the size of bulls, and in the second place, during

that business they didn't notice a thing—a house wasn't a house to them, a shed wasn't a shed; they smashed everything to splinters . . .

The intellectual type's eyes blazed and he listened avidly, constantly adjusting his glasses with outstretched fingers. Fritz called from the truck, "Hey, are you coming or not? Andrei?" The intellectual type glanced around at the truck, looked at his watch, groaned pitifully, and started mumbling apologies and thanks. Then he grabbed the bearded man's hand, shook it with all his might, and ran off. But Andrei stayed.

He himself didn't know why he had stayed. It was a rush of something like a fit of nostalgia. It wasn't even as if he were missing the sound of spoken Russian—after all, everyone around here spoke in Russian—and it wasn't as if this man with a beard seemed to him like the incarnation of his motherland, no way. But something about him definitely made Andrei feel thoroughly homesick, something or other that he couldn't get from the stern, sardonic Donald, or from the jolly and passionate but still somehow alien Kensi, or from Wang, always good natured, always affable, but really badly downtrodden. And even less from Fritz, a remarkable man after his own fashion but nonetheless yesterday's enemy . . . Andrei hadn't even suspected how badly he'd been pining for this mysterious "something."

The man with a beard gave him a sideways glance and asked, "From the home country, are you?"

"From Leningrad," said Andrei, feeling embarrassed, and in order to gloss over this embarrassment somehow, he took out his cigarettes and offered them to the bearded man.

"So that's the way of it," said the man, tugging a cigarette out of the pack. "We're fellow countrymen, then. But I'm from Vologda, brother. Cherepovets—ever heard of it? The wild and woolly Cherepovtsians . . ."

"Sure I have!" Andrei exclaimed, absolutely delighted. "They've built an iron and steel works there, a ginormous industrial plant."

"You don't say?" the bearded man responded rather indifferently. "So they've roped in Cherepovets too . . . Well, OK. And what do you do here? What's your name?"

Andrei told him.

"I'm working the land here," the bearded man continued. "A farmer, as they say here. Yurii Konstantinovich, and the surname's Davydov. Fancy a drink?"

Andrei hesitated. "It seems a bit early," he said.

"Well, maybe it is," Yurii Konstantinovich agreed. "I've still got to get to the market, haven't I? I arrived yesterday evening, you see, went straight to the workshops; they promised me a machine gun there a long time ago. Well, it was one thing and another: I tried out the gadget, offloaded some ham, you know, and a couple hundred liters of moonshine for them, then I look around—and they've turned the sun off already . . ." While he was telling Andrei all this, Davydov finished securing his load, untangled the reins, sat in the cart sideways, and started the horses moving. Andrei set off beside him.

"Yep, yep," Yurii Konstantinovich continued. "So here they've already switched off the sun, and this guy says to me: 'Come on, let's go,' he says. 'I know a place near here.' So we went and we had a drink and a bite to eat. You know how it is with vodka in the City, and I had moonshine. They provide the music, like, and I put up the drink. Well, women, of course . . ." Davydov waggled his beard as he reminisced, then went on, lowering his voice: "Out in our swamps, brother, women are kind of thin on the ground. You know, there's this widow, well, we go to her . . . her husband drowned the year before last . . . Well, you know the way that works out—you go visit her, no way around it, but afterward, it's fix her threshing machine, or lend her a hand with the harvest, or else it's the tiller . . . Ah, what a *paain!*" He lashed a baboon that had tagged along behind the cart with his whip. "Anyway, brother, where we are, it's like living in combat conditions—near as, dammit. Without a gun, there's just no way. And who's that bright-blond boy of yours? German, is he?"

"Yes," said Andrei. "A former sublieutenant, he was taken prisoner near Königsberg, and he came here from captivity . . ."

"I spotted something repulsive about that ugly mug," said Davydov. "Those wormy assholes drove me all the way to Moscow, drove me into hospital, blew off half my backside, clean as a whistle. I gave them what for afterward too. I'm a tank soldier, right? Last time I burned out was outside Prague . . ." He twisted his beard about. "Now, what do you reckon to this then? Of all the damned places to meet!"

"No, he's a decent enough, no-nonsense kind of guy," said Andrei. "And gutsy too. He likes to cut a strut, OK, but he's a good worker, lots of energy. For the Experiment, I reckon he's a very useful individual. An organizer."

Davydov said nothing for a while, clicking his tongue at the horses. "This guy comes out to us in the swamps last week," he said eventually. "Well, we got together at Kowalski's place—he's a farmer too, a Pole, about ten kilometers from me, got a good house, big. Yep, yep. So we got together. And then this type starts feeding us this hogwash: do we, like, have a correct understanding of the objectives of the Experiment? And he's from City Hall, the Agricultural Department. Well, we can see where he's heading: let's say we do have a correct understanding—then a tax increase would be a good idea . . . Are you married?" he suddenly asked.

"No," said Andrei.

"The reason I ask is, I could do with a place to stay tonight. I've got another piece of business set up for tomorrow morning."

"But of course!" said Andrei. "No need even to ask! Come and stay the night, I've got loads of space, I'd be delighted."

"Well, and so would I," Davydov said with a smile. "Fellow countrymen and all that."

"Make a note of the address," said Andrei. "Have you got something to write it on?"

"Just tell me," said Davydov. "I'll remember it."

"It's a simple address: 105 Main Street, apartment 16. Entrance from the courtyard. If I'm not there, call round to the caretaker's

place—he's a Chinese guy, Wang, I'll leave a key with him."
Andrei really liked Davydov, although they clearly didn't see eye
to eye on everything.

"What year were you born?" Davydov asked.

"Twenty-eight."

And when did you leave Russia?"

"In '51. Only four months ago."

"Aha. And I left Russia for here in '47 . . . So tell me then,
Andriukha, how are things in the countryside—have they gotten
better?"

"Well, of course!" said Andrei. "They've rebuilt everything,
they're reducing prices every year . . . I didn't get out into the
country after the war myself, it's true, but to judge from
the movies and the books, life in the country's really good now."

"Hmm . . . movies," Davydov said doubtfully. "You know,
when it comes to movies . . ."

"No, why say that? In town, the shops have got everything.
They abolished ration cards ages ago. So where's it all from?
From the country, right . . ."

"That's right," said Davydov. "From the country . . . But
you know, I got back from the front and my wife was gone,
she'd died. My son disappeared without a trace. The village was
deserted. OK, I think, we'll put this right. Who won the war?
We did! So now we're calling the shots. They wanted to make
me farm chairman. I agreed. There was no one in the village
but women, so there was no need even to get married. We just
about scraped through '46; right, I think, now things will get a
bit easier . . ." He suddenly stopped talking and said nothing for
a long time, as if he'd forgotten about Andrei. "Happiness for all
mankind!" he declared unexpectedly. "How about you—do you
believe it?"

"Of course."

"And I believed that too. No, I thought, the countryside's
a dead duck. Some kind of stupid blunder, I thought. Grabbed
by the tits before the war, grabbed by the throat after it. No, I

thought, this way they'll crush us. And the life, you know, as grim as a general's shoulder straps. I'd started drinking already, and then—the Experiment." He sighed heavily. "So, you reckon this Experiment of theirs will work out?"

"Why is it theirs? It's ours!"

"OK, so let say it's ours. Will it work out or not?"

"It's got to," Andrei said firmly. "It all depends on us, and only us."

"Whatever depends on us, we're doing it. We did it there, we're doing it here . . . Basically, of course, I can't really grumble. Life's tough, all right, but way better than it was. The main thing is, you do it for yourself, get what I mean? And if some stooge shows up, you can maybe drop him in the privy, and there you go, home free! Party member, are you?" he asked suddenly.

"Komsomol. Yurii Konstantinovich, you take altogether too gloomy a view of things. The Experiment is the Experiment. It's hard, there are plenty of mistakes, but probably it couldn't possibly be any other way. Everyone on duty at his own post—everyone doing what he can."

"And what's your post?"

"Garbage collector," Andrei said proudly.

"A really serious post, that," said Davydov. "And have you got a profession?"

"My profession's very specialized," said Andrei. "Stellar astronomer." He pronounced the title shyly, glancing sideways at Davydov, anticipating mockery, but on the contrary, Davydov was terribly interested.

"Really, you're an astronomer? Listen, brother, then you ought to know where this is we've all been fetched up. Is it a planet of some kind, or a star, maybe? Back out there, in the swamps I mean, folks fall out over that every evening—they come to blows, so help me! They get a skinful of moonshine and then they go at it hammer and tongs . . . There are some as think, you know, we're stuck in some kind of fish tank—still right here on Earth. This great, huge kind of fish tank, only instead of fish, it has people in it. So help me! But what do you think—from the scientific point of view?"

Andrei scratched the back of his head and laughed. In his apartment people almost came to blows for the same reason—even without any moonshine. And as for the fish tank, Izya Katzman had expatiated on that in exactly the same way, word for word, giggling and spraying. "How can I put it, you see . . ." he began. "It's all very complicated. Baffling. And from the scientific point of view, there's only one thing I can tell you: it's not likely that this is a different planet, even less a star. In my opinion, everything here is artificial, and it has nothing to do with astronomy."

Davydov nodded a few times. "A fish tank," he said decisively. "And the sun here's a sort of lightbulb, and that Yellow Wall running right up to the sky . . . Listen, if I follow this side street, will I get to the market or not?"

"Yes, you will," said Andrei. "You haven't forgotten my address?"

"I haven't forgotten it—expect me this evening."

Davydov lashed at the horses and let out a whistle, and the cart rumbled onto the side street and disappeared. Andrei set off for home. What a great guy, he thought, feeling moved. A soldier! Of course, he didn't join the Experiment, he ran away from his problems, but I've no right to judge him for that. He was wounded, his house and land were trashed—he was entitled to falter, wasn't he? His life here is clearly no bowl of cherries either. And he's not the only one here who's faltered; we have plenty of those here . . .

On Main Street the baboons were sauntering about, totally free and easy. Either Andrei had gotten used to them, or they themselves had changed in some way, but they no longer seemed anything like as brazen, let alone as frightening, as a few hours earlier. They placidly arranged themselves in groups in the hot sun, jabbering and searching themselves for lice, and when people walked by, they held out their shaggy, black-palmed paws and blinked pleadingly with their watery eyes. It was as if an immense number of beggars had suddenly shown up in the City.

Andrei saw Wang at the gates of his building. He was sitting on a stanchion, hunched over sadly with his work-worn hands lowered between his knees.

"Lost the cans, did you?" he asked, without raising his head.

"Look at what's happening."

Glancing into the passageway, Andrei was horrified. The heaps seemed to reach right up to the lightbulb. There was only a narrow little track leading to the door of the caretaker's lodge.

"God almighty!" Andrei said, suddenly getting jittery. "I'll go right now . . . hang on . . . I'll be right back . . ." He tried fever-ishly to recall which streets he and Donald had raced along last night and the spot where the fugitives had dumped the cans off the truck.

"Don't bother," Wang said in a hopeless voice. "A commis-sion's already been here. They took down the numbers of the cans and promised to bring them this evening. They won't bring them this evening, of course, but maybe they might by morning, eh?"

"You know, Wang," said Andrei, "it was sheer hell and hul-labaloo, I feel ashamed to remember it."

"I know. Donald told me what it was like."

"Donald's home already?" Andrei asked, brightening up.

"Yes. He said not to let anyone into his place. He said his teeth ached. I gave him a bottle of vodka and he left."

"So it's like that . . ." Andrei said, examining the heaps of trash again.

And he suddenly felt a desire so unbearably intense it was almost hysterical, enough to make him cry out, to get a wash, to strip off his stinking overalls and forget that tomorrow he would have to scrabble through all this stuff with a spade . . . Every-thing around Andrei was suddenly sticky and rank-smelling, and without saying another word, he dashed through the courtyard and onto his stairway, bounding up the steps three at a time and trembling in impatience, reached his apartment, grabbed the key from under the rubber mat, and swung open the door—and the fragrant coolness of eau de cologne received him into its tender embrace.

3

First of all he undressed, crumpling up his overalls and under-wear and flinging them into a box of filthy junk. Filth unto filth. Then, standing stark naked in the center of the kitchen, he looked around and shuddered with renewed revulsion. The kitchen was submerged under heaps of dirty dishes. Plates were banked up in the corners, covered with bluish cobwebs of mold that charita-bly concealed black lumps of something or other. The table was crammed with murky, finger-marked wineglasses, water glasses, and empty preserved-fruit jars. The sink was choked with cups and saucers; blackened saucepans, greasy frying pans, colanders, and casseroles sat on the stools, giving off a lethargic stench. He walked over to the sink and turned the faucet on. He was in luck! The water was hot! And he set to work.

After washing all the dishes, pots, and pans, he grabbed hold of a mop. He worked with zealous enthusiasm, as if he were washing the dirt off his own body, but he couldn't keep that up for all five rooms. He limited himself to the kitchen, the dining room, and the bedroom, merely glancing into the other rooms with a feeling of bewilderment—he simply couldn't get used to it, just couldn't understand what one man would need so many rooms for, and such monstrously huge, musty rooms at that. He closed their doors tightly, wedging them shut with chairs.

Now he ought to pop down to the shop to buy something for the evening. Davydov was coming, and some of the usual mob were bound to drop in too . . . But first he decided to get washed up. The water was running almost cold already, but it was still wonderful anyway. Then he put fresh sheets on the bed, and when he saw his own bed with clean sheets and crisp, starched pillowcases, when he caught the scent of freshness that they exuded, he was suddenly overcome by a desperate urge to lay his own clean body down for a while in this long-forgotten cleanness, and he collapsed with a crash, setting the trashy springs screeching and the old polished wood creaking.

Yes, it was wonderful, so cool, fragrant, and squeaky, and there on the right, within his reach, there turned out to be a pack of cigarettes with matches, and on the left, also within range, there was a small shelf of handpicked detective novels. It was slightly disappointing that there was no ashtray anywhere within reach, and it turned out that he had forgotten to wipe the dust off the small shelf, but these were merely insignificant details. He chose *Ten Little Indians*, lit up, and started reading.

When he woke, it was still light. He listened. The apartment and the building were silent, with only the water, dripping copiously from the defective faucets, weaving a strange pattern of sound. And apart from that, everything around him was clean, and that was strange too, but at the same time inexpressibly delightful. Then there was a knock at the door. He pictured Davydov, with his powerful build and tanned skin, scented with hay and reeking of fresh alcohol, standing outside on the landing, holding his horses by their bridles, with a bottle of moonshine at the ready. And then there was another knock and he woke up completely.

"Coming!" he yelled, springing up and running across the bedroom, searching for his underwear. He came across a pair of stripy pajama bottoms and hastily pulled them on. The elastic was weak, and he had to hold the pants up at one side.

Contrary to expectations, he couldn't hear any good-natured swearing from behind the front door, no neighing of horses or glugging of liquid. Smiling in anticipation, Andrei pulled back the latch, opened the door, gave a croak, and took a rapid step back, grabbing the cursed elastic with his other hand as well. Standing there in front of him was his recent acquaintance Selma Nagel, the new girl from number 18.

"Have you got any cigarettes?" she asked, without even a trace of neighborly conviviality.

"Yes . . . please . . . come in . . ." Andrei mumbled, backing away.

She came in and walked past him, scalding him with the mingled aromas of incredible perfumes.

She walked through into the dining room, then he closed the door, and with a despairing call of "Wait just a moment, I'll be right there!" dashed into the bedroom. *"Ay-ay-ay"* he said to himself. *"Ay-ay-ay,* how could I . . ." In fact, however, he didn't feel ashamed in the least; he even felt glad that he'd been caught out like this, so clean and washed, with his broad shoulders and smooth skin and magnificently developed biceps and triceps—it was actually a shame to get dressed. But after all, it was necessary to get dressed, and he stuck his hands in a suitcase and rummaged around in it, then pulled on a pair of gymnastics pants and a washed-out blue sports singlet with the intertwined letters "LU" (for Leningrad University) on the back and the chest. And that was how he appeared before Selma Nagel: chest thrust out, shoulders spread wide, with a slightly lingering gait and a pack of cigarettes in his outstretched hand.

Pretty Selma Nagel indifferently took a cigarette, clicked her lighter, and lit up. She didn't even look at Andrei, and she had an air about her as if she didn't give a damn for anything in the world. In fact, by daylight she didn't look so very pretty. Her face was rather irregular, even coarse, her nose was too short, and her large mouth was daubed too thickly with lipstick. However, her little legs, so thoroughly naked, were far above and beyond all praise. Unfortunately he couldn't get a proper look at all the rest—who in hell's name had taught her to wear such baggy clothes! A sweater, and with that neck! Like a frogman.

She sat there in a deep armchair, with one beautiful leg crossed over the other beautiful leg, and looked around indifferently, holding her cigarette soldier fashion, with the burning end cradled inside her palm. Andrei sat down jauntily but elegantly on the edge of the table and also lit up.

"My name's Andrei," he said.

She turned her indifferent gaze onto him. Her eyes weren't the way they had seemed last night either. They were large but quite definitely not black; they were pale blue, almost transparent.

"Andrei," she repeated. "Polish?"

"No, Russian. And your name's Selma Nagel—you're from Sweden."

She nodded. "Yes, from Sweden . . . So it was you they were beating in the police station yesterday?" she asked, abruptly setting a little lacquered box, slightly larger than a matchbox, on her knee. "Nothing but crackling and howling on every wavelength, no fun at all."

Andrei cautiously took the little box from her and realized with surprise that it was a radio. "Oh, wow!" he muttered. "Is it really transistorized?"

"How should I know?" She took the radio back from him and there was a burst of wheezing, crackling, and mournful howling. "It just doesn't work, that's all. So you've never seen any like this, then?"

Andrei shook his head. Then he said, "Actually, your radio shouldn't work. There's only one radio station here, and that broadcasts directly through the mains."

"Oh God," said Selma. "Then what are people supposed to do here? There's no box either."

"What box?"

"You know, the telly . . . TV!"

"Ah . . . Yes, that's not planned for any time soon around here."

"Well, what a drag!"

"We can crank up the phonograph," Andrei suggested shyly, feeling awkward. Really and truly, what was all this—no radio, no television, no movie theaters?

"The phonograph? What sort of thing is that, then?"

"You don't know what a phonograph is?" Andrei asked in amazement. "Well, it's a gramophone. You put on a record . . ."

"Ah, a record player . . ." Selma said in a totally uninspired voice. "Haven't you got a tape recorder?"

"What a question," said Andrei. "Do you think I'm a radio station or something?"

"You're some kind of savage," Selma Nagel declared. "*Russian*, that's the word. OK then, you listen to your phonograph, you probably drink vodka, and what else do you do? Race around on a motorbike? Or don't you even have a motorbike?"

Andrei got angry. "I didn't come here to race around on a motorbike. I'm here to work. But what about you, I wonder—what do you intend to do here?"

"He came here to work . . ." said Selma. "Tell me, what were they beating you for in the police station? Drugs?"

"No one was beating me in the police station! Where did you get that idea from? And in any case, our police don't beat anyone. You're not in Sweden now, you know."

Selma drew in her breath with a whistle. "Well, well," she said mockingly. "So I imagined it." She stuck her cigarette butt into the ashtray, lit another cigarette, got up, and set off around the room with a comical, waltzing movement. "And who lived here before you?" she asked, halting in front of a huge oval portrait of some woman in lilac with a toy dog on her knees. "In my place, for instance, it was obviously some sex maniac. Pornography in all the corners, used condoms on the walls, and an entire collection of women's garter belts in the wardrobe. I can't really tell what he was, a fetishist or a clit-licker . . ."

"You're lying," Andrei said, stunned. "That's all lies, Selma Nagel."

"What would I tell lies for?" Selma asked in astonishment. "Who was it who lived there? Do you know?"

"The mayor! The current mayor lived there, got it?"

"Ah," Selma said indifferently. "I see."

"What do you see?" said Andrei. "What is it that you see?" he yelled, growing frenzied. "What can you understand here anyway?"

He stopped. That wasn't something you could talk about. That was something you had to experience inside, for yourself.

"He's probably about fifty," Selma declared with the air of a connoisseur. "Old age creeping up on him, the man's freaking out. Male menopause!" She laughed and stared at the portrait with the toy dog again.

Silence fell. Andrei gritted his teeth, feeling distressed for the mayor. The man was expansive and imposing; he had an exceptionally engaging face, with a full head of noble gray hair. He spoke beautifully at meetings of the municipal citizens' council—about temperance, about proud asceticism, about strength of spirit, about inner moral fiber, charged with fortitude and virtue. And when they used to meet outside on the landing, he invariably held out his large, warm hand to be shaken and inquired with his perennial courtesy and consideration whether the tapping of his typewriter bothered Andrei at night.

"He doesn't believe it!" Selma suddenly burst out. She turned out not to be looking at the portrait anymore but to be examining Andrei with an angry kind of curiosity. "If you don't believe it, then don't. Only it disgusts me, having to wash it all off. Isn't there any way to hire someone for that here?"

"Hire someone . . ." Andrei repeated obtusely. "Screw you!" he said malevolently. "You can wash it off yourself. There's no place for whiners here."

For a while they examined each other with mutual animosity. Then Selma turned her eyes away and murmured, "Why the hell did I come here? What am I going to do here?"

"Nothing special," said Andrei. He had overcome his animosity. This person needed help. Andrei had already seen plenty of new arrivals in this place. "The same thing as everyone else, that's what you'll do. You'll go to the labor exchange, fill out a record card, drop it in the slot . . . We've got a job allocation device set up there. What were you in the other world?"

"A foxtailer."

"What?"

"Well, how can I explain it . . . One, two, spread those legs . . ."

Andrei felt stunned again. She's lying. The thought flashed through his mind. The minx is just feeding me a load of drivel. Trying to make a fool out of me. "And did you earn good money?" he asked sarcastically.

"You fool," she said, almost affectionately. "It's not for the money, just that it's interesting. It's out of boredom."

"But how could that happen?" Andrei asked mournfully. "What on Earth were your parents thinking? You're young, you could still be studying and learning for ages and ages . . ."

"What for?" Selma asked.

"What do you mean, what for? You could make a life for yourself . . . Be an engineer, or a teacher . . . You could join the Communist Party and fight for socialism . . ."

"Oh my God, my God . . ." Selma whispered hoarsely, collapsing into the armchair as if she'd been poleaxed and hiding her face in her hands. Andrei was frightened, but at the same time he felt a sense of pride, and his own prodigious responsibility.

"Oh, come on now, come on . . ." he said, awkwardly sliding closer to her. "What's happened has happened. It's over. Don't get upset. Perhaps it's good that things turned out this way for you. You'll make up for everything here. I've got lots of friends, all real human beings . . ." He recalled Izya and frowned. "We'll help. We'll fight together. There's a hell of a lot of work to do here! Lots of disorder and confusion, and simple trash—every honest person counts. You can't imagine just how much trash of all kinds has come flooding in here! I don't ask them, of course, but sometimes I'd really love to: What exactly brought you here anyway, what damn use are you to anyone here?"

He was on the point of giving Selma a friendly, even brotherly, pat on the shoulder, but at that moment, without taking her hands away from her face, she asked, "So not everyone here's like that?"

"Like what?"

"Like you. Idiots."

"Oh, for crying out loud!" Andrei jumped down off the table and started walking in circles around the room. What a bourgeois bitch. A whore, but she comes here too. Thinks it's interesting, don't you see . . . But then, Selma's directness actually impressed him. Directness was always good. Face-to-face, across the barricades. Not like Izya, for instance: neither ours nor yours, as slippery as an eel, and he'd squirm through anywhere . . .

Selma giggled behind him. "Well, what are you running around for?" she said. "It's not my fault if you're such a little idiot. OK, I'm sorry."

Determined not to relent, Andrei resolutely sliced his open hand through the air. "I'll tell you this," he said. "You, Selma, are a very badly neglected individual, and it will take a long time to scour you clean. And please don't imagine that I am personally offended by you. The people who reduced you to this state, yes, I have scores to settle with them. But not with you, none at all. You're here, and that means you're our comrade. Work well, and we'll be good friends. And you'll have to work well. Being here, you know, it's like being in the army: if you don't know how, we'll teach you; if you don't want to, we'll make you!" He liked the way he was speaking very much—it was so distinctly reminiscent of the speeches given by Lyosha Baldaev, the leader of the Communist Youth League group in his faculty at the university, before the unpaid working Saturdays. At this point he discovered that Selma had finally taken her hands away from her face and was gazing at him with frightened curiosity. He winked at her encouragingly. "Oh yes, we'll make you, what were you expecting? We used to get real loafers coming to the building site—at first all they wanted to do was slip down to the beer kiosk and into the woods. But we fixed them! And they were as good as gold! You know, work can even humanize a monkey."

"Do you always have monkeys roaming round the streets here?" Selma asked.

"No," said Andrei, pulling a long face. "That only started today. In honor of your arrival."

"Are you going to humanize them?" Selma inquired insinuatingly.

Andrei forced out a laugh. "We'll see how things go," he said. "Maybe we really will have to humanize them. The Experiment is the Experiment." For all its contemptuous insanity, the idea still seemed to have to some kind of rational kernel to it. I'll have to bring up the question this evening, he thought briefly, but then another idea immediately occurred to him. "What are you planning to do this evening?" he asked.

"I don't know. Whatever comes up. What do people do around here?"

There was a knock at the door. Andrei looked at the clock. It was seven already—the gathering was already starting to come together. "Today you're my guest here," he told Selma firmly. With this dissolute creature, the only way to act was firmly. "I don't exactly promise a load of fun and games. But I'll introduce you to some interesting people. Deal?"

Selma shrugged one little shoulder and started tidying her hair. Andrei went to open the door. Someone was already hammering on it with his heel. It was Izya Katzman. "Have you got a woman in here, or what?" he asked while he was still in the doorway. "And when will you finally get a doorbell put in, that's what I'd like to know."

As always, for the first few minutes of his appearance at a gathering, Izya's hair was neatly combed, his shirt collar was stiffly starched, and his cuffs positively gleamed. His narrow, well-ironed tie was arranged with great precision along the nose-navel axis. Nonetheless, Andrei would still have preferred to see Donald or Kensi right now. "Come in, come in, blabbermouth," he said. "What's wrong with you today, showing up before everyone else?"

"I knew you had a woman here," Izya replied, rubbing his hands and giggling, "so I hurried over to take a peek." They walked into the dining room and Izya made straight for Selma with broad, rapid strides. "Izya Katzman"—he introduced himself in a velvety voice—"garbage collector."

"Selma Nagel," Selma responded indolently. "Tramp."

Izya actually grunted in delight and solicitously kissed the hand held out to him. "By the way," he said, turning to Andrei and then back to Selma, "have you heard? The council of district commissioners is considering a draft resolution"—he lifted one finger in the air and raised his voice—"'concerning the regularization of the situation that has arisen in connection with the presence within the city limits of large aggregations of dog-headed monkeys' . . . *Oof!* It is proposed to register all the monkeys, fit them with metal collars and disks bearing their names, and then assign them to institutions and private individuals, who will be responsible for them henceforth!" He started giggling, then grunting, and then began hammering his right fist into the open palm of his left hand with shrill, lingering little groans. "Superb! All other work has been abandoned—all the factories are producing collars and name disks. Our Mr. Mayor is personally taking into his care three mature baboons and is calling on the public to follow his example. Will you take in a female baboon, Andrei? Selma will be against it, but such is the requirement of the Experiment! And as everyone knows, the Experiment is the Experiment. I hope you are in no doubt, Selma, that the Experiment *is* definitely an experiment—neither excrement, nor exponent, nor even a permanent—wave, that is—but precisely *the* Experiment?"

Struggling to make himself heard above the gurgling and groaning, Andrei said, "There you go again, waffle, waffle, waffle!" This was what he had dreaded most of all. This kind of nihilistic, couldn't-care-less attitude was bound to have a highly subversive impact on someone new. Of course, it was so incredibly alluring to wander from building to building like this, giggling and spraying disdainful spittle right and left, instead of gritting your teeth and—

Izya stopped giggling and started striding agitatedly around the room. "Perhaps it is waffle," he said. "Possibly. But as usual, Andrei, you understand damn-all about the psychology of the management. Exactly what, in your opinion, is the function of the management?"

"To manage!" said Andrei, rising to the challenge. "To manage and not to waffle, by the way, not to prattle. To coordinate the activities of the citizens and organizations—"

"Stop! Coordinate activities—to what end? What is the ultimate goal of this coordination?"

Andrei shrugged. "That's elementary. The universal good, order, the creation of optimal conditions for advancing—"

"Oh!" Izya thrust his finger into the air again. His mouth fell slightly open and his eyes rolled up. "Oh!" he repeated, and fell silent again. Selma watched him delightedly. "Order!" Izya proclaimed. "Order!" His eyes rolled back even farther. "And now imagine that in the city entrusted to you, countless herds of baboons appear. You can't drive them out—you haven't got the guts for it. You can't feed them on a centralized basis either—there isn't enough grub, not enough reserves. The baboons are begging in the street—outrageous disorder: we do not have and cannot have any beggars. The baboons crap without cleaning up after themselves, and no one intends to clean up after them. What is the conclusion begging to be drawn from all this?"

"Well, in any case, it's not to put collars on them," said Andrei.

"Correct!" Izya said approvingly. "Of course it's not to put collars on them. The very first no-nonsense conclusion begging to be drawn is: conceal the existence of the baboons. Pretend that they are not even here. But that, unfortunately, is also impossible. There are too many of them, and so far our management remains nauseatingly democratic. And then a brilliantly simple idea appears: regularize the presence of the baboons! Legitimize the chaos and outrage, thereby rendering them an element of the harmonious order intrinsic to the administration of our good mayor! Instead of herds and gangs of beggars and hooligans—we have sweet household pets. We all love animals! Queen Victoria loved animals. Darwin loved animals. Even Beria, so they say, loved some animals, not to mention Hitler . . ."

"Our king Gustaf loves animals too," Selma put in. "He has cats."

"Excellent!" Izya exclaimed, slamming his fist into his palm. "King Gustaf has cats, and Andrei Voronin has his own personal baboon. And if he really loves animals a lot, even two baboons . . ."

Andrei gave up and went off to the kitchen to check his food reserves. While he was rummaging in the little cupboards, unfolding and carefully sniffing at dusty little packets with stale, darkened contents, in the dining room Izya's voice carried on booming without a break and Selma's laughter rang out, mingling with Izya's own grunting and gurgling.

There was nothing to eat: a bag of potatoes that had already begun to sprout, a dubious can of sprats, and an absolutely stony loaf of bread. Then Andrei delved into the drawer of the kitchen table and counted his cash again. He had some cash— just enough to last until payday, as long as he was economical with it and didn't invite any guests but went visiting other people instead. They'll drive me into the grave, Andrei thought gloomily. Damn it, I've had enough. I'll bleed them all dry. What do they think I've got here, some kind of cookshop? The baboons!

At this point there was another knock at the door and Andrei went to open it, chuckling malevolently. He noticed in passing that Selma was sitting on the table with her hands stuck under herself and her painted mouth stretched out to her ears, like a real little bitch, and Izya was pontificating in front of her, waving his baboon-like arms around, and all his gloss had deserted him: the knot of his tie was under his right ear, his hair was standing up on end, and his shirt cuffs were gray.

It turned out that former noncommissioned officer of the Wehrmacht Fritz Heiger had arrived, along with his personal sidekick and private of the same Wehrmacht, Otto Friese. "So you've come!" Andrei greeted them with a malevolent smile.

Fritz immediately took this greeting as an attack on the dignity of a German noncommissioned officer and put on a stony face, but Otto, a gentle man of somewhat nebulous moral profile, merely clicked his boot heels and smiled ingratiatingly.

"What kind of tone is that?" Fritz inquired coldly. "Perhaps we should leave?"

"Have you brought anything to eat?" Andrei asked.

Fritz executed a thoughtful movement of his lower jaw. "Eat?" he repeated. "*Mmm*, how can I put it . . ." And he glanced inquiringly at Otto. Smiling shyly, Otto immediately pulled a flat bottle out of the pocket of his breeches and held it out to Andrei. Like an entry pass, with the label upward.

"Well, OK then . . ." said Andrei, mellowing and taking hold of the bottle. "But bear in mind, guys, there's absolutely nothing to eat. Maybe you have some money at least?"

"Maybe you'll let us in after all?" Fritz inquired, his head turned slightly to advance one ear: he was listening to the bursts of female laughter in the dining room.

Andrei let them into the hallway and said, "Money. Cash up front!"

"Even here we are unable to avoid reparations, Otto," said Fritz, opening his wallet. "Here!" He thrust a few bills at Andrei. "Give Otto some kind of bag and tell him what to buy—he'll run down to the shop."

"Wait, not so fast," Andrei said, and led them into the dining room. While heels clicked, slicked-down hairstyles stooped over, and soldierly compliments resounded, Andrei dragged Izya off to one side and, before he could gather his wits, frisked all his pockets, which Izya didn't even seem to notice—he just struggled feebly to break free, dying to finish the joke he had started telling. After Andrei had confiscated everything he could find, he moved away and counted the reparations. It wasn't really all that much, but it was about enough. He glanced around. Selma was still sitting on the table and dangling her legs. Her melancholy had evaporated; she was jolly. Fritz was lighting her cigarette, while Izya, choking and wheezing, was preparing to tell another joke, and Otto, red-faced from the tension and uncertainty about his manners, was a solitary pillar at the center of the room, standing to attention and visibly wiggling his large ears.

Andrei caught hold of Otto's sleeve and dragged him into the kitchen, intoning: "They'll manage without you, they'll manage . . ." Otto didn't object; he even seemed pleased. Once he found himself in the kitchen, he immediately went into action. He took the vegetable basket from Andrei, shook the rubbish out of it into the trash pail (which Andrei would never have thought of doing), rapidly and neatly covered the bottom of it with old newspapers, and instantly found the bag, which Andrei had lost the month before. Declaring "Maybe we'll find some tomato sauce . . ." he put an empty compote jar into the bag, after first rinsing it out, then stuck in a few folded newspapers in case of need ("What if they don't have any packaging . . . "), so that Andrei's contribution was limited to moving the money from one pocket to the other, stepping impatiently from one foot to the other, and intoning mournfully: "That'll do now . . . That's enough . . . let's go, shall we . . ."

"Are you going as well?" Otto asked in awed surprise when he finished getting everything together.

"Yes, why?"

"I can do it on my own," said Otto.

"On my own, on my own. It's quicker with two. You get in line for the counter, I get in line for the till."

"That's true," said Otto. "Yes. Of course."

They went out through the back entrance and walked down the back staircase. On the way they startled a baboon—the poor creature hurled itself straight out the window like a rocket, and they even felt afraid for its life, but everything was fine after all—the baboon was dangling from the fire escape ladder, baring its fangs in a grin.

"I could give him the scraps," Andrei said thoughtfully. "I've got enough leftover scraps for an entire herd."

"Shall I go and get them?" Otto suggested willingly.

Andrei merely looked at him, said "At ease!" and walked on. The stairway already stank a bit. In fact it had always stunk a bit here anyway, but now a distinctly new whiff had appeared, and after walking down another flight, they discovered its source—and more than just one.

"Yes, Wang will have a bit more work to do," said Andrei. "God forbid that I should end up as a caretaker right now. Who are you working as at the moment?"

"A minister's deputy," Otto replied despondently. "This is the third day already."

"Which minister?" Andrei inquired.

"What's it called . . . professional training."

"Is it hard?"

"I don't understand a thing," Otto said dismally. "Lots and lots of documents, instructions, reports . . . estimates, budgets . . . And no one else there understands anything either. They all run around, asking each other—Wait, where are you going?"

"To the shop."

"No. Let's go to Hofstadter's. He's cheaper, and he's German, after all."

They went to Hofstadter's. Hofstadter had a kind of combined greengrocer's and general grocery store on the corner of Main Street and Old Persian Street. Andrei had been there a couple of times, and every time he had left empty handed: Hofstadter didn't have very many foodstuffs, and he chose his own customers.

There was no one in the shop and the shelves were filled with neat ranks of identical jars of pink horseradish. Andrei went in first and Hofstadter, raising his pale, puffy face from the cash register, immediately said, "I'm closing." But then Otto turned up, after catching the basket on the door handle, and the pale, puffy face broke into a smile. The closing of the shop was, of course, postponed. Otto and Hofstadter withdrew into the depths of the establishment, where boxes immediately started rustling and creaking as they were moved, potatoes drummed as they were poured, a glass vessel filled with something jangled, and muted voices started talking in muted tones . . .

With nothing else to do, Andrei gazed around. Yes indeed. Mr. Hofstadter's little private trading business was a pitiful spectacle. The scales, of course, had not undergone the appropriate checks, and the sanitary conditions weren't all that great. But then, that's no concern of mine, thought Andrei. When everything got organized properly, all these Hofstadters would simply go bust. You could say they already had. In any case, Hofstadter wasn't capable of serving anyone and everyone. Just look at the way he camouflaged himself, standing all that horseradish everywhere. Kensi should be set on him—this was a black market he was running here, the lousy nationalist. Only for Germans . . .

Otto glanced out of the depths and spoke in a whisper: "The money, quick!" Andrei hastily handed him a bundle of crumpled bills. With equal haste Otto peeled off a few of them, gave the rest back to Andrei, and disappeared back into the depths. A minute later he appeared behind the counter with his arms completely stretched by a full bag and a full basket. Hofstadter's moonlike physiognomy loomed up behind him. Otto was streaming with sweat and kept smiling all the time, and Hofstadter kept repeating amiably, "Come again, come again, young men, I'm always glad to see you, always glad to see genuine Germans . . . And give Herr Heiger my special greetings . . . Next week they've promised to bring me a little bit of pork. Tell Herr Heiger I'll keep three kilograms or so for him."

"Yes indeed, Herr Hofstadter," Otto replied. "Everything will be conveyed precisely, don't you worry, Herr Hofstadter . . . And please don't forget to give Fräulein Elsa our best regards—from both of us, and especially from Herr Heiger . . ."

They carried on droning this duet all the way to the door of the shop, where Andrei took the massively heavy bag from Otto—it was stuffed full with robust, clean carrots, firm beets, and sugar-white onions, from beneath which protruded the neck of a bottle sealed with wax, while a jumble of leeks, celery, dill, parsley, and other green stuff bristled on the top.

When they turned the corner, Otto put the basket down on the sidewalk, pulled out a large checkered handkerchief, and started wiping off his face, panting for breath and intoning, "Wait . . . I need to take a rest . . . *Pheeew* . . ."

Andrei lit a cigarette and offered the pack to Otto.

"Where did you get those carrots?" asked a woman walking by in a man's leather coat.

"They're finished, all gone," Otto told her hastily. "We took the last ones. The shop's closed already . . . Damn, that bald old devil's exhausted me," he told Andrei. "All that nonsense I spun him in there! Fritz will tear my head off when he finds out. And I don't even remember now exactly what nonsense it was . . ."

Andrei didn't understand a thing, and Otto explained the situation to him in brief.

Herr Hofstadter, a greengrocer from Erfurt, had been filled with hope all his life, and all his life he had been unlucky. When in 1932 some Jew made a beggar of him by opening a large, modern greengrocer's shop across the street from his, Hofstadter realized that he was a true German and joined a brigade of storm troopers. In the storm troopers he was on the point of making a career, and in 1934 he personally pummeled the face of the aforementioned Jew and was about to close in on his business enterprise, but then came the disaster of Röhm's denunciation and Hofstadter was purged. And by that time he was already married, and his charming little blonde-haired Elsa was already growing up. He managed to get by more or less for a few more years, then he was called up into the army and was about to embark on the conquest of Europe, but at Dunkirk he was bombed by his own side's planes and received a massive piece of shrapnel in the lungs, so that instead of ending up in Paris, he found himself in a military hospital in Dresden, where he lay until 1945 and was on the point of being discharged when the Allied air forces made their famous raid that destroyed

Dresden in a single night. The horror he experienced made all his hair fall out, and he went a bit crazy, according to the way that he himself told the story. So after finding himself back in his native Erfurt, he sat out the most hectic period, when it was still possible to decamp to the West, in the cellar of his little house. When he finally plucked up the courage to emerge into the light of day, everything was all over. Admittedly, they did allow him to run a greengrocer's shop, but any kind of expansion of the business was out of the question. In '46 his wife died, and in his clouded state of mind he yielded to the blandishments of a Mentor and, without really understanding the choice that he was making, moved here, where he had improved a bit, but to this day he still seemed to suspect that he had ended up in a large, specialized concentration camp somewhere in Central Asia, to which all the Germans from East Germany had been exiled. His brainbox still hadn't been restored to completely normal functioning: he adored genuine Germans and was convinced that he had a special nose for detecting them, and he was mortally afraid of Chinese, Arabs, and blacks, whose presence here he didn't understand and couldn't explain, but above all he worshipped and adored Herr Heiger. The point was that during one of Heiger's first visits to Hofstadter's, while the greengrocer was filling the bag, the brilliant Fritz had briefly flirted, soldier fashion, with blonde-haired Elsa, who had been driven to a frenzy by the lack of any prospect of a decent marriage. And from that moment a blinding hope had been conceived in the heart of the insane, bald Hofstadter—the hope that this magnificent Aryan, a staunch supporter of the führer and scourge of the Jews, would at long last escort the unfortunate Hofstadter family out of turbulently heaving seas into some quiet backwater.

"What's it to Fritz!" Otto complained, constantly changing the arm that was stretched out of shape by the basket. "He only goes to Hofstadter's place once, maybe twice a month, when we've got nothing to eat—he paws that little fool a bit and that's the end of it . . . But I come here every week, even two or three times a week . . . Hofstadter's a fool all right, a fool, but he's a businessman, you know—the contacts he's built up with the farmers, his food's first class and it's not expensive . . . I've turned into a hopeless liar. I have to assure him of Fritz's eternal affection for Elsa. I have to assure him of the inexorable demise of international Jewry. I have to assure him of the implacable advance of the forces of the great Reich to his greengrocer's shop . . . I've got totally tangled up in it all myself, and I think I've driven him completely insane. I feel guilty, after all: I'm driving an insane old man into total insanity. Just now he asked me, *What are these baboons supposed to mean?* And without even thinking, I blurted out, 'It's an Aryan assault force, a cunning trick.' You wouldn't believe it—he hugged me and smooched me like he was sucking on a bottle."

"But what does Elsa think?" Andrei asked curiously. "She's not insane, is she?"

Otto flushed bright crimson and started wiggling his ears. "Elsa . . ." he cleared his throat. "I'm working away there too, like a horse. It's all the same to her: Fritz, Otto, Ivan, Abraham . . . The girl's thirty years old, and Hofstadter doesn't let anyone but Fritz and me get near her."

"Well, you and Fritz are bad bastards!" Andrei said sincerely.

"As bad as they come!" Otto agreed sadly. "And you know what's most terrible about it: I absolutely can't imagine how we're going to extricate ourselves from this business. I'm weak; I've got no character."

They stopped talking, and all the way back Otto merely panted as he changed the hand holding the basket. He didn't walk up the stairs.

"You take this up and put on some water in a large saucepan," he said. "And give me some money, and I'll run over to the shop—maybe I'll be able to get some canned stuff." He hesitated, turning his eyes away. "And don't you . . . tell Fritz. Or he'll shake the life out of me. You know what Fritz is like—likes to keep everything buttoned up and under wraps. Who doesn't?"

They parted, and Andrei lugged the basket and the bag up the back staircase. The basket was incredibly heavy, as if Hofstadter had loaded it with cast-iron cannonballs. Yes, brother, Andrei thought bitterly. What sort of Experiment is it if there are things like this going on? How much experimenting can you get done with this Otto and this Fritz? Would you believe it, what bastards—no honor and no conscience. Where would they get them from? The Wehrmacht. The Hitlerjugend. Trash. Yes, I'll have a word with Fritz! I can't leave this the way it is—the man's decaying morally in front of my very eyes. But he could be a real human being! He must! When you get right down to it, you could say he saved my life that time. They could have just slid a knife under my shoulder blade, and that would have been it. Everyone shit their pants, everyone all went belly-up. All except for Fritz. No, he is a human being. I have to fight for him . . .

He slipped on the traces of baboon activity, swore, and started watching where he put his feet.

The moment he stepped inside the kitchen, he realized everything in the apartment had changed. The phonograph was booming and hissing in the dining room. He heard the clatter of dishes and the shuffling of dancing feet. And rumbling out over and above all these other sounds was the familiar bass voice of his excellency Yurii Konstantinovich: "You, brother, all that stuff about the economics and sociology—we don't need it. We'll get by without. But freedom, brother, now that's a different matter. Freedom's worth breaking your back for."

Water was already boiling up in a large saucepan on the gas cooker, a freshly sharpened knife was lying, ready and waiting, on the kitchen table, and there was a ravishing aroma of meat coming from the oven. Two paunchy sacks were standing in the corner of the kitchen, propped against each other, and lying on top of them were an oil-soaked wadded jacket with burn holes, a familiar whip, and some kind of harness. The familiar machine gun was standing right there too—assembled and ready for use, with a flat, burnished metal magazine protruding from the breech. A glass carboy was gleaming with an oily glint under the table, with corn shuckings and pieces of straw stuck to it.

Andrei put down the basket and the bag. "Hey, you loafers!" he yelled. "The water's boiling!"

Davydov's rumbling bass fell silent, and Selma appeared in the doorway, red-faced and with her eyes glowing. Fritz towered up behind her shoulder. Apparently they had just been dancing, and the Aryan had no intention of taking his massive red paws off Selma's waist just yet.

"Hofstadter sends you his greetings!" said Andrei. "Elsa is concerned that you don't call round. The child will be a month old soon, after all!"

"Stupid jokes!" Fritz declared in disgust, but he took his paws away. "Where's Otto?"

"It's true, the water is boiling!" Selma declared in surprise. "Now what do we do with it?"

"Take the knife," said Andrei, "and start peeling the potatoes. And I think you're very fond of potato salad, aren't you, Fritz? So you get on with it, and I'll go and play the part of the host."

He was about to walk into the dining room, but Izya Katzman intercepted him in the doorway. His face was glowing ecstatically.

"Listen," he said, giggling and spraying. "Where did you get that remarkable character from? It seems like they've got a genuine Wild West down on the farms. American wide-open spaces!"

"Russian wide-open spaces are every bit as good as American ones," Andrei said peevishly.

"Oh yes! Oh yes!" Izya shouted. "'When the Jewish Cossacks rebelled, there was a coup, a coup in Birobidzhan, and if anyone tries to take our Berdichev, a boil will spring up on his belly!'"

"You drop that," Andrei said sternly. "I don't like it . . . Fritz, I'm placing Selma and Katzman under your command: work, and quickly. I'm hungry—I'm starving . . . And don't yell in here— Otto will be knocking, he dashed off to get some canned stuff."

Having put everyone in their places, Andrei hurried into the dining room, where first of all he exchanged a firm handshake with Yurii Konstantinovich.

Yurii Konstantinovich, still as red-faced and strong-smelling as ever, was standing in the middle of the room with his feet planted wide apart in their tarpaulin-fabric boots and his hands stuck into his soldier's belt. His eyes were merry and slightly wild—Andrei had often seen eyes like that in the faces of harum-scarum men who liked hard work and strong drink, and had no fear of anything on Earth. "There!" said Davydov. "I've come, just as I promised. Have you seen the big bottle? That's for you. The potatoes are for you too—two sacks. They wanted to give me, you know, a certain something for them, but I thought what the hell do I want all this for? I'll drive them round to a good man instead. They live here, rotting away in their stone mansions, never seeing the light of day . . . Listen, Andrei, I was just telling Kensi here, the Japanese, I told him: Give it all up, guys! What is there round here that you haven't seen already? Collect up your little kids, your women, your girls, and all come on out to us . . ."

Kensi, still in uniform after his spell of duty but with his tunic unbuttoned, was working away awkwardly with one hand, trying to set the table with miscellaneous dishes. His left hand was bound up with a bandage. He smiled and nodded to Davydov. "That's what it will come to, Yura," he said. "Next there'll be an invasion of squids, and then every last one of us will move out to those swamps of yours."

"Ah, why bother to wait for those . . . what-d'you-call-ems . . . To hell with those damned squids. Tomorrow morning I'm leaving empty, nothing in the cart—I can easily load up three families. You're not a family man, are you?" he asked, turning to Andrei.

"God has spared me," said Andrei.

"Then who's this girl to you? Or isn't she yours?"

"She's new here. Just arrived last night."

"So what could be better? A pleasant young lady. Take her and let's go, eh? We've got air out there. We've got milk out there. You probably haven't drunk any fresh milk in a year, have you? And I keep on wondering why there's no milk in your shops. I've got three cows all to myself. I hand over that milk to the state, I feed myself with it, I feed the pigs with it, I pour it away on the ground . . . You settle at our place, you'll see, and you'll wake up in the morning to go out into the field and your very own cow will give you a pitcher of steaming-fresh milk—straight from the cow, eh?" He winked strenuously with both eyes, one after the other, laughed, whacked Andrei on the shoulder, then set off across the room, making the floorboards creak loudly, stopped the phonograph, and came back again. "And the air there! You haven't even got any air left here— you've got a menagerie here, that's all the air you've got. Kensi, why keep making it so hard on yourself? Call the girl, let her set the table."

"She's peeling potatoes in there," Andrei said with a smile. Then he pulled himself up short and started helping Kensi. Davydov was a really great guy. He felt very close to him, as if they'd known each other for a whole year already. So . . . what if he really did it—took off to the swamps? Milk or no milk, the life there had to be really healthy. Just look at the way Davydov was standing there, like a statue!

"Someone's knocking," Davydov told him. "Shall I open up or will you go yourself?"

"Just a moment," Andrei said, and went to the front door. Standing outside the door was Wang—without his wadded jacket now, wearing a blue serge shirt down to his knees and a waffle-weave towel wrapped around his head.

"They brought the cans!" he said with a joyful smile.

"So screw them then," Andrei responded no less joyfully. "The cans can wait. Why are you alone? Where's Mei-lin?"

"She's at home," said Wang. "She's very tired. She's sleeping. Our son's taken sick."

"Well come in, don't just stand there . . . Come on, I'll introduce you to a fine human being."

"We've already met," Wang said as he walked into the dining room.

"Ah, Vanya!" Davydov shouted delightedly. "So you're here as well! Yes," he said, turning back to Kensi, "I knew Andrei was a regular guy. Look, all the good people get together at his place. Take you, now, or that little Jew . . . what's his name . . . Well, now we'll have a whale of a feast! I'll go and take a look at what they're fiddling with for so long in there. There's nothing at all to do, and they've made a huge job out of it . . ."

Wang quickly squeezed Kensi away from the table and began neatly and deftly rearranging the knives and forks. Kensi adjusted his bandage with his free hand and his teeth. Andrei waded in to help him. "Donald still hasn't shown up," he said in a concerned voice.

"He locked himself in," Wang responded. "Said he wasn't to be disturbed."

"He's been down in the dumps recently for some reason, guys. OK, forget about him. Listen, Kensi, what's wrong with your hand?"

Kensi pulled a wry face as he answered. "A baboon snapped at me. What a bastard—bit right through to the bone."

"You don't say!" Andrei exclaimed, astonished. "I thought they were kind of placid."

"Sure, very placid . . . When someone catches you and starts riveting a collar round your neck . . ."

"What collar?"

"Directive 57. All baboons are to be registered and fitted with a numbered collar. Tomorrow we're going to distribute them to members of the public. Well, we ringed about twenty of them and herded the others over into the next precinct; they can sort them out. Why are you just standing there with your mouth hanging open? Let's have some shot glasses—there aren't enough shot glasses . . ."

Ч

When the sun was turned off, the entire company was already flying high. In the darkness that instantly fell, Andrei clambered out from behind the table and made his way over to the light switch, along the way kicking over some saucepans or other standing on the floor. "Don' you be frightened, sweet fräulein," Fritz babbled behind him. "That's what always happens here . . ."

"Let there be light!" Andrei declared, articulating the words laboriously.

The dusty lightbulb on the ceiling lit up. The light was pitiful, just like in the passage to the courtyard. Andrei turned around and surveyed the gathering.

Everything was absolutely fine. Ensconced at the head of the table, swaying slightly on his kitchen stool, was Yurii Konstantinovich Davydov, who half an hour earlier had finally and irrevocably become "Uncle Yura" to Andrei. Uncle Yura had a brawny roll-up smoking between his firmly clenched teeth and a thick glass tumbler clutched in his right hand, and he was waving the calloused index finger of his left hand through the air in front of the nose of Izya Katzman, who was sitting beside him, now entirely bereft of his tie and jacket, and with traces of meat sauce clearly displayed on the collar and chest of his shirt.

Wang was sitting modestly on Uncle Yura's right; in front of him he had the very smallest plate, with a small piece of something on it, and the most battered fork, and for the moonshine he had taken himself a glass with a chipped edge. His head had sunk completely down into his shoulders and his face was raised, with the eyes closed and a blissful smile on the lips: Wang was basking in his peace.

Sharp-eyed Kensi, his cheeks brightly flushed, was snacking with gusto on sauerkraut and rendering an enthusiastic account

77

of something to Otto, who was battling heroically against drowsiness, exclaiming in his brief moments of victory, "Yes! Of course! Yes! Oh, yes!"

Selma Nagel, the Swedish tramp, was out-and-out gorgeous. She was sitting in an armchair, with her legs thrown over the soft armrest, and those gleaming legs were exactly level with the chest of the bold Unter-officer Fritz, so Fritz's eyes were blazing, and in his excitement he had broken out in red blotches. He kept thrusting his full glass at Selma, repeatedly attempting to drink to *Bruderschaft* with her, but Selma pushed him away with her own glass, laughed, swung her legs about, and from time to time brushed Fritz's hairy, fondling paw off her knees.

Andrei's chair on the other side of Selma was the only one that was empty, apart from the chair set out for Donald, also sadly vacant. What a pity Donald's not here, Andrei thought. But we'll survive—we'll even get through that! We've had to cope with worse things . . . His thoughts were a little confused, but his general mood was spunky, with a light veneer of the tragic. He went back to his place, picked up a glass, and roared, "A toast!"

No one took any notice of him except Otto, who merely jerked his head like a horse bitten by gadflies and responded, "Yes! Oh, yes!"

"I came here because I believed!" Uncle Yura boomed in his deep bass voice, not giving the giggling Izya a chance to remove that gnarled finger from under his nose. "And I believed because there was nothing else left to believe in. And a Russian has to believe in something, don't you see, brother? If he doesn't believe in anything, there'll be nothing left but vodka. Even to make love to a woman, you've got to have faith. You have to believe in yourself, without faith you'll never even get it up."

"That's right, that's right!" Izya responded. "Take away a Jew's belief in God and a Russian's belief in the Good Czar, and they become capable of all sorts of diabolical things."

"No . . . hang on! Jews are a special case . . ."

"The most important thing, Otto, is to take things easy," Kensi was saying at the same time, crunching with relish on his cabbage. "There isn't any training anyway—there simply *can't* be any. Think about it: who needs professional training in a city where everyone is constantly changing his profession?"

"Oh, yes!" Otto responded, his mind clearing for a second. "I said the same thing to the minister."

"And what did the minister say?" asked Kensi, picking up his glass of moonshine and taking a few small sips, as if he were drinking tea.

"The minister said that it was an extremely interesting idea and suggested that I should draft a detailed proposal." Otto sniffed and tears welled up in his eyes. "But instead of that I went to see Elsa . . ."

"And when the tank was only about two meters away from me," Fritz droned, spilling moonshine on Selma's white legs, "I remembered everything! You wouldn't believe it, fräulein, all the years of my life flashed by in front of my eyes . . . But I'm a soldier! With the name of the führer—"

"Ah, your führer's been gone for ages!" Selma kept trying to drum into his head, laughing so hard that she cried. "They burned that führer of yours!"

"Fräulein!" Fritz declared, thrusting his jaw forward menacingly. "In the heart of every true German, the führer still lives! The führer will live on down through the ages! You are an Aryan, fräulein, you can understand me: when th'Russian tank . . . only three meters away . . . with the name of the führer on my lips, I . . ."

"Ah, I'm sick of you and your führer!" Andrei yelled at him. "Guys! Come on, you bastards! Listen to the toast, will you?"

"A toast?" exclaimed Uncle Yura, suddenly getting the idea. "Come on! Go to it, Andriukha!"

"*Fortheladiespresent!*" Otto suddenly blurted out, shoving Kensi away from him.

"You shut up, will you!" Andrei barked. "Izya, stop grinning like that! I'm being serious! Kensi, damn you! Guys, I think we should drink . . . we've already drunk to it, but only sort of in passing, and we need to drink fundamentally, seriously, to our Experiment, to our noble cause, and especially—"

"To the inspirer of all our victories, Comrade Stalin!" Izya roared.

That put Andrei off his stride. "No, listen," he mumbled. "What are you interrupting me for? OK, to Stalin too, of course . . . Damn, now you've completely thrown me . . . I wanted us to drink to friendship, you fool!"

"Never mind, never mind, Andriukha," said Uncle Yura. "It's a good toast: we ought to drink to the Experiment, and we ought to drink to friendship too. Boys, raise your glasses, we'll drink to friendship and to everything turning out just fine."

"And I'll drink to Stalin," Selma piped up stubbornly. "And to Mao Tse-tung. Hey, Mao Tse-tung, do you hear, I'm drinking to you," she shouted at Wang.

Wang started, smiling pitifully, picked up a glass, and pressed it against his lips.

"Tse-tung?" Fritz asked menacingly. "Who's 'at?"

Andrei drained his glass in a single gulp and, feeling slightly stunned, started hastily jabbing his fork at the hors d'oeuvres. Suddenly it was as if all the conversations were reaching him from the next room. Stalin . . . Yes, of course. There has to be some kind of link . . . Why didn't that ever occur to me before! Phenomena of the same scale—cosmic. There has to be some kind of link and interconnection . . . Let's say this is the question: the choice between the success of the Experiment and the health of Comrade Stalin. Which one, for me personally, as a citizen, as a warrior . . . Of course, Katzman says Stalin's dead already, but that's not important. Let's suppose he's alive. And let's suppose the choice I'm facing is: the Experiment or the cause of Stalin . . . No, rubbish, that's not right. To continue the cause of Stalin under Stalin's leadership or continue the cause of Stalin in completely different conditions, exceptional conditions, unforeseen by any theory—that's how the question is posed.

"And what makes you think the Mentors are continuing the cause of Stalin?" Andrei suddenly heard Izya's voice say, and realized that he'd been speaking out loud for some time already.

"But what other work can they be doing?" he asked in astonishment. "There's only one cause on Earth worth working for—building communism! That *is* Stalin's cause."

"That's a D for you in the Basics of Scientific Communism," Izya retorted. "Stalin's cause is the building of socialism in one country, the consistent struggle against imperialism, and the extension of the socialist camp to include the whole world. Somehow I don't see how you can achieve those goals here."

"*Borrring!*" Selma whined. "Let's have some music! I want to dance!"

But Andrei was already blind and deaf to everything. "You dogmatist!" he barked. "You're a Talmudist and doctrinarian! And, in general, a metaphysician. You don't see anything but the form. It doesn't matter what form the Experiment takes! But it can only have the same content, and only one final result: the establishment of the dictatorship of the proletariat in alliance with the laboring farmers—"

"And the toiling intelligentsia!" Izya put in.

"What damned intelligentsia . . . What sort of shit-pie garbage is that—the intelligentsia!"

"Yes, true," said Izya. "That's from a different era."

"The intelligentsia is altogether impotent!" Andrei declared bitterly. "A lickspittle social stratum. It serves whoever holds the power."

"A gang of wimps," barked Fritz. "Wimps and blabbermouths, an eternal source of slackness and disorganization!"

"Precisely!" Andrei would have preferred to be supported by Uncle Yura, say, but support was useful even from Fritz's side. "There, if you please: Heiger. Basically the class enemy, but his position coincides perfectly with ours. So it turns out that from the viewpoint of any class, the intelligentsia is shit." He grated his teeth. "I hate them . . . I can't stand those spineless, four-eyed weaklings, blabbermouths, freeloaders. They've got no inner strength, no faith, no morality . . ."

"When I hear the word *culture*, I reach for my gun!" Fritz proclaimed in a metallic voice.

"Ah, no," said Andrei. "I part company with you there. You drop that! Culture is the great heritage of the liberated people. What's needed here is a dialectical . . ."

Somewhere close by the phonograph was thundering and Otto was stumbling around drunkenly, dancing with drunken Selma, but Andrei wasn't interested in that. The best part of all was just beginning, the thing for which he loved these get-togethers more than anything else in the world. The argument.

"Down with culture!" Izya howled, skipping from one empty chair to another in order to move closer to Andrei. "It's got nothing to do with our Experiment. What is the goal of the Experiment? That's the question! You just tell me that."

"I already told you: to create a model of communist society!"

"What in hell's name would the Mentors want with a model of communist society? Judge for yourself, cabbage-head!"

"And why not? Why not?"

"What I think, though, is this," said Uncle Yura. "The Mentors aren't real human beings. They're, how can I put it . . . a different species, I suppose . . . They've planted us in a fish tank . . . or something like a zoological garden . . . and they're watching to see what happens."

"Did you think that up for yourself, Yurii Konstantinovich?" Izya asked, and turned toward him, suddenly immensely interested.

Uncle Yura fingered his right cheekbone and replied evasively, "It emerged in the course of debate."

Izya actually slammed his fist down on the table. "How incredible!" he exclaimed enthusiastically. "Why? Where does it all come from? Why do the most different kinds of people, and people who basically think in entirely conformist terms, come up with this idea that the Mentors are not human in origin? The idea that the Experiment is being conducted by higher powers of some kind?"

"Well, for instance, I asked him straight out," Kensi put in. "'Are you aliens?' He avoided giving a direct answer, but he didn't actually deny it."

"And I was told they're human beings from a different dimension," said Andrei. It felt awkward talking about the Mentor, like discussing family matters with outsiders. "But I'm not sure I understood correctly . . . Maybe it was just allegorical."

"But I won't have it!" Fritz abruptly declared. "I'm not an insect. I am *myself*. Aha!" he exclaimed, swinging his hand through the air. "I'd never have ended up here if I hadn't been taken prisoner, would I?"

"But why?" said Izya. "Why? I feel some kind of internal protest all the time too, and I can't understand what's wrong. Maybe in the long run their goals are close to ours—"

"That's what I've been telling you!" Andrei exclaimed delightedly.

"Not in that sense," said Izya, gesturing impatiently. "It's not all as straightforward as you make it out to be. They're trying to figure out the human race, right? Make sense of it. And problem number one for us is the very same: making sense of the human race, of ourselves. Maybe by figuring things out for themselves, they'll help us figure things out as well?"

"Ah, no, my friends," said Kensi, swaying his head from side to side. "Ah, don't flatter yourselves. They're preparing to colonize the Earth, and they're using you and me to study the psychology of their future slaves."

"But why think that, Kensi?" Andrei said disappointedly. "Why these terrible assumptions? If you ask me, thinking about them that way is simply unfair."

"Well, I probably don't really think that," Kensi replied. "It's just that I have this strange sort of feeling . . . All these baboons, the transformation of the water, the general bedlam day after day . . . One fine day they'll hand us a confusion of tongues too . . . It seems like they're systematically preparing us for some appalling kind of world that we're going to live in henceforth, now and forever, and unto the ages of ages. It's like at Okinawa. I was just a little kid then, the war was going on, and the Okinawa boys and girls like me were forbidden to speak their own dialect. Nothing but Japanese. And when they caught some kid, they hung a sign around his neck: I Don't Know How to Talk Properly. And he walked around with that sign."

"Yes, yes, I understand," said Izya, tugging and pinching at the wart on his neck with a frozen smile on his face.

"But I don't understand!" Andrei declared. "All this is probably perverse supposition, it's delusory . . . The Experiment is the Experiment. Of course we don't understand anything. But then, we're not supposed to understand! That's a fundamental condition! If we understood what the baboons are for, what the switching around of professions is for . . . that understanding would immediately condition our behavior, the Experiment's integrity would be compromised, and it would fail. That's perfectly clear! What do you think, Fritz?"

Fritz shook his blond head. "I don't know. I'm not interested in that. I'm not interested in what *they* want. I'm interested in what *I* want. And I want to instill some order into this shambles. And, anyway, one of you, I don't remember who, said that perhaps the entire purpose of the Experiment is to select those who are the most energetic, the most active, the staunchest . . . It's not so people can prattle and babble, or dissolve into sloppy puddles like wet pastry, or start wallowing in philosophy, but to show that they can stick to their guns. Those are the ones they'll select—the ones like me, or like you, say, Andrei, and drop them back on Earth. Because if we haven't faltered here, we won't falter there either."

"It could well be!" Andrei said with a profound air. "I accept that as perfectly possible too."

"But Donald thinks," Wang said in a quiet voice, "that the experiment has already failed a long, long time ago."

Everyone looked at him. Wang was sitting in the same pose of tranquility as before—with his head pulled down into his shoulders and his face raised toward the ceiling; his eyes were still closed.

"He said the Mentors got all snarled up in this stunt of theirs ages ago, they've tried everything they can, and now even they don't know what to do. They're totally busted, he said. And now everything's just rolling along under its own inertia."

Totally bemused, Andrei reached up to scratch the back of his head. So that was Donald's problem! The reason he'd been so tetchy and out of sorts . . . Nobody else said anything either. Uncle Yura slowly rolled yet another crooked cigarette, Izya pinched and tormented his wart with a stony-faced smile, Kensi started guzzling cabbage again, and Fritz stared fixedly at Wang, thrusting out his jaw and then setting it back in place. This was the way demoralization set in, Andrei thought fleetingly. With conversations like this. The lack of understanding produced a lack of belief. And the lack of belief meant death. Very, very dangerous. The Mentor had told him bluntly: the essential thing was to believe in the idea to the very end, unconditionally. To realize that not understanding anything was an absolutely indispensable condition of the Experiment. That was the hardest part, naturally. The majority here had no real ideological toughness, no genuine certainty that the bright future was inevitable. That no matter how tough and difficult things might be today, and tomorrow as well, the day after tomorrow the star-spangled sky will surely unfurl above our heads, and life will be bright and festive . . .

"I'm not an educated man," Uncle Yura said suddenly, lovingly gluing together his new roll-up with his tongue. "I've only got four years of schooling, in case you'd like to know, and as I've already told Izya, to be quite frank, I bailed out to get here . . . The same way you did," he said, pointing the roll-up at Fritz. "Only for you the road led out of captivity, and for me it led out of the collective farm, you see. Not counting the war, I spent my entire life in the village, and in my entire life I never saw any light. But *here* I have seen it! I'll tell you straight, brothers, it's beyond me what fancy business they're up to with this Experiment of theirs, and I'm not all that interested. But here I'm a free man, and as long as they don't touch my freedom, I won't bother anyone either. But if anyone here suddenly decides they want to change the current status of the farmers, then I can promise you for certain that we won't leave a stone standing in this City of yours. We're not a fucking troop of baboons! We won't let you put any fucking collars round our throats! So that's the way of things, brother," he said, speaking directly to Fritz.

Izya giggled absentmindedly, and an awkward silence fell again. Andrei was rather surprised by Uncle Yura's tirade, and he decided that life must obviously have been especially hard on Yurii Konstantinovich, and if he said he'd never seen any light, then he must have special grounds of his own for that, and asking him about them would be tactless, especially right now. And so Andrei simply said, "We're probably raising all these questions too soon. The Experiment hasn't been going on for that long, there's a huge amount of work to be done, we have to work and believe in the correctness—"

"What makes you think the Experiment hasn't been going on for very long?" Izya interrupted him with a mocking grin. "The Experiment's been going on for a hundred years at least. I mean to say, it's definitely been going on for a lot longer, only I can personally vouch for a hundred years."

"And how do you know?"

"How far to the north have you gone?" Izya asked.

Andrei was at a loss. He had no idea that there even was a north here.

"You know, north!" Izya said impatiently. "Let us notionally consider that the direction toward the sun, the direction where the swamps and the farms are, is south, and the opposite direction, moving farther in through the City, is north. You haven't gone any farther than the garbage dumps, have you? But from there the City goes on and on: there are huge city districts, entire palaces . . ." He giggled. "Palaces and hovels. There's no one there now, of course, because there's no water, but someone used to live there once, and let me tell you, that 'once' was a pretty long time ago. The documents I discovered in empty houses there— *ay-ay-ay*! Have you ever heard of the monarch Velarius the Second? There, you see! Well, as it happens, he used to rule there. Only in the times when he used to rule there"—Izya tapped one fingernail on the tabletop—"there were swamps here, and their serfs labored in those swamps . . . or their slaves. And that was at least a hundred years ago."

Uncle Yura shook his head and clicked his tongue. Fritz asked, "And what about farther north?"

"I haven't gone any farther," said Izya, "but I know people who have gone very far, 100 or 150 kilometers, and plenty have gone and never come back."

"OK, so what's there?"

"The City," Izya said, and paused. "Mind you, they tell shameless lies about those places too. That's why I only talk about what I've discovered for myself. A hundred years for certain. Got that, have you, my friend Andriusha? A hundred years is long enough to give up on any experiment."

"Well OK, just hang on, will you . . ." Andrei muttered, flustered. "But they haven't given up on it!" he exclaimed, perking up. "If they're still bringing in new people all the time, they haven't dropped it, they haven't despaired. It's just that the problem that's been set is extremely complex." A new idea occurred to him and he perked up even more. "And anyway, how do you know what their time scale is like? Maybe our year is just a second to them?"

"I don't know anything about any of that," Izya said with a shrug. "I'm just trying to explain to you what kind of world you live in, that's all."

"OK!" Uncle Yura interrupted him decisively. "We've wasted enough time on empty talk Hey, kiddo! What's your name . . . Otto! Leave the girl alone and bring us . . . No he's totally wasted already. He'll break my carboy. I'll go get it myself." He slid down off the stool, picked the empty pitcher up off the table, and walked off into the kitchen.

Selma plumped down across her chair so that her legs were higher than her head again and petulantly nudged Andrei on the shoulder. "How long are you going to carry on with this tedious crap? Don't be such an incredible drag . . . The Experiment, the Experiment . . . Give me a light!"

Andrei gave her a light. The abrupt breaking off of the conversation had stirred up some kind of unpleasant sediment inside him—something had been left unsaid, something had been misunderstood, they hadn't let him explain, unity hadn't been achieved . . . And Kensi was sitting there looking sad somehow, and that was a rare thing for him. We think too much of ourselves, that's what, he thought. The Experiment is all well and good, but everyone insists on doing things his own way, clings to his own position, and we have to do it together, together!

At this point Uncle Yura dumped a new batch of booze on the table with a thud, and Andrei gave up on the whole damn business. They drank a glass and took a bite; Izya threw out a joke and it fell flat. Uncle Yura flung out a joke too, a monstrously obscene one, but it was very funny. Even Wang laughed, and Selma was in stitches from laughing so hard. "In the pitcher . . ." she gasped, choking and rubbing her eyes with the palms of her hands. "It won't fit in the pitcher!"

Andrei smashed his fist down on the table and launched into his mother's favorite song:

> For all them as drink, pour them plenty,
> For them as don't drink, don't pour any.
> We'll drink every day, singing God's praise,
> For us, for you, and for old nanny too,
> Who taught us to knock back a strong glass or two . . .

They joined in with him, everyone trying his best, and then Fritz, with his eyes bulging wildly, bawled out a duet with Otto, a song that Andrei didn't know, but an excellent one, about the quaking bones of the old, decrepit world—a magnificent battle song. Watching Andrei enthusiastically trying to sing along, Izya Katzman giggled and gurgled, rubbing his hands together, and then Uncle Yura fixed his drolly rakish, bright-eyed stare on Selma's naked thighs and abruptly roared out in a voice like a bear:

> *Through the village when you go,*
> *Coyly singing high and low,*
> *Torturing my poor heart so,*
> *Sweet sleep it can never know.*

This was an absolute hit, and Uncle Yura carried on:

> *You girls are all skilled to beguile,*
> *Luring in sweet, seductive style,*
> *Promising with a tempting smile,*
> *And yet deceiving all the while . . .*

At that Selma took her legs down off the armrest, shoved Fritz away, and said resentfully, "I'm not promising you anything. I don't need any of you."

"I didn't mean anything by it," said Uncle Yura, seriously embarrassed. "It's not like I've got any use for you either."

To smooth over the incident, they drank another glass. Andrei's head started spinning. He was vaguely aware that he was fiddling with the phonograph, and he was going to drop it in a moment, and the phonograph really did fall to the floor, but it wasn't damaged at all—quite the opposite. It seemed to start playing even louder. Then he was dancing with Selma, and Selma's sides turned out to be warm and soft, and her breasts were unexpectedly firm and large, which was one helluva of a pleasant surprise—finding something beautifully formed under those formless folds of prickly wool. They danced, and he held on to her sides, and she took his cheeks in her open palms and said he was a really nice boy and she really liked him, and in his gratitude he told her that he loved her and he had always loved her, and now he'd never let her get away from him again . . . Uncle Yura slammed his fist into the table, proclaiming, "I feel a sudden chill in here, time for another glass of cheer." Then he put his arms around Wang, who had completely wilted by this stage, and kissed him three times in the Russian fashion. Then Andrei found himself in the middle of the room, and Selma was sitting at the table again, throwing bread pellets at apathetic Wang and calling him Mao Tse-tung. That put Andrei in mind of the song "Moscow-Peking" and he immediately performed that beautiful composition with exceptional passion and fervor, then he and Izya Katzman suddenly found themselves standing, staring wide-eyed at each other, lowering their voices deeper and deeper in a sinister whisper and holding up their index fingers as they repeated, over and over: "*Lis*-tening to us! *Lis*-tening to us!" After that he and Izya somehow found themselves crammed into a single armchair, with Kensi sitting on the table in front of them, dangling his legs, while Andrei fervently tried to persuade him that he, Andrei, was willing to perform any kind of work here— that any work at all gave him especial satisfaction, and he felt just great working as a garbage collector. "Here I am—a garb- . . . age col-lector!" he exclaimed, enunciating the words with a struggle. "A grab- . . . grabbage collector!"

And Izya, spitting in Andrei's ear, kept harping on about something unpleasant, something offensive: saying that Andrei actually experienced a sweet humiliation from being a garbage collector ("Yes . . . I'm a grab-bage collector!"), that he was so intelligent, so well read and capable, fit for much greater things, but even so he bore his heavy cross with patience and dignity, unlike certain others . . . Then Selma appeared, bringing him immediate consolation. She was soft and affectionate, and she did everything he wanted, and she didn't contradict him, and at that point there was a sweet, devastating gap in his sense impressions, and when he surfaced from out of that gap, his lips were puffy and dry and Selma was already sleeping on his bed. He straightened her skirt with a paternal gesture, flung the blanket over her, adjusted his own attire appropriately, and went back out into the dining room, trying to walk with a brisk stride and stumbling on the way over the outstretched legs of poor Otto, who was sleeping on a chair in the hideously uncomfortable pose of a man killed by a shot to the back of the neck.

Towering up on the table was the large carboy itself, and all the revelers were sitting there, propping up their tousle-haired heads and warbling in a soft-voiced chorus, "In the desolate depths of the steppe a coachman was freezing . . ." and large tears were rolling down out of Fritz's pale, Aryan eyes. Andrei was about to join in when there was a knock at the door. He opened it, and a woman wrapped in a shawl, dressed in her underskirt with boots on her bare feet, asked if the caretaker was here. Andrei shook Wang awake and explained to him where he was and what was required of him. "Thanks, Andrei," Wang said after listening carefully to him, and left, feebly shuffling his feet. The others finished singing the song about the coachman in the steppe, and Uncle Yura suggested a drink "to folks at home not grieving," but then it turned out that Fritz was asleep, so he couldn't clink glasses. "That's it, then," said Uncle. "That means this will be the last one . . ." But before they drank one last glass, Izya Katzman, who had suddenly turned strangely serious, rendered one more solo—a song that Andrei didn't entirely understand, but apparently Uncle Yura understood it perfectly well. The song included the refrain "Ave Maria" and an absolutely appalling verse that seemed to come from a different planet:

> They sent the prophet up the river a short while later,
> And in the Komi Republic he gave up the ghost.
> The labor union committee gave the dour investigator
> A free month in Teberda for devotion to his post.

When Izya finished singing, there was silence for a while, then Uncle Yura abruptly smashed his massively heavy fist into the tabletop and swore at length in exceptionally florid style, following which he grabbed a glass and started swigging from it without any toasts at all. And Kensi, following some strange association that only he could understand, performed another song in an extremely unpleasant, squeaky, and vehement voice, about how, if the Japanese soldiers were all to start pissing at once against the Great Wall of China, a rainbow would appear above the Gobi Desert; about how the imperial army was in London today, tomorrow it would be in Moscow, and the next morning it would drink tea in Chicago; that the sons of Yamato had settled the banks of the Ganges and were catching crocodiles with fishing rods. Then he fell silent, tried to light a cigarette, broke several matches, and suddenly out of the blue told them about a little girl he used to be friends with in Okinawa—she was fourteen years old, and she lived in the house opposite his. One day some drunken soldiers raped her, and when her father went to the police to complain, gendarmes showed up and took him and the girl away, and Kensi never saw them again . . .

Nobody was saying anything when Wang stuck his head into the dining room, called Kensi's name, and beckoned to him.

"That's the way things go," Uncle Yura said gloomily. "And just look: the same thing in the West, and back home in Russia, and in the yellow-skinned countries—the same story everywhere. Power is unjust. Ah, no, brothers, what would I want to go back there for? I'd rather be here."

Kensi came back, pale-faced and preoccupied, and started looking for his belt. His uniform tunic was already fully buttoned.

"Has something happened?" Andrei asked.

"Yes. Something has happened," Kensi replied in a crisp, staccato voice, adjusting his holster. "Donald Cooper shot himself. About an hour ago."

PART II

THE
INVESTIGATOR

1

Andrei suddenly had a headache from hell. He crushed his cigarette butt into the overflowing ashtray with a sense of loathing,
pulled out the middle drawer of his desk, and looked to see if
there were any tablets in there. There weren't any. Just a massive army pistol lying on top of a jumble of old documents and
little tattered cardboard boxes of assorted petty stationery items
lurking in the corners, plus a littering of gnawed pencil stumps,
tobacco crumbs, and broken cigarettes. All this only made his
headache worse. Andrei slammed the drawer shut, propped
his head up with his hands over his face, and started watching
Peter Block through the cracks between his fingers

Peter Block, a.k.a. Tailbone, was sitting a short distance away
on a stool, with his red mitts calmly folded together on his knees,
blinking indifferently and licking his lips from time to time. He
clearly didn't have a headache, but it was obvious that he was
feeling thirsty. And he probably wanted a smoke too. Andrei tore
his hands away from his face with an effort, poured himself some
lukewarm water from a carafe, and drank half a glassful, subdu-
ing a mild spasm. Peter Block licked his lips. His gray eyes were
as inexpressive and empty as ever. His massive, gristly Adam's
apple set off on a long glide down the skinny, grubby neck protruding from his unbuttoned shirt collar and then bobbed back
up to his chin.

"Well?" said Andrei.

"I don't know," Tailbone replied hoarsely. "I don't remember
anything like that."

You bastard, thought Andrei. You animal. "So what's this
you've told us?" he asked. "You hit the grocery store on Wool
Lane; you remember when you hit it, you remember who you

hit it with too. Good. You hit Dreyfus's café, and you remember when you hit it and who with as well. But for some reason you've forgotten about Hofstadter's shop. And that was your latest job, wasn't it, Block?"

"I really couldn't say that, Mr. Investigator," Tailbone responded with excruciatingly loathsome politeness. "I beg your pardon, but that's just someone trying to set me up. Since we quit after the Dreyfus place, you know, since we chose the path of complete rehabilitation and socially useful employment, well, since then I haven't done any more jobs of that kind."

"Hofstadter identified you."

"I really do beg your pardon, Mr. Investigator"—the note of irony in Tailbone's voice was clearly audible now—"but Mr. Hof-stadter is a bit screwy, after all, everybody knows that. So he's got everything confused, hasn't he? I've been in his shop, sure I have—to buy a few potatoes or onions . . . I noticed before that he wasn't quite right in the head, begging your pardon, and if I'd known how things would turn out, I'd have stopped going to his place. I mean, just look, would you ever . . . ?"

"Hofstadter's daughter also identified you. It was you who threatened her with a knife, you in person."

"It never happened. Something did happen, but it wasn't anything like that. It was her that set the knife against my throat, that's what! One day she boxed me into that back room of theirs—and I had a really narrow escape. She's got this obsession with sex; all the men in the neighborhood hide away in the corners to avoid her . . ." Tailbone licked his lips again. "The main thing is, she says to me, you come in the back room yourself, she says, choose the cabbage yourself—"

"I've already heard that. Tell me again what you did and where you went on the night of the twenty-fourth. In detail, starting from the moment the sun was switched off."

Tailbone raised his eyes to the ceiling. "Right then," he began, "when the sun was switched off, I was sitting in a beer parlor on the corner of Jersey and Second, playing cards. Then Jack Lever invited me to another beer parlor, so we went, and on the way we dropped by Jack's place, we wanted to pick up his broad, but we stayed too long and started drinking there. Jack got tanked, and his broad put him to bed and threw me out. I went off home to sleep, but I was totally plastered, and along the way I tangled with these guys, three of them there were, they were drunk too. I don't know any of them; I'd never seen them before in my life. They gave me such a battering, I don't remember anything after that—I just came round in the morning right on the edge of the Cliff, barely made it back home. I went to bed, and then they came to get me."

Andrei leafed through the case file and found the medical evaluation. The sheet of paper was already slightly greasy.

"The only fact confirmed here is that you were drunk," he said. "The medical evaluation does not confirm that you had been beaten up. No traces of a beating were discovered on your body."

"So the guys did a tidy job, then," Tailbone said approvingly. "So they had stockings filled with sand . . . All my ribs are still aching even now . . . and they refuse to put me in the hospital . . . I'll croak in your cells here—then you'll all have to answer for me."

"They didn't ache for three days, then the moment we presented you with the medical evaluation, they suddenly started aching—"

"What d'you mean, they didn't ache? I was in agony, they were aching so bad, I couldn't stand it any longer, so I started complaining."

"Stop lying, Block," Andrei said wearily. "It's obscene just to listen to you."

He was sick and tired of this slimeball. A bandit, a gangster, literally caught with the goods, and Andrei still couldn't nail him . . . I haven't got enough experience, that's what it is. The others have his kind spilling their guts in no time flat . . . Meanwhile Tailbone began sighing woefully, screwed up his face pitiably, rolled his pupils back up under his forehead, and started swaying on his seat, moaning feebly and clearly intending to collapse in a faint as adroitly as he could so they would give him a glass of water and pack him off to sleep in his cell. Andrei watched these loathsome antics through the cracks between his fingers with hate in his heart. Come on, then, come on, he thought. Just you dare puke on my floor—I'll make you wipe it all up with blotting paper, you son of a bitch.

The door opened and Senior Investigator Fritz Heiger strode confidently into the office. Casting an indifferent glance at Tailbone doubled over on the stool, he walked across to the desk and perched sideways on the papers. Without bothering to ask, he shook several cigarettes out of Andrei's pack, stuck one in his teeth, and arranged the others neatly in a slim silver cigarette case. Andrei struck a match and Fritz took a drag, nodded as an expression of gratitude, and blew out a stream of smoke toward the ceiling.

"The boss told me to take the Black Centipedes case off you," he said in a low voice. "That's if you don't mind, of course." He lowered his voice even further and puckered his lips significantly. "Apparently the solicitor general came down on our boss like a ton of bricks. Now he's calling everyone to his office and giving them an earful too. Just wait—he'll get around to you soon."

Fritz took another drag and looked at Tailbone. The suspect, who had been straining his neck to catch what the bosses were whispering about, immediately cringed and emitted a pitiful moan.

"Looks like you're done with this one, right?"

Andrei shook his head abruptly. He felt ashamed. This was the second time in the last ten days that Fritz had come to take a case from him.

"Oh really?" Fritz said in surprise. He studied Tailbone for a few seconds, sizing him up, then spoke under his breath—"With your permission?"—and slipped off the desk without waiting for a reply.

Walking right up close to the suspect, he leaned down over him compassionately, holding his cigarette away at arm's length.

"Hurting all over?" he inquired sympathetically.

Tailbone moaned in the affirmative.

"Like a drink?"

Tailbone groaned again and reached out a trembling paw.

"And you'd probably like a smoke too, I suppose?"

Tailbone half-opened one eye distrustfully.

"He's hurting all over, the poor soul!" Fritz said loudly, but without turning toward Andrei. "It's a shame to watch a man suffering so badly. He hurts here . . . and he hurts here . . . and he hurts here too . . ."

As he repeated these words, varying the tone of his voice, Fritz made short, obscure movements with the hand that wasn't holding the cigarette: Tailbone's pitiful lowing suddenly broke off, to be replaced by squawking gasps of surprise, and his face turned pale.

"Get up, you bastard!" Fritz suddenly yelled at the top of his voice, taking a step back.

Tailbone immediately jumped to his feet, and Fritz swung a horrific punch into his stomach. Tailbone swayed forward and Fritz landed an open-palm uppercut on his chin with a dull thud. Tailbone swayed backward, knocking over the stool, and fell on his back.

"Get up!" Fritz roared again.

Sobbing and gasping for breath, Tailbone started hastily scrabbling across the floor. Fritz bounded over to him, grabbed his collar, and jerked him up onto his feet. Tailbone's face was completely white now, with a green glint to it, his eyes were goggling crazily, and he was sweating profusely.

Wrinkling up his face in disgust, Andrei looked down at the floor and started fumbling in the pack of cigarettes with trembling fingers, struggling to catch hold of a cigarette. He had to do something, but it wasn't clear what. On the one hand, Fritz's actions were abhorrent and inhuman, but on the other hand, the way this barefaced gangster and thief, this noxious boil on the body of society, made a mockery of justice was just as abhorrent.

"I believe you're dissatisfied with your treatment?" Fritz's ingratiating voice was saying in the meantime. "I believe you're even thinking of making a complaint. Well then, my name is Friedrich Heiger. Senior Investigator Friedrich Heiger . . ."

Andrei forced himself to look up. Tailbone was standing there stretched out to his full height, but with his entire body leaning back, and Fritz was standing right up close, leaning down toward Tailbone and hovering over him menacingly, with his fists propped against his sides.

"You can complain—you know who my present boss is . . . But do you know who used to be my boss before? A certain Reichsführer-SS Heinrich Himmler! Ever heard that name before? And do you know where I used to work before? In an organization that went by the name of the Gestapo! And do you know what I was famous for in that organization?"

The phone rang and Andrei picked up the receiver. "Investigator Voronin here," he said through his teeth.

"Martinelli," replied a slightly strangled voice that sounded short of breath. "Come to my office, Voronin. Immediately."

Andrei hung up. He realized he was going to get a humongous bawling-out from the boss, but right now he was glad to get out of this office—as far away as possible from Tailbone's crazed eyes, from Fritz's savagely thrust-out jaw, out of the congealing atmosphere of the torture chamber. What was Fritz doing this for . . . the Gestapo, Himmler . . . ?

"The boss wants me in his office," he announced in a strange, squeaky voice that didn't seem to be his own, mechanically pulling out the drawer of the desk and putting the pistol in his holster so that he would report in due form.

"Good luck," Fritz responded, without turning around. "I'll be here for a while, don't worry."

Andrei walked toward the door, moving faster and faster as he went, and shot out into the corridor like a rocket. Beneath the gloomy vaulted ceiling, a cool, odorous silence reigned, with several ragged individuals of the male sex sitting motionless on a long wooden garden bench under the strict gaze of the guard on duty. Andrei walked past a row of closed doors and into the detention cells, past a stairway landing on which several young investigators from the latest intake puffed continually on cigarettes as they passionately explained their cases to each other, went up to the third floor, and knocked on the door of his boss's office.

The boss was in a somber mood. His thick cheeks were drooping, his sparse teeth were bared in menace, he was breathing heavily through his mouth with a whistling sound, and he glowered at Andrei from under his brows.

"Sit down," he growled.

Andrei sat down, put his hands on his knees, and stared out the window . . . The window was covered with bars, and the darkness outside it was impenetrable. About eleven o'clock, he thought. I've wasted so much time on that slimeball . . .

"How many cases do you have?" asked the boss.

"Eight."

"How many do you intend to close by the end of the quarter?"

"One."

"That's not good."

Andrei didn't say anything.

"Your work record's poor, Voronin. Poor!" the boss said hoarsely, tormented by his shortness of breath.

"I know," Andrei said humbly. "I just can't get into the swing of it."

"Well, it's about time you did!" said the boss, raising his voice to a whistling hiss. "You've been working here all this time and you've only closed three pitiful cases. You're not fulfilling your duty to the Experiment, Voronin. And after all, you have people you can learn from, people you can ask for advice. Look at the way that friend of yours works, for instance, I mean . . . er, er . . . I mean Friedrich . . . er, er . . . He has his shortcomings, of course, but there's no point in you just adopting his faults. You can adopt his virtues too, Voronin. You came to us together, and he's already closed eleven cases."

"I don't know how to work like that," Andrei said gloomily.

"Learn. You have to learn. We're all learning. Your . . . er . . . Friedrich didn't come here from law school either, but he works, and he works pretty well . . . Just look, he's already a senior investigator. And some people think it's time he was made deputy head of the Criminal Sector . . . Yes . . . But they're not happy with you, Voronin. For instance, what progress are you making on the Building case?"

"None at all," said Andrei. "That isn't a case. It's just nonsense, some kind of mystification."

"Why is it mystification, when there's testimony from witnesses? When there are victims? People are disappearing, Voronin!"

"I can't see how it's possible to conduct a case based on legends and rumors," Andrei said morosely.

The boss strained and coughed, wheezing and whistling. "You've got to use your brains, Voronin," he hissed. "Rumors and legends—yes. A mystical atmosphere—yes. But what for? Who needs that? Where did the rumors come from? Who started them? Who's spreading them? What for? And most important of all—where are the people disappearing to? Do you understand me, Voronin?"

Andrei plucked up his courage and said, "I understand you, boss. But this case isn't for me. I prefer dealing with simple criminal matters. The City's swarming with lowlifes—"

"And I prefer growing tomatoes!" said the boss. "I adore tomatoes, and for some reason you can't get them here for love or money . . . This is your job, Voronin, and no one's interested in what you prefer. You've been given the Building case, so kindly get on with it. I can see for myself that you're a fumbler. Under different circumstances I wouldn't have given you the Building case. But under the present circumstances I am giving it to you. Why? Because you are one of us, Voronin. Because you are not just going through the motions, you're fighting a battle here! Because you didn't come here for your own sake but for the Experiment! There aren't many people like that, Voronin. And that's why I'm going to tell you something that officers of your rank aren't supposed to know."

The boss leaned back in his chair and said nothing for a while, with his chest whistling even more loudly and his teeth completely bared in a grin.

"We fight against gangsters, racketeers, and hooligans, everyone knows that. That's good, it's necessary. But they aren't our danger number one, Voronin. First, there's a natural phenomenon that exists here, it's called the Anticity. Ever heard of it? No, you haven't. And you shouldn't have. You shouldn't have heard of it. And don't let anyone ever hear of it from you! It's an official secret with a 'double 0' number. The Anticity. We have information that there are settlements of some kind to the north of us: one, two, several—we don't know. But they know all about us! There could be an invasion, Voronin. It's very dangerous. The end of our City. The end of the Experiment. Espionage is being committed, sabotage and acts of subversion are being attempted, panicky rumors and calumnies are being spread. Is the situation clear, Voronin? I can see that it is. To continue. Here, in the City itself, there are people living beside us and among us who didn't come here for the sake of the Experiment but for other, more or less selfish reasons. Nihilists, internal recluses, elements that have lost faith, anarchists. Not many of them are activists, but even the passive ones represent a danger. The erosion of morals, the breakdown of ideals, attempts to set some strata of the population against others, corrosive skepticism. Example: a good friend of yours, a certain Katzman . . ."

Andrei started. The boss shot a dark glance at him from between puffy eyelids, paused, and continued.

"Iosif Katzman. A curious individual. We have information that he often sets out and travels in a northerly direction, spends some time there, and then comes back. In so doing, he neglects his own direct responsibilities, but that's none of our business. To continue. Conversations. This is something you must be aware of."

Andrei nodded involuntarily but immediately realized what he was doing and put on a stony face.

"To continue. The most important thing for us. He has been spotted in the vicinity of the Building. Twice. Once he was seen emerging from it. I hope I have adduced a good example, successfully linking him with the Building case. You have to get to work on this case, Voronin. This, Voronin, is a case that I can't hand to anyone else now. There are people no less devoted than you, and with far more sense, but they're busy. All of them. Every last one. Up to their eyes in work. So you push on with the Building case, Voronin. I'll try to relieve you of the other cases. Tomorrow at 1600 hours come back to me to report and present your plan. Go."

Andrei got up.

"Oh yes! A piece of advice. I advise you to pay some attention to the Falling Stars case. Advise you very earnestly. There could be a connection. That case is being handled by Chachua now; drop into his office and familiarize yourself. Consult him."

Andrei bowed awkwardly and set off toward the door.

"One more thing!" the boss said, and Andrei halted right in front of the door. "Bear in mind that the solicitor general is taking a special interest in the Building case. A special interest! So apart from you, there's someone else from the Public Prosecutor's Office, and he'll still be dealing with it. Try to avoid any lapses arising from your personal inclinations, or the opposite. Go on, Voronin."

Andrei closed the door behind him and leaned against the wall. He could feel a sort of obscure emptiness inside himself, some kind of indeterminate void. He'd been expecting a severe reprimand, a huge dressing-down from the boss, maybe even the boot or a transfer to the police. Instead of that it seemed like he'd actually been praised, singled out from the others, trusted with a case that was considered a top priority. Only a year ago, when he was still a garbage collector, a bawling-out at work would have cast him into an abyss of woe and despair, and a responsible assignment would have raised him up on high to a peak of exultation and feverish enthusiasm. But now he sensed a kind of indefinite twilight inside himself; he cautiously attempted to figure himself out and at the same time feel out the inevitable complications and inconveniences which were, of course, bound to arise in this new situation.

Izya Katzman . . . A blabbermouth. A windbag. A vicious, venomous tongue. A cynic. And at the same time—there was no way around it—totally unmercenary, kindhearted, absolutely unselfish, even to the point of stupidity, basically helpless when it came to worldly matters . . . And the Building case. And the Anticity. Damn it all . . . OK, we'll figure this out . . .

He went back to his office and was rather nonplussed to discover Fritz there. Fritz was sitting at Andrei's desk, smoking Andrei's cigarettes, and carefully leafing through Andrei's cases, extracted from Andrei's safe. "Well then, did you get the full works?" Fritz asked, looking up at Andrei.

Without answering, Andrei took a cigarette, lit up, and inhaled deeply several times. Then he looked around for somewhere to sit and saw an empty stool. "Listen, where's that guy?"

"In the slammer," Fritz replied contemptuously. "I sent him off to the slammer for the night, with orders not to give him anything to eat, drink, or smoke. He coughed up the goods, meek as a lamb, a complete confession, and he named another two we didn't even know about. But to wrap things up the slimeball has to be taught a lesson. I'll give you the record of interrogation." He tossed a few files from one spot to another. "I've filed the record, you'll find it yourself. Tomorrow you can hand it on to the Prosecutor's Office. It has some curious things he told me in it—they'll come in handy sometime."

Andrei smoked, looking at that long, well-groomed face and those keen, watery eyes, and he couldn't help admiring the confident movements of those large, genuinely manly hands. Fritz had grown recently. There was almost nothing left in him of the pompous young noncommissioned officer. The rather blunt insolence had been replaced by focused confidence; he no longer took offense at jokes; he didn't put on a stony face and didn't play the jackass at all. At one point he had become a frequent visitor to Selma's place, and then they'd had some kind of bust-up, and Andrei had had a few words with him as well. And Fritz had calmly withdrawn.

"What are you gawping at me like that for?" Fritz inquired with benign curiosity. "Still can't pull yourself together after the shellacking? Never mind, old buddy, a shellacking from the boss is a subordinate's holiday of the heart!"

"Hey, listen," said Andrei. "What did you act out that little operetta for? Himmler, the Gestapo . . . What sort of innovative investigative practice is that?"

"Operetta?" said Fritz, jerking up his right eyebrow. "That, my old buddy, works like a shot from a gun!" He slammed shut an open case file and got up from the desk. "I'm surprised you haven't figured that out for yourself. I assure you, if you'd told him you used to work in the Cheka or the GPU and clicked a pair of manicure scissors under his nose, you'd have had him kissing your boots . . . You know, I've picked out a few of your cases—with the heap you have here, you'll never plow through them in a year . . . So I'll take them off your hands, and we can settle up somehow later."

Andrei gave him a grateful look and Fritz gave him a friendly wink in reply. A helpful kind of guy, Fritz. And a sound comrade. So maybe that was the way the work should be done? Why the hell bother using kid gloves on this garbage? And it was true, everyone over there in the West had been frightened half to death with talk of the Cheka's basement rooms, and when it came to filthy carrion like that Tailbone, any means were good.

"Well, any questions?" asked Fritz. "No? Then I'll be going."

He tucked the case files under his arm and stepped out from behind the desk. "Oh yes!" said Andrei, suddenly remembering.

"You haven't taken the Building case, by any chance, have you? Leave that one!"

"The Building case? My dear man, my altruism doesn't extend that far. You can figure out the Building case yourself somehow."

"Uh-huh," Andrei said with morose determination. "Myself . . . By the way," he said, remembering something else. "Falling Stars—what sort of case is that? I know the name all right, but what it's all about, what sort of stars they are, I don't recall . . ."

Fritz wrinkled up his forehead and gave Andrei a curious glance. "There is a case by that name," he said. "They haven't really handed it off to you, have they? Then you're a goner. Chachua's got it. A desperate case, absolutely hopeless."

"No," Andrei said with a sigh. "No one's handed it to me. It's just that the boss suggested I should familiarize myself with it. A series of some kind of ritual killings, isn't it? Or is it?"

"No, it's not exactly that. Although maybe it *is* that. That case, my friend, has been dragging on for years. Every now and then they find people smashed to smithereens at the foot of the Wall. They've obviously fallen off the Wall, from a great height . . ."

"What do you mean, off the Wall?" Andrei asked in amazement. "Is it really possible to climb up it? It's smooth . . . And what for? You can't even see the top of it."

"That's the point! At first some thought there was a city like ours up there too, on top, and they were throwing these people down to us over their Cliff, you know, the way we can throw things into our Abyss. But then they managed to identify a couple of the bodies: they were ours, all right, local residents . . . No one has the slightest idea how they managed to clamber up there. So far we can only assume that they're some kind of desperado rock climbers who were trying to get out of the City by the upward route . . . But on the other hand . . . Anyway, it's a pretty dismal case. A dead case, if you want my opinion. Well, OK, time I was going."

"Thanks. Cheers," Andrei said, and Fritz left.

Andrei moved across into his own chair, put away all the files except the Building case in the safe, and sat there for a while with his head propped on his hands. Then he picked up the phone, dialed a number, and started waiting. As usual, no one answered the phone for a long time, then someone picked up the receiver and a low male voice, clearly not sober, inquired, *"Heeello?"* Andrei said nothing, pressing the receiver hard against his ear: "Hello! *Hellooo?"* the drunken voice growled, then fell silent, and all that could be heard was heavy breathing and Selma's voice in the distance, crooning a heartrending song that Uncle Yura had brought to the City:

> *Get up, Katya, get up,*
> *The ships at anchor ride!*
> *Two ships of a dark blue,*
> *One bright blue as the sky . . .*

Andrei hung up, croaked and grunted, rubbing his cheeks, then muttered bitterly, "Lousy tramp, she's irredeemable . . ." and opened the case file.

The Building case had been opened during the time when Andrei was still a garbage collector and knew nothing at all about the murky backstage life of the City. In the sixteenth, eighteenth, and thirty-second districts, people had suddenly started disappearing on a regular basis. They disappeared absolutely without a trace, and there was absolutely no system, no sense, and no logic to the disappearances. Ole Svensson, forty-three years of age, a laborer at the paper mill, went out one evening to get bread and didn't come back, and he never showed up at the bread shop. Stepan Cibulski, twenty-five years of age, a policeman, disappeared at night from his post, his shoulder belt was found on the corner of Main Street and Diamond Avenue—and that was all; there were no other traces. Monica Lehrer, fifty-five years of age, a seamstress, took her spitz out for walk before bed; the spitz returned home cheerful and in good health, but the seamstress had disappeared. And so on, and so on—more than forty disappearances in all.

Fairly soon witnesses turned up who claimed that shortly before the missing people disappeared, they had entered a certain Building—from the descriptions it seemed like the same one, but the strange thing was that different witnesses provided different locations for the Building. Josef Humboldt, sixty-three years of age, a hairdresser, walked into a three-story redbrick building on the corner of Second Right Street and Graystone Lane in full view of Leo Paltus, who knew him personally, and since that time no one had seen Josef Humboldt again. A certain Theodore Buch testified that Semyon Zahodko, thirty-two years of age, a farmer, who subsequently disappeared, had entered a building of precisely the same description, but this time on Third Left Street, not far from the Catholic church. David Mkrtchan related how he had met an old acquaintance from work, Ray Dodd, forty-one years of age, a cesspool cleaner, in Wattle and Daub Lane—they stood there for a while, chatting about the harvest, family matters, and other neutral subjects, and then Ray Dodd said, "Hang on a moment, I've just got to drop into this place, I'll try to make it quick, but if I'm not back out in five minutes, you go on, it means I've been delayed." He went into some kind of redbrick building with windows that were whitewashed over. Mkrtchan waited a quarter of an hour for him, then gave up and went on his way, and as for Ray Dodd, he disappeared without a trace forever.

The redbrick building figured in the testimony of all the witnesses. Some asserted that it was three stories high, others said it had four floors. Some noticed windows that were whitewashed over, others mentioned windows that were covered with metal gratings. And no two witnesses gave exactly the same spot as its location.

Rumors started rippling through the City. In the lines to buy milk, in the hairdressing salons, in the restaurants, it was passed on by word of mouth in an ominous whisper—the bright, shiny, brand-new legend of the appalling Red Building that wandered around the City of its own volition, settling in somewhere between the ordinary buildings, opening the ghastly jaws of its doors and lying in wait there for the incautious. Then people appeared claiming to be friends of relatives of acquaintances who had managed to escape, tearing themselves out of the grip of that insatiable brick maw. These acquaintances had told terrifying stories, presenting by way of proof scars and fractures earned by jumping from the second, third, and even fourth floor. According to all these rumors and legends, the building was empty inside—there were no robbers or sadistic maniacs waiting for you in there, no shaggy-haired, bloodsucking beasts. But the stone bowels of the corridors suddenly contracted, straining to squash their victim; the black chasms of manholes gaped open underfoot, breathing out an icy graveyard stench; mysterious forces drove men along the black, constantly narrowing passages and tunnels until they got stuck, trying to force their way through the final stony crack—and in the empty rooms with tattered wallpaper, among slabs of plaster that had fallen from the ceilings, the crushed bones decayed, projecting ghoulishly from rags that were crusted hard with blood . . .

At first Andrei had actually taken an interest in this case. He marked the places where the Building had been seen with little crosses on a map of the City, tried to find some consistent principle in the locations of these little crosses, and drove out to investigate those places a good dozen times—and every time at the location of the Building he discovered either an abandoned garden or a gap between buildings, or even an ordinary apartment building that had nothing to do with any mysteries or riddles.

He was bemused by the circumstance that the Red Building had never been seen by the light of the sun; he was bemused by the circumstance that at least half the witnesses had seen the Building while in a state of greater or lesser alcoholic intoxication; he was bemused by the petty but seemingly compulsory inconsistencies in virtually every testimony; and he was especially bemused by the total senselessness and absurdity of what was happening.

Izya Katzman had once remarked concerning this business that a city of a million people, deprived of any systematic ideology, would inevitably acquire its own myths. That sounded convincing enough, but people were actually disappearing for real! Of course, it wasn't all that hard for someone to disappear in the City. They only had to be thrown over the Cliff and no one would ever be any wiser. But who would want to cast assorted hairdressers, old seamstresses, and petty shopkeepers into the Abyss? People with no money, with no reputation, and practically no enemies? Kensi had once voiced the perfectly sensible supposition that the Red Building, if it really existed, was evidently an integral part of the Experiment, so seeking an explanation for it was pointless—the Experiment is the Experiment. In the end Andrei had also settled for this point of view. There was a whole heap of work to be done, the Building case already ran to more than a thousand pages, and Andrei had stuck the file right down at the bottom of his safe, only occasionally extracting it in order to insert the latest witness testimony.

Today's talk with the boss, however, had opened up entirely new prospects. If there really were people in the City who had set themselves the task (or for whom someone else had set the task) of creating an atmosphere of panic and terror among the general population, that lent many aspects of the Building case some comprehensibility. And then the inconsistency of the testimony from the so-called witnesses could be explained by the distortion of rumors as they were passed on, and the disappearances were transformed into ordinary murders, intended to intensify the atmosphere of terror. The constantly active sources, the distribution centers of this murky, sinister haze, now had to be sought out among the welter of idle gossip, fearful whispers, and lies . . .

Andrei took a clean sheet of paper and began slowly drafting out a plan, word by word and point by point. A little while later he had come up with the following:

Primary goal: Identify sources of rumors, arrest said sources, and identify control center. Basic methods: Repeat questioning of all witnesses who have previously provided testimony in a sober condition; pursue links in the chain to identify and question individuals who claim they have been inside the Building; identify possible links between these individuals and the witnesses . . . Take into account: a) Information provided by agents b) Inconsistencies in the testimony . . .

Andrei chewed on his pencil for a moment, squinted at the lamp, and remembered another thing: contact Petrov. At one time this Petrov had really gotten Andrei's goat. His wife had disappeared, and for some reason he decided that the Red Building had swallowed her. Since then he had abandoned all his other business and devoted himself to searching for the Building: he wrote countless notes to the Prosecutor's Office—which were promptly forwarded to the Investigation Department and ended up with Andrei—he wandered around the City at night, was taken into the police station several times on suspicion of criminal intent, and raised Cain there, which got him locked up for ten days, and when he got out he carried on with his search.

Andrei wrote out summonses for him and two other witnesses, handed the summonses to the duty guard with orders to see they were delivered immediately, and went to see Chachua.

Chachua, an immense Caucasian who had run to fat, with almost no forehead but a gigantic nose, was reclining on the sofa in his office, surrounded by swollen case files, and sleeping. Andrei shook him.

"Eh!" Chachua said hoarsely as he woke up. "What happened?"

"Nothing happened," Andrei said angrily. He couldn't stand this kind of lax behavior in people. "Give me the Falling Stars case."

Chachua sat up, his face beaming with joy. "Are you taking it?" he asked with a predatory twitch of his phenomenal nose.

"Don't go getting all happy. It's only to take a look."

"Listen, what do you want to just look at it for?" Chachua exclaimed passionately. "Take the case off my hands completely. You're handsome, young, and full of energy; the boss holds you up as an example to everyone. You'll soon have this case unraveled—you'll just clamber up that Yellow Wall and unravel it, quick as a flash! It's a piece of cake for you!"

Andrei gazed at Chachua's nose. Immense and hooked, with a web of crimson veinlets covering its bridge and bunches of coarse black hairs protruding from its nostrils, this nose lived a life of its own, apart from Chachua. It obviously just didn't want to know about the concerns of Investigator Chachua. It wanted everyone around it to quaff ice-cold Kakhetian wine out of large glasses, following it down with juicy kebabs and moist, crunchy green herbs and salads; it wanted everyone to dance, clutching the hems of their sleeves in their fingers, with passionate cries of "*Ássa!*" It wanted to bury itself in fragrant blonde hair and hover above sumptuous naked breasts . . . Oh, it wanted many things, that magnificent, life-loving hedonist of a nose, and its multitudinous desires were all candidly expressed in its various independent movements and changes of color, and the range of sounds that it emitted!

"And if you can close this case," said Chachua, rolling the olives of his eyes back up under his low forehead, "oh my God! What fame that will earn you! What honor! Do you think Chachua would offer you this case if he could climb up the Yellow Wall himself? Not for anything would Chachua offer you this case! It's a gold mine! And I'm only offering it to *you*. Lots of people have come to me and asked for it. No, I thought, none of you can handle it. Voronin's the only one who can handle it, I thought—"

"OK, OK, that's enough," Andrei said in annoyance. "Just cut the gab, will you, and let me have the file. I haven't got time to waste on singing along here with you."

Still prattling, complaining, and boasting, Chachua lazily got up, shuffling his feet across the littered floor, walked over to the safe, and started rummaging around in it, while Andrei watched his massive, broad shoulders and thought that Chachua was probably one of the best investigators in the department—he was simply a brilliant investigator, he had the highest percentage of closed cases—but he hadn't been able to get anywhere with this Falling Stars case. No one had been able to get anywhere with this case—not Chachua, not the investigator before him, and not the investigator before that . . .

Chachua took out a pile of plump, greasy files, and they leafed through the final pages together. Andrei carefully noted down on a separate piece of paper the names and addresses of the two individuals who had been identified, and also the small number of distinguishing characteristics that had been determined for some of the unidentified victims.

"What a case!" Chachua exclaimed, clicking his tongue. "Eleven bodies! And you're turning it down. Oh yes, Voronin, you don't know your own good luck when you see it. You Russians always were idiots—you were idiots in the other world, and you're still idiots in this one! What do you want this for anyway?" he asked, suddenly curious.

Andrei explained what he intended to do as coherently as he could. Chachua grasped the essence quickly enough but didn't evince any particular delight at the idea.

"Try it, try it . . ." he said lethargically. "I have my doubts, though. What's your Building, compared to my Wall? The Building's a figment, but the Wall—there it is, just a kilometer away . . . Ah, no, Voronin, we'll never get to the bottom of this case." But then, when Andrei was already at the door, Chachua called after him, "Well, if something does come up—you get right back to me."

"OK," said Andrei. "Of course."

"Listen," said Chachua, wrinkling up his fat forehead in concentration and wiggling his nose. Andrei stopped and looked at him expectantly. "I've been wanting to ask you for a long time . . ." Chachua's face turned serious. "In 1917 you had a little bust-up in Petrograd. How did that turn out, ah?"

Andrei spat and walked out, slamming the door, to peals of laughter from the delighted Caucasian. Chachua had caught him out again with that idiotic joke. It would be better not to talk to him at all.

There was a surprise waiting for him in the corridor outside his office. A disheveled little character with drowsy eyes was sitting on the bench, huddling up in his coat to keep warm and looking frightened to death. The duty guard at the small desk with the telephone jumped to his feet and gallantly barked out, "Witness Eino Saari delivered in accordance with your summons, Mr. Investigator!"

Andrei gazed at him, dumbfounded. "In accordance with my summons?"

The duty guard was rather dumbfounded too. "You told me yourself," he said resentfully. "Half an hour ago . . . You handed me the summonses and ordered me to deliver them immediately."

"My God," said Andrei. "The summonses! I ordered you to deliver the summonses immediately, damn you! For tomorrow, at ten in the morning!" He glanced at pale, smiling Eino Saari with the white ankle ties of his long johns dangling out from under his trousers, then looked at the duty officer again. "And are they going to bring the others right now?" he asked.

"Yes sir," the duty officer replied morosely. "I did what I was told to do."

"I'll report you," said Andrei, barely able to control himself. "You'll be transferred to street duty—herding the crazies back home in the morning—then I'll watch you in your misery . . . Well then," he said, turning to Saari, "since this is the way things have turned out, come in."

He pointed out the stool to the witness, sat down at the desk, and glanced at the clock. It was shortly after midnight. His hopes of getting a good night's sleep before a heavy day tomorrow had miserably evaporated. "Right, then," he said with a sigh, opened the Building case file, leafed through the immense pile of reports, statements, references, and forensic testimony, found the sheet with the previous testimony provided by Saari (forty-three years of age, a saxophone player in the Second Municipal Theater, divorced), and ran his eyes over it one more time. "Right, then," he repeated. "Actually what I need to do is check a few things relating to the testimony you gave the police a month ago."

"By all means, by all means," said Saari, eagerly leaning forward and holding his coat closed across his chest in a womanish kind of gesture.

"You testified that at 2340 hours on September 8 of this year, your acquaintance Ella Stremberg entered the so-called Red Building as you watched, and at that time the building was located on Parrot Street, in the gap between delicatessen number 115 and Strem's pharmacy. Do you confirm that testimony?"

"Yes, yes, I confirm it. That's absolutely the way everything was. Only about the date . . . I don't recall the precise date—after all, it was more than a month ago."

"That's not important," said Andrei. "You remembered at the time, and it also happens to concur with other testimony . . . What I'm asking you to do now is to describe that so-called Red Building again, in greater detail."

Saari leaned his head over to one side and pondered. "Well then, it was like this," he said. "Three stories. Old brick, dark red, like a barracks, if you know what I mean. With sort of narrow, high windows. On the first floor they were all whitewashed over, and as I recall now, they weren't lit up . . ." He thought again for a moment. "You know, as far as I recall, there wasn't a single lit-up window. Well, and . . . the entrance. Stone steps, two or three . . . this heavy kind of door . . . an old-fashioned sort of brass handle . . . ornate. Ella grabbed hold of that handle and pulled the door toward her with a real effort, you know . . . I didn't notice the number of the building, I don't even remember if it had a number . . . Basically it looked like an old government building, something from late last century."

"Right, then," said Andrei. "So tell me, had you often been on this Parrot Street before?"

"It was the first time. And the last, actually. I live quite a long way from there, I'm never in that area, but this time it just happened that I decided to see Ella home. We'd had a party, and I . . . mmm . . . well, I flirted with her a bit, and I went to see her home. We had a very agreeable talk on the way, then she suddenly said, 'Well, it's time for us to part,' and kissed me on the cheek, and before I realized what was happening, she'd already slipped into this building. At the time I honestly thought that she lived there . . ."

"I see," said Andrei. "You were probably drinking at the party, right?"

Saari slapped himself on the knees regretfully with both hands. "No, Mr. Investigator," he said. "Not a drop. I can't drink—the doctors advise me not to."

Andrei nodded sympathetically. "You don't happen to remember if this building had chimneys, do you?"

"Yes, of course I remember. I really should tell you that the appearance of that building has an astounding impact on the imagination—it's as if it were standing there in front of my eyes right now. It had this tiled roof and three fairly tall chimneys. I remember there was smoke coming out of one of them, and I thought at the time how many buildings we still have that are heated by stoves . . ."

The moment had come. Andrei carefully laid his pencil across the reports and statements, leaned forward slightly, and peered intently through narrowed eyes at Eino Saari, saxophonist. "There are discrepancies in your testimony. First, as forensic analysis has demonstrated, if you were on Parrot Street, there was no way you could have seen the roof or the chimneys of a three-story building."

The jaw of Eino Saari, mendacious saxophonist, dropped open, and his eyes started darting about in confusion.

"To continue. The investigation has established that at nighttime Parrot Street is not lit at all, and therefore it is quite incomprehensible how, in the pitch darkness of night, three hundred meters from the nearest streetlamp, you could have made out such a host of details: the color of the building, the old brick, the brass door handle, the shape of the windows, and, finally, the smoke from the chimney. I would like to know how you account for these discrepancies."

For a while Eino Saari merely opened and closed his mouth without a sound. Then he gulped convulsively and said, "I don't understand a thing . . . You've completely flummoxed me . . . It never even dawned on me . . ."

Andrei waited expectantly.

"It's true, why didn't I think of it before . . . It was completely dark there on that Parrot Street! Never mind the buildings—I couldn't even see the sidewalk under my feet . . . Or the roof . . . I was standing right beside the building, by the porch . . . but I absolutely, distinctly remember the roof and the bricks and the smoke from the chimney—that white, nighttime smoke, as if it were lit up by moonlight."

"Yes, that is strange," Andrei said in a wooden voice.

"And the handle on the door . . . Brass, and polished by the touch of so many hands . . . such a subtle pattern of flowers and little leaves . . . I could draw it now, if I knew how to draw . . . And at the same time it was absolutely dark—I couldn't make out Ella's face, I could only tell from her voice that she was smiling when—"

A new idea appeared in Eino Saari's gaping eyes. He pressed his hands to his chest.

"Mr. Investigator!" he said in a despairing voice. "At this moment my head is filled with confusion, but I realize quite clearly that I'm testifying against myself, leading you to suspect me. But I'm an honest man—my parents were absolutely honest, deeply religious people . . . Everything I'm telling you now is the absolute, honest truth! That's exactly the way it was. It's just that it never dawned on me before. It was pitch dark, I was standing right beside the building, and at the same time I remember every brick, and I can see the tiles of that roof as if it were right here, beside me . . . and the three chimneys . . . And the smoke."

"Hmm . . ." said Andrei, and drummed his fingers on the desk. "And perhaps you didn't see all this yourself? Perhaps someone else told you about it? Had you ever heard about the Red Building before the incident with Miss Stremberg?"

Eino Saari's eyes started darting about again. "*Nnnn* . . . I don't recall," he said. "Afterward—yes. After Ella disappeared, when I went to the police, after she was declared missing . . . there was a lot of talk then. But before that . . . Mr. Investigator!" he declared solemnly. "I can't swear that I didn't hear anything about the Red Building before Ella disappeared, but I can swear that I don't remember anything about it."

Andrei picked up a pen and started writing the record of interrogation. At the same time he spoke in a deliberately monotonous, officious voice, intended to inspire in the suspect a state of dreary melancholy and a sense of implacable fate propelled by the impeccable mechanism of justice. "You must realize, Mr. Saari, that the investigation cannot be satisfied with your testimony. Ella Stremberg disappeared without a trace, and you, Mr. Saari, were the last person to see her. The Red Building that you have described in such detail here does not exist on Parrot Street. The description that you give of the Red Building is not credible, since it contradicts the elementary laws of physics. And finally, as the investigation is aware, Ella Stremberg lived in an entirely different district, a long way from Parrot Street. That in itself is not evidence against you, of course, but it does arouse additional suspicions. I am obliged to detain you from this moment until a number of circumstances have been clarified . . . Please read the report of the interrogation and sign it."

Not saying a word, Eino Saari approached the desk and signed each page of the report without even reading it. The pencil was trembling in his hand, his narrow jaw had dropped, and it was trembling too. Afterward he walked back to the stool, shuffling his feet, sat down limply, and said through gritted teeth, "I wish to emphasize once again, Mr. Investigator, that in providing my testimony . . ." His voice broke off and he gulped again. "In providing my testimony, I was aware that I was acting against my own interests . . . I could have made something up, I could have lied . . . I could easily not have become involved in the search at all—nobody knew that I had left to see Ella home."

"This declaration of yours," Andrei said in an indifferent voice, "is already included in the report. If you're not guilty of anything, you are in no danger. You will now be shown to a detention cell. Take this sheet of paper and pencil. You can render assistance to the investigation, and yourself, by writing down, in as much detail as possible, who spoke to you about the Red Building, when they did so, and under what circumstances. Before or after Ella Stremberg's disappearance, it doesn't matter. In the greatest possible detail: who—the name and address; when—the precise date and time of day; under what circumstances—where, for what reason, for what purpose, in what tone. Do you understand me?"

Eino Saari nodded and said a soundless *yes*.

Looking intently into his eyes, Andrei went on. "I'm certain that you learned all the details about the Red Building somewhere else. Quite possibly you yourself have never even seen it. And I earnestly recommend that you remember who provided you with these details—who, when, under what circumstances. And for what purpose."

He rang the bell for the duty guard, and the saxophonist was led away. Andrei rubbed his hands together, punched holes in the report of interrogation, added it to the case file, asked for hot tea, and called the next witness. He was feeling pleased with himself. Imagination and a knowledge of elementary geometry could come in useful after all. The mendacious Eino Saari had been exposed in keeping with all the laws of science.

The next witness, Matilda Husáková (sixty-two years of age, knitting work from home, a widow), was, at least in principle, a far simpler case. She was a powerfully built old woman with a small head that was covered with completely gray hair, ruddy cheeks, and cunning eyes. She didn't look in the least bit sleepy or frightened; on the contrary, she seemed to be quite pleased with this adventure. She had turned up at the Prosecutor's Office with her basket, balls of different-colored wool, and a selection of needles, and in the office she immediately perched on the stool, put on her eyeglasses, and started working away with her needles.

"It has come to the attention of the investigation, Pani Husáková, that some time ago, speaking among friends, you told the story of what had happened to a certain František, who supposedly entered the so-called Red Building, had various adventures there, and only escaped with some difficulty. Is that true?"

The aged Matilda laughed, deftly tugged out one needle and set in another, and answered without looking up from her knitting: "It is, that happened. I told people that story, and more than once, only I'd like to know how the investigation came to find out about it . . . I don't believe I have any acquaintances among the judiciary."

"I am obliged to inform you," Andrei said in a confidential tone, "that at the present time an investigation is being conducted concerning the so-called Red Building, and we are extremely interested in contacting at least one person who has been inside this building . . ."

Matilda Husáková wasn't listening to him. She put her knitting down on her knees and looked thoughtfully at the wall. "Who could have informed them?" she said. "Everyone at Liza's place is reliable, unless Carmen let it slip somewhere afterward . . . that old blabbermouth . . . At Frieda's place?" She shook her head. "No, it couldn't be at Frieda's place. There's that individual who visits Liuba . . . a repulsive kind of old man, with really shifty eyes, and always letting Liuba buy his drinks . . . Now that's something I never expected! And now it seems I'm supposed to figure out who it was and whose place it was at . . . Under the Germans we kept our lips buttoned up tight. After '48 it was keep *shtum* again and keep an eye out. We only opened our mouths just a little bit in our golden spring—then *bang*, the Russians arrived in their tanks, shut your mouth again, mind your tongue . . . So I came here and it's the same picture all over again—"

"Pardon me, Pani Husáková," Andrei interrupted her. "But in my opinion you're taking a perverse view of the situation. After all, as far as I understand, you haven't committed any crime. We regard you only as a witness, someone who can help, who—"

"Eh, sweetheart! What kind of helpers are there in this business? The police is the police."

"No, not at all!" said Andrei, pressing one hand to his heart for greater conviction. "We're looking for a gang of criminals. They abduct people and all the indications are that they kill them. Someone who has been in their clutches could render invaluable service to the investigation!"

"Are you telling me, sweetheart . . ." said the old woman, ". . . are you telling me that you believe in this Red Building?"

"Why, don't you believe in it?" asked Andrei, rather taken aback.

Before the old woman could even reply, the door of the office opened slightly, a hubbub of agitated voices burst in from the corridor, and a squat individual with a thick head of black hair appeared in the crack, shouting back into the corridor, "Yes, it's urgent! I have to see him urgently!" Andrei frowned, but then the figure was dragged back out into the corridor and the door slammed shut.

"I'm sorry we were interrupted," said Andrei. "I think you wanted to tell me that you yourself don't believe in the Red Building?"

Still working away with her needles, aged Matilda shrugged one shoulder. "Well, what grown-up person could believe in that? This house, you see, it runs around from one place to another, inside it all the doors have teeth, you go up the stairs and you end up in the basement . . . Of course, anything can happen in these parts, the Experiment is the Experiment, but this is really over the top, after all . . . No, I don't believe in it. Who do you take me for, to go believing in cock-and-bull stories like that? Of course, every city has buildings that swallow people up, and ours probably has some of its own too. But it's hardly likely that those houses go running around from one place to another . . . and as I understand it, the stairs in them are perfectly normal."

"I beg your pardon, Pani Husáková," said Andrei. "But then why do you tell everyone these cock-and-bull stories?"

"Why not tell them, if people listen? People are bored with things, especially old folks like us."

"So did you just make it up yourself?"

Aged Matilda opened her mouth to answer, but at that moment Andrei's phone started trilling desperately right in his ear. Andrei cursed and grabbed the receiver. "Andrei. Sweetie pie . . ." Selma's very drunk voice said in the earpiece. "I've locked. Them. All out. Locked. Them out. Why aren't you coming?"

"Sorry," said Andrei, chewing on his lip and squinting at the old woman. "I'm really busy right now, I'll call you—"

"But that's not what I want!" Selma declared. "I love you, I'm waiting for you. I'm all drunk and all naked, and waiting for you, I'm cold . . ."

"Selma," Andrei said, speaking right into the receiver, lowering his voice. "Quit acting like a fool. I'm very busy."

"You won't find another girl like me anyway, not in this shshsh- . . . shithouse. I've curled right up tight in a ball . . . *ab-solutely-ab-solutely* . . . naked . . ."

"I'll come in half an hour," Andrei said hastily.

"You *lit-tle* fool! In ha- . . . half an hour I'll be asleep already . . . Whoever takes half an hour?"

"OK then, Selma, see you in a while," said Andrei, cursing the day and the hour when he gave this dissipated female his office phone number.

"Well, you just go to hell!" Selma suddenly yelled, and hung up. She probably slammed the receiver down so hard that she smashed the phone into pieces. Gritting his teeth in fury, Andrei carefully put down his own receiver and sat there for a few seconds, not even daring to look up as his thoughts scattered in confusion. Then he cleared his throat.

"Well then," he said. "Aha . . . So you told the stories just for the sake of it, out of boredom . . ." He finally recalled his last question. "So should I take you to mean by that, that you made up the entire story about František yourself?"

The old woman opened her mouth again to answer, but once again nothing came of it. The door swung open: the duty officer appeared in the doorway, saluted smartly, and reported, "I beg your pardon, Mr. Investigator! The witness Petrov is demanding that you question him immediately, because he has something to tell."

Andrei's eyes misted over darkly . . . He slammed both fists down on the desk and yelled so loud it set his own ears ringing: "Damn you, duty guard! Don't you know the regulations? What do you mean by butting in here with your Petrov? Where do you think you are, in the bathroom at home? About turn, quick march!"

The duty guard disappeared in a flash. Andrei, feeling his lips trembling, poured himself some water from his carafe with trembling hands and drank it. His throat was raw after that wild bellow. He glanced sullenly at the old woman. Aged Matilda was still knitting away as if nothing at all had happened.

"I beg your pardon," he mumbled.

"Never mind, young man," Matilda reassured him. "I'm not offended by you. So, you asked if maybe I made it all up myself. No, sweetheart, I didn't. How could I possibly think up something like that? Of all things—stairs that you walk up but end up going down . . . I could never imagine anything like that, not even in a dream. I told it the way I was told it."

"And who exactly told it to you?"

Still carrying on with her knitting, the old woman shook her head. "Now *that* I can't recall. A woman was telling people about it in a line somewhere. Supposedly this František was the son-in-law of some woman she knew. She was lying too, of course.

Standing in line you can sometimes hear things they'll never print in any newspapers."

"And when was this, more or less?" Andrei asked, gradually recovering his composure and already annoyed with himself for charging head-on at things like a bull at a gate.

"About two months ago, probably . . . maybe three."

Right, I've screwed up the interrogation, Andrei thought bitterly. Damn it, I've screwed up the interrogation because of that slut and that jackass guard. No, I won't let that go—I'll give that bonehead a real roasting. I'll make him dance. He'll be chasing lunatics through that chilly morning air . . . Right, OK, but now what do I do with the old woman? The old woman's clammed up, hasn't she, doesn't want to name any names. "But are you sure, Pani Husáková, that you don't remember that woman's name?"

"I don't, sweetheart, I don't remember it at all," aged Matilda responded cheerfully, working away deftly with her glittering needles.

"But perhaps your friends remember?"

The needles' movement slowed a little.

"After all, you did tell them the name, right?" Andrei went on. "So it's quite possible, isn't it, that their memories might be slightly better?"

Matilda shrugged one shoulder again and said nothing. Andrei leaned back in his chair.

"Well, this is the situation in which you and I find ourselves, Pani Husáková. You have either forgotten the name of that woman or you simply don't want to tell it to us. But your women friends do remember it. That means we'll have to detain you here for a little while so that you can't warn your friends, and we'll be obliged to keep you here until either you or one of your friends remembers who you heard this story from."

"That's up to you," Pani Husáková said meekly.

"That's all well and good," said Andrei. "But while you're try-ing to remember and we're wasting time on your friends, people will carry on disappearing, the bad guys will be chortling and rubbing their hands in glee, and all this will happen because of your strange prejudice against the investigative agencies."

Aged Matilda didn't answer. She just pursed her wrinkled lips stubbornly.

"You must understand what an absurd situation we have here," Andrei continued, trying to hammer home the point. "Here we are, kept busy day and night by all sorts of slimeballs, lowlifes, and scum, and then an honest person comes in and absolutely refuses to help us. What are we supposed to make of that? It's totally bizarre! And this childish trick of yours is pointless in any case. If you won't remember, your friends will, and we'll find out that woman's name anyway, we'll get to František, and he'll help us take out the entire nest of villains. As long as the thugs don't take him out first, as a dangerous witness . . . And if they do kill him, you'll be the guilty one, Pani Husáková! Not in the eyes of the court, of course, not in the eyes of the law, but from the viewpoint of conscience, the viewpoint of humanity!"

Having invested this brief speech with the entire force of his conviction, Andrei languidly lit up a cigarette and began waiting, casting inconspicuous glances at the face of the clock. He set himself exactly three minutes to wait, and then, if the absurd old woman still didn't cough up, he would send the old crone off to a cell, even though that would be completely illegal. But he had to push this damned case along somehow, didn't he? How much time could he waste on every old woman? A night in a cell sometimes had a positively magical effect on people . . . And if there were any problems about him exceeding his authority . . . there wouldn't be any, she wouldn't complain, it didn't look like she would . . . but if problems did come up anyway, the solicitor general was taking a personal interest in this case, wasn't he, and it was a reasonable assumption that he wouldn't hang Andrei out to dry. Well, let them hit me with a reprimand. I don't work just to earn their gratitude, do I? Let them. Just as long as I can push this damned case on even a little bit . . . just a tiny little bit . . .

He smoked, politely wafting aside the clouds of smoke, the second hand ran cheerfully around the face of the clock, and Pani Husáková remained silent, merely clacking away quietly with her needles.

"Right," said Andrei when four minutes had elapsed. He crushed his cigarette butt into the ashtray with a determined gesture. "I am obliged to detain you. For obstructing the course of the investigation. It's entirely up to you, Pani Husáková, but to my mind this is some kind of puerile nonsense . . . Here, sign the record of interrogation and you'll be escorted to a cell."

After aged Matilda had been led away (she wished him goodnight as they parted), Andrei remembered that they still hadn't brought him any hot tea. He stuck his head out into the corridor, reminded the duty guard of his obligations in harsh terms and at considerable length, and ordered him to bring in the witness Petrov.

The witness Petrov was so stocky that he was almost square, with hair as black as a crow—he looked like the classic gangster, a twenty-four-karat mafioso. He sat down firmly on the stool without saying a word and started watching sullenly as Andrei sipped his tea.

"What is it then, Petrov?" Andrei said to him good-naturedly. "You come bursting in here, creating havoc, preventing me from working, and now you don't say anything . . ."

"What's the point of talking to you spongers?" Petrov said spitefully. "You should have moved your ass sooner, it's too late now."

"And what's happened that's such an emergency?" Andrei inquired, turning a deaf ear to the "spongers" and all the rest.

"What's happened is that while you were blabbing in here, sticking to your shitty regulations, I saw the Building!"

Andrei carefully put his spoon in his glass. "What building?" he asked.

"You can't possibly be serious!" said Petrov, instantly flying into a rage. "Are you joking around with me here? What building . . . the Red one. *That* Building. The bastard's standing right there on Main Street, and people are walking into it, and here you are sipping on your tea . . . tormenting some silly old women—"

"Hang on now, hang on," said Andrei, taking a map of the City out of the file. "Where did you see it? When?"

"It was just now, when they were driving me here . . . I tell the idiot, stop!—and he steps on the gas . . . I tell the duty guard here, get a police unit there, quick—and he dithers like a fart in a trance."

"Where did you see it? At what spot?"

"You know the synagogue?"

"Yes," said Andrei, finding the synagogue on the map.

"Well then, it's between the synagogue and the movie the-ater—there's this dingy dump down there."

On the map there was a small square with a fountain and a children's playground marked between the synagogue and the New Illusion movie theater. Andrei chewed on the end of his pencil. "When was it you saw it?" he asked.

"It was twelve twenty," Petrov said morosely. "And now it's probably almost one already. Don't expect it to wait for you . . . Sometimes I've run there in fifteen or twenty minutes and it was gone already, so this time . . ." He gestured hopelessly.

Andrei picked up the phone and gave an order. "A motorcycle with a sidecar and one police officer. Immediately."

2

The motorcycle roared along Main Street, bouncing over the battered asphalt surface. Andrei hunched over, hiding his face behind the windscreen of the sidecar, but he was still chilled to the bone. He ought to have brought his uniform greatcoat.

Every now and then loonies who were completely blue from the cold leaped off the sidewalk, skipping and weaving toward the motorcycle and yelling something that was drowned out by the noise of the motor—then the police motorcyclist braked, swearing through his teeth as he dodged away from the outstretched, clutching hands, broke through the lines of striped robes, and immediately revved up the motorbike again so hard that Andrei was flung backward.

Apart from the loonies, there wasn't anyone else in the street. Only once did they come across a patrol car slowly cruising along with an orange light blinking on its roof, and they saw a baboon running across the square in front of City Hall. The baboon was tearing along at full speed, and unshaven men in striped pajamas were chasing after it with shrill giggles and piercing howls. Turning his head, Andrei saw them finally overtake the baboon, knock it to the ground, stretch out its front and back legs in different directions, and start swinging it regularly to and fro to the strains of some ghoulish, otherworldly song.

Infrequent streetlamps came hurtling toward them, between dark blocks of neighborhoods without a single light, where life seemed to have died out, and then up ahead the hazy, yellowish bulk of the synagogue appeared, and Andrei saw the Building.

It was standing there firmly and confidently, as if it had always occupied that space between the wall of the synagogue, daubed all over with swastikas, and the trashy movie theater, which had been fined the previous week for showing pornographic films at night—standing in the very same spot where yesterday scraggy little trees were growing, an anemic little fountain was splashing in a preposterously large, drab concrete basin, and a motley assortment of little kids were squealing as they dangled from rope swings.

It really was red, built of brick, with four stories, the windows of the first floor were closed off with shutters, and several windows on the second and third floors glowed yellow and pink, but the roof was covered with galvanized tin, and a strange antenna with several crosspieces had been installed beside the one and only chimney. There really was a porch with four stone steps leading up to the door, and a gleaming brass door handle, and the longer Andrei looked at this building, the more distinctly he heard a strange melody, solemn and gloomy, ringing in his ears, and he recalled in passing that many of the witnesses had testified that there was music playing in the Building . . .

Andrei adjusted the visor of his uniform cap so that it didn't obstruct his view and glanced at the police motorcyclist. The fat, surly man was sitting there huddled up, with his head pulled down into his raised collar, and smoking drowsily, holding the cigarette in his teeth.

"Do you see it?" Andrei asked in a low voice.

The fat man awkwardly swung his head around and turned down his collar. "Eh?"

"The building. I asked if you can see it," Andrei said, starting to get annoyed.

"I'm not blind," the policeman replied morosely.

"And have you seen it here before?"

"No," said the policeman. "Not here. But I've seen it in other places. What of it? You see weirder things than that around here at night."

The music was roaring in Andrei's ears with such tragic power that he couldn't really hear the policeman very well. There was some kind of immense funeral taking place, with thousands and thousands of people weeping as they saw off their near ones and dear ones, and the roaring of the music gave them no chance to compose themselves, calm down, and disconnect themselves from it all . . .

"Wait for me here," Andrei told the policeman, but the policeman didn't answer, which wasn't really very surprising, since he was already on the far side of the street, and Andrei was standing on the stone porch, facing the oak door with the brass handle.

Then Andrei looked to the right along Main Street, into the murky haze, and to the left along Main Street, into the murky haze, and said good-bye to all of this, just in case, and set his gloved hand on the ornately patterned, gleaming brass.

Behind the door was a small, quiet entrance hall, illuminated by a dim, yellowish light, with bunches of greatcoats, overcoats, and raincoats dangling from a coat stand with splayed branches, like a palm tree. Underfoot was a worn carpet with pale, indistinct patterns, and straight ahead there was a broad marble staircase with a soft, red runner, squeezed tight against the steps by well-polished metal rods. There were also pictures of some kind on the walls, and something else behind an oak barrier on the right, and someone nearby, who politely took Andrei's portfolio and whispered, "Upstairs, please . . ." Andrei couldn't make out any of this very clearly, because the visor of his cap obstructed his view very badly by sliding down right over his eyes, so that he could only see what was right under his feet. Halfway up the stairs it occurred to him that he ought to have checked the damned cap at the cloakroom with that gold-braid-festooned character who had sideburns right down to his waist, but it was too late now, and everything here was arranged so that you had to do things at the right time or not do them at all, and it was impossible to take back a single move or a single action that he had made. And with a sigh of relief he strode up the final step and took off the cap.

The moment he appeared in the doorway, everyone got to their feet, but he didn't look at any of them. He saw only his partner, a short, elderly man in a prewar-style uniform and gleaming box-calf-leather boots, who reminded him painfully of someone and at the same time was entirely unfamiliar.

Everyone stood motionless along the walls, the white marble walls decorated in gold and purple and draped with bright, multicolored banners . . . no, not multicolored—everything was red and gold, only red and gold, and huge panels of purple and gold fabric hung down from the infinitely distant ceiling, like the materialized ribbons of some incredible northern lights. They all stood along the walls with their tall, semicircular niches, and hiding in the twilight of the niches were haughtily modest busts of marble, plaster, bronze, gold, malachite, stainless steel . . . those niches breathed out the chill of the grave, everyone was freezing, everyone was furtively rubbing their hands together and huddling up against the cold, but they all stood at attention, looking straight ahead, and only the elderly man in the semimilitary uniform, Andrei's partner, Andrei's adversary, strode about slowly with silent steps in the empty space at the center of the hall, with his massive, graying head tilted slightly forward and his hands held behind his back, with the left hand clutching the wrist of the right. And when Andrei walked in, and when everyone got up and had already been standing for some time, and when the faint sigh, as if of relief, had already faded away under the vaults of the hall, after tangling itself in the purple and the gold, this man continued to stride about, and then suddenly, in midstride, he stopped and looked at Andrei very intently, without smiling, and Andrei saw that the hair on the large cranium was sparse and gray, the forehead was low, the magnificent mustache was really sparse, but neatly trimmed, and the indifferent face was yellowish, with bumpy skin, as if it had been dug over.

There was no need for introductions, and there was no need for speeches of greeting. They sat down at a small encrusted table, and Andrei turned out to have the black pieces, while his elderly partner had the white ones, not actually white but yellowish, and the man with the dug-over skin reached out a small, hairless hand, picked up a pawn between his finger and thumb, and made the first move. To meet it Andrei immediately moved out his own pawn—the quiet, reliable Wang, who had always wanted only one thing, to be left in peace, and here he would be granted a certain peace, dubious and relative though it was, here, in the very center of events, which would unfold, of course, which were inevitable, and Wang would have a tough time of it, but here was the precise spot where Andrei could bolster him, cover him, protect him—for a long time and, if he so wished, an infinitely long time.

The two pawns stood facing each other, forehead to forehead—they could touch each other, they could exchange meaningless words, they could simply be quietly proud of themselves, proud of the fact that they, simple pawns, had defined the main axis around which the entire game would now unfold. But they couldn't do anything to each other, they were neutral toward each other, they were in different combat dimensions—small, yellow, shapeless Wang with his head pulled down into his shoulders in customary fashion, and a thickset little individual with crooked cavalryman's legs, wearing a Caucasian felt cloak and a tall astrakhan hat, with a prodigiously opulent mustache, high cheekbones, and slightly slanting eyes.

Equilibrium had been restored on the board again, and this equilibrium ought to last for quite a long time, because Andrei knew that his partner was a genius of caution, who always considered men to be the most valuable thing of all, which meant that for the immediate future nothing could threaten Wang, and Andrei sought out Wang in the ranks along the walls and smiled ever so slightly at him, but immediately turned his eyes away, because they had caught Donald's intent, sad gaze.

His partner thought, slowly and deliberately tapping the cardboard tube of his long *papirosa* on the mother-of-pearl-encrusted surface of the small table, and Andrei squinted once again at the frozen ranks, but this time he was looking not at his own men but at the men whom his adversary had at his disposal. There were almost no faces that he knew: some surprisingly cultured-looking men in civilian clothes, with beards and pince-nez, wearing old-fashioned neckties and vests; some military men in unfamiliar uniforms, with numerous diamonds on their collar tabs, with medals bolted onto mounts covered with shot-silk ribbons . . . Where did he get men like that from? thought Andrei, feeling rather surprised, and looked again at the white pawn that had been moved out. This pawn, at least, was very familiar to him—a man of once-legendary fame who, so the adults whispered, had failed to justify the hopes placed in him and had now, so to speak, left the stage. The man clearly knew that himself but was not particularly mournful—he stood there with his crooked legs firmly planted on the parquet floor, twirling the wings of his gigantic mustache, peering around under his brows, and giving off an acrid smell of vodka and horse sweat.

Andrei's partner raised his hand above the board and moved a second pawn. Andrei closed his eyes. He hadn't been expecting this at all. How could it be—immediately, like this? Who was it? A handsome, pale face, inspired, yet at the same time rendered repulsive by a strange hauteur, a bluish pince-nez, an elegant, curly beard, a shock of black hair above a light forehead—Andrei had never seen this man before and couldn't say who he was, but he was evidently someone of importance, because he was talking peremptorily and briskly with the crooked little man in the felt cloak, who only twitched his mustache, twitched his jaw muscles, and kept turning his slanting eyes off to the side, like some huge wildcat facing a confident trainer.

But Andrei had no interest in their relationship—Wang's fate was in the balance, the fate of little Wang, who had suffered torment all his life, who had his head pulled right down into his shoulders now, prepared already for the very worst, hopelessly submissive in his preparedness, and now there were only three possibilities: Wang is taken, Wang takes, or Andrei leaves everything just as it is, suspending the lives of these two in uncertainty—in the exalted language of strategy that would be called Queen's Gambit Declined—and Andrei was familiar with that continuation, and he knew it was recommended in the textbooks, he knew that it was elementary, but he couldn't bear the idea of Wang hanging by a thread for hour after hour, breaking out in a cold sweat in fear of imminent death, and the pressure on him would keep building up and up, until finally the monstrous tension at this point became absolutely intolerable, the gigantic, bloody abscess burst, and not a trace would be left of Wang.

I couldn't bear that, thought Andrei. And after all, I don't know this man in the pince-nez at all—why should I feel pity for him, if even my brilliant partner thought for no more than a few minutes before deciding to make this sacrifice . . . And Andrei removed the white pawn from the board and set his own, black pawn in its place, and in that moment he saw the wildcat in the felt cloak suddenly, for the first time in its life, glance directly into its tamer's eyes and bare its yellow, smoke-stained fangs in a carnivorous grin. And immediately a man with dusky, olive-dark skin, not Russian or even European looking, slipped through between the ranks along the walls to the blue pince-nez and swung an immense rusty blade, and the blue pince-nez flashed aside like a streak of blue lightning, and the man with the pale face of a great tribune and failed tyrant gasped feebly, his legs buckled, and his small, well-proportioned body tumbled down the ancient, chipped steps that were heated to incandescence by the tropical sun, becoming soiled with white dust and bright red, sticky blood . . . Andrei caught his breath, swallowed the lump that was obstructing his throat, and looked at the board again.

Two white pawns were already standing there side by side; the center had been firmly seized by the Brilliant Strategist, and in addition, from out of the depths the gaping pupil of impending doom was aimed directly at Wang's chest—there could be no lengthy deliberations here, this wasn't a matter of just Wang; the slightest procrastination and the white bishop would break through into open space with room to maneuver—he had been dreaming for a long time of breaking out into open space, this tall, statuesque, handsome man, a great commander, decorated with constellations of medals, badges, diamonds, and stripes, this proud Adonis with eyes of ice and the plump lips of a youth, the pride of a young army, the pride of a young country, the successful rival of other, equally haughty and arrogant individuals, bedecked with the medals, badges, diamonds, and stripes of the Western science of warfare. What was Wang to him? He had hacked down dozens of Wangs with his own hand; at a single word from him thousands of such Wangs—dirty, lice-ridden, and hungry, inspired with blind faith in him—had marched, steady and erect, against tanks and machine guns, and those who had miraculously survived, now well-groomed and paunchy, were willing to march even now, willing to do everything all over again . . .

No, Andrei must not let this man have either Wang or the center. And he quickly advanced a pawn that was waiting there to be used, without looking to see who it was and thinking of only one thing: covering Wang, bolstering him, defending him, if only from the rear, showing the great tank commander that Wang was, of course, in his power, but he could not move beyond Wang. And the great tank commander realized this, and the fresh glint in his eyes was drowsily concealed once again by those handsome, heavy eyelids, but evidently he had forgotten, exactly as Andrei had forgotten and now suddenly realized with some appalling inner flash of insight, that it was not they, the pawns and bishops, who decided everything here—and not even the castles, and not even the queens. And immediately the small, hairless hand slowly rose over the board, and Andrei, already realizing what was about to happen, croaked hoarsely, *"J'adoube."* And in accordance with the noble code of the game, and so hastily that his fingers actually cramped, he swapped Wang and the piece that was supporting him. Fortune favored him with a pale smile: Wang was now supporting, and Wang's place had been taken by Valka Soifertis, with whom Andrei had shared a school desk for six years, and who had already died anyway in '49, during an operation on a stomach ulcer.

His brilliant partner's eyebrows slowly rose up and the brownish, speckled eyes narrowed in mocking surprise. Of course he found this move ludicrous and incomprehensible; it was nonsensical from both the tactical and, especially, the strategic point of view. Continuing the movement of his small, weak hand, he halted it above the bishop, paused for a few more seconds, pondering, and then his fingers closed confidently on the lacquered head of the piece, and the bishop lunged forward and knocked gently against the black pawn, pushing it aside and establishing itself in its place. The Brilliant Strategist then slowly carried the taken pawn off the board, and a small group of intent, businesslike people in white coats had already surrounded the gurney on which Valka Soifertis was lying—Andrei's eyes caught one last glimpse of the dark features, corroded by illness, and the gurney disappeared through the doors of the operating theater . . .

Glancing at the great tank commander, Andrei saw in his gray, transparent eyes the same terror and oppressive perplexity that he felt himself. The tank commander was blinking rapidly, watching the Brilliant Strategist without understanding a thing. He was accustomed to thinking in terms of the movements through space of immense masses of machines and men; in his naivety and simplemindedness, he was accustomed to believing that everything would always be decided by his armor-plated armadas, rolling on confidently through foreign lands, and by the multi-engined airborne fortresses, stuffed with bombs and parachutists, sailing through the skies above foreign lands; he had done everything possible to make sure that this clear dream could be realized at any moment necessary . . . Of course, he had sometimes indulged in certain doubts as to whether the Brilliant Strategist was really so very brilliant and would be able to unequivocally determine that moment and the necessary directions of the armor-plated blows, but even so, it was impossible for him to understand how it was possible to sacrifice precisely *him*, so talented, so assiduous, and so unique, how it was possible to sacrifice everything that had been created by such immense labor and effort . . .

Andrei quickly removed him from the board, away with him, and set Wang in his place. Men in blue peaked caps squeezed through the ranks, grabbed the great tank commander crudely by the shoulders and arms, took away his weapon, punched the handsome, thoroughbred face with a crunch, and dragged him off to a prison cell, and the Brilliant Strategist leaned bank in his chair, narrowed his eyes in satisfaction, folded his hands together on his stomach, and started twiddling his thumbs. He was content. He had given a bishop for a pawn and was very content. And then Andrei suddenly realized that in the Strategist's eyes everything looked entirely different; he had deftly and unexpectedly removed the bishop that had been hindering him and received a pawn into the bargain—that was how things looked in reality . . .

The Great Strategist was more than a strategist. A strategist always circles around within the limits of his strategy. The Great Strategist had abandoned all limits. Strategy was merely an insignificant element of his game; it was as incidental for him as it was for Andrei—a casual kind of move made on a whim. The Great Strategist had become great precisely because he had realized (or perhaps he had known since the day he was born) that it is not the one who knows how to play according to all the rules who wins; the one who wins is the one who is able to abandon all the rules at any moment when it is necessary, to impose his own rules, unknown to his opponent, on the game and, when necessary, abandon them too. Whoever said that one's own pieces are less dangerous than the pieces of one's opponent? Rubbish, one's own pieces are far more dangerous than the pieces of one's opponent! Whoever said that the king has to be protected and moved out of danger of check? Rubbish, there are no kings that cannot be replaced if necessary by some knight or even pawn. Whoever said that a pawn, after breaking through to the final row of squares, is obliged to become another piece? Nonsense, sometimes it can be far more useful to leave it as a pawn—let it stand on the edge of the abyss as an example to the other pawns . . .

The damned cap kept sliding farther and farther down over Andrei's eyes, making it harder and harder for him to follow what was going on around him. However, he could hear that the dignified silence no longer existed in the hall: he heard the clattering of tableware, a babble of many voices, the sounds of an orchestra tuning up. He caught a whiff of kitchen fumes. Someone declared in a loud, squeaky voice that rang through the entire house, "Georges! I'm deviwishwy hungwy. Teww them to bwing me a gwass of cuwaçao and some pine-app-uw, quickwy."

"I beg your pardon," someone said with austere politeness, right in Andrei's ear, squeezing in between Andrei and the board—he caught a glimpse of black coattails and polished lacquer shoes, and a hand raised high in the air, bearing a loaded tray, drifted over his head. And a white hand also placed a glass of champagne by Andrei's elbow.

The Brilliant Strategist had finally tapped and kneaded his *papirosa* into a state fit for smoking. He lit up and hazy, bluish smoke drifted out of his hairy nostrils, getting tangled in his magnificent but rather sparse mustache.

And meanwhile the game continued. Andrei defended convulsively, retreated, maneuvered, and so far he had managed to act so that only people who were already dead anyway were lost. There they had carried away Donald with a bullet through his heart, and beside the wineglass on the table they had placed his pistol and suicide note: "Rejoice not in arriving, in departing do not grieve. Give the pistol to Voronin. It will come in handy sometime." And there his brother and father had already carried the body of his grandmother, Evgenia Romanovna, sewn into old sheets, down the icebound stairway and added it to the stack of corpses . . . There now they had buried his father in a mass grave somewhere in the Piskariovskoye Cemetery, and the morose driver, sheltering his unshaven face from the biting wind, had driven his steamroller to and fro over the frozen corpses, tamping them down so that more could be fitted into a single grave . . . But the Great Strategist generously, cheerfully, and sardonically disposed of friends and strangers alike, and all his well-groomed men with little beards and medals shot themselves in the temple, threw themselves out windows, died as a result of hideous tortures, trampled over each other's dead bodies to become queens and still remained pawns.

And Andrei carried on agonizingly trying to understand what sort of game this was that he was playing, what its purpose was, what the rules were, and why all this was happening, and he was transfixed to the depths of his soul by the question: How had he become the adversary of the Great Strategist—he, a faithful soldier in the Strategist's army, prepared at any moment to die for him, prepared to kill for him, not knowing any other goals except *his* goals, not believing in any means except the means indicated by *him*, not distinguishing the plans of the Great Strategist from the plans of the Universe? He greedily gulped down the champagne, without tasting anything at all, and then suddenly he was overwhelmed by a blinding flash of insight. But of course, he wasn't an adversary of the Great Strategist at all. He was his ally, his faithful helper. That was it—the main rule of this game. It was played not by adversaries but by partners, allies; the game had only one set of goalposts, nobody lost, everybody won . . . apart, of course, from those who would not survive until the victory.

Someone touched his legs and spoke under the table. "Would you be so kind as to move your foot?" Andrei looked down at his feet. There was a dark, glistening puddle down there, and a bald dwarf on his hands and knees was fidgeting beside it, holding a dried-out rag covered in dark blotches. Andrei suddenly felt nauseous and started looking at the board again. He had already sacrificed all the dead; now he only had the living left. The Great Strategist at the other side of the table curiously watched what he was doing and even seemed to be nodding in approval, baring his small, sparse teeth in a polite smile, and at that point Andrei felt that he couldn't go on. It was a great game, the most noble of all games, a game in the name of the greatest of all goals that

humankind had ever set itself, but Andrei couldn't carry on playing it any longer.

"I'll step outside . . ." he said hoarsely. "Just for a moment."

It came out so quietly that he hardly even heard himself,
but everybody immediately looked at him. Silence fell in the hall
again, and somehow the visor of his cap didn't bother him anymore, and now he could see them clearly, eye to eye, all of his
own people, all of those who were still alive.

Massive Uncle Yura with his faded army tunic gaping
wide open and his roll-up cigarette crackling, looked at Andrei
morosely; Selma smiled drunkenly, sprawling in an armchair with
her legs hoicked up so high that he could see her little bottom in
its pink, lacy panties; Kensi looked at him sagely and seriously,
and standing beside him was Volodka Dmitriev, tousle-headed
and as savagely unshaven as ever; and ensconced on the high,
old chair that Seva Barabanov had only just abandoned to set off
on his latest and final work assignment was wizen-faced Borka
Chistyakov, with his aristocratic aquiline nose, looking as if he
were about to ask, "Oh really, why are you bellowing like a sick
elephant?"—they were all here, all his nearest and all his dearest, and they were all looking at him, and all differently, and at
the same time their gazes all had something in common too,
some common attitude toward him. Sympathy? Trust? Pity? No,
it wasn't that, and before he managed to understand what exactly
it was, he suddenly spotted among these old, familiar faces someone he didn't know at all, some Oriental with a yellowish face
and slanting eyes—no, not Wang, but some subtle, even elegant
Oriental, and he also got the feeling that someone very small was
hiding behind this stranger, someone very, very small, dirty and
ragged, probably a stray, homeless child . . .

He got up abruptly, moved the chair back with a scraping
sound, and turned away from them all, and after gesturing indefi-
nitely in the direction and for the attention of the Great Strategist,
he walked out of the hall, squeezing through between shoulders
and stomachs, pushing some people aside, and as if to console

him, someone mumbled somewhere close by, "Well, the rules allow it—let him take a moment to think and reflect on things . . . We just have to stop the clock . . ."

Absolutely exhausted and soaked in sweat, he managed to reach the landing of the stairway and sat down directly on the carpet, not far from a torridly blazing fireplace. His cap had slipped down over his eyes again, so he didn't even try to make out what sort of fireplace this was and what sort of people were sitting around the fireplace; he only sensed the soft, dry heat on his wet body that felt as if it had been badly beaten, and saw the half-dried but still sticky blotches on his shoes, and through the cozy crackling of the blazing logs he heard someone telling a story with measured elegance, listening closely to the sound of his own voice.

". . . Just imagine—a handsome fellow, shoulders like a barn door, a holder of all three degrees of the Order of Glory—and let me tell you, they didn't award a full set of those orders to just anybody, they were even rarer than Heroes of the Soviet Union. Well, a fine comrade, an excellent student, and all the rest of it. And yet, let me tell you, he had a certain strange quirk. He would turn up for a party at the pad of some pampered son of a general or marshal, but as soon as everyone paired up and started wandering off, it was out into the hallway, set his cap at a jaunty angle, and bye-bye. At first they thought he must have some abiding love of his own. But no—every now and again the boys would meet him in public places—in Gorky Park, say, or in various different clubs—with these absolute sluts, and always with different ones! I met him like that myself once. I looked—well, what a choice! As ugly as sin, stockings flapping round skinny legs, plastered with makeup—it's horrible to speak of it . . . and back then, by the way, there wasn't any makeup like there is nowadays—the girls used to line their eyebrows with boot blacking, as near as, dammit . . . Anyway, a glaring *mésalliance*, as they say. But he didn't mind. Leading her along arm in arm, spinning her some kind of line, all in due order, and she's simply melting, she's proud and ashamed at the same time, happy as a pig in a peach orchard . . . And then one day at a bachelor get-together, we cornered him: come on, out with it, what is it with these perverted tastes of yours, how can you even walk with those whores without feeling sick, when the very finest beauties are pining for you . . . And, let me tell you, in the academy we had a Department of Education, a privileged little spot—they only accepted girls from the most illustrious families there . . . Well, at first he tried to laugh it off, then he gave in and told us something quite amazing. Comrades, he said, I know that I'm blessed with all the appurtenances, so to speak: I'm handsome, with medals, bright-eyed and bushy-tailed. I know all this about myself, he said, and I've received plenty of notes about it too. But there was this thing, he said, that just happened to me. I suddenly saw the misery of our women. Right through the war they never saw a single chink of light, they were starving all the time, they slaved away doing real men's work—poor and homely, without even the slightest idea of what it's like to be beautiful and desired. And so, he said, I set myself the goal of giving at least a few of them an experience so bright and vivid that they would have something to remember for the rest of their lives. I meet this streetcar driver, he said, or a worker from the Hammer and Sickle factory, or a miserable little teacher, who couldn't have counted on any particular happiness even without the war, and now that so many men have been killed, she can't see any ships at all coming in through the waves. I spend two or three evenings with them, he said, and then I disappear. Of course, when we part, I lie, I say I'm going on a long work assignment or something else that sounds plausible, and they're left with this bright memory . . . at least some kind of bright spark in their lives, he said. I don't know, he said, how it all looks from the viewpoint of high morals, but I have the feeling that by doing this I'm fulfilling at least some tiny little part of our male duty . . . When he told us all this, we were dumbfounded. Later on, of course, we started arguing, but the whole thing made a quite exceptional impression on us. He disappeared soon afterward, in fact. Back then a lot of us disappeared like that: orders from army command, and in the army you don't ask where you're going and what for . . . I never saw him again."

Neither did I, thought Andrei. I never saw him again either. There were two letters—one to our mother, and one to me. And our mother received a notification: "Your son, Sergei Mikhailovich Voronin, died an honorable death while carrying out a combat mission from the army command." It was in Korea. Under the pink watercolor sky of Korea, where the Great Strategist first tried his strength in a skirmish with American imperialism. He played his great game there, and Seryozha was left there, with his full set of Orders of Glory . . .

I don't want it. I don't want this game. Maybe that's the way everything has to be; maybe nothing is possible without playing this game. Maybe. Pretty certainly. But I can't do it . . . I don't know how. And I don't even want to learn . . . So all right, then, he thought bitterly, it means I'm a poor soldier. Or rather, I'm just a soldier. And no more than a soldier. That selfsame soldier who doesn't know how to reflect on things, so he has to obey blindly. And I'm not any kind of chess partner or ally of the Great Strategist, but just a tiny little cog in his colossal machine, and my place is not at the table in his inscrutable game but beside Wang, with Uncle Yura, with Selma . . . I'm a little stellar astronomer of average ability, and if I had managed to prove the existence of some connection between wide double stars and Schilt's star streams, that would have been a very, very big deal for me. But as for solving great problems and achieving great things . . .

And at this point he remembered that he was no longer a stellar astronomer, that he was an investigator in the Public Prosecutor's Office, and he had achieved quite a lot: using a specially trained network of agents and distinct investigative procedures to pinpoint this mysterious Red Building and infiltrate it, exposing its sinister secrets and creating all the necessary conditions for the successful elimination of this malignant phenomenon from our life . . .

Lifting himself up on his hands, he slid down a step lower. If I go back to the table now, he thought, I'll never get out of the Building. It will devour me. That's quite clear: it has already devoured many people, we have witness testimony to that. But that's not what's most important. What's important is that I have to get back to my office and untangle this ball of thread. That's where my duty lies. That's my responsibility, what I have do now. Everything else is a mirage . . .

He slid down another two steps. He had to break free of the mirage and get back to work. There was nothing accidental about all this. Everything here had been superbly thought through. It was a hideous illusion, fabricated by provocateurs in an attempt to destroy belief in the ultimate victory, to pervert the concepts of morality and duty. And it was no accident that the sordid little New Illusion movie theater was there at one side of the Building. New! There was nothing new about pornography, but that place called itself new! Who were they fooling? But what was on the other side? The synagogue . . .

He slid down the steps, going full tilt, and reached a door with the word Exit on it. And after he had already taken hold of the handle, when he was still overcoming the resistance of the creaking spring, he suddenly realized what the common element was in all the eyes fixed on him up there. Reproach. They knew that he wouldn't come back. He still hadn't realized it himself, but they already knew for certain . . .

He tumbled out into the street, avidly gulped down a huge mouthful of the damp, misty air, and his heart thrilled with joy to see that everything was still the same out here: murky gloom along Main Street to the right, murky gloom along Main Street to the left, and there in front of him, just across the street, was the motorcycle with the sidecar and the police driver, soundly asleep, with his head completely submerged in his collar. The fat bastard's dozing, Andrei thought affectionately. He's worn out.

And then a voice inside him suddenly declared loudly, "Time!" and Andrei groaned and burst into tears of desperation, only now recalling the most important, the most terrible rule of the game. The rule invented specially to deal with namby-pamby sissies from the intelligentsia like him: anyone who breaks off the game loses all his pieces.

Andrei swung back around with a howl of "Don't!" and reached out for the brass door handle. But it was too late. The Building was already leaving, slowly backing away into the impenetrable gloom of the shadowy back alleys behind the synagogue and the New Illusion. It crept away with a palpable rustling and grating, with its windowpanes rattling and floor beams creaking. A tile fell off the roof and smashed on a stone step of the porch.

Andrei clutched the brass handle with every ounce of his strength, but it seemed to have fused with the timber of the door, and the house was moving faster and faster, and Andrei was already running, almost being dragged after it, as if it were a departing train. He jerked and tugged on the door handle, and suddenly stumbled over something and fell, his cramped and twisted fingers slipped off the smooth brass whorls, he smashed his head very painfully against something, he saw a shower of bright stars, and something crunched in his skull, but he could still see the Building backing away, extinguishing its windows as it went; he saw it swerve behind the yellow wall of the synagogue, then reappear, as if it peeping out with its last two lit-up windows, and then those windows went out too, and darkness fell.

3

He was sitting on a bench facing the idiotic concrete basin of the fountain and pressing a damp handkerchief that was already warm against a massive bump over his right eye. The bump was horrific to touch and he was in absolute agony; the ache in his head felt so bad, he was afraid his skull might be fractured; his skinned knees stung; his bruised elbow had gone numb, but there were indications that it would soon be demanding his attention. Perhaps, however, all this was really for the best. All this lent what was happening an emphatic, crude reality. There was no more Building, there was no Strategist or dark, sticky puddle under a table, there was no game of chess, there was no betrayal, there was nothing but a man who was strolling absentmindedly through the dark and had tumbled over the low concrete barrier straight into the idiotic basin, smashing his stupid head and the rest of his body against the damp concrete . . .

In fact, of course, Andrei realized only too well that it wasn't all as simple as that, but it was comforting to think that it had all really been a delirious delusion, that he really had tripped and smashed his head—that really made it all quite amusing, and it was certainly convenient. What do I do now? he thought hazily. So I've found the Building; I've been inside it and seen it for myself . . . But what next? Don't go trying to stuff my head—my poor, aching head—with all that bombastic garbage about rumors and myths and all the rest of that stupid propaganda. That's just for starters. So don't forget . . . Actually, that was my mistake— I think I was the one stuffing everyone else's heads. I have to release that guy right away . . . what's his name . . . the flute man. I wonder if that Ella of his played chess in there too? Shit, but my head is hurting like hell . . .

147

The handkerchief had gotten really warm now. Andrei got up with a grunt, hobbled across to the fountain, leaned over the edge, and held the damp rag in the ice-cold stream for a while. Someone was hammering on his lump with passionate fury—from the inside. How about that for a myth! A.k.a. a mirage . . . He squeezed out the handkerchief, pressed it against the painful spot again, and looked across the street. The fat policeman was still sleeping. Fat scumbag, Andrei thought rancorously. Some sentry you are. Why did I bother to bring you? Just so you could catch up on your shut-eye, was it? I could have been bumped off a hundred times here. And then, of course, after that jerk had caught up on his sleep, he would have shown up at the Public Prosecutor's Office in the morning and reported as a matter of routine that the investigator went into the Red Building last night and never came back out again. Andrei spent some time imagining how glorious it would feel right now to fill a bucket with icy water, sneak up to the fat bastard, and pour the entire bucketful down the back of his neck. Wouldn't that just make him freak! That was how the boys used to amuse themselves at the training camp: if someone dozed off, they tied a shoe to his private parts with the laces, then put that huge, filthy shit-crusher on his face. Still half asleep, the guy would go berserk and savagely launch the shoe into space with all his might. It was very funny.

Andrei went back to the bench and found that he had acquired a companion. A scraggy little man dressed completely in black—even his shirt was black—was sitting there with one leg crossed over the other, holding an old-fashioned bowler hat on his knees. Probably the caretaker from the synagogue. Andrei gingerly sat down beside him, cautiously probing the boundaries of the lump through the damp handkerchief.

"Well, all right," the little man said in a clear, old voice. "But what comes next?"

"Nothing special," said Andrei. "We'll catch all of them. I won't just leave things like this."

"And then?" the old man persisted.

"I don't know," Andrei said after a moment's thought. "Maybe some other abomination will turn up. The Experiment is the Experiment. It's not for long."

"It's for ever and ever," the old man remarked. "According to every religion—it's forever."

"Religion's got nothing to do with this," Andrei objected.

"You still think that, even now?" the old man asked in surprise.

"Of course. That's what I've always thought."

"All right, let's not talk about that for now. The Experiment is the Experiment, a rope is just a piece of string—plenty of people here console themselves like that, almost everybody. Which, by the way, is something that not a single religion foresaw. But I'm talking about something else. Why have we been left with freedom of will, even here? You'd think that in the kingdom of absolute evil, in a kingdom with ABANDON HOPE . . . written on its gates . . ."

Andrei waited for a continuation, but none came, and he said, "You have a rather strange perspective on all this. This isn't a kingdom of absolute evil. It's more like chaos, and we're here to put it in order. And how can we put it in order if we don't possess free will?"

"An interesting idea," the old man said thoughtfully. "That had never occurred to me. So you believe that we've been given another chance. Something like a penal battalion—to wash away the blood of our transgressions at the front line of the eternal battle between good and evil."

"What's the battle with evil got to do with anything?" asked Andrei, starting to get annoyed. "Evil is something deliberate and purposeful—"

"You're a Manichean!" the old man interrupted.

"I'm a Komsomol member!" Andrei protested, getting even more annoyed and feeling a terrific upsurge of belief and certainty. "Evil is always a class phenomenon. There's no such thing as evil in general. But everything's all muddled up here, because this is the Experiment. We have been given chaos. And if we can't cope with it, we'll go back to what we had there—to class stratification and all the rest of the garbage. Either we master chaos and transform it into the new, beautiful forms of human relations that are called communism . . ."

The old man listened for a while in bemused silence. "Well, well," he said eventually with immense surprise. "Who could ever have thought it, who could ever have expected it . . . Communist propaganda—here! It's not even a schism, it's . . ." He paused for a moment. "But then, the ideas of communism are akin to the ideas of early Christianity, aren't they?"

"That's a lie!" Andrei protested angrily. "An invention of the priests. Early Christianity was an ideology of resignation, the ideology of slaves. But we are rebels! We won't leave a single stone unturned here, and then we'll go back there, we'll go home and rebuild everything there the same way as we've rebuilt it here!"

"You're Lucifer," the old man said with reverential horror. "The proud spirit! Have you really not resigned yourself to your lot?"

Andrei carefully turned the handkerchief cold side down and looked at the little old man suspiciously. "Lucifer? I see. And who exactly would you be, then?"

"I'm a louse," the old man replied tersely.

"Hmm . . ." That was kind of hard to argue with.

"I'm an insignificant insect, no one," the old man explained. "I was no one there, and I'm no one here too." He paused for a moment. "You have inspired hope in me," he declared unexpectedly. "Yes, yes, yes. You can't even imagine . . . how strange, how strange . . . What a joy it was to listen to you! Truly, if free will has been left to us, then why does there have to be resignation and patient suffering? Yes, I regard this meeting as the most significant episode in all the time that I have been here . . ."

Andrei examined him with alert hostility. He was mocking him, the old coot . . . No, it didn't look like it . . . The synagogue caretaker? The synagogue! "Pardon me for asking," he inquired ingratiatingly, "but have you been here for long? I mean sitting here on this bench?"

"No, not very long. At first I was sitting on a stool over there in that entranceway—there's a stool in there . . . But after the Building went away, I moved to the bench."

"Aha," said Andrei. "So you saw the Building, then?"

"Of course I did!" the old man replied with dignity. "I sat there, listening to the music and crying."

"Crying," Andrei repeated, agonizingly racking his brains to figure all this out. "Tell me, are you a Jew?"

The old man started. "Good Lord, no! What kind of question is that? I'm a Catholic, a faithful and—alas!—unworthy son of the Roman Catholic Church . . . I have nothing against Judaism, of course, but . . . But why did you ask about that?"

"No special reason," Andrei said evasively. "So you don't have anything to do with the synagogue, then?"

"Not really," said the old man. "Apart from the fact that I often sit here in this little square and the caretaker comes here sometimes . . ." He giggled in embarrassment. "He and I engage in religious disputes."

"But what about the Building?" Andrei asked, squeezing his eyes shut to fight the pain in his skull.

"The Building? Well, when the Building comes, obviously we can't sit here. In that case we have to wait until it leaves."

"So this isn't the first time you've seen it, then?"

"Of course not. It comes almost every night . . . Of course, today it stayed longer than usual."

"Hang on," said Andrei. "And do you know what Building that is?"

"It's hard not to recognize it," the old man said in a quiet voice. "Before, in the other life, I saw images and descriptions of it quite often. It's described in detail in the confessions of Saint Anthony—that's not a canonical text, now . . . for us Catholics . . . Anyway, I've read it: 'And there appeared unto me a house, living and moving, and it did make obscene movements, and within I saw through the windows people who walked through its rooms, slept, and took food . . .' I can't vouch for the accuracy of the quotation, but it's very close to the text . . . And also, obviously, Hieronymus Bosch . . . I would call him Saint Hieronymus Bosch—I owe him a great deal; he prepared me for this . . ." The old man made a broad, sweeping gesture with his hand. "His remarkable paintings . . . The Lord must surely have allowed him to visit here. Like Dante . . . By the way, there is a manuscript that is attributed to Dante, in which this Building is also mentioned. How does it go now . . ." The old man closed his eyes and raised one hand with widespread fingers to his forehead. "Er, er . . . 'And my companion, reaching out his hand, dry and bony . . .' *Mmm* . . . No . . . 'The tangle of bloody, naked bodies in twilit chambers . . .' *Mmm* . . ."

"Hold on," said Andrei, licking his dry lips. "What sort of nonsense is it you're spouting? What have Saint Anthony and Dante got to do with anything? Just what are you driving at?"

The old man was surprised. "I'm not driving at anything," he said. "You asked me about the Building, didn't you, and I . . . Of course, I must thank God that in His eternal wisdom and infinite benevolence He enlightened me and allowed me to prepare myself. I shall learn a very, very great deal here, and my heart breaks when I think of the others who have arrived here and don't understand, who aren't capable of understanding where they have come to. A harrowing failure to grasp the reality of things and the harrowing memory of one's sins in the bargain. Perhaps that is also the great wisdom of the Creator, the eternal awareness of one's sins without the awareness of retribution for them . . . Take you, for instance, young man: Why has He cast you down into this abyss?"

"I don't know what you're talking about," Andrei muttered sullenly, and thought to himself, Religious fanatics are just about all that was missing here.

"No need to be shy about it," the old man said encouragingly. "There's no point in hiding anything here, for the Judgement has already been made . . . I, for instance, sinned against my own people: I was a traitor, an informer—I saw how the people whom I betrayed to the servants of Satan were tortured and killed. I was hanged in 1944." The old man paused. "And when did you die?"

"I didn't die," Andrei said, his blood running cold.

The old man nodded with a smile. "Yes, that's what many people think," he said. "But they're mistaken. History records cases in which people have been taken up to heaven while alive, but no one has ever heard of them being exiled alive—as a punishment!—to hell."

Andrei listened, staring at him in a daze.

"You've simply forgotten," the old man went on. "There was a war, bombs were falling in the streets, you were running to a bomb shelter and suddenly—a blast, pain, and everything disappeared. And afterward, a vision of an angel, speaking benignly in parables—and here you are." He nodded sagely again, thrusting out his lower lip. "Yes, yes, undoubtedly that is where the impression of free will comes from. Now I understand: it's inertia. Merely inertia, young man. You spoke with such conviction that you even shook me somewhat . . . the organization of chaos, a new world . . . No, no, it's merely inertia. It should pass off in time. Don't forget, hell is eternal, there is no way back, and you're still only in the first circle . . ."

"Are you serious?" Andrei asked in a slightly squeaky voice.

"You know all this yourself," the old man said gently. "You know it all perfectly well! It's just that you're an atheist, a young man, and you don't want to admit to yourself that all your life—short as it was—you were wrong. Your obtuse and ignorant teachers taught you that ahead of you there was nothing, an empty void, putrefaction, that you could expect neither gratitude nor retribution for what you had done. And you accepted these squalid ideas, because you were so very young, you possessed excellent bodily health, and death was merely a distant abstraction for you. Having committed evil, you always hoped to escape punishment, because the ones who could punish you were men exactly the same as you. And if you happened by chance to do good, you demanded immediate reward from those who were exactly like you. You were ludicrous. Now you understand that, of course—I can see it in your face . . ." He suddenly laughed. "We had an engineer in our underground organization, a materialist; he and I often argued about life after death. My God, how he used to mock me! 'Pop,' he used to say, 'you and I will finish off this pointless argument in heaven . . .' And you know, I'm still searching for him here—I search, but I simply can't find him. Perhaps there was some truth in his joke; perhaps he really did go to heaven—as a martyr. He certainly died an agonizing death . . . And I'm here."

"Nocturnal disputes about life and death?" a familiar voice suddenly croaked right in Andrei's ear, and the bench quaked as Izya Katzman, in his customary disheveled and shock-headed condition, plumped himself down on the other side of Andrei. In his left hand he was clutching a light-colored document file and with his right he immediately started fiddling with his wart. As always, he was in state of ecstatic exaltation.

Trying to sound as casual as possible, Andrei said, "This elderly gentleman here believes that we are all in hell."

"The elderly gentleman is absolutely right," Izya immediately retorted, and started giggling. "At least, if it's not hell, it's something entirely indistinguishable from it in all its manifestations. However, you must admit, Pan Stupalski, that you have not yet discovered in my career while alive even a single transgression for which I deserved to be dispatched to this place! I didn't even commit adultery, I was so stupid."

"Pan Katzman," the old man declared, "I can easily accept that you yourself are entirely unaware of that fateful transgression of yours!"

"Possibly, possibly," Izya readily agreed. "From the look of you," he said, addressing Andrei, "you have been in the Red Building. Well, how did you like it in there?"

And at that moment Andrei finally recovered his wits. As if the murky, sticky membrane of his nightmare had suddenly burst and melted, the pain in his head had faded away, and now he could distinguish everything around him sharply and clearly, and Main Street stopped being murky and misty, and it turned out that the policeman wasn't sleeping on the motorcycle at all but sauntering along the sidewalk with the red tip of his cigarette glowing, casting glances in the direction of the bench. My God, Andrei thought, almost in horror, what am I doing here? After all, I'm an investigator, time's passing by, and here I am engaging in idle banter with this crackpot, and then Katzman's here . . . Katzman? How did he get here? "How do you know where I've been?" he asked abruptly.

"It's not hard to guess," said Izya, giggling. "You should take a look at yourself in the mirror . . ."

"I'm asking you a serious question!" said Andrei, raising his voice.

The old man suddenly got up. "Good night, *pánové*," he said, transferring the bowler hat to his head with a smooth movement. "Pleasant dreams."

Andrei took no notice of him. He looked at Izya. But Izya, plucking at his wart and gently bobbing up and down on the spot, watched as the old man moved away, grinned from ear to ear, and was already choking and grunting in anticipation. "Well?" said Andrei.

"What a character!" Izya declared admiringly. "Ah, what a character! You're a fool, Voronin, as always—you don't have a clue about anything! Do you know who that is? That's the famous Pan Stupalski, Stupalski the Judas! He betrayed 248 people to the Gestapo in Lodz, he was exposed twice, and both times he somehow managed to wriggle out of it and put someone else in his place. It was only after the liberation that they finally nailed him, and he was given a fair and speedy trial, but even then he ducked out of it. The esteemed Mentors deemed it useful to extract him from the noose and send him here. To complete the bouquet. He lives in a madhouse here, acts as if he's crazy, but meanwhile he carries on with his favorite line of work . . . Do you think he just happened by chance to be here on the bench, right beside you? Do you know who he works for now?"

"Shut up!" said Andrei, summoning up the willpower to smother the eager curiosity that consumed him every time Izya told his stories. "I'm not interested in all that. How did you come to be here? And how the hell did you know that I'd been inside the Building?"

"I was inside it myself," Izya said calmly.

"I see," said Andrei. "So what happened in there?"

"Well, you know best what happened in there. How should I know what happened as you saw it?"

"And what happened as you saw it?'

"Now, that is absolutely none of your business," said Izya, adjusting the voluminous document file on his knees.

"Did you get the file in there?" asked Andrei, reaching out his hand.

"No," said Izya. "Not in there."

"What's in it?"

"Listen," said Izya. "What business is that of yours? What are you pestering me for?"

Izya still didn't understand what was going on. But then, Andrei himself didn't fully understand what was going on, and his mind raced feverishly as he tried to decide what to do next.

"Do you know what's really in this file?" said Izya. "I discovered the old City Hall—it's about fifteen kilometers from here. I was rummaging around in there all day long; they switched the sun off and it was as dark as hell—you know there hasn't been any lighting there for about twenty years now . . . I wandered round and round in circles, barely managed to find the way out onto Main Street—ruins on all sides, these wild voices yelling . . ."

"I see," said Andrei. "Didn't you know it's forbidden to rummage around in the old ruins?"

The glint of excitement faded from Izya's eyes and he looked intently at Andrei, as if he were beginning to catch on.

"What's wrong with you?" Andrei continued. "Do you want to carry an infection back into the City?"

"I don't much like the tone of your voice," Izya said with a crooked smile. "The way you're talking to me, it's not right somehow."

"And I don't like anything at all about you!" said Andrei. "Why did you hammer it into my head that the Red Building was a myth? You knew it wasn't a myth. You lied to me. What for?"

"What is this, an interrogation?" Izya asked.

"What do you think?" said Andrei.

"I think you've taken a hard knock on the head. I think you need to wash your face with cold water and generally pull yourself together."

"Give me that file," said Andrei.

"You go to hell!" said Izya, getting up. He had turned very pale.

Andrei got up too. "You're coming with me," he said.

"No damned way," Izya said abruptly. "Show me the arrest warrant."

And then Andrei, his blood running cold with hatred, slowly unbuttoned his holster and pulled out the pistol, keeping his eyes fixed on Izya. "Walk forward," he ordered.

"You idiot . . ." Izya muttered. "You've totally lost your mind."

"Silence!" Andrei barked. "Walk!"

He prodded Izya in the side, and Izya obediently hobbled across the street. Apparently his feet were badly chafed and he limped heavily. "You'll die the death of shame," he said over his shoulder. "When you've had some sleep, you'll burn up with shame."

"No talking!"

They reached the motorcycle, the policeman deftly flung back the flap of the sidecar, and Andrei pointed into it with the barrel of the pistol.

"Get in."

Izya got in and sat down very clumsily, without saying a word. The policeman quickly leaped into the saddle. Andrei sat behind him, shoving the pistol into its holster. The engine roared and backfired; the motorcycle swung around and set off back to the Public Prosecutor's Office, bouncing over the potholes and scattering the loonies who were wearily and senselessly wandering around the street, which was damp with fresh dew.

Andrei tried not to look at Izya hunched up in the sidecar. The first blast of anger had passed, and what he felt now was something like embarrassment—it had all happened too fast somehow, too hastily, in a rush, like that joke about the bear rocking the hare in a cradle with no bottom. Well, OK, we'll get things straightened out . . .

In the lobby of the Public Prosecutor's building, without looking at Izya, Andrei ordered the policeman to register the arrested man and take him upstairs to the duty guard. Andrei himself went up to his office, taking three steps at a time.

It was about four o'clock, the most hectic time of all. In the corridors suspects and witnesses stood along the walls or sat on the benches polished bright by backsides. They all looked equally hopeless and sleepy; almost all of them were yawning convulsively, with their eyes goggling blearily. Every now and then the duty guards bawled from their little desks: "Quiet! No talking!" From behind the office doors upholstered in leatherette, Andrei heard the clatter of typewriters, the droning of voices, and tearful wailing. It was stifling, dirty, and gloomy. Andrei suddenly felt nauseous—he wanted to drop into the cafeteria and drink something bracing: a cup of strong coffee, or at least a shot of vodka. And then he saw Wang.

Wang was squatting down, leaning back against the wall, in a pose of infinitely patient waiting. He was wearing his distinctive wadded jacket and his head was pulled down into his shoulders, so that the collar of the jacket pushed his ears out. His round, hairless face was calm. He was dozing.

"What are you doing here?" Andrei asked in amazement

Wang opened his eyes, got up smoothly, and said with a smile, "I've been arrested. I'm waiting to be called."

"What do you mean, arrested? What for?"

"Sabotage," Wang said in a quiet voice.

A huge thug in a filthy raincoat who was dozing nearby also opened his eyes—or, rather, one eye, because the other had swollen up in a bright purple bruise. "What sabotage?" Andrei exclaimed, dumbfounded.

"Avoidance of the right to work—"

"Article 112, paragraph 6," the thug with the shiner explained briskly. "Six months of swamp therapy—and you're done."

"You keep quiet," Andrei told him.

The thug flashed his purple eye at him and chuckled (immediately remembering the bump on his own forehead, Andrei felt it quite distinctly) and wheezed peaceably, "I can keep quiet. Why not keep quiet, when everything's clear without words anyway?"

"No talking!" the duty guard bawled menacingly. "Who's that there slouching against the wall? Right, unslouch yourself!"

"Wait," Andrei said to Wang. "Where have you been summoned to? Here?" He pointed to the door of room number 22, trying to recall whose office that was.

"That's right," the thug wheezed helpfully. "We're for number 22. We've been propping up the wall for an hour and a half already."

"Wait," Andrei said to Wang again, and pushed open the door.

Ensconced at the desk was Heinrich Ruhmer, a junior investigator and Friedrich Heiger's personal bodyguard, formerly a middleweight boxer and Munich bookmaker. Andrei asked, "May I come in?" but Ruhmer didn't reply. He was very busy. He was sketching something on a large sheet of drawing paper, leaning down his brutish physiognomy with the flattened nose to each shoulder by turns, panting and even moaning in his creative efforts. Andrei closed the door behind himself and walked right up to the desk. Ruhmer was copying a pornographic post-card. The sheet of drawing paper and the postcard were ruled off into squares. The work had only just begun, and so far only the general outlines had been plotted out on the paper. The job in prospect was titanic in scope.

"What's this you're doing during working hours, you vile brute?" Andrei asked reproachfully.

Ruhmer started visibly and looked up. "Ah, it's you . . ." he said with evident relief. "What do you want?"

"Is this the way you work?" Andrei asked mournfully. "People are waiting for you out there, and you—"

"Who's waiting?" Ruhmer asked, startled. "Where?"

"Your suspects are waiting!" said Andrei.

"Aah . . . Well, what of it?"

"Never mind," Andrei said malignly. What he probably should do was make this character feel ashamed somehow, remind the brute that Fritz had vouched for him, after all, vouched on his own good name for an idle cretin, for a bonehead, but Andrei felt he didn't have the strength for that right now.

"Who lamped you on the forehead?" Ruhmer asked with pro-fessional interest, examining Andrei's bump. "Someone lamped you handsomely."

"It's not important," Andrei said impatiently. "I'll tell you why I called in: Have you got Wang Li-hung's case?"

"Wang Li-hung?" Ruhmer stopped examining the bump and thoughtfully stuck one finger into his right nostril. "Why, what's up?" he asked warily.

"Have you got it or not?"

"And why are you asking?"

"Because he's sitting outside your door and waiting while you're working on this filthy smut in here!"

"Why is it filthy smut?" Ruhmer asked resentfully. "Just look at the tits on her! *Moooo!* Eh?"

Andrei fastidiously pushed the photograph aside. "Hand over the case file," he demanded.

"What case?"

"Hand over the Wang Li-hung case!"

"I haven't got any such case," Ruhmer said angrily. He pulled out the middle drawer of his desk and glanced into it. Andrei glanced into the drawer too. The drawer really was empty.

"Where are all your case files anyway?" Andrei asked, restraining himself.

"What's that to you?" Ruhmer asked aggressively. "You're not my boss."

Andrei grabbed the receiver of the phone with a resolute gesture.

Alarm glinted in Ruhmer's piggy little eyes. "Hang on," he said, hastily setting his huge mitt on the base of the phone. "Where are you going to take it? What for?"

"I'm going to call Heiger now," Andrei said spitefully. "And he'll give you a roasting, you idiot."

"Wait," Ruhmer muttered, trying to take the receiver away from him. "Ah, come on, will you . . . Why call Heiger? We can settle this between the two of us, can't we? First of all, you explain properly what you want."

"I want to take the case of Wang Li-hung."

"That Chinese, you mean? The caretaker?"

"Yes!"

"Well, why didn't you say so to begin with? There isn't any case against him. They've only just brought him in. I'm going to take his initial interrogation."

"What was he arrested for?"

"Refuses to change his profession," said Ruhmer, gently pulling the telephone receiver toward himself, along with Andrei. "Sabotage. He's on his third term as a caretaker. Do you know article 112?"

"Yes," said Andrei. "But this is a special case. They're always fouling something up. Where's the accompanying letter?"

Wheezing loudly, Ruhmer finally got the phone away from Andrei, put it back in its place, and turned back to the desk. This time he opened the drawer on the right, rummaged around in it, concealing the contents behind his gigantic shoulders, pulled out a piece of paper, and handed it to Andrei. He was running with sweat. Andrei ran his eyes over the letter.

"It doesn't say here that he's been allocated to you specifically," he stated.

"So what?"

"So I'm taking him," said Andrei, sticking the sheet of paper in his pocket.

Ruhmer was bothered by that. "He's been registered to me! At the duty desk."

"Well, call the duty officer and tell him that Wang Li-hung has been taken by Voronin. He can reregister him."

"You can call him yourself," Ruhmer said pompously. "Why should I bother to call him? You're taking him, so you call. And give me a receipt to say you took him."

Five minutes later all the formalities had been completed. Ruhmer put the receipt in a desk drawer and looked at Andrei, and then at the photograph. "Oh, those tits!" he said. "Real udders!"

"You'll come to a bad end, Ruhmer," Andrei promised on the way out.

In the corridor he took Wang by the elbow without saying a word and drew him along. Wang submitted without asking any questions, and it occurred to Andrei that Wang would have gone just as silently and uncomplainingly to the firing squad, the torture chamber, and any other form of humiliation. Andrei couldn't understand that. There was something bestial and subhuman about this resignation, and at the same time something exalted that aroused an inexplicable respect, because vaguely discernible behind this resignation was some unearthly kind of understanding of the profound, hidden, eternal, essential nature of what was happening, an understanding of its eternal futility, and therefore of the unworthiness of resistance. East is East and West is West. A deceitful and unjust line, but somehow in this case it seemed apt.

"Well, what's this that's happened to you? Tell me about it."

And Wang was immediately telling the story in his measured storytelling voice. "A week ago the district employment officer came to my caretaker's lodge and reminded me that I was in blatant contravention of the law on diversified labor. He was right, I really am in blatant contravention of that law. The labor exchange has sent me a notification three times, and three times I have thrown it in the trash. The officer informed me that if I continued to shirk my responsibilities, I could be in serious trouble. And then it occurred to me that there were cases when the machine left someone in their former job. So that day I went to the labor exchange and put my record card in the machine. I was unlucky. I was given a job as director of a footwear plant. But I had decided in advance that I wouldn't move to a new job, and I stayed on as a caretaker. This evening two policemen came for me and brought me here. That's how it all happened."

"I get it," Andrei drawled. But he didn't really get anything. "Listen, would you like some tea? We can order tea and sandwiches here. For free."

"That would be a great inconvenience," Wang protested. "Please don't bother."

"What do you mean, inconvenience!" Andrei said angrily, and ordered two glasses of tea and sandwiches over the phone. After he put the phone down, he looked at Wang and asked cautiously, "Wang, I still don't completely understand why you didn't want to work as the director of a footwear plant. It's a respectable position; you would have acquired a new profession and made a real difference—after all, you're a very efficient and industrious person . . . And I know that footwear plant—pilfering goes on there all the time; they carry out shoes by the crateful . . . That wouldn't happen with you there. And then the pay's much better there, and you have a wife and a child, don't you? What's the problem?"

"Well, I think it will be hard for you to understand," Wang said thoughtfully.

"What is there to understand?" Andrei asked impatiently. "It's obvious that it's better to be the director of an industrial plant than to spend your whole life raking up trash . . . Or even worse, to slave away in the swamps for six months . . ."

Wang shook his round head. "No, it isn't better," he said. "The best place of all to be in is one from which you can't fall. You can't understand that, Andrei."

"Why do you have to fall at all?" asked Andrei, puzzled.

"I don't know why. But it's bound to happen. Or you have to make such a great effort to hold on that it's better to fall immediately. I know, I've been through all that."

A policeman with a sleepy face brought the tea and saluted, swaying on his feet, then edged back out into the corridor. Andrei set a glass of tea in a tarnished metal glass-holder in front of Wang and pushed the plate of sandwiches toward him. Wang thanked him, took a sip from the glass, and took the very smallest sandwich. "You're simply afraid of responsibility," Andrei said disappointedly. "I'm sorry, but I have to say that's not entirely fair to everybody else."

"I always try to do only good for people," Wang objected calmly. "And as for responsibility, I bear a supreme responsibility. My wife and child."

"That's true," said Andrei, feeling rather confused again. "That's right, of course. But you must agree that the Experiment demands from every one of us . . ."

Wang listened carefully, nodding. When Andrei finished, he said, "I understand you. You are right in your own way. But then, you came here to build, didn't you? And I ran away to get here. You seek battle and victory, I seek repose. We are very different, Andrei."

"What does that mean—repose? You're slandering yourself. If you sought repose, you would have found a cozy little corner somewhere and lived there like a pig in clover. Cozy little corners are ten a penny around here. But you've chosen the dirtiest, most unpopular job of all, and you work honestly, without begrudging the effort or the time . . . What sort of repose is that?"

"Repose of the soul, Andrei. Inner repose," said Wang. "At peace with oneself and the universe."

Andrei drummed his fingers on the table. "Well then, do you intend to be a caretaker for the rest of your life?"

"Not necessarily a caretaker," said Wang. "When I arrived here, I was a laborer in a warehouse at first. Then the machine appointed me the mayor's secretary. I refused and I was sent to the swamps. I worked off my six months and came back, and by law, as a punished convict, I was given the very lowest job. But then the machine started pushing me upward again. I went to the director of the labor exchange and explained everything to him, as I have to you. The director of the exchange was a Jew, he had arrived here from an extermination camp, and he understood me very well. For as long as he was the director, they didn't bother me." Wang paused. "About two months ago, he disappeared. They say he was found murdered, you probably know about that. And it all started all over again . . . Never mind, I'll do my time in the swamps and go back to being a caretaker. It will be a lot easier for me now—my son's a big boy now, and Uncle Yura will help me out in the swamps . . ."

At this point Andrei caught himself gawping wide-eyed at Wang in a way that was incredibly rude, as if it weren't Wang sitting there in front of him but some strange, outlandish creature. But then, Wang really was outlandish. My God, thought Andrei, what kind of life must a man have had to be reduced to a philosophy like this? Yes, I have to help him. I'm duty bound. But how? "Well, all right," he said eventually. "Have it your own way. Only there's absolutely no point in you going to the swamps. Do you happen to know who's the director of the labor exchange now?"

"Otto Friese," said Wang.

"What? Otto? Then what's the problem?"

"Yes, I would go to him, only he's such a little child, isn't he? He doesn't understand anything and he's afraid of everything."

Andrei grabbed the telephone directory, found the number, and picked up the phone. He had to wait a long time; Otto was obviously sleeping like a log. Eventually he answered in a halting voice that was angry and frightened. "Director Otto Friese here."

"Hello, Otto," said Andrei. "This is Voronin, from the Public Prosecutor's Office."

"The Public Prosecutor's Office? What can I do for you?"

"What is this, aren't you awake yet?" Andrei asked angrily. "Has Elsa worn you out, then? This is Andrei here! Voronin!"

"Ah, Andrei?" Otto said in a completely different voice. "What are you doing, calling in the middle of the night like this? My heart's pounding, dammit . . . What do you want?"

Andrei explained the situation. As he expected, everything went through without a hitch. Yes, Otto had always thought that Wang was in the right place. Yes, he definitely did think that Wang would never make a director of an industrial plant. He quite openly and unambiguously admired Wang's desire to remain in such an unenviable job ("We could do with more people like that here—everyone's trying to climb upward, like a bunch of mountain rangers"), he indignantly rejected the very idea of sending Wang to the swamps, and as far as the law was concerned, he was filled with pious outrage at the idiots and bureaucratic cretins who had replaced the living spirit of the law with its dead letter. After all, the law existed to hinder the efforts of various tricksters to worm their way up, and it shouldn't affect people who wanted to stay at the bottom in any way. The director of the labor exchange clearly understood all this. "Yes!" he repeated. "Oh, yes, of course!"

Andrei was left, however, with the vague, ludicrous, and annoying impression that Otto would have agreed to any proposal that he, Andrei Voronin, made—for instance, to appoint Wang as mayor or, on the contrary, lock him away in a cell. Otto had always felt a certain morbid gratitude to Andrei, probably because Andrei was the only person in their set (and perhaps in the entire City) who treated Otto like a human being . . . But, after all, the point at hand was really the most important thing, wasn't it?

"I'll see that it's done," Otto repeated for the tenth time. "You can stop worrying, Andrei. I'll issue the instructions, and no one will bother Wang again."

They left it at that. Andrei put down the phone and started writing out an exit pass for Wang. "Will you go right now?" he asked, still writing. "Or will you wait for the sun? Think about it, the streets are dangerous at this hour."

"Thank you," Wang murmured. "Thank you."

Andrei looked up in amazement. Wang was standing in front of him, repeatedly bowing rapidly and shallowly, with his hands folded together in front of his chest.

"Ah, drop all the Chinese ceremony," Andrei growled in embarrassed annoyance. "As if I'd done you some kind of good deed!" He handed Wang the pass. "I asked if you were going to go right now."

Wang accepted the pass with yet another bow. "I think I had better go immediately," he said, as if apologizing. "Right away. The garbage collectors have probably arrived already."

"The garbage collectors . . ." Andrei repeated. He looked at the plate of sandwiches. Large, fresh sandwiches, with excellent ham. "Hang on," he said, taking an old newspaper out of a drawer and starting to wrap the sandwiches in it. "You can take them home, for Mei-lin."

Wang resisted feebly, murmuring something about it being an excessive inconvenience, but Andrei stuffed the bundle inside Wang's jacket, put one arm around his shoulders, and led him to the door. Andrei felt terribly awkward somehow. Both Otto and Wang had reacted strangely to his actions. After all, he'd only tried to be just, to do everything correctly and rationally, and it had turned out like the damnedest sort of thing—some kind of charity work or string-pulling or cronyism . . . He hastily tried to find the right words—dry and matter-of-fact words—that would emphasize the official nature and legality of the situation . . . And suddenly he thought he'd found them. He stopped, raised his chin, looked Wang over from head to foot and said coolly,

"Citizen Wang, on behalf of the Public Prosecutor's Office, I offer you our profound apologies for your illegal detention. I assure you that it will never happen again."

And after that he felt totally embarrassed. What kind of nonsense was that? In the first place, Wang's detention had not, strictly speaking, been illegal. And second, the investigator Voronin couldn't give any assurances about anything; he didn't have that right . . . And at that point he saw Wang's eyes—that strange look, so familiar in its strangeness, and he suddenly remembered and the memory was like a wave of scalding heat.

"Wang," he said, his voice suddenly hoarse. "I want to ask you something, Wang."

He stopped. It was stupid to ask, pointless. And already too late not to ask. Wang looked up at him, expectant.

"Wang," said Andrei, and cleared his throat. "Where were you at two o'clock this morning?"

Wang wasn't surprised. "They came for me at two," he said. "I was washing down the stairs."

"And before that?"

"Before that I collected the trash. Mei-lin helped me, then she went to bed and I went to wash down the stairs."

"Yes," said Andrei, "that's what I thought. OK, good-bye, Wang. Sorry things turned out like this . . . No, hang on, I'll see you out . . ."

Ч

Before he summoned Izya, Andrei thought the whole thing through again.

First, he forbade himself to take a biased approach to Izya. The fact that Izya was a cynic, a know-it-all, and a blabbermouth, that he was prepared to ridicule—and he did ridicule—everything in the world, that he was slovenly and sprayed saliva when he spoke, giggled repulsively, and lived with a widow like a kept man and nobody had any idea how he earned a living . . . in this instance all of that must be absolutely irrelevant.

Andrei also had to discard root and branch the primitive idea that Katzman was a simple disseminator of panicky rumors about the Red Building and other mystical phenomena. The Red Building was a reality—a mysterious, fantastic reality; it wasn't clear what it was for and who needed it—but it was a reality. (At this point Andrei checked in the first aid kit and spread disinfectant on his oozing bump, looking in a little mirror.) In this plan Katzman was primarily a witness. What was he doing in the Red House? How often did he visit it? What could he tell Andrei about it? What file had he brought out of it? Or was the file really not from there after all? Was it really from the old City Hall?

Stop, stop! Katzman had repeatedly let slip . . . well, not let slip, of course, but simply told them about his journeys to the north. What was he doing there? The Anticity lay somewhere to the north too.

Yes, I was right to detain Katzman, even if it was done in haste. That's the way it always goes. It all starts with simple curiosity—someone sticks his curious nose in where it doesn't belong, and before he can say boo, he's been recruited . . . Why did he refuse point-blank to give me that document file? The file is obviously from there. And the Red Building is from there! The boss obviously failed to put two and two together somewhere. No, it's understandable—he didn't have the facts. And he hasn't been in there. Yes, spreading rumors is a terrible thing, but the Red Building is more terrible than any rumor. And the really terrible thing is not even that people disappear inside it forever; the terrible thing is that sometimes they come back out! They come back out, they return to live among us, like Katzman . . .

Andrei felt that now he had a tight grasp of the most important thread, but he didn't have the courage to follow the analysis all the way through to the end. He knew only that the Andrei Voronin who went in through that door with the brass handle was not entirely the same Andrei Voronin who came out of that door. Something had snapped inside him in there, something had been irretrievably lost . . . He gritted his teeth. Oh no, you've miscalculated this time, my fine gentlemen. You shouldn't have let me out. We're not so easily broken . . . or bought . . . or moved to pity.

Grinning crookedly, he took a clean sheet of paper and wrote on it in large letters, "RED BUILDING—KATZMAN. RED BUILDING—ANTICITY. ANTICITY—KATZMAN." That was the way it all panned out. No, boss, he thought, it's not the rumor-spreaders we have to search for. We need to search for the people who have emerged from the Red Building alive and well—search for them, catch them, isolate them . . . or place them under rigorous observation . . . He wrote down, "People who have been in the Building—the Anticity." So Pani Husáková would have to tell them all she knew about her František after all. The flute player could probably be released, though. But then, it wasn't really about them . . . Maybe I should call the boss? Ask his blessing for the change of direction? No, it's probably a bit too soon for that. No, if I can get Katzman to talk . . . He picked up the phone.

"Duty guard? Bring detainee Katzman to me in 36."

And not only did he need to get Katzman to talk, he could. The file. There was no way Katzman could worm his way out of that . . . It flashed through Andrei's mind that it wasn't entirely ethical for him to handle Katzman's case; he had drunk with the man on numerous occasion, and in general . . . But he pulled himself up short there.

The door opened and detainee Katzman, with a huge grin on his face and his hands stuck in his greasy pockets, entered the room with a slack, jaunty stride.

"Sit down," Andrei said coolly, jerking his chin in the direction of the stool.

"Thank you," said the detainee, grinning even more widely. "I see you haven't snapped out of it yet."

It was all water off a duck's back to him, the creep. Katzman sat down, tugged at the wart on his neck, and glanced curiously around the office.

And then a cold shiver ran down Andrei's spine. The detainee didn't have the file with him.

"Where's the file?" Andrei asked, trying to speak calmly.

"What file?" Katzman inquired brazenly.

Andrei grabbed up the phone. "Duty guard! Where is detainee Katzman's document file?"

"What file?" the duty guard asked obtusely. "I'll just take a look . . . Katzman . . . Aha . . . The following items were confiscated from detainee Katzman: handkerchiefs, 2; wallet, 1, empty, worn . . ."

"Is there a document file in the inventory?" Andrei barked.

"There isn't any file," the duty guard answered in a sinking voice.

"Bring me the inventory," Andrei said hoarsely, and hung up. Then he glowered briefly at Katzman. His hatred for the man was buzzing in his ears. "Jewish pranks . . ." he said, restraining himself. "Where did you put the file, you bastard?"

Katzman responded immediately, in melodramatic literary style: "She grabbed hold of his hand and asked him over and over again: 'Where did you put the file?'"

"All right," said Andrei, breathing heavily through his nose. "It won't do you any good, you lousy, spying scum."

A look of astonishment flashed across Izya's face. But a second later he already had that repulsive, taunting grin stuck on it again. "Why, of course, of course!" he said. "Iosif Katzman, chairman of the 'Joint' organization, at your service. Don't beat me, I'll tell you everything anyway. The machine guns are hidden in Berdichev, the landing site is marked by campfires . . ."

The frightened duty guard walked in, holding the sheet of paper with the inventory on it out in front of him. "There isn't any file here," he muttered, putting the inventory down on the edge of the desk in front of Andrei and retreating. "I rang the front desk, and they don't—"

"All right, go," Andrei said through his teeth. He took a blank interrogation form and asked, without looking up: "Full name with patronymic?"

"Iosif Mikhailovich Katzman."

"Year of birth?"

"Thirty-six."

"Nationality?"

"Yes," Katzman said, and giggled.

Andrei raised his head. "Yes what?"

"Listen, Andrei," said Izya. "I don't understand what's going on with you today, but bear in mind that you'll destroy your entire career with me like this. I'm warning you as an old friend—"

"Answer the questions!" Andrei said in a strangled voice. "Nationality?"

"Just don't you forget how they took Dr. Timashuk's medal away from her," said Izya.

But Andrei didn't know who Dr. Timashuk was. "Nationality!"

"Jewish," Izya said with loathing.

"Citizenship?"

"U! S! S! R!"

"Religious affiliation?"

"None."

"Political affiliation?"

"None."

"Education?"

"Higher. Herzen Pedagogical Institute, Leningrad."

"Criminal record?"

"None."

"Earthly year of departure?"

"Nineteen sixty-eight."

"Point of departure?

"Leningrad."

"Reason for departure?"

"Curiosity."

"Period of residence in the City?"

"Four years."

"Present profession?"

"Statistician at the Department of Municipal Services."

"List previous professions."

"General laborer, senior municipal archivist, office clerk at the municipal slaughterhouse, garbage collector, blacksmith. I think that's all."

"Family status."

"Adulterer," Izya replied, smirking.

Andrei put down the pen, lit up, and studied the detainee through the blue smoke for a while. Izya was grinning, Izya was unkempt and shock-headed, Izya was sardonic, but Andrei knew this man well, and he could see that Izya was nervous. He obviously had something to be nervous about, even though he had managed to ditch the file—and very deftly, it must be said. He obviously realized now that he was being dealt with in earnest; that was why his eyes were narrowed nervously and the corners of his grinning mouth were trembling.

"Well then, suspect Katzman," Andrei said in a tried and tested chilly tone of voice. "I seriously recommend you adopt a respectful attitude toward the investigation if you don't wish to make your own situation any worse."

Izya stopped smiling. "All right," he said. "Then I demand to be informed of the charge against me and also the article under which I have been detained. Furthermore, I demand a lawyer. From this moment on I won't say another word without a lawyer."

Andrei chuckled to himself. "You have been detained under article 12 of the Criminal Procedural Code concerning the preventive detention of individuals whose continued presence at liberty could constitute a public danger. You are accused of illegal contacts with hostile elements, concealing or destroying material evidence at the time of arrest . . . and also of violating the municipal ordinance that forbids travel beyond the city limits for public health reasons. You have violated this ordinance on a regular basis . . . And as for a lawyer, the Public Prosecutor's Office cannot provide you with a lawyer until three days have elapsed following the time of arrest. In accordance with the aforementioned article 12 of the Criminal Procedural Code . . . In addition, let me clarify: you may formally protest, register complaints, and enter appeals only after you have satisfactorily replied to the questions of the initial interrogation. All in accordance with the said article 12. Is all that clear?"

He had been studying Izya's face and he could see that everything was clear to him. It was also absolutely clear that Izya would answer the questions and wait until the three days were over. At the mention of the three-day period Izya had unmistakably caught his breath.

"Now that you have received this clarification," Andrei said, picking up the pen again, "let us proceed. Your family status."

"Unmarried," said Izya.

"Home address?"

"What?" asked Izya. He had clearly been thinking about something else.

"Your home address? Where do you live?"

"Nineteen Second Left Street, apartment 7."

"Do you have anything to tell me regarding the charges brought against you?"

"By all means," said Izya. "Concerning the hostile elements: delirious drivel. This is the first time I've even heard that there are any hostile elements. I regard it as a deliberately provocative invention on the part of the investigation. Material evidence . . . I did not have and could not have had any material evidence with me, because I have not committed any crimes. Therefore I can neither conceal nor destroy anything. And as for the municipal ordinance—I am a former employee of the municipal archive, where I continue to work on a voluntary basis; I have access to all archival materials, and therefore also to those that lie outside the city limits. That's all."

"What were you doing in the Red Building?"

"That is my own personal business. You have no right to intrude into my personal affairs. First prove that they are relevant to the substance of the charges. Article 14 of the Criminal Procedural Code."

"Have you been in the Red Building on more than one occasion?"

"Yes."

"Can you name the people whom you met there?"

Izya gave a ghastly grin. "I can. Only that will not assist the investigation."

"Name these people."

"By all means. From modern times: Pétain, Quisling, Wang Ching-wei, Vasil Bilak—"

Andrei raised his hand. "I request that above all else you name individuals who are citizens of our City."

"And why would the investigation require that?" Izya inquired aggressively.

"I am not obliged to account for anything to you. Answer the questions."

"I don't wish to answer your idiotic questions. You don't understand a damn thing. You imagine that if I met someone in there, it means he really was there. But that's not so."

"I don't understand. Please explain."

"I don't understand it myself," said Izya. "It's something like a dream. The delirious ravings of an agitated conscience."

"I see. Like a dream. Were you in the Red Building today?"

"Yes, I was."

"Where was the Red Building when you entered it?"

"Today? Today it was there beside the synagogue."

"Did you see me in the Building?"

Izya grinned again. "I see you every time I go in there."

"Including today?"

"Yes."

"What was I doing?"

"Engaging in lewd behavior," Izya said with relish.

"Specifically?"

"You were copulating, Citizen Voronin. Copulating with numerous girls at the same time and simultaneously preaching high principles to eunuchs. Impressing on them that you were not engaging in this activity for your own pleasure but for the good of all mankind."

Andrei gritted his teeth. "And what were you doing?" he asked after a brief pause.

"I won't tell you that. That's my right."

"You're lying," Andrei said. "You didn't see me there. Here are your own words: 'From the look of you, you've been in the Red Building . . .' Consequently, you did not see me there. Why are you lying?"

"I wouldn't dream of it," Izya replied breezily. "It's just that I felt ashamed for you and decided to make you think I hadn't seen you there. But now, of course, things have changed. Now I am obliged to tell the truth."

Andrei leaned back and flung the pen behind his chair. "You say it's a kind of dream. Then what difference does it make if you saw me or didn't see me in a dream? Why try to make me think anything?"

"That's not it," said Izya. "I was simply embarrassed to let you know what I really think of you sometimes. But I shouldn't have been."

Andrei shook his head dubiously. "Well, all right. Did you bring the document file out of the Red Building too? From out of your own dream, so to say?"

Izya's face froze. "What file?" he asked nervously. "What is this file you keep asking about all the time? I didn't have any file."

"Drop it, Katzman," said Andrei, closing his eyes wearily. "I saw the file, the police officer saw the file, that old man saw the file . . . Pan Stupalski. You'll have to provide an explanation at the trial in any case . . . Don't exacerbate matters!"

Izya's eyes wandered across the wall. He sat there stony-faced and said nothing.

"Let's assume the file wasn't from the Red House," Andrei continued. "Then did you obtain it outside the city limits? Who from? Who gave it to you, Katzman?"

Izya said nothing.

"What was in that file?" Andrei got up and walked around the office with his hands clasped behind his back. "An individual has a file in his hands. The individual is arrested. On the way to the Prosecutor's Office the individual disposes of the file. Secretly. Why? The file evidently contains documents that are compromising for this individual . . . Do you follow the train of my logic, Katzman? The file was obtained outside city limits. What kind of documents, obtained outside city limits, can compromise an inhabitant of our City? What kind, tell me, Katzman?"

Izya looked up at the ceiling, worrying away relentlessly at his wart.

"Only don't try to worm your way out of it, Katzman," Andrei warned him. "Don't try to sell me another of your cock-and-bull stories. I can see right through you. What was in the file? Lists? Addresses? Instructions?"

Izya suddenly slapped himself on the knee. "Listen, you idiot!" he roared. "What sort of garbage are you spouting here? Who put all this into your head, you poor simpleton? What lists, what addresses? You crummy, pathetic Major Pronin! You've known me for three years—you know that I rummage around in the ruins, that I study the history of the City. Why the hell do you keep trying to pin some idiotic charge of spying on me? Think about it: Who can do any spying here? What for? Who for?"

"What was in the file?" Andrei barked out at the top of his lungs. "Stop prevaricating and give me a straight answer: What was in the file?"

At that Izya snapped. His eyes bulged out, suffused with blood. "You can just . . . go to hell with your files!" he squealed in a falsetto voice. "I'm not going to tell you anything. You're a fool, an idiot, a gendarme scumbag!"

He squealed, sprayed, swore, and gestured obscenely, and then Andrei took a clean sheet of paper and wrote at the top of it, "Testimony of the suspect I. Katzman concerning the document file that was seen in his possession and subsequently disappeared without a trace." He waited until Izya quieted down and said good-naturedly, "Let me tell you this, Izya. Unofficially. Your case is petty trash. I know you got tangled up in this business without even thinking, thanks to that idiotic curiosity of yours. If you'd like to know, we've had you in our sights for six months already. And my advice to you is to sit over here and write down everything just the way it is. I can't promise you much, but I'll do everything that lies in my power for you. Sit down and write. I'll come back in half an hour."

Trying not to look at Izya, who had fallen quiet out of sheer exhaustion, and feeling disgusted by his own hypocrisy but consoling himself with the thought that in this instance the goal quite definitely justified the means, he locked the drawers of his desk, got up, and walked out.

In the corridor he beckoned to the assistant duty guard, stood him at the door, and went off to the cafeteria. He had an ugly feeling in his heart and a foul, sticky taste in his mouth, as if he had gorged himself on shit. The interrogation had turned out skewed and unconvincing somehow. He'd screwed up the Red Building connection totally and absolutely; he shouldn't even have gotten into it at this stage. And the way he'd lost the file was a real blunder—the file was the only real clue, and he had ignominiously let it slip through his fingers. For gaffes like that he ought to be thrown out of the Public Prosecutor's Office in disgrace . . . Fritz probably wouldn't have let it slip away from him. Fritz would immediately have realized what the real goods were. Damned sentimentality. Of course it was—they'd drunk together, shot the breeze together; he was Andrei's buddy, a Soviet guy . . .

But what a chance it was, he thought, to rake them all in at once! And the boss goofed too: rumors, gossip . . . There's an entire network of them working away right under his nose, and I'm supposed to search for the source of the rumors . . .

Andrei walked up to the counter, took a shot glass of vodka, and tossed it down with a feeling of revulsion. Where had Izya put that damned file after all? Had he really just thrown it out on the road? Probably—he hadn't eaten it, had he? Maybe Andrei should send someone to look for it? Too late. Loonies, baboons, caretakers . . . No, the way our work's organized is all wrong, it's all wrong. Why is such important information as the existence of the Anticity kept secret even from employees of the Investigation Department? Why, they ought to write about it every day in the newspapers and put up posters in the streets! We need show trials! I'd have had this Katzman pegged ages ago . . . On the other hand, of course, you have to know how to think for yourself too. Since such a grandiose undertaking as the Experiment exists, and since people of the most various classes and political persuasions have been roped into it, it means that a certain stratification will inevitably arise . . . contradictions . . . dynamic contradictions, if you like . . . an antagonistic struggle . . . The opponents of the Experiment must be exposed sooner or later, those people who disagree with it in class terms and also those who try to warp it to suit their own interests—the déclassé element, those who lack moral fiber, and corrupted individuals, like Katzman . . . all sorts of cosmopolitans . . . a natural process. I could have figured out for myself the way all this ought to develop—

A small, firm hand was laid on his shoulder, and he swung around. It was the crime reporter from the *City Gazette*, Kensi Ubukata. "What are you musing about, investigator?" he asked. "Untangling a knotty case? Share your thoughts with the public. The public loves knotty cases. Eh?"

"Hi, Kensi," Andrei said in a tired voice. "Have a glass of vodka?

"Yes, if there's information to go with it."

"I've got nothing for you except vodka."

"OK, I'll take the vodka without the information."

They drank a shot each and snacked on limp pickles.

"I've just come from your boss," said Kensi, spitting out the tail of a pickle. "He's a very flexible sort of individual. One trend is rising and another is falling, the process of equipping solitary cells with washbasins is almost complete—and not a single word about the question that I'm interested in."

"And what are you interested in?" Andrei asked absentmindedly.

"Right now I'm interested in disappearances. In the last fifteen days eleven people have disappeared without a trace in the City. Maybe you know something about that?"

"I know they disappeared. I know they haven't been found."

"Who's handling the case?"

"It's not likely to be just one case," said Andrei. "You should ask the boss that."

Kensi shook his head. "Somehow just recently the gentlemen investigators have been referring me to their boss, or to Heiger, a bit too often . . . There's been a sudden proliferation of mysteries in our little democratic community. You wouldn't happen to have metamorphosed into a secret police at some odd moment, would you?" He glanced into his empty shot glass and complained, "What's the use of having friends among the investigators if you can never find out anything?"

"Duty before friendship."

Neither of them spoke for a while.

"By the way, you know, Wang's been arrested," said Kensi. "I warned him all right, but he wouldn't listen—he's as stubborn as a mule."

"It's OK, I fixed everything already," said Andrei.

"How so?"

Andrei enthusiastically told Kensi how deftly and quickly he had fixed everything. Set everything straight. Restored justice. He got a kick out of telling the story of this single successful incident in such a long, ludicrously disastrous day.

"Hmm," said Kensi after he heard Andrei out. "Interesting . . . 'When I arrive in a foreign country,'" he said, quoting, "'I never ask if the laws there are good or bad. I only ask if they are enforced . . .'"

"What do you mean by that?" Andrei asked him with a frown.

"What I mean is that as far as I'm aware the law on the right to diversified labor does not specify any exceptions."

"So you think that Wang should have been shipped out to the swamps?"

"If that's what the law requires—yes."

"But that's plain stupid!" Andrei said, getting annoyed. "Why the hell would the Experiment want a bad production plant director instead of a good caretaker?"

"The law on the right to diversified labor—"

"That law," Andrei broke in, "was devised for the good of the Experiment, not to harm it. A law can't anticipate everything. We enforcers of the law have to know how to think for ourselves."

"My view of the enforcement of the law is somewhat different," Kensi said drily. "In any case, you don't decide such matters, the court does."

"The court would have shipped him off to the swamps," said Andrei. "But he has a wife and a child."

"*Dura lex, sed lex*," said Kensi.

"That adage was invented by bureaucrats."

"That adage," Kensi said gravely, "was invented by people who wished to preserve a unified legal basis for the social coexistence of a disparate mass of free human beings."

"That's exactly it, disparate!" said Andrei, seizing on the word. "There simply cannot be a single law for all. There is no single law for the exploiter and the exploited. Now, if Wang had refused to move from being a director to being a caretaker . . ."

"It's not your job to interpret the law," Kensi said coldly. "The court exists to do that."

"But the court doesn't know Wang like I do, and it never can!"

Kensi shook his head with a crooked smile. "God almighty, what great experts you have here in the Prosecutor's Office!"

"OK, OK," Andrei growled. "So why not write an article about it? Idiot investigator releases criminal caretaker."

"I would, too. Only I'd feel sorry for Wang. I wouldn't feel sorry for you at all, you fool."

"Well, I feel sorry for Wang too, don't I?" said Andrei.

"But you're an investigator," Kensi retorted. "And I'm not. I'm not bound by the laws."

"You know what," said Andrei. "Just stop hassling me, for Christ's sake. My head's spinning already without you lending a hand."

Kensi looked up and chuckled. "Yes, I can see that. It's written on your forehead. Was there a raid?"

"No," said Andrei. "I just tripped over something." He looked at his watch. "Another shot?"

"Thanks, but no more," said Kensi, getting up. "I can't drink so much with every investigator. I only drink with the ones who give me information."

"Well, screw you then," said Andrei. "Chachua's just shown up over there. Go ask him about the Falling Stars. He's been making really great progress—he was boasting about it today . . . Only don't forget that he's a very modest guy: he'll deny everything, just don't let him off the hook, pump him really hard, and you'll end up with a real gem!"

Moving chairs aside, Kensi set off toward Chachua, who was dejectedly hunched over a skinny little meat rissole, and Andrei gently strolled over to the door, smirking vengefully. I'd just love to wait and watch Chachua bellow, he thought. Too bad there's no time for that . . . Right, then. Citizen Katzman, how have you been getting on? And God help you, Citizen Katzman, if you feed me any more of that hogwash. I won't stand for it, Citizen Katzman . . .

In room 36 every possible light had been turned on. Citizen Katzman was standing there, leaning his shoulder against the open safe, avidly leafing through some case or other, fiddling with his wart in his usual fashion, and grinning like a Cheshire cat at something.

"What the hell!" said Andrei, caught off-guard. "Who gave you permission? What sort of behavior is this, dammit?"

Izya looked up at him with a mindless expression in his eyes, grinned even wider, and said, "I never realized what a huge, tangled mess you'd made of the Red Building."

Andrei tore the file out of Izya's hands, slammed the metal door shut with a clang, grabbed him by the shoulder, and shoved him toward the stool. "Sit down, Katzman," he said, straining every nerve to control himself. Fury blurred everything in front of his eyes. "Have you written that statement?"

"Listen," said Izya, "this place is simply full of idiots . . . There's 150 of you cretins sitting here and you still can't understand . . ."

But Andrei wasn't looking at him any longer. He was looking at the sheet of paper with the title "Testimony of the suspect I. Katzman . . ." There wasn't any testimony, but there was a pen drawing instead: a male sex organ, life size.

"You bastard," Andrei exclaimed, and choked. "You scumbag." He tore the phone off the hook and dialed a number with a trembling finger. "Fritz? It's Voronin here . . ." With his free hand he ripped open his collar. "I really need your help here. Please, come over to my room right now."

"What's the problem?" Heiger asked in annoyance. "I'm about to go home."

"Please, please!" said Andrei, raising his voice. "Just come over here!"

He hung up and looked at Izya, and immediately discovered he couldn't look at him, so he started looking through him instead. Izya burbled and giggled on his stool, rubbing his hands together and talking nonstop, pontificating about something with a repulsive, self-righteous sort of glibness, something about the Red Building, about conscience, about idiotic witnesses . . . Andrei didn't listen; he didn't hear anything. The decision he had taken filled him with fear and a sort of diabolical merriment. Everything inside him was jigging about in excitement—he simply couldn't wait for that moment, any time now, when the door would open and somber, angry Fritz would stride into the room, and then he would see that repulsively smug face change, contorting in horror and ignominious fear . . . Especially if Fritz showed up with Ruhmer. The mere sight of Ruhmer would be enough—those bestial, hairy features of his, with the flattened nose. Andrei suddenly felt a chilly sensation on his back. He was completely covered in perspiration. He could still change his move after all, couldn't he? He could still say, "Everything's OK, Fritz, it's all been squared away, sorry I bothered you . . ."

The door swung open and in walked Fritz Heiger, sullen and irascible. "Well, what's the problem?" he inquired, and then he spotted Izya. "Ah, hi!" he said, breaking into a smile. "What are you two up to in the middle of the night? It's time to sleep; it's almost morning."

"Listen, Fritz!" Izya howled joyfully. "Explain to this blockhead, will you? You're a big boss around here—"

"Silence, suspect!" Andrei bellowed, slamming his fist onto the desk.

Izya fell silent and Fritz instantly gathered himself, giving Izya a different kind of look.

"This bastard is treating the investigation with contempt," Andrei said through his teeth, trying to calm down and stop trembling all over. "This bastard is refusing to talk. Take him, Fritz, make him answer the questions he's asked."

Fritz's transparent Nordic eyes opened wide.

"And just what questions is he being asked?" he inquired with brisk glee.

"That's not important," said Andrei. "Give him a piece of paper, he'll write it himself. And I want him to say what was in the file."

"Got it," said Fritz, and turned toward Izya.

Izya still didn't understand anything. Or he didn't believe it. He slowly rubbed his hands together and grinned uncertainly.

"Right, then, my Jewish friend, shall we go?" Fitz inquired affectionately. His grim sullenness had disappeared without a trace. "Move it, bucko!"

Izya carried on dragging his feet, and Fritz took hold of his collar, swung him around, and shoved him toward the door. Izya lost his balance and grabbed hold of the doorpost. His face turned white. Now he understood.

"Guys," he said in a choking voice. "Guys, wait . . ."

"If anything comes up, we'll be in the basement," Fritz purred in velvet tones, smiled at Andrei, and prodded Izya out into the corridor.

That was it. Feeling a repulsive, sickening chill inside him, Andrei walked around the office, turning off the unnecessary lights. That was it. He sat down at the desk and stayed there for a while, with his head lowered into his hands. He was covered in perspiration, as if he were about to faint. His ears were buzzing, and through the buzzing he kept hearing Izya's soundlessly deafening, desperate, choking voice: "Guys, wait . . . Guys, wait . . ." And there was the sound of music solemnly roaring, feet clacking and shuffling across a parquet floor, the clatter of dishes and indistinct mumbling: "A gwass of cuwaçao and some pine-app-uw, quickwy!" He tore his hands away from his face and stared blankly at the drawing of the male sex organ. He took the sheet of paper and started tearing it into long, narrow strips, then threw the paper noodles into the trash basket and buried his face in his hands again. That was it. He had to wait. Summon up his patience and wait. Then everything would be justified. The nauseous feeling would pass off, and he'd be able to breathe a sigh of relief.

"Yes, Andrei, sometimes one even has to resort to this," he heard a familiar, calm voice say.

Sitting there on the stool where Izya had been sitting only a minute ago, with one leg crossed over the other and his slim white fingers clasped on his knee, gazing at Andrei with a sad, weary expression, was the Mentor. He was nodding gently and the corners of his mouth were dolefully turned down.

"For the sake of the Experiment?" Andrei asked hoarsely.

"For the sake of the Experiment as well," said the Mentor. "But above all for one's own sake. There is no way around it. You had to go through this too. We don't want just any kind of people. We need a special kind of people."

"What kind?"

"That's something even we don't know," the Mentor said with quiet regret. "We only know the kind of people we don't need."

"People like Katzman?"

The Mentor told him *yes* with just his eyes.

"And people like Ruhmer?"

The Mentor laughed. "People like Ruhmer aren't people. They're living weapons, Andrei. By using people like Ruhmer in the name of and for the good of people like Wang, Uncle Yura . . . you understand?"

"Yes. That's what I think too. And after all, there isn't any other way, right?"

"Right. There isn't any way around it."

"But what about the Red Building?" Andrei asked.

"We can't manage without that either. Without that anyone could become like Ruhmer without even realizing. Have you not sensed already that the Red Building is a necessity? Are you really the same as you were this morning?"

"Katzman said the Red Building is the delirious raving of an agitated conscience."

"Well now, Katzman is smart. I hope you wouldn't argue with that."

"Of course not," said Andrei. "That's precisely why he's dangerous."

Once again the Mentor showed Andrei *yes* with just his eyes.

"Oh God," Andrei exclaimed wearily. "If only I could know for certain what the goal of the Experiment is! It's so easy to get confused, everything's such a muddle . . . Me, Heiger, Kensi . . . Sometimes I think I know what we have in common, but sometimes it's a kind of blind alley, it's totally absurd . . . After all, Heiger is a former fascist, and even now he . . . Even now I sometimes find him odious—not as an individual, but as a type, as . . . Or Kensi. He's something like a social democrat, some kind of pacifist or Tolstoyan . . . No, I don't understand."

"The Experiment is the Experiment," said the Mentor. "It's not understanding that is required of you but something quite different."

"What?"

"If one only knew . . ."

"But it's all for the sake of the majority, isn't it?" Andrei asked, almost in despair.

"Of course," said the Mentor. "For the sake of the benighted, downtrodden, entirely innocent, ignorant majority . . ."

"Which must be raised up," Andrei eagerly put in, "enlightened, and made the master of the Earth! Yes, yes, that I understand. You can go to any lengths for the sake of that . . ." He paused, agonizingly gathering his scattered thoughts. "And there's still the Anticity," he said hesitantly. "And that's very dangerous, right?"

"Very," said the Mentor.

"And then, even if I'm not entirely certain about Katzman, I still acted correctly. We have no right to take any risks."

"Absolutely!" said the Mentor. He was smiling. He was pleased with Andrei; Andrei could sense it. "The only man who never makes a mistake is the man who does nothing. It's not mistakes that are dangerous—passivity is dangerous, specious fastidiousness is dangerous, devotion to the old commandments is dangerous. Where can old commandments lead? Only to the old world."

"Yes," Andrei said excitedly. "I understand that very clearly. That's exactly what we must all take as our foundation. What is the individual? A social unit! A zero without the digit one. It's not a matter of the individual units but the public good. In the name of the public good we must be willing to lay any burden, no matter how heavy, on our Old Testament consciences, to transgress all written and unwritten laws. We have only one law: the public good."

The Mentor stood up. "You're maturing," he said almost triumphantly. "Slowly, but you are maturing."

He raised one hand in salutation, walked soundlessly across the room, and disappeared out the door.

For a while Andrei sat there without thinking, leaning against the back of his chair, smoking and watching the bluish smoke slowly eddying around the yellow lamp hanging from the ceiling. He caught himself smiling. He didn't feel tired anymore; the sleepiness that had tormented him since the evening had disappeared. He felt an urge to act, to work, and felt annoyed at the thought that anytime now he would have to go and sleep for a few hours anyway, in order not to burn out later.

He pulled the phone toward him with an impatient gesture, lifted the receiver, and then remembered that there was no phone in the basement. He got up, locked the safe, checked that the drawers of the desk were locked, and walked out into the corridor.

The corridor was empty, and the police officer on duty was dozing at his little desk. "You're asleep at your post!" Andrei remarked reproachfully as he walked by.

The building was filled with a resounding silence, as it always was at this time, a few minutes before the sun was switched on.

A sleepy cleaning lady was slowly trailing a damp rag across the concrete floor. The windows in the corridors were wide open; the stinking vapors of hundreds of human bodies crept out into the darkness and dispersed as they were displaced by the cold morning air.

With his heels clattering on the slippery iron stairway, Andrei went down into the basement, gestured casually with his hand for the guard who had jumped to his feet to sit back down, and swung open the low iron door.

Fritz Heiger, with no jacket and the sleeves of his shirt rolled up, was standing beside the rusty washbasin, whistling a little march that Andrei vaguely knew and rubbing his hairy, rawboned hands with eau de cologne. There was no one else in the room.

"Ah, it's you," said Fritz. "That's good. I was just going to come up to see you . . . Give me a cigarette, I've run out."

Andrei handed him the pack. Fritz pulled out a cigarette, kneaded it, stuck it in his mouth, and looked at Andrei with a smirk on his face.

"Well," Andrei asked impatiently.

"Well what?" Fritz lit up and dragged on it with relish. "You were way off the mark. He's no spy, he's not even—"

"But how come?" said Andrei, stunned. "What about the file?"

Fritz chortled, squeezing the cigarette into the corner of his large mouth, and splashed out more eau de cologne onto his broad palm.

"Our little Jew is a superhuman womanizer," he said pedantically. "He had love letters in that file. He was on his way from a woman's place—he'd quarreled with her and taken back his letters. But he's scared shitless of that widow of his, so being no fool, as you know very well, he tried to get rid of that file at the first convenient moment. He says he dumped it down a manhole in the road . . . And that's a great pity!" Fritz continued even more pedantically. "That file, Citizen Investigator, ought to have been confiscated immediately—it would have made grade-one dirt, and we would have had our little Jew by the short and curlies!" Fritz demonstrated where the short and curlies were. Fresh bruises were visible on his knuckles. "But anyway, he signed a little report of interrogation for us, so at least we got a tuft of wool from our mangy sheep."

Andrei fumbled for a chair and sat down. His legs wouldn't hold him up. He glanced around again.

"I'll tell you what," said Fritz, rolling down his sleeves and fiddling with his cufflinks. "I see you've got a bump on your forehead. Now, you go to the doc and get that bump logged. I've already broken Ruhmer's nose and sent him to the infirmary. Just as a precaution. During interrogation the suspect Katzman attacked investigator Voronin and junior investigator Ruhmer, causing them bodily harm. Forced to defend themselves . . . and so on. Got it?"

"Got it," Andrei muttered, mechanically feeling at his bump. He looked around again. "But where is . . . he?" he asked with an effort.

"Ah, that gorilla Ruhmer went overboard again," Fritz said in annoyance, buttoning up his jacket. "Broke his arm, right here . . . We had to send him to the hospital."

PART III

THE
EDITOR

1

Four daily newspapers had been published in the City since time out of mind, but first of all Andrei picked up the fifth, which had put out its first issue about two weeks before the onset of the "Egyptian darkness." It was a small newspaper, only one double sheet—not so much a newspaper, more of a handbill, and this handbill was published by the Party of Radical Rebirth, which had broken away from the left wing of the Radical Party. Bearing the title *Under the Banner of Radical Rebirth*, the handbill was vitriolic, vituperative, and aggressive, but the people who put it out were always superbly well informed: as a general rule, they *knew* what was going on in the City as a whole and in the government in particular.

Andrei reviewed the headlines: "Friedrich Heiger warns: You have plunged the City into darkness, but we are on the alert"; "But really, Mr. Mayor, what did happen to the grain from the municipal granaries?"; "Forward shoulder to shoulder! Friedrich Heiger meets the leaders of the Peasants' Party"; "Steel plant workers say: String up the grain dealers!"; "That's the way, Fritz! We're with you! PRR housewives' rally"; "Baboons again?" A cartoon: the fat-assed mayor, enthroned on a heap of grain—presumably the same grain that had disappeared from the municipal granaries—handing out guns to lugubrious characters of criminal appearance. Caption: "Come on now, guys, you tell them where the grain went!"

Andrei dropped the handbill on his desk and scratched his chin. Where the hell did Fritz get all the money for the fines? God, how sick Andrei was of everything. He got up, walked across to the window, and glanced out. In the dense, damp darkness, only faintly backlit by the streetlamps, he heard carts rumbling past, gruff voices swearing, and the loud hacking of a smoker's cough. Every now and then a horse gave a high-pitched whinny. For the second day in a row the farmers were flocking into the City.

There was a knock at the door and his secretary came in with a bundle of proofs. Andrei peevishly waved her away. "Ubukata. Give them to Ubukata."

"Mr. Ubukata is with the censor," the secretary replied timidly.

"He's not going to spend the night in there," Andrei said irritably. "Give them to him when he comes back—"

"But the compositor—"

"That's all!" Andrei said rudely. "On your way."

The secretary withdrew. Andrei yawned, wincing at the pain in the back of his head, went back to the desk, and lit a cigarette. His head was splitting open and he had a foul taste in his mouth. And in general everything was murky, foul, and scummy. Egyptian darkness . . . Andrei heard the sound of shots somewhere in the distance—a faint crackling, like someone breaking dry branches. He winced again and picked up the *Experiment*, the government newspaper printed on eight double sheets:

MAYOR WARNS PRR: THE GOVERNMENT IS VIGILANT, THE GOVERNMENT SEES EVERYTHING!

THE EXPERIMENT IS THE EXPERIMENT. Our science correspondent considers solar phenomena.

DARK STREETS AND SHADY CHARACTERS. The municipality's political consultant comments on Friedrich Heiger's latest speech.

A JUST SENTENCE. Alois Tender sentenced to death for carrying a firearm.

"SOMETHING UP THERE'S BROKEN. IT'S OK, THEY'LL FIX IT," says master electrician Theodore U. Peters.

TAKE CARE OF THE BABOONS—THEY'RE GOOD FRIENDS OF YOURS! A resolution from the latest meeting of the Society for the Protection of Animals.

FARMERS ARE THE STAUNCH BACKBONE OF OUR SOCIETY. The
  mayor meets the leaders of the Peasants' Party.
THE MAGICIAN FROM THE LABORATORY ON THE EDGE OF THE
  ABYSS. Dispatches on the latest research into cultivating
  plants without light.
"FALLING STARS" AGAIN?
WE HAVE ARMORED VEHICLES. An interview with the comman-
  dant of police.
CHLORELLA: NOT A PALLIATIVE, BUT A PANACEA.
ARON WEBSTER LAUGHS, ARON WEBSTER SINGS! The celebrated
  comic's fifteenth charity concert . . .

Andrei raked all these sheets of paper together in a heap,
clumped them into a tight ball, and tossed it into the corner. All
that seemed unreal. What was real was the darkness, now hanging over the City for the twelfth day. Reality was the lines of
people in front of the bread stores; reality was that ominous rumbling of rickety wheels below the windows, the little red sparks
of crude hand-rolled cigarettes flaring up in the darkness, the dull,
metallic clanking under the tarpaulins in the heavy country carts.
Reality was the shooting, although so far no one really knew who
was shooting at whom . . . And the most hideous reality of all was
that blunt, hungover buzzing in his own poor head and the huge,
furry tongue that he wanted to spit out because it didn't fit into
his mouth. Fortified port and raw spirit—they must have been
out of their minds! It was fine for her, lounging under the blanket,
sleeping it off, but he had to hang around here . . . If only the
whole damn kit and caboodle would just fall apart, collapse . . .
I'm sick and tired of wasting my life away; they can stick all their
experiments, mentors, radical rebirths, mayors, farmers, and that
lousy stinking grain right up their ass . . . Some great experimenters they are—they can't even guarantee the sun will shine. And
today I've still got to go to the jail and take Izya his food par-
cel . . . How much time has he got left to do? Four months . . .
No, six. That bastard Fritz—if only all that energy could be put
to peaceful purposes! Now there's a man who never loses heart.

It's all grist to his mill. They flung him out of the Public Prosecutor's Office, so he set up a party, he's laying plans of some sort,
the fight against corruption, all hail the new rebirth—he's locked
horns with the mayor now. Right now it would be good to go to
City Hall, grab Mr. Mayor by his shock of noble gray hair, and
smash his face into the desk: "Where's the grain, you creep? Why
isn't the sun shining?" and then land a good kick on his ass—and
again, and again . . .

The door swung open and crashed into the wall, and little
Kensi came tearing in. Andrei could see immediately that he was
in a fury—eyes narrowed to slits, teeth bared, raven black thatch
standing up on end. Andrei groaned to himself. Now he'll drag
me into another fight with someone, he thought drearily.

Kensi walked over and slammed down a pile of proofs, savagely crisscrossed with red pencil, onto Andrei's desk. "I'm not
going to print this!" he declared. "It's sabotage."

"Now what's your problem?" Andrei asked. "Been scrapping
with the censor, have you?" He took the proofs and stared at
them without understanding anything, without even seeing anything apart from the red lines and squiggles.

"The pick of the letters—with one letter!" Kensi said furiously. "The editorial won't do—too provocative. The comments
on the mayor's speech won't do—too trenchant. The interview
with the farmers won't do—a sensitive issue, now's not the right
time . . . I can't work like this, Andrei, it's up to you. You have to
do something. Those bastards are killing the paper!"

"Hang on now," said Andrei, wincing. "Hang on, let's figure
this out . . ."

A large, rusty bolt was suddenly screwed into the back of his
head, right into the little depression at the base of his skull. He
closed his eyes and gave a quiet moan.

"Moaning won't do any good here!" said Kensi, slumping into
the chair for visitors and nervously lighting up a cigarette. "You
moan and I groan, but that bastard's the one who should be
moaning, not you and me."

The door swung open again. The fat censor tumbled into the room, sweating and breathing heavily, with his face covered in red blotches. He yelled stridently on his way in, "I refuse to work in such conditions! I'm not some little kid, Mr. Senior Editor. I'm a government employee! I don't sit here because I get any pleasure out of it, and I don't intend to tolerate obscene language from your colleagues! Or let them call me abusive names!"

"Why, you ought to be strangled, not just called names!" Kensi hissed from his chair, with his eyes glinting like a snake's. "You're a saboteur, not a government employee!"

The censor's face turned to stone, and he shifted his eyes from Kensi to Andrei and back again. Then he suddenly spoke in a very calm, solemn voice: "Mr. Senior Editor, I wish to register a formal protest!"

At that point Andrei finally pulled himself together with a horrendous effort, slapped his hand down on the desk, and said, "Will you please be quiet! Both of you! Please sit down, Mr. Paprikaki."

Mr. Paprikaki sat down facing Kensi. No longer looking at anyone, he tugged a large checkered handkerchief out of his pocket and started mopping at his sweaty neck, his cheeks, the back of his head, and his Adam's apple.

"Right, then . . ." said Andrei, leafing through the proofs. "We prepared a selection of ten letters—"

"It's a biased selection!" Mr. Paprikaki immediately declared.

Kensi hit the roof. "Yesterday alone we received nine hundred letters about bread!" he bellowed. "And the tone was the same in all of them, if not harsher!"

"Just a moment!" said Andrei, raising his voice and slapping his hand down on the desk again. "Let me speak! And if you don't want to, you can both go out in the corridor and carry on haggling there. Well now, Mr. Paprikaki, our selection is based on a thoroughgoing analysis of the letters received by our office. Mr. Ubukata is absolutely right. We are in possession of correspondence that is far harsher and far less restrained in tone. And furthermore, we have even included in the selection one letter that directly supports the government, although it was the only one of its kind in all the seven thousand letters that we—"

"I have no objection to that letter," the censor interrupted.

"I should think not," said Kensi. "You wrote it yourself."

"That's a lie!" the censor exclaimed in a squeal that screwed the rusty bolt back into that little depression under Andrei's skull.

"Well, if not you then someone else from your mob," said Kensi.

"You're the blackmailer!" the censor shouted, breaking out in red blotches again. This was a strange outburst, and for a while there was silence.

Andrei picked through the proofs. "So far we have worked with you reasonably well, Mr. Paprikaki," he said in a conciliatory tone. "I'm sure we just need to find a compromise of some kind now too."

The censor flapped his cheeks. "Mr. Voronin!" he said soulfully. "What does all this have to do with me? Mr. Ubukata is an intemperate individual, always looking for a chance to vent his spleen, and he doesn't care who he vents it on. But you must understand that I am acting strictly in accordance with my instructions. A rebellion is brewing in the City. The farmers are ready to launch a massacre at any moment. The police are unreliable. Do you really want blood? Conflagrations? I have children, I don't want any of that. And you don't want it either! At times like this the press should serve to alleviate the situation, not exacerbate it. That's the official position, and I must say that I entirely agree with it. But even if I didn't agree, I am obliged—it is my official responsibility . . . Only yesterday the censor of the *Express* was arrested for collusion, for aiding and abetting subversive elements."

"I understand you perfectly, Mr. Paprikaki," Andrei said with every last ounce of goodwill that he could muster. "But after all, you must see that the selection is perfectly moderate. And you must understand that precisely because these are such difficult times, we cannot act as the government's yes-men. Precisely because there is a danger of insurgency by the déclassé elements and the farmers, we must do everything we can to bring the government to its senses. We are performing our duty, Mr. Paprikaki."

"I won't sign the selection," Paprikaki said in a quiet voice.

Kensi swore in a whisper.

"We shall be forced to put the paper out without any sanction from you," said Andrei.

"Oh, very good," Paprikaki said wearily. "Very nice. Absolutely charming. The paper will be fined, I shall be arrested. The edition will be impounded. And you'll be arrested too."

Andrei picked up the broadsheet *Under the Banner of Radical Rebirth* and waved it under the censor's nose. "And why don't they arrest Fritz Heiger?" he asked. "How many censors of this little paper have been arrested?"

"I don't know," Paprikaki said in quiet despair. "What business is that of mine? They'll get around to arresting Heiger too—he certainly has it coming."

"Kensi," said Andrei. "How much do we have in the kitty? Will it cover the fine?"

"We'll take up a collection among the staff," Kensi said briskly, getting to his feet. "I'll tell the compositor to start typesetting the edition. We'll scrape through somehow." Kensi set off toward the door.

The censor sighed and blew his nose as he watched him go. "You've got no heart," he muttered. "And no brains either. Greenhorns . . ."

Kensi stopped in the doorway. "Andrei," he said. "If I were you, I'd go to City Hall and try pulling all the levers I can."

"What levers?" Andrei inquired morosely.

Kensi immediately came back to the desk. "Go to the deputy political consultant. After all, he's Russian too. You used to drink vodka with him."

"And I used to smash his face too," Andrei said cheerlessly.

"That's OK, he doesn't bear grudges," said Kensi, "and then, I know for certain that he's on the take."

"Who isn't on the take in City Hall?" said Andrei. "That's not the problem, is it?" he sighed. "OK, I'll go. Maybe I'll find out something . . . But what are we going to do about Paprikaki? He'll just go running off and call in—you will, won't you?"

"Yes," Paprikaki agreed without any great enthusiasm.

"I'll tie him up right now and dump him behind the safe!" said Kensi, his teeth glinting in a grin of delight.

"Don't get carried away, now," said Andrei. "Tying him up, dumping him . . . Just lock him in the archive room, there's no phone in there."

"That would be coercion," Paprikaki remarked in a dignified voice.

"And if they arrest you, won't that be coercion?"

"Well, I'm not actually objecting!" said Paprikaki. "It was just a comment."

"Go on, Andrei, go on," Kensi said impatiently. "I'll see to everything here while you're gone, don't worry."

Andrei got up with a grunt, shambled over to the coat stand, dragging his feet, and took his raincoat. His beret had disappeared, and he searched for it on the floor, among the galoshes forgotten by visitors in the good old days, but failed to find it, swore abruptly, and walked out into the front office. The weedy secretary cast a rapid glance at him with her frightened gray eyes. Scraggy little slut. What was it that her name was?

"I'm going to City Hall," he said morosely.

Out in the newsroom everything seemed to be carrying on as usual. People yelling on the phone, people perching on the edges of desks writing something, people examining damp photographs and drinking coffee, office boys dashing about with files and documents. The whole area was thick with smoke and littered with trash, and the head of the literary section, a phenomenal ass in a gold pince-nez, a former draftsman from some quasi-state or other like Andorra, was holding forth pompously to a mournful-looking author: "There are places where you've tried too hard, places where you lack a sense of measure, where the material has proved too powerful and volatile for you . . ."

A good kick right on the ass, and again, and again, Andrei thought as he walked by. He suddenly recalled how dear to his heart all this had been only a very short time ago, how new and fascinating! How challenging, necessary, and important it had all seemed . . . "Boss, just a moment," shouted Denny Lee, the head of the letters department, all set to dash after him, but Andrei just waved him away without even looking back. Right on the ass, and again, and again . . .

Once outside the door, he stopped and turned up the collar of his raincoat. Carts were still rumbling along the street—and all in the same direction, toward the center of the City, toward City Hall. Andrei thrust his hands as deep into his pockets as he could and set off in the same direction, slouching over. About two minutes later he noticed he was walking along beside a monstrously huge cart with wheels the height of a man. The cart was being drawn along by two gigantic cart horses that were obviously tired after a long journey. He couldn't see the load in the cart behind the high wooden sides, but he did have a good view of the driver at the front—or, rather, not so much the driver as his colossal tarpaulin raincoat with a three-cornered hood. All Andrei could make out of the driver himself was a beard jutting forward, and through the creaking of the wheels and clatter of hooves, he could hear the driver making incomprehensible sounds of some kind: he was either urging on his horses or releasing excess gas in his simpleminded country manner.

He's going into the City too, thought Andrei. What for? What do they all want here? They won't get any bread here, and they don't need bread anyway—they've got bread. They've got everything, in fact, not like us city folks. They've even got guns. Do they really want to start a massacre? Makhno's peasant anarchists . . . Maybe they do. Only what will they get out of it? A chance to pillage the apartments? I don't understand a thing.

He remembered the interview with the farmers, and how disappointed Kensi had been with it, even though he did it himself, questioning almost fifty peasants on the square in front of City Hall. "What the people think, that's what we're for"; "Well, I had a bellyful, you know, sitting out there in the swamps—why don't I take a trip, I thought . . ."; "You said it, mister, why *are* the people all piling in, what for? We're as surprised as anyone . . ."; "Well, I see everyone's going into the City. So I came into the City. I'm as good as the rest, ain't I?"; "The machine gun? How could I manage without the machine gun? In our parts you can't set one foot in front of the other without a machine gun . . ."; "I come out to milk the cows this morning and I see they're all going. Syomka Kostylin's going, Jacques-François is going, that . . . what's-his-name . . . ah, darn it, I'm always forgetting what he's called, lives out beyond Louse Head Hill . . . He's going too! I ask, where're you going, guys? Look here, they say, there's been no sun for seven days, we ought to pay the City a visit . . ."; "Well, you ask the bosses that. The bosses know everything"; "They said, didn't they, they were going to give us automatic tractors! So we could sit at home, scratching our bellies, and it would do the work for us . . . More than two years now they've been promising . . ."

Evasive, vague, unclear. Ominous. Either they were simply being cunning, or they were all being whisked together in a heap by some kind of instinct, or maybe some kind of secret, well-camouflaged organization . . . So what was it . . . peasant insurrection, like the Jacquerie? Maybe like the Tambov partisan army? In some ways he could understand them: there hadn't been any sun for twelve days now, the harvest was going to ruin, no one knew what was going to happen. They'd been blown off their warm, comfortable perches . . .

Andrei passed a short, quiet line of people waiting outside a meat market, then another line outside a bakery. Most of the people standing there were women, and for some reason many of them had white armbands on their sleeves. Of course, Andrei immediately thought of the events of Saint Bartholomew's Eve—then it occurred to him that it was daytime now, not nighttime; it was one o'clock in the afternoon, but the stores were still closed. Three policemen were standing bunched together on a corner, below the neon sign of the Quisisana Night Café. They looked strange somehow—uncertain, was that it? Andrei slowed down, listening.

"So now what do we do, will they order us in to fight them? Why, there's twice as many of them."

"We'll just go and report: there's no way through there and that's it."

"And he'll say, 'How come there's no way through? You're the police.'"

"The police—so what? We're the police, and they're the militia . . ."

So there's some kind of militia now, Andrei thought as he walked on. I don't know any militia . . . He passed another line of people and turned onto Main Street. Up ahead he could already see the bright mercury lamps of Central Square, its wide-open space completely filled with something gray that was stirring about, enveloped in steam or smoke, but just then he was stopped.

A big, strapping young man—or, rather, a youth, an over-grown juvenile, wearing a flat peaked cap pulled down right over his eyes, blocked the way and asked in a low voice, "Where are you going, sir?"

The youth held his hands at his sides, with white armbands on both sleeves, and several other men, all very different but also with white armbands, were standing by the wall behind him.

Out of the corner of his eye Andrei noticed that the country-man in the tarpaulin raincoat drove straight on unhindered in his unwieldy cart.

"I'm going to City Hall," Andrei said when he was forced to stop. "What's the problem?"

"To City Hall?" the youth repeated loudly, glancing back over his shoulder at his comrades. Two other men detached them-selves from the wall and walked up to Andrei.

"Do you mind if I ask what you're going to City Hall for?" inquired a stocky man with unshaven cheeks, wearing greasy overalls and a helmet with the letters *G* and *M* on it. He had a vigorous, muscular face with cold, piercing eyes.

"Who are you?" asked Andrei, feeling in his pocket for the brass kitchen pestle he had been carrying for four days now because the times were so uncertain.

"We're the voluntary militia," the stocky man replied. "What business have you got in City Hall? Who are you?"

"I'm the senior editor of the *City Gazette*," Andrei said angrily, clutching the pestle tightly in his hand. He didn't like the way the juvenile approached him from the left while he was speaking and the third volunteer militiaman, another young guy who was obviously strong too, wheezed into his ear from the right. "I'm going to City Hall to protest against the actions of the censor."

"Ah," the stocky man said in an indefinite tone of voice. "I see. Only why go to City Hall? You could arrest the censor and put out your newspaper, no bother."

Andrei decided to act brazenly for the time being. "Don't you go telling me what to do," he said. "We've already arrested the censor without any advice from you. Anyway, just let me through."

"A representative of the press . . ." growled the one who was wheezing in his right ear.

"Why not? Let him go in," the youth on Andrei's left said condescendingly.

"Yes," said the stocky man. "Let him go in. Only don't let him try to blame us afterward . . . Have you got a gun?"

"No," said Andrei.

"That's a mistake," said the stocky man, stepping aside. "Go on through."

Andrei walked through. Behind him he heard the stocky man say in a high, squeaky voice, "Jasmine is a pretty little flower! And it smells very good too . . ." and the militiamen laughed. Andrei knew that little rhyme, and he felt an angry urge to turn back, but he only lengthened his stride.

There were quite a lot of people on Main Street. Most of them were sticking close to the walls or standing bunched together in courtyard entrances, and they all had white armbands. A few were loitering in the middle of the road, approaching the farmers driving past and telling them something before the farmers drove on. The stores were all closed, but there were no lines in front of them. Outside one bakery an elderly militiaman with a knotty walking stick was trying to get through to an old woman who was standing on her own: "I assure you quite definitely, madam. The stores will not open today. I myself am the owner of a grocery store, madam—I know what I'm talking about." But the old biddy replied in a screechy voice to the effect that she would die right here on these steps before she gave up her place in line . . .

Trying hard to smother his mounting sense of alarm and a strange feeling that everything around him was somehow unreal—it was all like in a movie—Andrei reached the square. Where the mouth of Main Street opened out onto the square, it was choked with carts great and small, farm wagons and drays. The air stank of horse sweat and fresh dung, and horses of every shape and size swung their heads to and fro, while the sons of the swamps shouted to each other in deep, loud voices and crude hand-rolled cigarettes glimmered on all sides. Andrei caught the smell of smoke—somewhere nearby they were lighting a campfire. A fat man with a mustache and a cowboy hat came out of an archway, buttoning up his fly as he walked, and almost ran into Andrei. The man swore good-naturedly and started picking his way between the carts, calling out in a barking voice to someone named Sidor: "Come this way, Sidor! Into the yard, you can do it there! Only watch your step, don't put your foot in it!"

Biting on his lip, Andrei walked on. At the very entrance to the square the carts were already standing on the sidewalk. Many of the horses had been unharnessed and hobbled, and they were shuffling around, sniffing dejectedly at the asphalt. In the carts people were sleeping, smoking, and eating—Andrei could hear the appetizing sounds of liquid glugging and lips smacking. He climbed up onto the porch of a building and looked across the vast camp. It was only about fifty paces to City Hall, but it was a maze. Campfires crackled and smoked, and the smoke, tinted gray-blue by the mercury lamps, drifted over the covered wagons and massive carts and was drawn into Main Street, as if into some gigantic chimney. Some motherfucker buzzed as it settled on Andrei's neck and bit, like a pin being thrust into his skin. With a feeling of loathing Andrei swatted something large and prickly that crunched juicily under his palm. They've dragged all the damned bugs in with them from the swamps, he thought angrily, catching a distinct whiff of ammonia coming from under the building's half-open front door. Jumping down onto the sidewalk, he set off decisively into the maze of horses, stepping in something soft and crumbly in his first few strides.

The ponderous, rounded form of City Hall towered up over the square like a five-story bastion. Most of the windows were dark, with only a few lit up, and the elevator shafts set on the outside of the walls glowed a dim yellow. The farmers' camp surrounded the building in a ring, and between the carts and City Hall there was an empty space, illuminated by bright streetlamps on fancy cast-iron columns. Farmers, almost all of them armed, were jostling together under the streetlamps, and at the entrance to City Hall a line of policemen stood facing them, their badges of rank indicating that they were mostly sergeants and officers.

Andrei was already pushing his way through the armed crowd when someone called his name. He stopped and turned his head.

"Here I am, over this way!" barked a familiar voice, and Andrei finally spotted Uncle Yura.

Uncle Yura was waddling toward him, already holding out his hand to be shaken—still in the same old tunic, with his fore-and-aft cap cocked to one side, and the machine gun that Andrei knew so well hanging on a broad strap over his shoulder.

"Howdy-do, Andriukha, you old townie!" he exclaimed, slapping his rough hand loudly into Andrei's palm. "Here I've been looking for you everywhere; there's a ruckus on, I think, no way our Andriukha's going to miss that! He's a spunky fellow, I think, he's got to be hanging around here somewhere."

Uncle Yura was pretty plastered. He tugged the machine gun off his shoulder, leaned his armpit on the barrel like a crutch, and carried on talking with the same vehement passion. "I go this way, I go that way—and still no Andriukha. Son of a bitch, I think, what the hell's going on? That blond-haired Fritz of yours—he's here. Rubbing shoulders with the country folk, making speeches . . . But I can't find you anywhere."

"Hang on, Uncle Yura," said Andrei. "What did you come here for?"

"To demand my rights!" Uncle Yura chuckled, his beard splaying out like a twig broom. "That's what I came here for, and only for that—but it doesn't look like we're going to get anywhere here." He spat and scraped the gobbet into the ground with his immense boot. "The people are lousy vermin. They don't know themselves what they came here for. Whether they came to ask or they came to demand, or maybe neither one thing nor the other, just because they missed the big-city life—we'll camp here for a while, shit all over your City, and then go back home. The people are shit. Look . . ." He swung around and waved to someone. "For instance, take Stas Kowalski, my little friend here . . . Stas! Stas, fuck it . . . Come over here!"

Stas came over—a skinny, round-shouldered man with mournfully dangling ends to his mustache and a sparse head of hair. He gave off a devastating reek of home brew and only stayed on his feet by instinctive reflex response, but every now and then he defiantly flung up his head, grabbed at the strange-looking short-barreled machine gun hanging around his neck, raised his eyelids with an immense effort, and glanced around menacingly.

"This here is Stas," Uncle Yura went on. "Stas fought in the war, he did—tell him! No, tell him: Did you fight or didn't you?"

Uncle Yura demanded, fervently grasping Stas around the shoulders and swaying in time with him.

"Heh! Ho!" Stas responded, straining every fiber to demonstrate that he did fight, that he fought real hard, that no words could express how hard he fought.

"He's drunk right now," Uncle Yura explained. "He can't stand it when there's no sun . . . Where was I? Right! You ask this fool what he's doing hanging around here . . . There are guns. There are boys with fire in their belly. What more do you need, I ask you?"

"Hang on," said Andrei. "What is it you want?"

"That's what I'm telling you!" Uncle Yura said intensely, letting go of Stas, who immediately drifted off to one side, following a long, gentle curve. "What I'm trying to get through to you! Hammer the bastards just once, that's all! They haven't got any machine guns! We'll trample them with our boots, smother them under our caps." He abruptly stopped talking and slung his machine gun back over his shoulder: "Let's go."

"Where to?"

"We'll go have a drink. We've got to drink this damned nonsense to hell and get out of here, go back home. What's the point in wasting time? I've got potatoes rotting back there . . . Let's go."

"No, Uncle Yura," Andrei said in an apologetic voice. "I can't right now. I've got to go into City Hall."

"Into City Hall? Let's go! Stas! Stas, fuck you . . ."

"Hang on there, Uncle Yura! You're . . . you know . . . they won't let you in."

"*Mmme?*" Uncle Yura roared with his eyes glittering. "Right, let's go! We'll see who's not going to let me in. Stas!"

He put his arm around Andrei's shoulder and dragged him across the empty, brightly lit space, straight toward the line of policemen.

"Understand this," he muttered ardently straight into Andrei's ear as Andrei tried to resist. "I'm afraid, OK? I haven't told anyone, but I'll tell you. Terrified! What if the fire never flares up again, eh? They've dragged us here and dumped us . . . No, let them explain, let them tell us the truth, the bastards—we can't live like this. I've stopped sleeping, got it? That never happened to me even at the front . . . You think I'm drunk? No damned way am I drunk—I've got fear running through my veins."

Andrei felt a shiver run down his spine at this delirious muttering. He stopped about five steps from the police line, feeling as if everyone in the square had gone silent and all of them, policemen and farmers, were watching him. Trying hard to sound convincing, he declared, "I'll tell you what, Uncle Yura. I'll just go in for a minute and settle one question to do with my paper, and you wait for me here. Then we'll go to my place and have a proper talk about everything."

Uncle Yura shook his beard furiously. "No, I'm with you. There's a certain question I have to settle too."

"But they won't let you in. And because of you they won't let me in!"

"Come on, let's go . . . Let's go . . ." Uncle Yura repeated. "What does that mean—they won't let us in? Why not? We'll be quiet . . . and dignified."

They were already right beside the line, and a stout police captain in a natty uniform, with an unbuttoned holster on the left side of his belt, stepped toward them and inquired drily, "Where are you going, gentlemen?"

"I am the senior editor of the *City Gazette*," said Andrei, furtively shoving away Uncle Yura so that he wouldn't embrace him. "I have to see the deputy political consultant."

"May I see your credentials?" A palm clad in kidskin was extended toward Andrei.

Andrei took out his editor's pass, handed it to the captain, and squinted at Uncle Yura. To his surprise, Uncle Yura was now standing there calmly, sniffing and occasionally adjusting the strap of his machine gun, although there was absolutely no need for that. His eyes, which didn't look drunk at all, ran along the police line in casual curiosity.

"You can go through," the captain said politely, handing back the pass. "Although I should tell you . . ." But without finishing what he was saying, he turned to Uncle Yura. "And you?"

"He's with me," Andrei said hastily. "A representative, so to speak . . . er . . . from the farmers."

"Credentials!"

"What kind of credentials can a peasant have?" Uncle Yura asked bitterly.

"I can't let you in without credentials."

"Why can't I go in without credentials?" asked Uncle Yura, totally distressed now. "Without some lousy piece of paper, I'm not even a human being, is that it?"

Someone breathed hotly on the back of Andrei's neck. It was Stas Kowalski, still twitching belligerently and swaying about as he brought up the rear. Several more men were feebly straggling across the brightly lit space, as if reluctant to cross it.

"Gentlemen, gentlemen, don't group together!" the captain said nervously. "You go through, sir!" he shouted angrily at Andrei. "Gentlemen, go back. Congregating is forbidden!"

"So, if I haven't got a piece of paper with scribble on it," Uncle Yura lamented despondently, "that means I won't be let through anywhere at all."

"Smash him in the face!" Stas suggested from behind in a surprisingly clear voice.

The captain grabbed Andrei by the sleeve of his raincoat and jerked, so that Andrei immediately found himself behind the backs of the police line. The line quickly closed up, blocking out the farmers who had crowded together in front of the captain, and without waiting to see how events developed, Andrei strode quickly toward the gloomy, feebly lit portal. He heard a buzz of voices behind him.

"Give them grain, give them meat, but if we want to get in anywhere . . ."

"If you please, do not congregate! I have orders to arrest . . ."

"Why won't you let our representative through, eh?"

"The sun! The sun, you bastards, when are you going to light it again?"

"Gentlemen, gentlemen! Now what has that got to do with me?"

More police came spilling down the snow-white marble steps toward Andrei, with their metal boot tips clattering. They were armed with rifles with bayonets fixed. A tense voice ordered, "Grenades at the ready!" Andrei reached the top of the steps and looked back. Men were scattered across the brightly lit space now. Farmers, some moving slowly and some at a run, were advancing from their camp toward the large black throng that was gathering.

With an effort, Andrei pulled open the door—tall and heavy, bound in copper—and walked into the vestibule. It was dark in here too, and the air had the distinctive harsh smell of a barracks. Policemen were sleeping jammed up against each other, covered with their greatcoats, in the luxurious armchairs, on the sofas, and right there on the floor. Indistinct figures of some kind hovered on the feebly lit gallery that ran around three sides of the vestibule below the ceiling. Andrei couldn't make out if they had guns or not.

He ran up the soft carpet runner to the second floor, where the press office was, and set off along the broad corridor. He suddenly felt overwhelmed by doubt. There was something too quiet about this huge building today. Usually there were scads of people hanging around here, typewriters clacking, telephones jangling, the air was filled with the buzz of conversation and imperious shouting, but now there was none of that. Some of the offices were wide open, with darkness inside, and even in the corridor only every fourth lamp was lit.

His premonition hadn't deceived him: the political consultant's office was locked, and two strangers were sitting in the deputy's office, wearing identical gray coats, buttoned right up to the chin, and identical bowler hats, tipped forward over their eyes.

"Excuse me," Andrei said angrily. "Where can I find the deputy political consultant?

The heads in the bowler hats lazily turned in his direction. "What do you want him for?" asked the shorter of the two men.

Suddenly this man's face didn't seem so very unfamiliar, and neither did his voice. And suddenly it seemed strange and worrying that this man was here. He had no business being here . . . Andrei stooped down and, trying to speak curtly and resolutely, explained who he was and what he wanted.

"Well, come in, will you?" said the half-familiar man. "Why are you standing in the door like that?"

Andrei stepped inside and looked around, but he didn't see anything; that smoothly shaved eunuch's face was hovering in front of his eyes. Where have I seen him before? An unsavory kind of character . . . and dangerous . . . I shouldn't have come in here, I'm just wasting time.

The little man in the bowler hat was studying him intently too. It was quiet. The tall windows were covered with heavy drapes, and the noise from outside barely even reached them in here. The small man in the bowler hat suddenly jumped to his feet and moved right up close to Andrei. His little gray eyes, with almost no lashes, blinked repeatedly, and a massive, gristly Adam's apple skipped up from the top button of his coat all the way to his chin and slid back down again.

"Senior editor?" said the little man, and at that moment Andrei finally recognized him, and he felt his legs turn numb under him as he realized with paralyzing anguish that he had been recognized too.

The eunuch's face grinned, revealing sparse, bad teeth, the little man crouched down, and Andrei felt a vicious pain in his belly, as if all his insides had burst, and through the nauseous haze in his eyes he suddenly saw the waxed floor . . . Run, run . . . A display of fireworks flared up in his brain, and the dark, distant ceiling, cobwebbed with cracks, started swaying and slowly revolving high above him . . . White-hot spikes thrust out of the suffocating darkness that had descended on him and jabbed into his ribs . . . He'll kill me . . . he's going to kill me! Andrei's head suddenly swelled up and jammed itself into a narrow, stinking crack, skinning his ears, and a thunderous voice kept repeating languidly, "Cool it, Tailbone, cool it, not all at once . . ." Andrei shouted out with all his might, a thick, warm slush filled his mouth, and he choked on it and puked.

There was no one in the room. The immense drapes had been pulled back, the window was open, there was a draft of damp, cold air, and he could hear a distant roaring. Andrei struggled up onto all fours and crept along the wall. Toward the door. He had to get out of here . . .

In the corridor Andrei puked again. He lay on the floor for a while in blank, mindless exhaustion, then tried to get up onto his feet. I'm in a bad way, he thought. A really bad way. He sat down and felt at his face, and it was damp and sticky, then he discovered that he could only see with one eye. His ribs hurt and it was hard to breathe. His jaws hurt, and his lower belly was cramped in appalling, unbearable agony. That bastard, Tailbone. He's maimed me . . . Andrei burst into tears. He sat on the floor in the empty corridor, leaning back against the gilded flourishes, and cried. He simply couldn't help himself. Weeping, he tugged up the hem of his raincoat with a struggle and reached in under his trouser belt. The pain was appalling, but not down there, higher up. His entire belly hurt. His shorts were wet.

Someone came running out of the depths of the corridor with his boots thudding heavily and stopped, standing over him. Some policeman—sweaty and red faced, with no cap and bewildered eyes. He stood there for a few seconds as if uncertain what to do, then suddenly went dashing on, and a second policeman came running out of the depths of the corridor, tearing off his tunic as he ran.

And then Andrei realized there was a roaring, multitudinous hubbub coming from the same direction they'd come from. He got up with a struggle and dragged himself toward that hubbub, clinging to the wall, still sobbing, feeling in horror at his face and repeatedly stopping to stand for a while, hunching over and clutching his belly.

He reached the stairway and grabbed at the slippery marble banister. Down below a thick human mush was heaving about in the immense vestibule. It was impossible to understand what was happening. Searchlights installed along the gallery illuminated the mush with a cold, blinding light, and Andrei glimpsed beards of various shapes and sizes, uniform caps, the gold laces of police shoulder knots, fixed bayonets, hands with splayed fingers and pale bald patches, and from all this a warm, moist stench rose up toward the ceiling.

Andrei closed his eyes in order not to see any of it and started moving down, feeling his way, hand over hand, along the banister, advancing any way he could—backward, sideways—not really understanding why he was doing this. He stopped several times to catch his breath and groan, opened his eyes and looked down, and the sight made his agony unbearable again; he squeezed his eyes shut and started moving again, hand over hand along the banister. At the bottom of the stairs his arms finally gave out and he fell and tumbled down the last few steps onto a marble landing decorated with immense bronze spittoons. Through the haze and hubbub he suddenly heard a hoarse, strident roar: "Lookee here, it's Andriukha! Boys, they're killing our people up there!" Opening his eyes, Andrei saw Uncle Yura only a short distance away, mussed and disheveled, still in his dilapidated tunic, with his eyes goggling wildly and his beard splayed out, and Andrei saw Uncle Yura raise his machine gun in his outstretched hands, still roaring like a bull, and fire a long burst along the gallery, at the searchlights, at both tiers of windows in the broad hall of the vestibule . . .

After that there were fragmentary impressions, because consciousness ebbed and flowed together with the ebb and flow of the pain and the nausea. First he found himself at the center of the vestibule and discovered that he was stubbornly crawling on all fours toward the wide-open door in the distance, clambering over motionless bodies, with his hands skidding in something wet and cold. Someone was moaning monotonously right beside him, intoning, "Oh God, oh God, God . . ." The carpet was thickly strewn with splinters of glass, spent cartridges, and lumps of plaster. Some terrible men with blazing torches in their hands burst in through the open door and ran straight toward him . . .

Then he came to outside, in the portal. He was sitting there with his legs spread wide, propping himself up with his palms pressed against the cold stone, and there was a rifle with no bolt lying on his knees. He could smell fresh smoke, somewhere on the edge of consciousness a machine gun was roaring, and horses were squealing frantically, and he kept monotonously repeating out loud, hammering the words into his own head: "They'll trample me to death here, they're bound to trample me to death . . ."

But they didn't trample him. He came to again in the road, at one side of the steps. He was pressing his cheek against the rough granite, a mercury lamp was glowing brightly above his head, the rifle was gone, and it felt as if he didn't have a body, as if he were suspended in the air with his cheek pressed against the granite, and some kind of grotesque tragedy was being played out on the square in front of him, as if it were a stage.

He saw an armored car hurtling along, clanking and roaring, following the line of streetlamps bordering the square and the ring of interlocked carts and wagons, swinging its machine gun turret from side to side, belching out fire and sending glittering trails spurting right across the square, and there was a horse galloping along in front of the armored car with its head thrown back, dragging its snapped traces. Then suddenly a covered wagon trundled out from among the thick mass of carts, right across the armored car's path; the horse jerked aside wildly, crashing into a streetlamp, the armored car braked sharply and skidded, and at that moment a tall man in black ran out into the open space, swung his arm, and fell full length on the asphalt. There was a flash of flame under the armored car, a low, rumbling blast, and the entire metal bulk subsided heavily to the rear. The man in black was running again. He rounded the armored car, thrust something into the driver's observation port, and jumped aside, and then Andrei saw that it was Fritz Heiger, and the observation port was lit up from the inside; there was a loud blast inside the armored car and a long, smoky tongue of flame flew out of the observation port. Moving on half-bent legs, with his long arms stretched right down to the ground, Fritz sidled around the vehicle like a crab, and then the armored door opened and a shaggy bale of something enveloped in flames tumbled out onto the asphalt and started rolling about, howling piercingly and scattering sparks . . .

After that Andrei blacked out and the curtain came down again; then there were savage voices and shrieks that didn't sound human, and the tramping of a multitude of feet. The burning armored car gave off a stink of red-hot iron and gasoline. Fritz Heiger, surrounded by a crowd of men with white armbands on their sleeves and towering head and shoulders above them, was shouting out commands, gesturing abruptly in various directions with his long arms, with his face and mussed blond hair covered in soot. Other men with white armbands, who had clustered around the streetlamps in front of the entrance to City Hall, climbed up the streetlamps for some reason and lowered long ropes that dangled in the wind. Someone was dragged down the steps, struggling and jerking his legs about, someone squealed in a high womanish voice that left Andrei's ears blocked, and suddenly the steps were completely covered with people. Andrei glimpsed black-bearded faces and heard the clatter of gun bolts. The squealing stopped and a dark body crept upward along the column of the streetlamp, squirming and shuddering convulsively. Shots were fired out of the crowd, the jerking legs went limp, stretching out full length, and the dark body started slowly twisting and turning in the air.

And afterward Andrei was shaken awake by a terrible jolting. His head was bobbing about on coarse, smelly knots of sackcloth;

he was being driven away, being taken somewhere, and a familiar, frenzied voice was shouting, "Gee-up now! Gee-up there, you damned whore! Move on!" And right there in front of him, against the backdrop of the black sky, City Hall was burning. Hot tongues of flame burst out of windows, scattering sparks into the darkness, and he saw long, stretched bodies dangling from the streetlamps, swaying to and fro.

2

Washed and changed, with a bandage over his right eye, Andrei was reclining in an armchair, watching morosely as Uncle Yura and Stas Kowalski, with his head also swathed in bandages, greedily slurped down some kind of steaming slop, spooning it straight from the saucepan. Selma was sitting beside him, sighing tearfully, and she kept trying to take hold of his hand. Her hair was mussed, the mascara from her lashes was smeared across her cheeks, and her face was puffy and covered with hot, red blotches. And her frivolous, transparent little robe looked freakish on her, with its front soaked in soapy water.

". . . He was going to finish you off," Stas explained, carrying on slurping. "Working you over carefully, you know, dragging it out as long as possible. I know that trick; the state's blue hussars worked me over the same way too. Only I got the full treatment, you see—they'd already started stamping on me and then, thanks be to God, it turned out that I was the wrong one; it was someone else they wanted."

"They broke your nose—that's nothing," Uncle Yura confirmed. "The nose isn't the most important thing . . . and a broken one will do. And the rib . . ." He waved the hand holding his spoon. "I've broken so many of them ribs. The important thing is, your innards are in good shape: liver, spleen, kidneys . . ."

Selma sighed fitfully and tried once again to take hold of Andrei's hand. He looked at her and said, "Stop bawling. Go and get changed, and anyway . . ."

She obediently got up and went into the other room. Andrei felt around in his mouth with his tongue, came across something hard, and pushed it out onto his finger.

"They broke out a filling," he said.

"Oh really?" said Uncle Yura, surprised.

Andrei showed him. Uncle Yura inspected it and shook his head. Stas shook his head too and said, "Unusual thing, that. Only when I was recuperating afterward, for instance—I spent three months in bed, you know—it was mostly teeth I spat out. My woman steamed my ribs every day. She died later, but here I am, still alive. And as right as rain."

"Three months!" Uncle Yura said contemptuously. "After they blew my backside off at Yelnya, I was knocking around the hospitals for half a year. It's a terrible thing, brother, to have your buttock ripped off. You see, all the major blood vessels are interwoven in the buttock. And that slab of iron sliced it right off me at a tangent! Boys, I asked, what is this, where's my backside got to? And would you believe it, my trousers were ripped off too, right down to the tops of my boots, as if I never had any trousers... There was something left in my boots, but above that... well, nothing!" He licked his spoon. "Fedka Cheparev got his head ripped off that time," he announced. "Ripped off by the very same slab."

Stas licked his spoon too, and they sat there for a while in silence, looking into the saucepan. Then Stas delicately cleared his throat and lowered his spoon into the steam again. Uncle Yura followed his example.

Selma came back. Andrei glanced at her and turned his eyes away. The fool had dolled herself up. Stuck on her gigantic earrings and a dress with a plunging neckline, and painted herself like whore again... She was a whore... He couldn't look at her—to hell with her anyway. First that shameful scene in the hallway, then the shameful scene in the bathroom when she wailed out loud as she pulled off his urine-soaked shorts, and he looked at the blue-black patches on his belly and his sides and wept again—out of pity for himself and sheer helplessness... And of course she was drunk, drunk again, every single day she was drunk, and now, while she was getting changed, she was sure to have taken a swig from the bottle...

"That doctor..." Uncle Yura said pensively. "The bald one who was just here—where have I seen him before?"

"You could easily have seen him here," said Selma, smiling seductively. "He lives in the next entrance. What job is he doing now, Andrei?"

"He's a roofer," Andrei said dismally.

She cheerfully slept with this bald doctor, not giving a damn for the consequences. The whole building knew it. He didn't make any particular effort to conceal it. In fact, no one tried to conceal it.

"How come he's a roofer?" Stas asked in amazement, and the spoon stopped halfway to his mouth.

"He just is," said Andrei. "Covers roofs, covers women." He got up with a groan, reached into the chest of drawers, and took out some cigarettes. Two packs were missing again.

"Never mind the women," Stas muttered, dumbfounded. "But why roofs? What if he falls off? He's a doctor."

"They're always thinking up something new in the City," Uncle Yura said venomously. He was about to tuck the spoon into the top of his boot, but remembered just in time and put it on the table. "It's like the way it was in Timofeevka just after the war: they sent a Georgian to be the chairman of this collective farm, a former political commissar—"

The phone rang. Selma picked it up. "Yes," she said. "Uh-huh, uh-huh . . . No, he's not well, he can't come—"

"Give the phone here," said Andrei.

"It's the paper," Selma said in a whisper, putting her hand over the mouthpiece

Andrei reached out his hand. "Give me the phone!" he repeated, raising his voice. "And don't make a habit of speaking for someone else!"

Selma gave him the phone and grabbed the pack of cigarettes. Her hands were trembling—and so were her lips.

"Voronin here," said Andrei.

"Andrei?" It was Kensi. "Where did you disappear to? I've been searching for you everywhere. What are we going to do? There's a fascist coup in the City."

"Why fascist?" Andrei asked, stunned.

"Will you come into the office? Or are you really unwell?"

"I'll come, of course I'll come," said Andrei. "You just explain—"

"We have lists," Kensi said hurriedly. "Special correspondents and all the rest of it . . . Archives . . ."

"I get it," said Andrei. "Only why do you think the coup's fascist?"

"I don't think so, I know so," Kensi said impatiently.

Andrei gritted his teeth and grunted. "Wait," he said irritably. "Don't be so hasty . . ." He tried feverishly to grasp the situation. "OK, you get everything ready, I'll leave right now."

"Yes, come on," said Kensi. "Only be careful on the streets."

Andrei hung up and turned toward the farmers. "Guys," he said, "I've got to go. Will you give me a ride to the office?"

"Sure we'll give you a ride." Uncle Yura responded. He was already getting up from the table, gluing together a roll-up on the way. "Come on, Stas, no more sitting around here. The pair of us are sitting around here and they're taking power, aren't they?"

"Yes," Stas agreed regretfully, also getting up. "It's all turning out kind of stupid. Seems like we've taken off the head, hanged every one of them, and there's still damn-all sign of the sun. Screw it all, where did I stick that little shooter of mine?"

He rummaged in all the corners, searching for his ugly automatic rifle, Uncle Yura puffed on his roll-up as he lazily pulled a tattered wadded jacket over his army tunic, and Andrei was about to get a coat too, but he ran into Selma, who was standing there, blocking his way, looking very pale and very determined. "I'm going with you!" she declared in the same special, high, brazen voice that she used to start a quarrel.

"Let me through," said Andrei, trying to move her out of the way with his good arm.

"I won't let you go anywhere," said Selma. "Either you take me with you or you stay at home!"

"Get out of the way," Andrei bellowed, flying off the handle. "You're the very last thing we need there, you fool!"

"I. Won't. Let. You. Out!" Selma said spitefully.

Then Andrei hit her, without taking a swing but very hard, across the cheek with his open hand. Silence fell. Selma didn't budge, but her white face with the lips stretched out into a fine thread broke into red blotches again.

Andrei came to his senses. "I'm sorry," he said through his teeth.

"I won't let you go . . ." Selma repeated in a very quiet voice.

Uncle Yura cleared his throat a couple of times and said, as if he were talking to no one in particular, "In general, at a time like this, a woman all alone in the apartment . . . you know . . . it's probably not a good idea . . ."

"Definitely not," Stas backed him up. "She wouldn't be safe now on her own, but if she's with us, no one will touch her, we're farmers . . ."

But Andrei carried on standing in front of Selma, looking at her. Even at this stage he was still trying to understand something about this woman, and as usual he couldn't understand a thing. She was a slut, a born slut, a slut by the grace of God—he understood that. He had understood that a long time ago. She loved him, she had loved him from the very first day—he knew that too, and he knew it was no obstacle to her. And staying in the apartment alone right now was no problem to her either; she'd never been afraid of anything anyway. He knew that perfectly well too. He knew all the separate things about himself and about her, but taking them all together . . .

"All right," he said. "Put on something warm."

"Do your ribs hurt?" Uncle Yura inquired, trying to change the subject to something as different as possible.

"It's OK," Andrei growled. "It's bearable. We'll battle through."

Trying not to meet anyone's eyes, he stuck the cigarettes and matches in his pocket and stood in front of the sideboard in the far corner of the room, where Donald's pistol lay under a pile of napkins and towels. Should he take it or not? He imagined various scenes and circumstances in which the pistol could come in handy, and decided not to take it. To hell with it, I'll manage without it somehow. I'm not planning to fight a war with anyone anyway . . .

"Right, are we off, then?" said Stas.

He was already standing by the door, cautiously threading his bandaged head through the strap of his automatic. Selma was standing beside him in her coarse, long sweater, which she had pulled on straight over her low-necked dress. She had a raincoat over her arm.

"Let's go," Uncle Yura commanded, clattering the butt of his machine gun against the floor.

"Take off the earrings," Andrei growled to Selma, and went out onto the stairs.

They started walking down. On the landings, residents of the building were whispering to each other in the dark, and they moved aside when they saw the armed men. Someone said: "It's Voronin . . ." and then immediately called to him, "Mr. Editor, can you tell us what's happening in the City?"

Andrei didn't get a chance to reply, because the man who asked was shushed from all sides, and someone said in an ominous whisper, "Can't you see the man's being taken away, you fool!" Selma giggled hysterically.

They came out into the courtyard and clambered into the cart, and Selma flung the raincoat across Andrei's shoulders. Uncle Yura suddenly said, "Quiet!" and they all started listening.

"There's shooting somewhere," Stas said in a low voice.

"Long bursts," Uncle Yura added. "Not sparing the ammunition. And where do they get it from? Ten cartridges is half a liter of home brew, and just listen to him blast away . . . *Gee-up*," he roared. "Can't hang around here any longer."

The cart rumbled into the archway. Little Wang was standing on the porch of the caretaker's lodge with his broom and shovel.

"Lookee, it's Vanya!" Uncle Yura exclaimed. "*Whooah* there! Hi there, Vanya! What are you doing here, eh?"

"Sweeping up," Wang replied with a smile. "Hello."

"Drop that, no more sweeping up!" said Uncle Yura. "Come on, what are you up to? You come along with us, we'll make you a minister, you know—you'll walk around in shantung silk and ride in a swanky 'Victory' automobile."

Wang laughed politely.

"All right, Uncle Yura," Andrei said impatiently. "Let's go, let's go!"

His side was hurting badly, sitting in the cart was uncomfortable, and he already regretted that he hadn't set out on foot. Without even noticing, he had slumped against Selma.

"OK then, Vanya, if you don't want to come, then don't," Uncle Yura decided. "But about being a minister—you get yourself ready! Comb your hair, you know, wash your neck . . ." he flourished the reins. "Gee-up."

They rumbled out onto Main Street.

"Whose cart is this, do you know?" Stas suddenly asked.

"Damned if I know," Uncle Yura replied without turning around. "The horse looks like it's that skinflint's . . . you know, lives right on the edge of the Cliff, ginger hair and freckles . . . Canadian, I reckon . . ."

"Really?" said Stas. "He's probably swearing a blue streak."

"No," said Uncle Yura. "He was killed."

"Really?" said Stas, and left it at that.

Main Street was empty and veiled in thick night fog, although by the clock it was five in the afternoon. The fog ahead of them had a reddish tinge and it was glimmering restlessly. Every now and then bright patches of white light flared up in it—either searchlights or powerful headlamps—and from that direction, muffled by the fog but still sometimes drowning out the rumble of the wheels and clopping of hooves, they heard shooting. Something was happening up there.

In the buildings lining the street many of the windows were lit up, but mostly on the higher floors, above the second. There were no queues at the locked stores and kiosks, but Andrei noticed that people were standing in some of the courtyard entrances and doorways, cautiously glancing out then hiding again, and the most audacious came out onto the sidewalk and looked in the direction of the glittering and crackling in the fog. Objects looking like dark sacks were lying here and there on the sidewalk. Andrei didn't realize what they were at first, and after a while he was surprised to realize that they were dead baboons. A solitary horse was grazing in a small park square beside a dark school.

The cart rumbled and rattled, and no one spoke. Selma quietly felt for Andrei's hand and he gave way to the pain and exhaustion, slumping completely against her warm sweater and closing his eyes. I'm in bad shape, he thought. Oh, really bad shape . . . What garbage was that Kensi was spouting—what fascist coup did he mean? It's just that the cold, the anger, and hopelessness have driven everyone wild . . . The Experiment is the Experiment . . .

At that moment the cart gave a sudden jolt, and above the rumbling of the wheels Andrei heard a shriek so savage and piercing that he came to instantly, covered in sweat. He straightened up and started swinging his head to and fro crazily.

Uncle Yura swore fiercely, hauling on the reins with all his might to hold back the horses, which were straining hard to one side, and at the same time something on fire, a bundle of flames, hurtled along the sidewalk on the left, uttering inhuman screeches that were somehow entirely human, filled with pain and terror, and scattering splashes of fire behind it, and before Andrei could even gather his wits, Stas had jumped smartly down off the cart and cut down the living torch with two short bursts from his automatic, setting the panes of glass jangling in a shop window. The fiery bundle somersaulted along the sidewalk, tumbling over and over, gave one last pitiful squeal, and froze.

"That's an end to its suffering, poor creature," Stas said hoarsely, and Andrei finally realized that it was a baboon, a burning baboon. What crazy nonsense was this . . . Now it was lying there, hanging off the edge of the sidewalk, still burning slowly, and the heavy stench it gave off was spreading along the street.

Uncle Yura set the horse moving, the cart pulled away, and Stas set off beside it on foot, with his hand resting on the planking side. Andrei strained his neck out, looking forward into the pink, glimmering fog, which had turned very bright. Yes, something was happening up there, something absolutely incomprehensible—they could hear strange howling from that direction, shots, the roar of engines, and every now and a bright flash of crimson flared up and immediately faded away.

"Listen, Stas," Uncle Yura said suddenly, without looking around. "You run on ahead, brother, take a look at what's happening up there. And I'll follow on after you, softly, softly . . ."

"OK," said Stas, taking his automatic under his arm, and he jogged forward, sticking to the wall of the building. Very soon he was lost to sight in the glimmering fog, and Uncle Yura carried on pulling the horses up until they stopped completely.

"Sit more comfortably," Selma whispered.

Andrei jerked his shoulder.

"Nothing like that happened," Selma went on, still whispering. "It was the building manager, he was going round all the apartments, asking if anyone was concealing weapons—"

"Shut up," Andrei said through his teeth.

"Honestly," Selma whispered. "He only called in for a moment, he was just on his way out—"

"So he was leaving without his trousers?" Andrei inquired icily, desperately struggling to drive away the hideous memory of hanging on Yura and Stas in limp exhaustion while he watched the scene in the hallway of his own apartment: some short-ass with white eyes furtively closing his robe, with his flannel long johns showing underneath it. And then watching Selma's revoltingly innocent, drunken face over the short-ass's shoulder as the expression of innocence on that face changed to fright, and then to despair.

"But that's how he was going round the apartments, in his robe!" Selma whispered.

"Listen, just shut up," said Andrei. "Shut up, for God's sake. I'm not your husband, you're not my wife. What concern is all this of mine?"

"But I love you, honey," Selma whispered despairingly. "Only you."

Uncle Yura started loudly clearing his throat. "Someone's coming," he announced.

A huge, dark shape loomed out of the darkness ahead and came toward them, then bright headlamps flashed—it was a truck, a massive dump truck. It stopped about twenty paces from the cart, with its engine rumbling. They heard a raucous voice giving orders, then some men clambered out over the side of the truck and started dejectedly wandering around in the road. A door slammed and another dark figure separated from the truck, stood still for a moment, then headed straight toward the cart at a stroll.

"He's coming this way," Uncle Yura announced. "I tell you what, Andrei . . . don't you interfere in the conversation. I'll do the talking."

The man reached the cart. He was clearly one of the so-called militiamen, wearing a short little coat with white armbands on the sleeves. He had a rifle hanging over his shoulder, barrel downward.

"Ah, farmers," said the militiaman. "Howdy, guys."

"Howdy, if you're not joking," Uncle Yura responded after a short pause.

The militiaman hesitated, twisted his head this way and that, as if he were uncertain, then asked diffidently, "Have you got any bread to sell?"

"No bread," said Uncle Yura.

"Well maybe you've got some meat, a few potatoes . . ."

"Potatoes he wants," said Uncle Yura.

The militiaman became completely embarrassed; he sniffed, sighed, looked in the direction of his truck, and then roared, as if in sudden relief, "It's over there, still lying over there!

You blind assholes! It's lying over there, all burned up!" Then
he darted off, tramping noisily on his flat feet, and ran along
the roadway. They saw him waving his arms about and giving
instructions, and heard the dejected men snarling back feebly
and indistinctly, as they dragged along something dark, strained
hard to swing it to and fro, then tossed it into the back of the
dump truck.

"Potatoes he wants," Uncle Yura growled. "Meat!"

The truck set off and drove past them, right up close. It gave
off a terrible smell of scorched fur and flesh. It was loaded right
up to the top; appalling, twisted silhouettes drifted by against
the background of the faintly illuminated wall of a building, and
Andrei suddenly felt a cold frost creep across his skin: sticking
up out of this appalling heap was a distinctly white, human hand
with the fingers splayed out. The dejected men standing in the
truck clutched at each other and the sides of the truck, and huddled close to the cab. There were five or six of them, respectable-
looking men in hats.

"The burial detail," said Uncle Yura. "That's right. Now they'll
take them to the dump—all done and dusted . . . Hey, that's Stas
waving to us over there! Gee-up!"

They could see Stas's ungainly figure in the illuminated mist
ahead of them. When the cart drew level with him, Uncle Yura
suddenly leaned down from the front edge and asked, almost
as if he were frightened, "What's the problem, brother? What's
wrong with you?"

Without answering, Stas tried to jump up sideways onto the
cart, fell off, gritted his teeth loudly, took hold of the side with
both hands, and started muttering in a stifled voice.

"What's wrong with him?" Selma asked in a whisper

The cart moved slowly toward the roaring of engines and
crackling of shots, and Stas held on to the cart with both hands,
walking alongside, as if he didn't have the strength to climb up,
until Uncle Yura leaned down from the cart and dragged him up
onto the front.

"So what is wrong with you?" Uncle Yura asked in a voice loud enough for everyone to hear. "Can we drive on? Just tell me what you're mumbling about, will you?"

"Mother of God," Stas said in a clear voice. "What are they doing it for? Who could have ordered that?"

"*Whooah!*" Uncle Yura called, loud enough for the whole City to hear.

"No, you keep going, keep going," said Stas. "We can drive on. Only it's best not to look . . . *Pani*," he said, turning to Selma, "turn away, you mustn't look, look over that way . . . better still, don't look at all."

Andrei felt his throat tighten; he looked at Selma and her eyes were open so wide, they seemed to cover her entire face.

"Go on, Yura, go on . . ." Stas muttered. "Drive her on, the bitch, stop plodding along! Move fast!" he roared. "Gallop on! Gallop on!"

The horse shot off at a gallop, the buildings on the left came to an end, and the mist suddenly receded and dispersed, revealing Baboon Boulevard—this was definitely the source of all the noise. A line of trucks with their engines idling blocked off the boulevard in a semicircle. Standing in the trucks and between them were men with white armbands, and running along the boulevard between burning trees and bushes, howling and screaming, were men in striped pajamas and baboons absolutely frantic with fear. They stumbled and fell, clambered up trees, tried to hide in the bushes, and all the time the men with white armbands shot at them with rifles and machine guns. The boulevard was strewn with large numbers of motionless bodies, some of them smoldering and smoking. A jet of fire enveloped in swirling black smoke gushed out of one of the trucks with a long hiss, and yet another tree hung with black clusters of baboons flared up like an immense torch. And above all the noise someone howled in an unbearably high falsetto voice, "I'm fit and well! It's a mistake! I'm normal! It's a mistake!"

All this went rushing past, shuddering and skipping, leaving them with a sharp pain in their ribs, scorching them with its heat and drenching them with its stink, deafening them and punching them in the eyes, and a minute later it was all behind them and the glimmering mist had closed back together, but Uncle Yura drove the horse hard for a long time, desperately whooping and brandishing the reins. "What in hell's name is all this?" Andrei kept repeating stupidly to himself, slumping in exhaustion against Selma. "What in hell's name is all this! They're madmen, the blood has driven them berserk . . . Madmen have taken control of the City, insane butchers have taken over, now it's the end of everything, they won't stop, they'll come for us next . . ."

The cart suddenly stopped. "*Ohh* no," said Uncle Yura, swinging around bodily. "You know what this calls for . . ." He rummaged among the sacks in the cart, pulled out a large bottle, dragged out the cork with his teeth, spat it out, and started swigging. Then he handed the bottle to Stas, wiped his mouth, and said, "So you're exterminating them . . . The Experiment . . . Right, then." He took a folded sheet of newsprint out of his breast pocket, neatly tore off one corner, and reached for his tobacco. "So you're going for broke. All the way! Really going for broke!"

Stas held out the bottle to Andrei. Andrei shook his head. Selma took the bottle, downed two gulps from it, and handed it back to Stas. No one said anything. Uncle Yura smoked his crackling roll-up, growled in his throat like an immense dog, then suddenly turned around and untangled the reins.

There was only one block left to the turn onto Stool Closet Lane when the mist ahead of them was brightly lit up again and they heard a cacophonous hubbub of voices. Right at the intersection, a huge, rumbling crowd, illuminated by searchlights, was heaving about in the middle of the street. The intersection was crammed solid; there was no way they could drive through it.

"Some kind of meeting," said Uncle Yura, looking back over his shoulder.

"That's the way of it," Stas agreed despondently. "Once they start shooting people, the meetings come next . . . Is there no way to drive around?"

"Hang on there, brother, why would we want to drive around?" said Uncle Yura. "We ought to listen to what the people are saying. Maybe they'll say something about the sun . . . Lookee, there's plenty of our folks here."

The rumbling died down and a furious, rasping voice, amplified through microphones, rang out over the crowd.

". . . And let me say that once again: mercilessly! We will purge the City! Of filth! Of scum! Of every last, single parasite! String up the crooks!"

"*Aaah!*" the crowd roared.

"String up the bribe-takers!"

"*Aaah!*"

"Anyone who comes out against the people will dangle from a streetlamp!"

"*Aaah!*"

Andrei recognized the speaker now. The riveted flank of some kind of military vehicle rose up out of the very center of the crowd, with a figure rising farther up above it, clutching the riveted flank with both hands. Illuminated by the blue beam of a searchlight, the long, black-clad torso swayed back and forth as the figure opened its parched mouth in a shout—the figure of the former noncommissioned officer of the Wehrmacht and present leader of the Party of Radical Rebirth, Friedrich Heiger.

"And this will only be the beginning! We shall establish a genuine order of the people, a genuinely human order, in this, our City! We care nothing for any experiments! We are not guinea pigs! We are people! Our weapons are reason and conscience! We will not allow anyone! To control our destiny! We shall be masters of our own destiny! The destiny of the people is in the hands of the people! The people has entrusted its destiny to me! Its rights! Its future! And I swear! I shall justify this trust!"

"*Aaah!*"

"I shall be ruthless! In the name of the people! I shall be cruel! In the name of the people! I shall not permit the slightest discord! No more struggle between people! No more communists! No

more socialists! No more capitalists! No more fascists! No more
fighting against each other! We shall fight *for* each other!"

"*Aaah!*"

"No more parties! No more nationalities! No more classes!
Anyone who preaches discord will be strung up!"

"*Aaah!*"

"If the poor continue to fight against the rich! If the communists continue to fight against the capitalists! If the blacks continue
to fight against the whites! We shall be trampled down! We shall
be exterminated! But if we! Stand shoulder to shoulder! Grasping
our guns in our hands! Or our sledgehammers! Or the handles
of our plows! Then no power will ever be found that can crush
us! Our weapon is unity! Our weapon is the truth! No matter
how hard it might be! Yes, we have been lured into a trap! But
I swear in the name of God, the beast is too large for this trap!"

"Ah!" the crowd roared and broke off, stunned, when the
sun flashed on.

For the first time in twenty days the sun flashed on: the golden
disk blazed up at its usual spot, blinding them, searing their gray
faces, glinting with unbearable brightness in the windowpanes,
reanimating and enkindling millions of colors—the black smoke
above distant roofs, the faded greenery of the trees, the red brick
beneath the crumbling plaster . . .

The crowd roared wildly, and Andrei howled with them.
Something unimaginable was happening. Caps went flying way
upward, men hugged each other, some started firing wildly into
the air, some flung bricks at the searchlight in their wild ecstasy,
and Fritz Heiger, towering over them all like the Lord God Himself after he proclaimed, "Let there be light!" pointed his long,
black arm at the sun, with his eyes glaring and his chin proudly
thrust out. Then his voice rang out over the crowd again.

"Do you see? They are already frightened! They tremble at
the sight of us! The sight of us! Too late, gentlemen! Too late!
Do you wish to slam the trap shut again? But people have already
broken out of it! No mercy for the enemies of mankind! The

speculators! The parasites! The plunderers of the people's wealth! The sun is with us again! We have torn it out of the black talons! Of the enemies of mankind! And we will never! Give it away again! Never! Not to anyone!"

"*Aaah!*"

Andrei came to his senses. Stas was no longer in the cart. Uncle Yura was standing on the front of the cart with his feet planted wide apart, brandishing his machine gun, and the crimson flush on the back of his neck showed that he was roaring inarticulately too. Selma was crying, hammering her little fists on Andrei's back.

Very neat, Andrei thought coolly. All the worse for us. What am I doing sitting here? I ought to run for it, and I'm just sitting here . . . Fighting against the pain in his side, he stood up and jumped out of the cart. The crowd was roaring and swirling all around him. Andrei started bulldozing through it. At first he still tried to spare himself, protecting himself with his elbows, but how could he protect himself in a shambles like this! Soaked in sweat from the pain and the mounting nausea, he forced his way forward, shoving his way through, stepping on feet, even butting with his head, and eventually forced his way out onto Stool Closet Lane. And all this time he was pursued by Heiger's thundering voice.

"Hatred! Hatred will guide us! No more false love! No more Judas kisses! From traitors to mankind! I myself set the example of sacred hatred! I blew up an armored car of murderous gendarmes! In front of your very eyes! I ordered the thieves and gangsters to be hanged! In front of your very eyes! I am sweeping the scum and the subhumans out of our City with a broom of iron! In front of your very eyes! I have not pitied myself! And I have earned the sacred right not to pity others!"

Andrei shoved his way into the entrance of the *Gazette*'s offices. The door was locked. He kicked it furiously, setting the panes of glass jangling. He started hammering on it with all his might, whispering appalling obscenities.

The door opened. The Mentor was standing in the doorway. "Come in," he said, moving aside.

Andrei walked in. The Mentor bolted the door behind him and turned around. His face was pasty white, with dark circles under the eyes, and he kept licking his lips. Andrei's heart sank—he had never seen the Mentor in such a dejected state before.

"Is everything really all that bad?" Andrei asked in a dismal voice.

"Oh yes." The Mentor gave a wan smile. "What could be good about any of this?"

"But the sun?" said Andrei. "Why did you switch it off?"

The Mentor clasped his hands together and strode backward and forward across the hallway. "But we didn't switch it off!" he said sorrowfully. "An accident. Totally and absolutely unplanned. No one was expecting it."

"No one was expecting it," Andrei repeated bitterly. He pulled off his raincoat and tossed it onto a dusty sofa. "If the sun hadn't gone out, none of this would have happened . . ."

"The Experiment has run out of control," the Mentor muttered, turning away.

"Run out of control . . ." Andrei repeated again. "I never thought the Experiment could run out of control."

The Mentor cast a sullen glance at him. "Well now . . . That is, in a manner of speaking. You could also look at it this way . . . If the Experiment has run out of control, it is still the Experiment. Possibly something will have to be modified somewhat . . . recalibrated. And so in retrospect—in retrospect!—this 'Egyptian night' will come to be regarded as an integral, programmed part of the Experiment."

"In retrospect," Andrei repeated once again. A blind fury swept over him. "But what do you want us to do now? Try to save ourselves?"

"Yes. Save yourselves. And save others."

"So we'll save ourselves, and Fritz Heiger will conduct the Experiment?"

"The Experiment remains the Experiment," the Mentor retorted.

"Oh yes," said Andrei. "From baboons to Fritz Heiger."

"Yes, to Fritz Heiger, and through Fritz Heiger, and regardless of Fritz Heiger. You can't put a bullet through your brains because of Fritz Heiger! The Experiment must go on . . . Life goes on, doesn't it, regardless of some Fritz Heiger or other? If you're disenchanted with the Experiment, then think about the struggle for life . . ."

"The struggle for survival," Andrei said with a crooked grin. "What sort of life is there now?"

"That will depend on you."

"And on you?"

"Not much depends on us. There are many of you. We don't decide everything here, you do."

"That isn't what you used to say before," said Andrei.

"You were different before too!" the Mentor objected. "And you spoke differently!"

"I'm afraid I acted like a fool," Andrei said slowly. "I'm afraid I was simply stupid."

"That's not all you're afraid of," the Mentor remarked in a sly tone of voice.

Andrei's heart stood still, the way it does when you fall in a dream. And he answered harshly, "Yes, I am afraid. Afraid of everything. A real scaredy-cat. Has anyone ever kicked you repeatedly in the crotch with his boot?" A new idea suddenly occurred to him. "And you're afraid yourself, aren't you? Eh?"

"Of course! Didn't I tell you the Experiment had run out of control—"

"Ah, come off it! The Experiment, the Experiment. It's not a matter of the Experiment. First the baboons, then us, and then you—isn't that right?"

The Mentor didn't answer. The most terrible thing of all was that the Mentor didn't say even a single word in reply. Andrei carried on waiting, but the Mentor merely prowled around the hallway without speaking, aimlessly shifting chairs from one spot to another and wiping the dust off tables with his sleeve, without even looking at Andrei.

Someone knocked on the door with a fist, and then immediately started kicking it. Andrei drew back the bolt and saw Selma standing there. "You abandoned me!" she said indignantly. "I almost couldn't fight my way through!"

Andrei glanced around in embarrassment. The Mentor had disappeared. "I'm sorry," said Andrei. "I had other things on my mind."

It was hard for him to speak. He was trying to suppress a terrifying sense of loneliness and vulnerability. He slammed the door shut with a crash and hastily slid the bolt home.

3

The offices were empty. The staff had obviously fled when the shooting started up around City Hall. Andrei walked through the rooms, indifferently surveying the scattered sheets of paper and overturned chairs, the dirty plates with the remains of sandwiches and cups with the remains of coffee. Loud, rousing music was coming from somewhere farther inside, and that was strange. Selma plodded after him, holding on to his sleeve. She kept saying something over and over, something shrewish, but Andrei wasn't listening to her. What did I come here for, he thought. They've all bolted, every last one of them, and they were right. I should be safe at home now, lying in bed, hugging my poor battered side and dozing, not giving a rotten damn for any of this . . .

At first he didn't realize it was Izya. Standing at the table farthest away, in the corner, stooped over an open binder of back issues and propping himself up on hands set wide apart, was a stranger with his hair carelessly trimmed in wedges, wearing a suspicious-looking gray garment with no buttons, and it was only when this man suddenly grinned in a familiar way a moment later and started plucking at a wart on his neck with a familiar gesture that Andrei realized he was looking at Izya.

Andrei stood in the doorway for a while, watching him. Izya hadn't heard Andrei come in. He couldn't hear or notice a thing—first, he was reading, and second, a loudspeaker hanging directly above his head was blasting out the thunderous jangling of a victorious march. Then Selma exclaimed in an appalling wail, "Oh, look, it's Izya!" and she darted forward, pushing Andrei aside.

Izya quickly looked up and spread out his arms, grinning even more broadly. "Aha!" he yelled delightedly. "So here you are!"

While Izya hugged Selma, delightedly smothering her cheeks and lips in kisses, while Selma squealed something unintelligible and ecstatic and ruffled up Izya's ugly hair, Andrei walked across to them, struggling to overcome his acute sense of awkwardness. The searing feeling of guilt and betrayal that had almost knocked him off his feet that morning in the basement had been blunted and almost forgotten over the last year, but now it transfixed him again, and after he got close, he hesitated for a few seconds before daring to hold out his hand. He would have found it perfectly natural if Izya had ignored this hand of his, or even said something witheringly contemptuous—that was probably exactly what Andrei would have done. But Izya freed himself from Selma's embrace, grabbed Andrei's hand with eager passion, shook it, and asked with keen interest, "Where did they give you that beautiful shiner?"

"I was beaten," Andrei replied tersely. He was astounded by Izya. There were many things he wanted to tell him, but all he did was ask, "So how come you're here?"

Instead of answering, Izya flipped over several pages of the bound newspapers and gestured in exaggerated fashion as he declaimed with gusto, "'. . . No rational arguments can possibly explain the fury with which the government press attacks the Party of Radical Rebirth. But if we recall that it is precisely the PRR—this tiny, young organization—that speaks out most uncompromisingly against every case of corruption—'"

"Drop it," said Andrei, wrinkling up his face, but Izya merely raised his voice.

"'—lawlessness, administrative stupidity, and shiftlessness; if we recall that it was precisely the PRR that brought up the Widow Batton case, if we recall that the PRR was the first party to warn the government of the futility of the swamplands tax . . .' Belinsky! Pisarev! Plekhanov! Did you write this yourself, or was it your idiots?"

"OK, OK . . ." said Andrei, starting to get annoyed, and he tried to take the binder away from Izya.

"No, wait!" shouted Izya, wagging his finger at Andrei and tugging the binder toward himself. "Here is yet another pearl! . . . Where is it now? . . . Ah, yes. 'Our City has a wealth of honest people, like any city populated by working folk. However, when it comes to political factions, surely Fritz Heiger is the only one who can lay claim to the exalted title—'"

"That's enough!" Andrei yelled, but Izya tore the binder out of his hands, darted behind Selma, who was exultant, and continued from there, still plucking and spraying.

"'Let us not speak of words, let us speak of deeds! Friedrich Heiger rejected the post of minister of information; Friedrich Heiger voted against a law providing major privileges to distinguished employees of the Public Prosecutor's Office; Friedrich Heiger was the only eminent public figure to oppose the creation of a regular army, in which he was offered a senior position . . .'" Izya flung the binder under the desk and rubbed his hands together. "You always were an incredible ass in politics! But in the last few months, you've become catastrophically more stupid. You deserve that ornament on your noggin! Is your eye still in one piece at least?"

"Yes, my eye's still in one piece," Andrei said slowly. He had only just noticed that Izya moved his left arm kind of awkwardly, and three fingers on his left hand didn't bend at all.

"Will you turn off that damned noise!" roared Kensi, appearing in the doorway. "Ah, Andrei, you're here already . . . That's good. Hello, Selma!" He dashed across the room and jerked the plug of the speaker out of its socket.

"What did you do that for?" Izya shouted. "I want to hear the speeches of my leaders! Let the martial music thunder forth!"

Kensi merely cast a furious glance at him. "Andrei, let's go, I'll tell you what we've done," he said. "And we have to think about what to do next."

His face and hands were covered in soot. He dashed out and Andrei dashed after him, realizing for the first time that the offices smelled of burnt paper. Izya and Selma followed behind.

"A general amnesty!" Izya told her, hissing and gurgling. "The great leader has flung open the doors of the prisons! He needed the space for different prisoners." He whooped and groaned. "Every single criminal has been set free, and we all know what a criminal I am, don't we? Even the lifers have been let out."

"You've gotten thin," Selma said in a voice filled with pity. "Your clothes are hanging off you, you've turned kind of mangy . . ."

"Well, at the end—for the last three days—they didn't give us any food, or let us get washed."

"So you must be hungry, then?"

"No, not a damn bit—I stuffed myself full in here."

They walked into Andrei's office. It was appallingly hot in there: the sun was shining straight in the window and the fireplace was blazing fiercely. Andrei's little floozy of a secretary was squatting in front of the fireplace, as smutty-faced as Kensi, stirring a heap of burning paper with a poker. Everything in the office was covered in soot and black clumps of paper ash.

When she saw Andrei, his secretary jumped up and gave him a frightened, ingratiating smile. She's the last person I expected to stay, thought Andrei. He sat down at his desk, feeling guilty, and forced himself to nod and smile back at her.

"Lists of all the special correspondents, names and addresses of members of the editorial board," Kensi ticked off briskly. "The originals of all political articles, the originals of weekly reviews . . ."

"Dupain's articles have to be burned," said Andrei. "He was our greatest opponent of the PRR, I think."

"Burned already," Kensi said impatiently. "Dupain, and Filimonov too, just to be on the safe side . . ."

"Why are you making all this fuss?" Izya asked merrily. "They'll carry you shoulder high."

"That all depends," Andrei said morosely.

"What do you mean, it all depends? Want to bet on it? A hundred finger flicks!"

"Just hang on, will you, Izya!" said Kensi. "For God's sake shut up for ten minutes at least! I've destroyed all the correspondence with City Hall, but left the correspondence with Heiger for the time being . . ."

"The minutes of the editorial board!" Andrei suddenly remembered. "For the last month . . ." He hastily reached into the bottom drawer of the desk, took out a file, and handed it to Kensi, who winced as he leafed through a few pages.

"Right, right . . ." he said, shaking his head. "I forgot about that . . . This has Dupain's speech in it." He took a step toward the fireplace and flung the file into the fire. "Keep stirring, keep stirring," he testily ordered the secretary, who was listening openmouthed to her bosses.

The head of the letters section appeared in the doorway, looking sweaty and very agitated. He was lugging a heap of files in his arms, pressing them down with his chin. "There," he panted, dumping the heap beside the fireplace with a heavy thud. "There are some opinion polls here, I didn't even try to sort them out . . . I could see names, addresses . . . My God, boss, what happened to you?"

"Hi, Denny," said Andrei, "thanks for staying."

"Is your eye OK?" asked Denny, wiping the sweat off his forehead.

"It's OK, it's OK," Izya reassured him. "You're destroying all the wrong stuff," he declared. "No one's going to touch you, are they? You're a yellowish liberal opposition newspaper. You'll just stop being liberal and oppositionist . . ."

"Izya," said Kensi. "I'm asking you for the last time: stop gabbling or I'll throw you out."

"But I'm not gabbling!" Izya exclaimed in annoyance. "Let me finish! The letters, destroy the letters. Some intelligent people probably wrote to you . . ."

Kensi gaped at him. "*Dammit!*" he hissed, and darted out of the office. Denny raced after him, still wiping his face and neck as he went.

"You don't understand a thing," said Izya. "All of you here are cretins. And it's not only intelligent people who are in danger."

"Cretins is what we are," said Andrei. "You're right there."

"Aha! You're getting brighter!" Izya exclaimed, waving his mutilated arm about. "You shouldn't. It's dangerous. That's what so tragic about the whole thing. Many, many people will get a bit brighter now, but not bright enough. They won't realize in time that this is when they should pretend to be fools."

Andrei looked at Selma. Selma was gazing admiringly at Izya. And the secretary was gazing admiringly at Izya too. And Izya was standing there with his feet set wide apart in their prison shoes, unshaven and dirty, a total mess, with his shirt sticking out of his trousers, because there weren't enough buttons on the fly—standing there in all his glory, still the same as ever, not changed in the least—and pontificating and sermonizing. Andrei got up from his desk, walked over to the fireplace, squatted down beside the secretary, took the poker from her, and started stirring and turning the reluctantly burning paper.

"And so," Izya sermonized, "you have to destroy not just the letters that abuse our leader. There are different ways of abusing someone. You have to destroy the letters written by intelligent people!"

Kensi stuck his head into the office and shouted, "Listen, someone give us a hand . . . Girls, why are you just hanging around in here, come on, follow me!"

The secretary immediately jumped up and ran out, straightening out her little skirt that had twisted around. Selma stood there for a moment, as if expecting someone to stop her, then stubbed out her cigarette in the ashtray and walked out too.

"But no one will touch you!" Izya carried on pontificating, seeing nothing and hearing nothing, like a wood grouse singing his mating song. "They'll say thank you to you, toss you more paper so you can increase your print run, raise your salaries, and give you more staff. But afterward, if you suddenly take it into your heads to get uppity, that's when they'll grab you by the balls, and then you can be sure they'll remind you about everything—that Dupain of yours, and that Filimonov, and all your liberal opposition ravings. Only why would you want to get uppity? You won't even think of getting uppity—on the contrary!"

"Izya," said Andrei, looking into the flames. "Why didn't you tell me what you had in that file?"

"What? In what file? Ah, in that file . . ." Izya suddenly turned quiet, came over to the fireplace, and squatted down beside Andrei.

For a while neither of them spoke. Then Andrei said, "Of course, I was a stupid jackass then. An absolute blockhead. But I've never been a rumormonger and gossip. You ought to have realized that then . . ."

"In the first place, you weren't a blockhead," said Izya. "You were worse. You were zombified. It was impossible to talk to you like a human being. I know, I was like that for a long time myself . . . And then—what have rumors got to do with it? You must admit that simple citizens really shouldn't know that kind of thing. That way the whole damn shooting match could go to hell."

"What?" Andrei asked, confused. "Because of your little love letters?"

"What little love letters?"

For a while they gazed into each other's eyes in astonishment. Then Izya grinned. "Oh Lord, of course . . . What made me think he'd tell you all that? Why would he tell you? He's our soaring eagle, our leader! He who controls information, controls the world—he learned that lesson well from me!"

"I don't understand a thing," Andrei muttered almost despairingly. But he could sense that he was about to learn something loathsome about this already loathsome business. "What are you talking about? Who is *he*? Heiger?"

"Heiger, Heiger," said Izya, nodding. "Our great Fritz . . . So it was love letters I had in the file, then? Or maybe compromising photographs? The jealous widow and the womanizer Katzman . . .

That's right, that's what the record I signed said too." Izya got up with a croak and started walking around the office, rubbing his hands together and giggling.

"Yes," said Andrei. "That's what he told me. The jealous widow. So it was all lies?"

"Well of course, what did you think?"

"I believed it," Andrei said curtly. He clenched his teeth and started frenziedly stirring the poker in the hearth. "And what was really in the file?" he asked.

Izya didn't answer. Andrei glanced around. Izya was standing there, slowly rubbing his hands together, looking at Andrei with a frozen smile and glassy eyes. "Now that's interesting . . ." he said uncertainly. "Maybe he simply forgot? That is, not exactly forgot . . ." He suddenly darted over and squatted down beside Andrei again. "Listen, I'm not going to tell you anything, got that? And if they ask you, that's what you say: he didn't tell me anything, he refused. All he said was that it was to do with some big secret of the Experiment; he said it was dangerous to know the secret. And he also showed me several sealed envelopes and explained with a wink that he was going to deliver those envelopes to reliable people, and the envelopes would be opened if he, Katzman, were arrested or, let's say, his life came to a sudden end. Do you understand? He didn't name the reliable people. That's what you tell them, if they ask."

"All right," Andrei said slowly, looking into the flames.

"That will be the right thing," said Izya, also looking into the flames. "It's just that, if they beat you . . . That Ruhmer's a real bastard, you know." Izya shuddered. "And maybe no one will ask. I don't know. It all needs thinking over. I can't figure everything out at once."

He stopped speaking. Andrei was still stirring the hot pile with its shimmering red flames, and after a while Izya started tossing files full of papers into the hearth. "Don't throw the files themselves in," said Andrei. "Look, they don't burn well . . . But aren't you afraid they'll find that file?"

"What should I be afraid of?" said Izya. "Let Heiger be afraid . . . And they won't find it now if they didn't find it immediately. I tossed it into a manhole, and then I kept wondering if I'd missed or not . . . But what did they work you over for? I thought you and Fritz were on excellent terms."

"It wasn't Fritz," Andrei said reluctantly. "I was just unlucky."

The women and Kensi barged noisily into the room, lugging an entire mound of letters on a stretched-out raincoat. Denny walked in after them, still wiping away his sweat. "Well, I think that's all now," he said. "Or have you come up with something else?"

"Come on, move over!" Kensi demanded.

The raincoat was set down beside the fireplace, and everyone started throwing letters into the flames. The hearth immediately started buzzing. Izya sank his good hand into the depths of this multicolored heap of paper covered with writing, extracted someone's letter, and grinned in anticipation as he started reading it.

"Who was it that said manuscripts don't burn?" Denny asked, panting for breath. He sat down at the desk and lit up a cigarette. "They burn wonderfully well, in my opinion . . . Phew, it's hot. Maybe I should open the windows?"

The secretary suddenly squealed, jumped to her feet, and ran out, repeating over and over, "I forgot, I completely forgot."

"What's her name?" Andrei hastily asked Kensi.

"Amalia!" Kensi growled. "I've told you a hundred times . . . Listen, I just phoned Dupain . . ."

"Well?"

The secretary came back with an armful of notebooks. "That's all of them—your instructions, boss," she squeaked. "I forgot all about them. We probably ought to burn them too?"

"Of course, Amalia," said Andrei. "Thank you for remembering. Burn them, Amalia, burn them . . . So what did Dupain say?

"I wanted to warn him," said Kensi, "let him know everything's all right, all the tracks have been covered. And he was terribly surprised—what tracks? Did he ever really write anything of that kind? He's just finished a detailed dispatch on the heroic storming of City Hall, and now he's working on an article called 'Friedrich Heiger and the People.'"

"What a bastard," Andrei said in a feeble voice. "But then, we're all bastards."

"You speak for yourself, when you say things like that!" Kensi snarled.

"OK, I'm sorry," Andrei said weakly. "OK, we're not all bastards. Just the majority."

Izya suddenly started giggling. "There, now—an intelligent man!" he proclaimed, shaking the piece of paper in his hand. "'It is absolutely clear,'" he recited, "'that people like Friedrich Heiger simply wait for some great disaster or other to come along, some disturbance of the equilibrium, even if it is only temporary, in order to whip up passions so that the muddy waters of turmoil will raise them up . . .' Who writes that?" He looked at the reverse side of the sheet of paper. "Ah, well, who else! Into the flames with it! Into the flames!" He crumpled up the letter and flung it into the hearth.

"Listen, Andrei," said Kensi. "Isn't it time we thought about the future?"

"What is there to think about it?" Andrei growled, working away with the poker. "We'll survive somehow, we'll get by . . ."

"I don't mean our future!" said Kensi. "I'm talking about the future of the paper, about the future of the Experiment!"

Andrei looked at him in amazement. Kensi was the same as he had always been. As if nothing had happened. As if absolutely nothing at all had happened in the last few sickening months. He actually seemed even more ready for a fight than usual. Only now the fight was in the name of legality and ideals. Like a cocked firing hammer. But maybe nothing really had happened to him? "Have you been talking to your Mentor?" Andrei asked.

"Yes, I have," Kensi replied defiantly.

"Well, and?" asked Andrei, overcoming that familiar awkwardness, the way he always had to in a conversation about the Mentors.

"That's nobody else's business and it has no significance. What have the Mentors got to do with this? Heiger has a Mentor too. Every bandit in the City has a Mentor. That doesn't stop any of them from thinking for themselves."

Andrei pulled a cigarette out of a pack, kneaded it, and lit it from the red-hot poker, narrowing his eyes against the heat. "I'm fed up with the whole thing," he said quietly.

"What are you fed up with?"

"Every damn thing . . . I think we need to escape, get out of here, Kensi. To hell with all of them."

"What does that mean—escape? What are you talking about?"

"We have to clear out, before it's too late, make tracks for the swamps, for Uncle Yura's place, as far away as possible from this whole mess. The Experiment has run out of control, you and I can't bring it back under control, so there's no point even trying. In the swamps at least we'll have weapons, we'll have strength—"

"I'm not going to any swamps!" Selma suddenly declared.

"No one's asking you to," Andrei said without looking around.

"Andrei," said Kensi, "that's desertion."

"In your book it's desertion, in mine it's a rational maneuver. Anyway, you suit yourself. You asked me what I think about the future and I'm telling you. There's nothing for me to do here. They'll shut down the paper anyway, and send us to clear away the dead baboons. Under armed guard. And that's the best scenario."

"Now here's another intelligent individual!" Izya proclaimed admiringly. "Listen: 'I'm an old subscriber to your newspaper and on the whole I approve of its line. But why do you always come out in defense of F. Heiger? Perhaps you are inadequately informed? I know for certain that Heiger has a dossier on anyone who is even slightly noteworthy in the City. His people permeate the entire municipal establishment. They are probably in your newspaper too. I assure you, the PRR is by no means as small as you think. I know that they have weapons too . . .'" Izya looked at the reverse of the letter. "Ah, that's who it is . . . 'I ask you please not to publish my name . . .' Into the fire with it, into the fire."

"Anyone would think you know all the intelligent people in the City," said Andrei.

"Well, as it happens, there aren't all that many of them," Izya retorted, lowering his hand into the heap of paper again. "Not to mention the fact that intelligent people don't often write to the newspapers."

Silence fell. Denny, who had smoked his fill, also came over to the fireplace and started tossing large armfuls of paper into the flames. "Stir it, boss, stir it!" he said. "Put more life into it! Let me have that poker . . ."

"I think it's simply cowardice, running away from the City now," Selma said defiantly.

"Every honest man counts now," Kensi agreed. "If we go, who'll be left? Will you tell them to give the newspaper to the Dupains?"

"You'll be left," Andrei said wearily. "You can hire Selma for the paper, or Izya—"

"You know Heiger well," Kensi interrupted. "You could use your influence . . ."

"I haven't got any influence," said Andrei. "Or if I do, I don't want to use it. I don't know how to do things like that and I can't stand it."

Again everyone fell silent, with just the flames humming in the chimney.

"I wish they'd get here soon," Denny growled, flinging the final pile of letters into the fire. "I'm dying for a drink, and there isn't anything here."

"They won't come straight round, just like that," Izya immediately retorted. "They'll call first!" He threw the letter he was reading into the hearth and started walking around the office. "You don't know that, you don't understand. It's a ritual! A procedure developed in three countries, honed to a fine edge, tried and tested . . . Girls, isn't there anything to eat here?" he suddenly asked.

Skinny Amalia immediately jumped up, squeaking, "Just a moment, just a moment!" and disappeared into the front office.

"By the way," Andrei asked out of the blue. "Where's the censor?"

"He really wanted to stay," said Denny. "But Mr. Ubukata threw him out. He was screaming bloody murder, that censor. 'Where will I go?' he shouted. 'You're killing me!' We even had to bolt the door so he couldn't get back in. He kept throwing himself against it at first, then he gave up hope and left. Listen, I'm going to open the window after all. It's too hot, I can't bear it."

The secretary came back in, smiled shyly with her pale, unpainted lips, and handed Izya a greasy paper bag of pies.

"Mmm!" Izya exclaimed, and immediately started champing on them.

"Are your ribs hurting?" Selma asked in a quiet little voice, leaning down to Andrei's ear.

"No," Andrei said curtly. He got up, moved her away, and walked over to the desk. And at that moment the telephone rang. Everyone turned their heads to stare at the white phone. It carried on ringing.

"Well, Andrei!" Kensi said impatiently.

Andrei picked up the receiver. "Yes?"

"The *City Gazette* offices?" a brisk voice inquired.

"Yes," said Andrei.

"I'd like Mr. Voronin, please."

"Speaking."

There was the sound of someone breathing into the phone, followed by a loud dial tone as they hung up. Andrei carefully put down the receiver, with his heart pounding. "It's them," he said.

Izya champed out something unintelligible, frenziedly nodding his head. Andrei sat down. Everyone looked at him—Denny with a forced smile on his face, Kensi stooped over and tousle-headed, Amalia pitiful and frightened, Selma pale but collected.

Izya looked at him too, chewing and grinning at the same time, wiping his greasy fingers on the flaps of his coat.

"Well, what are you all staring at?" Andrei asked irritably. "Come on now, all of you, clear out of here."

No one stirred.

"What are you so worried about?" said Izya, examining the last pie. "It will be a breeze, a walk in the park, all calm and quiet, as Uncle Yura says. Calm and quiet, honest and respectable . . . Only don't make any sudden movements. Just like with cobras."

From outside they heard an engine rumbling and brakes squealing, and a strident voice commanded, "Kaiser, Velichenko, follow me! Mirovich, stay here!" A fist was immediately hammered against the door downstairs.

"I'll go and open up," said Denny, and Kensi sprang over to the fireplace and started stirring the heap of smoking ash with all his might. Ash flew everywhere in the room.

"Don't make any sudden movements!" Izya shouted after Denny.

The door downstairs shuddered and its panes of glass jangled plaintively. Andrei stood up, clasped his hands behind his back, squeezing them together as hard as he could, and stood in the middle of the room. The recent sensation of dark lethargy and weakness in his legs swept over him again. The hammering and rattling downstairs ended; he heard grumbling voices and then the sound of large numbers of feet stamping in the empty offices. As if there's an entire battalion of them, Andrei thought fleetingly. He backed away, bracing his rump against the wall. His knees were trembling repulsively. I won't allow them to beat me, he thought in despair. Let them kill me. I didn't bring the pistol . . . I should have brought it . . . Or maybe I was right not to bring it?

A short, stout man strode resolutely in through the door opposite Andrei. He was dressed in a good-quality coat with white armbands over it and a huge beret with a badge of some kind. His feet were encased in magnificently polished boots and his coat was pulled in slightly at the waist, in a very ugly way, by a broad belt, with a shiny, brand-new holster tugging it down heavily on the left. Some other men piled in behind him, but Andrei didn't see them. He stared, spellbound, into the pale, puffy face with the blurred features and sour-looking little eyes. Has he got conjunctivitis, then? Andrei thought somewhere on the very edge of his consciousness. And he's shaved so close he actually gleams, like he's been varnished . . .

The man in the beret quickly glanced around the room before staring straight at Andrei. "Citizen Voronin?" he declaimed in a high, piercing voice, but with an interrogative intonation.

"Yes," said Andrei, forcing out the word and clutching at the edge of the desk with both hands.

"Senior editor of the *City Gazette*?"

"Yes."

The man in the beret saluted deftly but casually with two fingers. "I have the honor, Citizen Voronin, to present you with a personal communication from President Friedrich Heiger!"

He had obviously intended to pluck the personal communication out from under his coat in a single, smart gesture, but something in there got hooked on something else, and he had to scrabble around in the depths of his coat for a long time, skewed over slightly to the right and looking as if he were being assaulted by insects. Andrei watched him fatalistically, not understanding a thing. This was all wrong somehow. This wasn't what he had been expecting. Maybe it will all blow over, he thought fleetingly, but dismissed the idea in superstitious haste.

Eventually the communication was extracted, and the man in the beret handed it to Andrei with a dissatisfied and rather offended air. Andrei took the crisp, sealed envelope. It was an ordinary postal envelope, a pale blue oblong bearing a stylized representation of a heart embellished with little bird's wings. The address written on the envelope in familiar handwriting with large letters was "To Andrei Voronin, Senior Editor of the City Gazette, in person, confidential. F. Heiger, President." Andrei tore open the envelope and pulled out an ordinary sheet of letter paper edged in blue.

My dear Andrei,

First of all allow me to thank you with all my heart for the help and support that I have constantly felt from your newspaper in the course of the recent decisive months. Now, as you can see, the situation has fundamentally changed. I am sure that you will not be confused by the new terminology and certain unavoidable excesses: the words and the means have changed, but the goals remain the same. Take control of the newspaper yourself—you have been appointed its permanent senior editor and publisher with full authority. Employ staff according to your own preferences, increase the number of employees, demand new printing capacity—I give you complete carte blanche. The deliverer of this letter is Junior Adjutor Raymond Cvirik, who has been appointed to your newspaper as the political representative of my Department of Information. As you will soon realize for yourself, he is not a man of great intellect, but he knows his job well and will be helpful to you, especially during the early stages, in getting the hang of the general policy line. Naturally, if any conflicts should arise, come directly to me. I wish you success. We'll show these drooling liberals how to work.

In friendship,

Your Fritz

Andrei read this personal and confidential missive twice, then lowered the hand holding the letter and looked around. They were all looking at him again—pale-faced, resolute, and tense. Only Izya was beaming like a newly polished samovar, and secretly releasing finger flicks into space where the others couldn't see. The junior adjutor (dammit, what the hell could that mean, it was a familiar word . . . adjutor, coadjutor . . . something out of history . . . or out of *The Three Musketeers*) . . . Junior Adjutor Raymond Cvirik was looking at him too—looking sternly but protectively. And over by the door some odd-looking characters with carbines and white armbands on their sleeves were shifting from foot to foot and watching him too.

"I see," said Andrei, folding the letter and putting it back in the envelope. He didn't know where to begin.

Then the junior adjutor began. "Are these your colleagues, Citizen Voronin?" he inquired briskly, with a brief side-to-side gesture.

"Yes," said Andrei.

"Hmm," Citizen Raymond Cvirik declared dubiously, looking point-blank at Izya.

But at that moment Kensi abruptly asked him, "And who exactly might you be?"

Citizen Raymond Cvirik glanced at him, and then turned in amazement to Andrei. Andrei cleared his throat. "Gentlemen," he announced. "Allow me to introduce to you Junior Coadjutor Citizen Cvirik—"

"Adjutor!" Cvirik corrected him indignantly.

"What? Ah yes, adjutor. Not coadjutor, but simply adjutor . . ." (For no reason at all Selma gave a sudden splutter of laughter and put her hand over her mouth.) "Junior adjutor and political representative at our newspaper. From now on."

"Representative of what?" Kensi asked intransigently.

Andrei was about to look in the envelope again, but Cvirik declared in an even more indignant tone of voice, "Political representative of the Department of Information!"

"Your credentials!" Kensi said brusquely.

"What?" Citizen Cvirik's sour little eyes started blinking indignantly.

"Your credentials, your authorization—do you have anything, apart from that idiotic holster of yours?"

"Who is this?" Citizen Cvirik exclaimed in a piercing shriek, turning back toward Andrei. "Who is this man?"

"This is Citizen Kensi Ubukata," Andrei said hastily. "The deputy editor . . . Kensi, no credentials are required. He delivered a letter to me from Fritz."

"What Fritz?" Kensi said disdainfully. "What has some Fritz or other got to do with anything?"

"Sudden movements!" Izya appealed. "I implore you, don't make any sudden movements!"

Cvirik swung his head to and fro from Izya to Kensi and back. His face wasn't gleaming any longer; it was slowly flooding with crimson. "Citizen Voronin," he eventually enunciated, "I see that your colleagues do not have a very clear idea of exactly what has happened today! Or perhaps on the contrary!" He kept raising his voice. "They have some strange, distorted idea of it! I see burnt paper here, I see gloomy faces, and I do not see any readiness to set to work. At an hour when the entire City, our entire people—"

"And who are they?" Kensi interrupted, pointing to the characters with carbines. "Are they the new staff?"

"Believe it or not, they are! Citizen *Former* Deputy Editor! They are the new staff. I cannot promise you that they—"

"We'll see about that," Kensi declared in an unfamiliar, squeaky voice, taking a step toward Cvirik. "By what authority—"

"Kensi!" Andrei said helplessly.

"By what authority are you haranguing us here?" Kensi went on, taking no notice of Andrei. "Who are you? How dare you behave like this! Why don't you present your credentials? You're nothing but a bunch of armed bandits who have broken in to pillage the place!"

"Shut your mouth, you yellow asshole!" Cvirik suddenly howled out savagely, reaching for his holster.

Andrei swayed forward to stand between them, but at that moment someone shoved him hard on the shoulder, and Selma was suddenly standing in front of Cvirik.

"How dare you swear like that in the presence of women, you bastard!" she yelled. "You fat-assed scumbag! You ugly thug!"

Andrei was completely dazed. Cvirik and Kensi and Selma all screamed hideously at the same time. Out of the corner of his eye, Andrei noticed the characters in the doorway glancing uncertainly at each other and moving to hold their carbines at the ready, and Denny Lee suddenly appeared beside them, holding a heavy editor's stool with a metal seat by one leg, but the most frightening and unbelievable sight of all was the little floozy Amalia, hunched over in a strange, predatory pose and baring long, white teeth that looked spine-chilling on her haggard, corpse-like face, stealthily creeping toward Cvirik, raising the smoking poker over her right shoulder, as if it were a golf club . . .

"I remember you, you son of a bitch!" Kensi shouted furiously. "You embezzled the money for schools, you sleazeball, and now you've risen to be a coadjutor!"

"I'll trample you all into shit! I'll make you eat shit! You enemies of mankind!"

"Shut it, you piece of scum. Shut it, while you're still in one piece!"

"No sharp movements! I implore you!"

Like a man under a spell, Andrei followed the movement of the smoking poker, unable to stir a muscle. He could sense, he knew, that something terrible and irrevocable was about to happen, and it was already too late to prevent this terrible thing.

"We'll string you up on a streetlamp!" the junior adjutor howled wildly, waving a huge automatic pistol around in the air. In all this hubbub and uproar he had somehow managed to pull out his pistol, and now he was brandishing it mindlessly and yelling continuously in his piercing voice, and then Kensi bounded up to him, and grabbed him by the lapels of his coat, and Cvirik started pushing him off with both hands, and suddenly a shot rang out, followed immediately by a second and a third. The poker flashed through the air without a sound, and everyone froze.

Cvirik was standing alone in the center of the office, with his crimson face rapidly turning gray. He was rubbing the shoulder bruised by the poker with one hand, and his other hand was shaking, still held out in front of him. The pistol was lying on the floor. The characters in the doorway stood there with their mouths all hanging open in the same way and their carbines lowered.

"I didn't mean to . . ." Cvirik said in a trembling voice.

The stool fell out of Denny's hand and crashed heavily against the floor, and that was when Andrei realized where everyone was looking. They were all looking at Kensi, who was tumbling backward with a strange, extremely slow movement, pressing both hands to the lower part of his chest.

"I didn't mean to . . ." Cvirik repeated in a tearful voice. "As God's my witness, I didn't mean to!"

Kensi's legs buckled and he collapsed gently, almost without a sound, into the heap of ash beside the fireplace, uttering an inarticulate, painful sound as he strained to pull his knees up to his stomach.

And then, with a terrible shriek, Selma sank her nails into Cvirik's fat, gleaming, dirty-white face, and everyone else went dashing to the man lying on the floor, tramping loudly, and screened him off, piling up over him, and then Izya straightened up, turned to look at Andrei with his face strangely contorted and his eyebrows raised in astonishment, and mumbled, "He's dead. They killed him . . ."

The telephone rang thunderously. Not understanding a thing, Andrei held out his hand as if this were a dream and picked up the receiver.

"Andrei? Andrei!" It was Otto Friese. "Are you alive and well? Thank God, I was so worried about you! Well, everything will be fine now. Fritz will look out for us now if need be . . ." He said something else—about sausage, about butter. Andrei wasn't listening to him any longer.

Selma was squatting down on her haunches with her arms wrapped around her head and weeping uncontrollably, and Junior Adjutor Raymond Cvirik was smearing the blood from the deep, oozing scratches across his gray cheeks and repeating over and over again, like a broken piece of clockwork, "I didn't mean to . . . I swear to God, I didn't mean to . . ."

PART IV

MR. COUNSELOR

1

The water flowed out lukewarm and tasted vile. The showerhead was set unnaturally high, beyond his reach, and the feeble jets watered absolutely everything except what they were meant to. The drain was blocked, as usual, and the water above the grating sloshed about under his feet. And anyway, it was outrageous that he'd had to wait. Andrei listened: they were still droning and jabbering in the locker room. He thought he heard his name mentioned. Andrei twisted around and started squirming with his back, trying to catch the flow on his spine—he slipped, grabbed hold of the rough concrete wall, and swore under his breath. Damn them all to hell, why didn't they realize they ought to build a separate shower for government employees? I hate hanging around here like some kind of bad smell . . .

On the door in front of his nose someone had scratched, LOOK RIGHT. Andrei automatically looked to the right, where someone had scratched, LOOK BACK. Andrei got the idea. OK, we know the deal, we learned that in school, we used to write the same stuff ourselves . . . He shut off the water. It was quiet in the locker room. He cautiously opened the door and glanced out. Thank God, they'd gone . . .

He walked out, squeamishly turning up his toes as he hobbled across the dirty tiles toward his clothes. Out of the corner of his eye he spotted some kind of movement over by the wall. Peering in that direction, he discovered a pair of skinny buttocks, overgrown with black wool. So that was it, the usual picture: a naked man kneeling on the bench, staring into the women's locker room through a chink in the corner. Frozen absolutely still in his intent concentration.

Andrei took a towel and started wiping himself down. The towel was a cheap one, government issue, impregnated with the smell of carbolic, and it didn't really absorb the water but just smeared it across his skin.

The naked man was still ogling. His pose was unnatural, like a hanged man's—the hole in the wall had evidently been made by a teenager, in a low, inconvenient spot. And then the moment must have come when there was nothing left for the man to watch, because he sighed loudly and sat down, lowering his feet onto the floor. And then he saw Andrei.

"She got dressed," he announced. "A beautiful woman."

Andrei didn't say anything.

"I burst a blister again—there you go . . ." the naked man declared, examining the palm of his hand. "Yet again." He unfolded a towel and examined it suspiciously on both sides. "I'll tell you what I don't understand," he went on, toweling his head. "Why the hell couldn't they send some excavators over here? All of us could be replaced by a single excavator, couldn't we? And here we are scrabbling away with spades, like . . ."

Andrei shrugged and mumbled something that he didn't even understand himself.

"Ah?" asked the naked man, freeing his ear from under the towel.

"I said, there are only two excavators in the City," Andrei growled irritably. The lace on his right shoe had snapped, and now it was impossible to escape a conversation.

"That's what I'm saying—they should send one over here!" the naked man protested, energetically scrubbing at one side of his hairy pigeon chest. "But with spades . . . Let me tell you, you have to know how to work with a spade, and how, I ask you, are we supposed to know that, if we're from City Planning?"

"The excavators are needed somewhere else," Andrei growled. The damned shoelace just wouldn't tie.

"Where else is that?" asked the naked man from City Planning, pouncing immediately. "If I understand right, this here is the Great Construction Project. So where are the excavators? Gone to the Greatest Construction Project, have they? I haven't heard about that one."

Why the hell do I have to argue with you? Andrei thought balefully. And why *am* I arguing with him anyway? I ought to agree with him, not argue. If I'd backed him up a couple of times, he'd have left me in peace . . . No, he wouldn't have left me in peace anyway, he'd have started talking about naked women— how good it is for his health to ogle them. Obsessive-delusional creep. "What are you beefing about, anyway?" he said, straightening up. "They only ask you to work one hour a day, but you're whining like they were screwing a pencil up your ass . . . So he burst a blister! An industrial injury . . ."

Stunned, the naked man from City Planning stared at Andrei with his mouth half open. Skinny and hairy, with gouty little knees and a crooked little belly . . .

"You're all working for your own sake, after all!" Andrei continued, furiously knotting his necktie. "They're asking you to work for yourselves, not for someone else's uncle! But no, they're still dissatisfied, nothing's right for them. Before the Turning Point he probably carted shit, but now he works in City Planning, and he's still whining . . ."

He put on his jacket and started rolling up his overalls. And at that point the man from City Planning finally spoke up. "I beg your pardon!" he exclaimed resentfully. "I didn't mean anything of the kind. I was only thinking of rationality, efficiency . . . You surprise me! If you'd like to know, I stormed City Hall in person! And I tell you that if this is the Great Construction Site, then the very best of everything ought to be sent here . . . and don't you take the liberty of shouting at me!"

"Aah, it's pointless trying to talk to you . . ." Andrei said, and walked out of the locker room, wrapping his overalls in newspaper as he went.

Selma was already waiting for him, sitting on a bench a short distance away. She was smoking pensively, looking in the direction of the foundation pit, with her legs crossed in her usual manner, fresh and pink after her shower. Andrei felt an unpleasant twinge—it could very easily have been her that the hairy little bastard was ogling and drooling over. He walked across, stopped beside her, and laid his palm on her cool neck. "Shall we go?"

She looked up at him, smiled, and rubbed her cheek against his hand. "Let's just have a cigarette," she suggested.

"Right," he agreed, sitting down beside her and lighting up too.

In the foundation pit hundreds of people shuffled about, earth flew off spades, the sun flashed on polished iron. A line of drays loaded with dirt was moving across the opposite slope, and the next shift was gathering by the stacks of concrete slabs. The wind swirled around the reddish dust, carrying fragments of marches from the loudspeakers installed on concrete columns to their ears, and swaying immense sheets of plywood bearing faded slogans: "Heiger said: We must! The City replied: We shall!"; "The Great Construction Site is a blow struck at the nonhumans!"; "The Experiment—on the Experimenters!"

"Otto promised the rugs would come today," said Selma.

"That's good," Andrei answered delightedly. "Take the biggest one there is. We'll put it on the floor in the parlor."

"I was going to put it in your study. On the wall. Remember, I said so last year, when we'd only just moved in?"

"In the study?" Andrei said thoughtfully. He imagined his study, the rug, and his guns. It looked great. "Good idea," he said. "Right. Let's put it in the study."

"Only you have to call Ruhmer," said Selma. "Get him to send a man."

"You call him," said Andrei. "I won't have time . . . But then . . . OK, I'll call. Where shall I get him to send the man? Our place?"

"No, straight to the depot. Will you be back for lunch?"

"Yes, probably. By the way, Izya's been asking for a long time if he can come by."

"Well, that's great! Invite him this evening. It's ages since we got together. And we should invite Wang, with Mei-lin . . ."

"Uh-huh . . . *mmm* . . ." said Andrei. Somehow he hadn't thought of inviting Wang. "Apart from Izya, are you thinking of inviting anyone else from our crowd?" he asked cautiously.

"Our crowd? We could ask the colonel . . ." Selma said uncertainly. "He's a really nice man . . . But anyway, if we do invite anyone from our crowd today, the Dolfusses should be first in line. We've been to their place twice already, it's awkward."

"If only it could be without his wife," said Andrei.

"We can't possibly invite him without his wife."

"You know what," said Andrei, "don't call them yet, and we'll see how things look this evening." It was absolutely clear to him that there was no way Wang and the Dolfusses fitted together. "Maybe we ought to invite Chachua instead?"

"Brilliant," said Selma. "We'll set him on Madam Dolfuss. And everyone will have a good time." She dropped her cigarette butt. "Shall we go?"

Raising dust, yet another crowd of Great Builders made its way from the foundation pit toward the shower block—sweaty, loud-voiced, chortling workers from the foundry.

"Yes, let's," said Andrei.

Following a grubby little sandy lane between two rows of puny, freshly planted lime trees, they came out at a bus stop, where two battered and peeling buses were still standing, absolutely packed. Andrei looked at his watch: there were seven minutes until the buses left. Red-faced women were pushing a drunk out of the first bus. The drunk was hollering in a hoarse voice, and the women were hollering too, in high, hysterical voices.

"Shall we ride with the louts or walk?" Andrei asked.

"Do you have time?"

"Yes. Let's go. We'll walk along the Cliff. It's a bit cooler there."

Selma took him by the arm and they turned left into the shade of a five-story building covered in scaffolding, then set off along a small, cobblestoned street toward the Cliff.

This was a desolate, abandoned district. The empty, shabby little houses stood at crooked angles; the roads were overgrown with grass. Before the Turning Point and immediately afterward, it wasn't really safe to show your face here during the day, let alone at night—the whole area was full of thieves' hangouts, shady dives, and dens of iniquity. It had been populated by moonshiners, fences handling stolen goods, professional gold hunters, prostitutes who fingered victims for muggers, and other lowlifes. And then measures had been taken: some of them were caught and sent to settlements in the swamps, to work as farm laborers; others—the petty riffraff—were simply scattered to the four winds. In the hurly-burly some of them were put up against the wall, and everything of value that was found here was requisitioned for the City. The city blocks were left deserted. At first, patrols still used to come in here, then they were canceled as unnecessary, and just recently it had been announced that the slums were due for demolition and would be replaced by a belt of recreational land running along the entire cliff edge within the city limits—a promenade and amusement park.

Selma and Andrei rounded the final tumbledown ruin and set off along the cliff top, walking up to their knees in tall, luscious grass. It was cool here—damp, cold air billowed up out of the Abyss. Selma sneezed, and Andrei put his arm around her shoulders.

The granite parapet didn't extend as far as this stretch yet, and Andrei instinctively tried to keep a good distance away from the cliff edge—five or six steps.

Everyone felt strange on the cliff top. And apparently everyone got the same feeling here—that the world, if you looked at it from this spot, was clearly divided into two equal halves. Looking to the west, there was a boundless, blue-green void—not sea, and not even sky, but precisely a void of a bluish-greenish color. Blue-green Nothing. To the east, towering up vertically and blotting out the sky, was an unbounded expanse of solid yellow, with a narrow protruding terrace, along which the City stretched. The Yellow Wall. A solid, yellow Firmament.

Infinite Void to the west and infinite Solidity to the east. It was absolutely impossible to comprehend these two infinities. You could only grow accustomed to them. Those who couldn't grow accustomed to them, who simply didn't know how, tried not to come to the Cliff, so it was a rare thing to meet anyone here. Nowadays lovebirds were pretty much the only ones who came out here, and mostly at night. At night something in the Abyss glowed with a weak, greenish light, as if down there in the depths something was slowly rotting, century by century. This glow gave the black, ragged cliff edge a clearly defined outline, and everywhere here the grass was incredibly tall and soft . . .

"And when we build the airships," Selma suddenly said, "what will we do then, go up into the air in them or go down into this Abyss?"

"What airships?" Andrei asked absentmindedly.

"You know, the airships!" Selma exclaimed in surprise, and Andrei realized what she meant.

"Ah, the airships!" he said. "Down. Down, of course. Into the Abyss."

It was believed among the majority of the citizens working their daily hour at the Great Construction Site that a gigantic airship factory was being built. Heiger thought it best to encourage this opinion in every way that he could—without, however, specifically confirming anything.

"But why down?" Selma asked.

"Well, you see . . . We've tried sending up balloons— unmanned, of course. Something happens to them up there; they explode for some reason we don't understand. So far not one has gone higher than a kilometer."

"But what can there be down there? What do you think?"

Andrei shrugged. "I have no idea."

"Ah, you great scientist! Mr. Counselor." Selma picked up a fragment of an old wooden board with a rusty nail in it out of the grass and tossed it into the Abyss. "To give someone down there a smack on the noggin," she said.

"Don't be such a hooligan," Andrei said good-humoredly.

"But that's the way I am," said Selma. "Or had you forgotten?"

Andrei looked her over from head to toe. "No, I hadn't forgotten," he said. "Want me to tumble you over into the grass right now?"

"Yes," said Selma.

Andrei looked around. Two characters in peaked caps were sitting and smoking on the roof of the nearest ruin, with their legs dangling. Right beside them, standing at a skewed angle on a mound of garbage, was a crudely made tripod with a wrecking ball dangling on a crooked chain. "They're staring," he said. "A pity. I'd have showed *you*, Mrs. Counselor."

"Go on, tumble her over, stop wasting time!" someone shouted in a loud voice from the roof. "You young dork!"

Andrei pretended he hadn't heard. "Are you going straight home now?" he asked.

Selma looked at her watch. "I've got to call in to the hair salon," she said.

Andrei suddenly got an unfamiliar, exciting feeling. Suddenly he was very clearly aware that here he was, a counselor, an important member of the president's personal chancellery and a highly respected man, who had a wife—a beautiful wife—and a gracious home, and here was his wife, about to go to the hair salon, because in the evening they would be receiving guests, and the guests would be not just anybody but all respectable and important people, the right kind of people, the best in the City. A sensation of sudden awareness of his own maturity, his own importance and responsibility—could that be it? He was a complete adult, a fully developed, independent individual, married. He was a mature man, standing firmly on his own two feet. The only thing missing was children—he had everything else that real adults had . . .

"Good day to you, Mr. Counselor!" a respectful voice declared.

They had already emerged from the derelict district. The granite parapet was there, running along on their left, there were patterned concrete slabs under their feet on their right, and ahead of them stood the colossal white bulk of the Glass House, and immediately in their path, standing to attention and holding two fingers to the visor of his uniform cap, was a young, dapper, black-skinned policeman in the light blue uniform of external security.

Andrei nodded to him absentmindedly and said to Selma, "I'm sorry, you were saying something, I got lost in thought . . ."

"I was saying, don't forget to call Ruhmer. I'll need the man for more than the rug now. We have to get in wine, and vodka . . . The colonel likes whiskey, and Dolfuss likes beer . . . I think I'll get a whole crate."

"Yes! Get him to change the ceiling lamp in the lavatory!" said Andrei. "And you make beef bourguignonne. Shall I send Amalia round?"

They parted at the path leading off from their road to the Glass House. Selma walked on, and Andrei savored watching her walk before he turned to the side and walked toward the west entrance.

The broad plaza, paved with concrete slabs, that surrounded the building was empty, with only the blue uniforms of security men dotted around here and there. As always, new arrivals were loitering idly under the trees bordering the plaza, avidly gawping at the seat of power, and pensioners with walking canes were giving them explanations.

Dolfuss's old jalopy was already standing at the entrance with the hood raised as always and the bottom half of the driver, encased in glittering chrome leather, protruding from the engine. Standing right beside it was a filthy, stinking farm truck, straight out of the swamps, with grubby, scraped, red and blue legs of beef jutting up untidily above its sides. Flies circled around above the meat. The owner of the truck, a farmer, was arguing abusively with the security guard in the doorway. They had apparently been arguing for quite a long time: the duty head of security was already there, as well as three policemen, and another two were approaching at a leisurely pace, walking up the broad steps from the plaza.

Andrei thought the farmer looked familiar—a skinny beanpole of a man with dangling ends to his mustache. He reeked of sweat, gasoline, and stale alcohol fumes. Andrei showed his pass and walked through into the vestibule, and on the way he heard the farmer demanding to see President Heiger in person and the security guard trying to impress on him that this was the staff entrance and the farmer should go around the building and try his luck at the reception office. As they argued, the men's voices gradually grew louder and louder.

Andrei rode up in the elevator to the fifth floor and stepped inside a door embellished with an inscription in gold and black: PERSONAL CHANCELLERY OF THE PRESIDENT FOR SCIENCE AND TECHNOLOGY. The couriers sitting at the entrance got to their feet when he entered, and all hid their smoking cigarette butts behind their backs with identical gestures. In the broad, white corridor there was no one else to be seen, but from behind the doors, exactly the way it used to be in the newspaper offices, he could hear telephones ringing, voices briskly dictating, and typewriters clattering. The chancellery was working at full tilt. Andrei opened a door with a plaque that said COUNSELOR A. VORONIN and stepped into his own reception office.

Here too people rose to their feet to greet him: the fat, constantly sweating head of the Geodesy Sector, Quejada; the apathetic, mournful-looking chief of the personnel department, Vareikis; a fidgety, aging woman from the finance office; and some unfamiliar, athletic-looking young boy—he had to be a new arrival, waiting to be presented. And his personal secretary, Amalia, smiling at him as she quickly got to her feet at her little desk with a typewriter by the window.

"Good day, good day, ladies and gentlemen," Andrei said in a loud voice, putting on his most benign smile. "I beg your pardon!

The damned buses are packed solid—I had to foot it all the way from the Construction Site . . ."

He started shaking hands: Quejada's massive, sweaty paw, Vareikis's flaccid fin, the finance lady's bunch of dry bones (Why the hell has she come to see me? What could she possibly want here?), and the cast-iron blade of the sullen-looking new arrival.

"I think we'll let the lady to the front of the line," he said. "Madam, if you please . . ."—that was to the finance woman. "Is there anything urgent?"—that was to Amalia, in a low voice. "Thank you . . ." He took the phonogram that she held out to him and opened the door into his own office. "After you, madam, after you . . ."

He unfolded the telephonogram as he walked over to the desk. Glancing at the piece of paper, he pointed out a chair for the woman to sit on, then sat down and placed the phonogram in front of him.

"What can I do for you?"

The woman started jabbering. Andrei listened to her attentively, smiling with just the corners of his lips and tapping a little pencil on the telephonogram. Everything was clear to him from the first few words she uttered.

"Pardon me," he said, interrupting her after a minute and a half. "I understand you. It is not actually our practice to hire people as a personal favor. However, in your case, we are undoubtedly dealing with an exception. If your daughter really is so interested in cosmography that she has studied it independently while still in school . . . Please call my head of personnel. I'll have a word with him." He stood up. "Such ambition in our young people should definitely be welcomed and encouraged in every possible way . . ." He showed her to the door. "This is entirely in the spirit of the new times . . . Don't thank me, madam, I am simply performing my duty. All the very best to you . . ."

He went back to the desk and reread the phonogram: "The president invites Mr. Counselor Voronin to his office at 1400." That was all. On what business? What for? What should I take with me? Strange . . . Probably Fritz is simply feeling bored and wants to chew the fat for a while. Fourteen hundred hours— that's the lunch break. So we're having lunch with the president . . .

He picked up the internal phone. "Amalia, let me have Quejada."

The door opened and Quejada walked in, leading the athletic-looking youth after him by the sleeve. "Allow me to introduce you, Mr. Counselor," he began straight from the doorway, "to this young man . . . Douglas Ketcher . . . He is a new arrival, who arrived here only a month ago, and he gets bored with being stuck in the same place all the time."

"Well," Andrei laughed, "we all get bored with being stuck the same place all the time. Pleased to meet you, Mr. Ketcher. Where are you from? And from what time?"

"Dallas, Texas," the youth replied in a surprisingly deep voice, smiling shyly. "Sixty-three."

"Have you graduated from anywhere?"

"A regular college. Then I went on a lot of expeditions with geologists. Oil prospecting."

"Excellent," said Andrei. "That's just what we need." He toyed with the little pencil. "Perhaps you don't know this, Ketcher, but here it's customary to ask: Why? Did you run away from something? Or were you seeking adventure? Or were you intrigued by the Experiment?"

Douglas Ketcher frowned, grasped the thumb of his left hand in his right hand, and looked out the window. "You could say I ran away," he mumbled.

"Their president was shot," Quejada explained, mopping his face with a handkerchief. "Right there in his home city."

"Ah, so that's it," Andrei said in an understanding tone of voice. "Did you fall under suspicion for some reason?"

The youth shook his head, and Quejada said, "No, that's not it. It's a long story. He had very high hopes of this president, the president was his idol—in short, it's psychological."

"Goddamn country," the youth declared. "Nothing will ever save them."

"I see, I see," said Andrei, nodding sympathetically. "But you do know that we no longer recognize the Experiment?"

The youth shrugged his powerful shoulders. "That's all the same to me. I like it here. Only I don't like being stuck in one place all the time. I get bored in town. And Mr. Quejada has suggested I could go on an expedition . . ."

"For a start I want to send him to Son's group," said Quejada. "He's a strong youngster, he has some sort of experience, and you know how hard it is to find men to work in the jungle."

"Well then," said Andrei. "Very glad to have met you, Ketcher. I like the look of you, and I hope things will continue that way."

Ketcher nodded awkwardly and got up. Quejada got up too, panting.

"One more thing," said Andrei, raising his finger. "I'd like to warn you, Ketcher, that the City and the Glass House are interested in you continuing your studies. We don't need people who simply do things—we have enough of them here. We need qualified people. I'm sure you'd make an excellent oil engineer . . . What's his Intelligence Index like, Quejada?"

"Eighty-seven," said Quejada, chuckling.

"There, you see . . . I have grounds for my confidence in you."

"I'll try my best," Douglas Ketcher mumbled, and looked at Quejada.

"That's all we have to say," said Quejada.

"And that's all I have to say," said Andrei. "The best of luck to you . . . And let Vareikis in to see me."

As usual, Vareikis didn't walk in but advanced into the office one part at a time, repeatedly looking back through the crack of the half-open door. Then he closed the door firmly, hobbled soundlessly over to the desk, and sat down. The expression on his face became more emphatically doleful and the corners of his lips turned all the way down.

"Just so I don't forget," said Andrei. "That woman from the finance office was here."

"I know," Vareikis said quietly. "Her daughter."

"Yes. Well then, I have no objections."

"For Quejada," Vareikis half-asked, half-stated.

"No, I think for the data processors."

"All right," said Vareikis, and pulled a notepad out of his inside pocket. "Regulation 017," he said in a quiet voice.

"Yes?"

"The latest assessment has been completed," Vareikis said in an even quieter voice. "Eight employees have been identified with an index below the required level of 75."

"Why 75? According to the regulation the minimum intelligence index is 67."

"According to a clarification from the President's Personal Chancellery for Personnel"—Vareikis's lips barely even moved—"the minimum intelligence index for employees of the President's Personal Chancellery for Science and Technology is 75."

"Ah, so that's it . . ." said Andrei, scratching the top of his head. "Hmm . . . Well now, that's logical."

"In addition," Vareikis continued, "five of the eight are even ranked below 67. Here is the list."

Andrei took the list and looked through it. Half-familiar names, two men and six women . . . "Oh, come on now," he said, frowning. "Amalia Torn . . . That's my Amalia! What sort of hocus-pocus is this?"

"Fifty-eight," said Vareikis.

"And the last time?"

"I wasn't here the last time."

"She's a secretary!" said Andrei. "My secretary! My personal secretary!"

Vareikis remained dismally silent.

Andrei glanced though the list again. Rashidov . . . he's a geodesist, I think . . . Someone praised him to me. Or did they lambaste him? Tatyana Postnik. A technician. Ah, she's the one with the curls and that cute little face, Quejada had something going on with her . . . ah, no, that's a different one . . . "All right," he said, "I'll deal with this and we'll talk about it again. It would be good if you could request clarification through your own channels concerning posts such as secretary, technician . . . concerning auxiliary personnel. We can't make the same demands of them as we do of the scientific workers. After all, we have couriers listed on our staff . . ."

"Very well," said Vareikis.

"Anything else?" Andrei asked.

"Yes. Regulation 003."

Andrei frowned. "I don't recall that one."

"Advocating the idea of the Experiment."

"Ah," said Andrei. "Well?"

"There are regular alarm signals concerning the following individuals." Vareikis put another sheet of paper in front of Andrei. There were only three names on the list. All were men. All three of them were heads of sectors. Fundamental sectors. Cosmography, Social Psychology, and Geodesy. Sullivan, Butz, and Quejada. Andrei drummed his fingers on the list. What a damned disaster, he thought. Back to the same old dreck. But keep calm. We need to watch our step here. There's no way to get through to this blockhead, and I still have to work with him for a long, long time . . . "Disturbing," he declared. "Very disturbing. I assume the information has been checked? There are no errors?"

"Crosschecked and repeatedly confirmed information," Vareikis said in a colorless voice. "Sullivan claims that the Experiment on the City is still going on. According to him, the Glass House is continuing the line of the Experiment, regardless of its own intentions. He claims that the Turning Point is only one stage of the Experiment."

Hallowed words, thought Andrei. Izya says the same thing, and Fritz doesn't like it at all. Only Izya is allowed to say it, and the unfortunate Sullivan isn't.

"Quejada," Vareikis continued. "Expresses admiration for the scientific and technical prowess of the hypothetical experimenters in the presence of his subordinates. Belittles the value of the president's work and the work of the presidential council. Has twice compared these activities to the scrabbling of mice in a cardboard shoebox . . ."

Andrei listened with his eyes lowered, keeping a stony face.

"And finally, Butz. Makes hostile remarks about the president. In an inebriated state has referred to the current political leadership as the dictatorship of mediocrity over cretins."

Andrei couldn't restrain himself—he groaned. What the hell makes them say it, he thought irritably, pushing the sheet of paper away. The elite, they're called, and they saw off the branch they're sitting on . . . "But even so, you know," he said to Vareikis. "But even so, you are aware . . ."

He shouldn't have said that. It was stupid. Vareikis stared mournfully into his face, without blinking.

"Excellent work, Vareikis," said Andrei. "I've got nothing to worry about with you there looking out for me . . . I assume this information"—he tapped his fingernail on the sheet of paper—"has already been forwarded through the usual channels?"

"It will be forwarded today," said Vareikis. "I was obliged to inform you first."

"Excellent," Andrei said cheerfully. "Forward it." He fastened both pieces of paper together with a pin and placed them in the blue folder with the title REPORT TO THE PRESIDENT. "We'll see what our Ruhmer decides concerning this matter."

"Since this is not the first time that we have received information of this kind," Vareikis said, "I assume that Mr. Ruhmer will recommend removing these men from their senior positions."

Andrei looked at Vareikis, trying to focus his eyes somewhere behind Vareikis's back. "Yesterday I went to a screening of a new movie," he said. "*The Naked and the Bosses*. We approved it, so it will soon be released for the big screen. I really, really do recommend you watch it. You know, it's such . . ."

He launched into a leisurely, detailed exposition of this gruesome example of hideous banality, which Fritz had genuinely liked—and he wasn't the only one. Vareikis listened in silence, nodding every now and then in the most unexpected places—as if suddenly recalling where he was. His face still expressed nothing but gloom and despondency. It was obvious that he had lost the thread long ago and didn't understand a single thing. At the most crucial point in the plot, when Vareikis had clearly realized that he would have to listen right through to the very end, Andrei broke off with a blatant yawn and said complacently, "Well, and so on, in the same vein. You must watch it . . . By the way, what kind of impression did young Ketcher make on you?"

"Ketcher? So far I have the impression that he is all right."

"And so do I," said Andrei. He picked up the phone. "Do you have anything else for me, Vareikis?"

Vareikis got up. "No," he said. "Nothing else. May I go?"

Andrei benevolently nodded to him and spoke into the receiver. "Amalia, is there anyone else?"

"Ellisauer, Mr. Counselor."

"What Ellisauer?" Andrei asked, observing Vareikis cautiously exiting the office, one part at a time.

"The deputy head of the transport department. Concerning the subject of 'Aquamarine.'"

"Let him wait. Bring in the mail."

Amalia appeared in the doorway a minute later, and Andrei spent that entire minute moaning gently as he massaged his biceps and squirmed his waist about; everything ached pleasantly after an hour of intensive work with a spade in his hands, and as always he absentmindedly thought what good exercise it was for a man who led a mostly sedentary life.

Amalia closed the door firmly behind her, clattered across the parquet floor in her high heels, stopped beside him, and put the correspondence file on the desk. In a habitual gesture, he put his arm around her firm, narrow hips sheathed in cool silk and patted her on the thigh while he opened the file with his other hand.

"Right, then, what do we have here?" he said cheerfully.

Amalia simply dissolved under his palm—she actually stopped breathing. A funny girl, and devoted as a dog. And she knows her job. He looked up at her. As always happened in these tender moments, her face had turned pale and frightened. When their eyes met, she hesitantly laid her hot, slim hand on his neck below the ear. Her fingers were trembling.

"Well then, babe," he said endearingly. "Is there anything important in this trash? Or shall we lock the door right now and assume a different position?" That was their code name for fun and games in the armchair and on the carpet. He could never have told anyone what Amalia was like in bed. He had never been in bed with her even once.

"Here are the draft budget figures," Amalia said in a weak little voice. "Then all sorts of proposals and submissions . . . Well, and the personal letters—I haven't opened them."

"Quite right too," said Andrei. "What if there was one from some little cutie . . ."

He let go of her and she gave a feeble sigh.

"Sit down for a moment," he said. "Don't go, I'll be quick."

He took the first letter that came to hand, tore open the envelope, rapidly glanced through it, and frowned. The technician Yevseenko informed Andrei that Yevseenko's immediate superior, Quejada, "passes remarks concerning the administration and concerning Mr. Counselor Voronin personally." Andrei knew this Yevseenko well. He was an extremely strange individual and a hopeless loser—nothing he tried ever went right. He had once stunned Andrei by singing the praises of life in the year 1942 near Leningrad. "Those were good times," he had said in a strange, dreamy kind of voice. "Just living, without thinking about anything, and if you need something—just tell the men and they'll get it." He had served his time as a captain, and in the entire war he had killed only one man—his own political commissar. They were fighting their way out of encirclement at the time. Yevseenko saw the Germans had caught the political commissar and were rummaging through his pockets. He fired at them out of the bushes, killing the political commissar, and then took to his heels. He thought very highly of himself for this exploit: they would have tortured him to death.

Well, what can I do with this fool? This is the sixth denunciation he's written. And he doesn't write to Ruhmer, does he, or to Vareikis, but to me. A very amusing psychological twist, that. If he writes to Vareikis or Ruhmer, Quejada will be held accountable for his words. But I won't touch Quejada—I know all about him, but I won't touch him, because I value him and I forgive him, everyone knows that. So this way it turns out that Yevseenko has sort of fulfilled his civic duty but no one's life has been ruined . . . God almighty, what a creep he is!

Andrei crumpled up the letter, flung it in the wastebasket, and picked up the next one. The writing on the envelope looked familiar to him; it was very distinctive. There was no return address. Inside the envelope was a sheet of paper with text written on a typewriter—a carbon copy, not the top sheet—and below the text a note had been added by hand. Andrei read it without understanding a thing, read it again, turned cold, and glanced at his watch. Then he grabbed the receiver off the white phone and dialed a number.

"Counselor Ruhmer, urgently!" he barked in an altered voice.

"Counselor Ruhmer is busy."

"This is Counselor Voronin! I said—urgently!"

"I'm sorry, Mr. Counselor, Counselor Ruhmer is with the president—"

Andrei flung down the receiver, pushed aside dumbfounded Amalia, and dashed for the door. He had already grabbed the plastic handle before he realized it was too late—he couldn't get there in time anyway. If it was all true, of course. If it wasn't all an idiotic hoax . . .

He walked slowly across to the window, took hold of the velvet-covered handrail, and started watching the plaza. It was empty, as it always was. Light blue uniforms hovering, idle onlookers mooching under the trees, an old woman hobbling past, pushing a baby stroller along in front of her. A car driving past. Andrei waited, clutching the handrail.

Amalia came up to him from behind and gently touched him on the shoulder. "What's happened?" she asked in a whisper.

"Move away," he said without turning around. "Sit in the chair."

Amalia disappeared. Andrei looked at the time again. On his watch an extra minute had already gone by. Of course, he thought. It's not possible. An idiotic hoax. Or blackmail . . . And just at that moment a man appeared from under the trees. He looked very small from this height and this distance, and Andrei didn't recognize him. He remembered the man as being slim and erect, but *this* man looked bulky and swollen, and Andrei only realized why at the very last moment. He squeezed his eyes shut and backed away from the window.

A short, rumbling boom shattered the silence of the plaza. The windows shuddered and jangled and somewhere below him shards of glass scattered with an irritating tinkling sound. Amalia gave a stifled screech and down below in the plaza frantic voices started shrieking.

With one hand Andrei pushed aside Amalia, who was straining to get to him, or maybe to the window, then forced himself to open his eyes and look. Where the man had been there was a yellowish column of smoke, and he couldn't see anything beyond it. From every direction light blue uniforms were running toward the spot, and farther away, under the trees, a crowd was rapidly gathering. It was all over.

Andrei walked back to the desk with no feeling in his legs, sat down, and picked up the letter again:

To all the powerful of this trashy world!
I hate lies, but your truth is worse than lies. You have transformed the City into a well-organized pigsty, and the citizens
of the City into gorged swine. I don't want to be a gorged

swine, but I don't want to be a swineherd either, and in your chomping, champing world, there is no other choice. You are smug and mediocre in your correctness, although there was a time when many of you were real human beings. Some of my former friends are among you, and I am writing to them first. Words have no effect on you, and I shall reinforce them with my death. Maybe you'll feel ashamed, maybe you'll feel afraid, or maybe you'll simply stop feeling so comfortable in your pigsty. This is all I have left to hope for. May God punish your boredom! These are not my words, but I fervently subscribe to them.

Denny Lee

All this was typed with carbon paper—the third or even fourth copy. And below it was a note added by hand:

Dear Voronin, good-bye!
I'm going to blow myself up today at 1300 in the plaza in front of the Glass House. If this letter doesn't arrive too late, you can watch it happen, but don't try to stop me—that would only cause unnecessary casualties.

Your former friend and head of the letters department in your former newspaper,
Denny

Andrei raised his eyes and saw Amalia. "Do you remember Denny?" he asked. "Denny Lee, our letters editor . . ."

Amalia nodded without speaking, then her face suddenly crumpled in horror. "It's not possible!" she said hoarsely. "It's not true . . ."

"He blew himself up," said Andrei, finding it hard to move his lips. "Probably strapped dynamite around himself. Under his jacket."

"What for?" said Amalia. She bit on her lip and tears welled up in her eyes, overflowing and running down her little white face and hanging from her chin.

"I don't understand," said Andrei. "I don't understand any-thing . . ." He stared blankly at the letter. "We saw each other not long ago . . . Sure, we cussed and swore at each other; sure, we quarreled . . ." He looked at Amalia again. "Maybe he tried to get in to see me? Maybe I wouldn't see him?"

Amalia put her hands over face and shook her head.

And suddenly Andrei felt anger. Not even anger but the same furious exasperation he had felt earlier that day in the locker room after his shower. What the hell! What more do they damn well want? What else do they need, these riffraff? The idiot! What has he proved with this? He doesn't want to be a swine, he doesn't want to be a swineherd . . . He's bored! Well you can go to hell and take your damned boredom with you! "Stop bawling!" he yelled at Amalia. "Wipe off your nose and get back to your place."

He tossed the sheet of paper away, jumped up, and went over to the window again.

A huge, dark crowd filled the plaza. At the center of the crowd was an empty, gray space, cordoned off by light blue uniforms, with people in white coats swarming about in it. An ambulance was hysterically howling with its siren, trying to clear a path for itself . . .

And just what have you really proved? That you don't want to live with us? What did you have to prove that for, and to whom? That you hate us? You shouldn't. We do everything that has to be done. It's not our fault they're swine. They were swine before us, and they'll still be swine after us. We can only feed and clothe them, and relieve them of brutish animal suffering, but they've never known any spiritual suffering in their lives and they never can. Have we done so very little for them? Look what the City is like now. Clean and orderly, without a trace of the old shambles, chow to spare, duds to spare, soon there'll be amusements to spare, just give us time—and what else do they need? And you, what have you achieved? Now the ambulance men will scrub your guts off the asphalt—and you're done . . . But we have to keep on and on working, keeping the whole behemoth moving, because everything we've achieved so far is only the beginning—it still has to be secured, my friend, and once it has been secured, increased . . . Because maybe on Earth there's neither God nor devil standing above people, but here there is . . . You stinking democrat, populist weasel, the brother of my brothers . . .

But Denny was still there in front of his eyes, the way he was the last time they met, a month or two ago—completely withered somehow, ground down, as if he were ill, and some kind of secret horror was lurking in his sad, extinct eyes—and the words he said right at the end of their rowdy, senseless argument, after he had already gotten up and tossed the crumpled bills onto the little silver dish: "God, what have you been bragging about to me? He's laying his life on the altar . . . What for? To stuff people's bellies! But is that really the goal? In crummy little Denmark they've known how to do that for years and years already. OK, so maybe I don't have the right, as you put it, to crucify myself in the name of everyone. Maybe not everyone knows, but you and I certainly do—that's not what people need; you'll never build a genuinely new world that way!"

"And just how, damn and blast it, *do* you build it? How?" Andrei had bellowed, but Denny merely waved that aside and wouldn't talk anymore after that.

The white phone rang. Andrei reluctantly went back to the desk and picked it up.

"Andrei? This is Heiger here."

"Hello, Fritz."

"Did you know him?"

"Yes."

"And what do you think about this?"

"A hysterical wimp," Andrei said through his teeth. "Trash."

Heiger said nothing for a moment. "Did you get a letter from him?"

"Yes."

"A strange man," said Heiger. "All right, then. I'm expecting you at two."

Andrei put down the receiver, and the phone rang again. This time it was Selma calling. She was badly shaken. Rumors of the explosion had already reached White Court; naturally, along the way they had been distorted beyond all recognition, and now all White Court was in a state of quiet panic.

"Fine, everyone's safe and sound," said Andrei. "I'm fine, and Heiger's fine, and the Glass House is fine . . . Did you call Ruhmer?"

"To hell with Ruhmer!" Selma exclaimed, infuriated. "I ran back from the salon almost out of my mind—Madam Dolfuss burst in, as white as a ghost, and set the walls shaking, howling that someone had tried to kill Heiger and half the building had been blown to pieces . . ."

"Oh, come on," Andrei said impatiently. "I haven't got time."

"Can you tell me what happened?"

"Some psychopath—" Andrei stopped, realizing what he was saying. "Some blockhead was lugging explosives across the plaza and he dropped them, probably."

"It definitely wasn't an assassination attempt?"

"I don't know, do I? Ruhmer's handling it, but I don't know anything."

Selma breathed into the phone for a while. "You're just lying, probably, Mr. Counselor," she said, and hung up.

Andrei walked around the desk and glanced out into the reception office. Amalia was in her place—stern, with her lips pursed, absolutely unapproachable—and her fingers were flying over the keyboard at her usual furious speed; not a trace was left on her face of tears, snot, or any kind of emotion. Andrei looked at her tenderly. That's my girl. Screw you, Vareikis, he thought with boundless malice. I'll throw you out on your ass first . . . His view of Amalia was suddenly blocked off. Obsequiously looming over him at a superhuman height was a face, squashed in from both sides, that belonged to Ellisauer from the transport department.

"Ah," said Andrei. "Ellisauer . . . I'm sorry, I won't see you today. Tomorrow, first thing in the morning, please."

Without saying a word, Ellisauer bowed, breaking himself in half, and disappeared. Amalia was already standing with her notepad and pencil at the ready. "Mr. Counselor?"

"Come in for a moment," said Andrei. He went back to his desk, and the white phone immediately rang.

"Voronin?" said a nasal voice, hoarse from smoking. "It's Ruhmer here. Well, how are you doing?"

"Fine," said Andrei, gesturing for Amalia to stay: *Don't go, I'll just be a moment.*

"How's your wife?"

"Just fine—she told me to say hello. By the way, send her two men from the service department today, something needs to be done around the house."

"Two? OK. Where to?"

"They can call her, she'll tell them. Tell them to call right now."

"OK," said Ruhmer. "I'll do it. Not immediately, but I'll do it . . . I'm totally swamped, you know, with this garbage. Do you know the official version?"

"How could I?" Andrei asked angrily

"Basically, it goes like this. An accident with explosives. While explosive substances were being carried . . . Or let's say someone was driving them somewhere. Drunk."

"I get it, I get it," said Andrei. "That's right. Good move."

"Aha," said Ruhmer. "Well, then he stumbled, or . . . Anyway, the details are being clarified. The culprits will be punished. They'll duplicate the information in a minute and bring it to you. Only you just answer me this. You got a letter, didn't you? Who else there read it?"

"No one."

"What about your secretary?"

"I told you: no one. I always open the personal letters myself."

"That's right," Ruhmer said approvingly. "That's the right arrangement you've got there. But, you know, some people have made a real rat's nest of their letters . . . Absolutely anyone reads them . . . So no one read yours, then. That's good. You keep it well hidden, that letter—the double-zero file. One of my flunkeys will drop by right now, you give it to him, OK?"

"What for?" Andrei asked.

Ruhmer was stuck for an answer. "Well, how can I put it . . ." he mumbled. "It might come in handy . . . Apparently you knew him."

"Who?"

"You know, the guy." Ruhmer giggled. "That worker . . . with the explosive . . ."

"Yes, I did."

"Well, we won't talk about it on the phone; this lackey of mine will ask you a couple of questions, you answer him."

"I've got no time for that," Andrei said angrily. "Fritz has asked me to go to see him."

"Ah, come on, just five minutes," Ruhmer whined. "What bother is that to you, honest to God . . . You can't even answer two questions now . . ."

"OK then, OK," Andrei said impatiently. "Is that all?"

"I've already sent him over to you; he'll be there in a minute. His name's Cvirik. A senior adjutor . . ."

"All right, all right, agreed."

"Just two questions, that's all. He won't hold you up."

"Is that all?" Andrei asked again.

"That's it. Now I've got to call around to the other counselors."

"Don't you forget to send those men to Selma."

"I won't forget. I've already noted it down here. See you."

Andrei hung up and said to Amalia, "Don't forget, you didn't see or hear a thing."

Amalia gave him a frightened glance and jabbed her finger toward the window without saying anything.

"Exactly," said Andrei. "You don't know any names and you don't know anything about what happened."

The door opened slightly and a vaguely familiar pale face with sour little eyes was thrust into the office.

"Wait!" Andrei said curtly. "I'll call you."

The face disappeared.

"You understand?" Andrei asked. "There was a big bang outside, and you don't know anything else. The official version is this: a drunk worker, carrying explosive from the depot, the culprits are being identified." He paused for a moment, pondering. Where have I seen that ugly mug before? And the name's familiar . . . Cvirik . . . Cvirik . . .

"Why did he do it?" Amalia asked in a quiet voice. Her eyes turned suspiciously damp again.

Andrei frowned. "Let's not talk about that now. Later. Go and call that lackey in."

2

When they were seated at the table, Heiger said to Izya, "Help yourself, my Jew. Help yourself, my dear fellow."

"I'm not your Jew," Izya objected, heaping salad onto his plate. "I've told you a hundred times that I'm my own Jew. That's your Jew there." He jabbed his finger in Andrei's direction.

"Is there any tomato juice?" Andrei asked sullenly, looking around the table.

"You want tomato juice?" Heiger asked. "Parker! Tomato juice for Mr. Counselor!"

A burly, ruddy-cheeked individual—Heiger's personal adjutant—appeared in the doorway, jangling his spurs mellifluously, approached the table, gave a shallow bow, and set down a dew-spangled carafe of tomato juice in front of Andrei.

"Thank you, Parker," said Andrei. "It's all right, I'll pour it myself."

Heiger nodded, and Parker was gone.

"Great training!" Izya mumbled with his mouth stuffed full.

"A fine young man," Andrei said.

"But at Manjuro's place they serve vodka with lunch," said Izya.

"You stoolie!" Heiger told him reproachfully.

"Why's that?" Izya asked in astonishment.

"If Manjuro swigs vodka during working hours, I have to punish him."

"You can't shoot everyone," Izya said.

"The death penalty has been abolished," said Heiger. "Actually, I don't exactly remember. I should ask Chachua . . ."

"And what happened to Chachua's predecessor?" Izya inquired innocently.

"That was a complete accident," said Heiger. "An exchange of fire."

"He was an excellent administrator, by the way," Andrei observed. "Chachua knows his job, but his boss! . . . He was phenomenal."

"Yep, yep, we were pretty reckless back then," Heiger said pensively. "Young and green . . ."

"All's well that ends well," Andrei said.

"Nothing's ended yet!" Izya objected. "What makes you think everything's already over?"

"Well, the shooting's all over, anyway," Andrei growled.

"The real shooting hasn't even started yet," Izya declared. "Listen, Fritz, have there been any attempts on your life?"

Heiger frowned. "What sort of idiotic idea is that? Of course not."

"There will be," Izya promised.

"Thank you," Heiger said frostily.

"There'll be assassination attempts," Izya continued. "There'll be an explosion of drug addiction. There'll be affluence riots. The hippies have already appeared, I won't even mention them. There'll be protest suicides, self-immolations, people blowing themselves up . . . In fact, this has already happened."

Heiger and Andrei exchanged glances.

"There, you see," Andrei said. "He knows already."

"I wonder how," said Heiger, peering at Izya through narrowed eyes.

"What do I know?" Izya asked quickly. He put down his fork. "Hang on, now! Ah! So that was a protest suicide! I was wondering about all that bullshit! Blasters staggering around drunk with dynamite . . . So that's it! But to be honest, I imagined it was an assassination attempt . . . Now I get it . . . And who was it really?"

"A certain Denny Lee," Heiger said after a pause. "Andrei knew him."

"Lee . . ." Izya said thoughtfully, absentmindedly smearing splashes of mayonnaise across the lapel of his jacket. "Denny Lee . . . Wait, he's a skinny guy . . . A journalist?"

"You knew him too," said Andrei. "Remember, in my news-paper . . ."

"Yes, yes, yes!" Izya exclaimed. "That's right! I remember now."

"Only, for God's sake, keep your mouth shut," said Heiger.

Wearing his habitual frozen smile, Izya started plucking at the wart on his neck. "So that's what it was . . ." he muttered. "I get it . . . I get it . . . So he wrapped himself in explosives and went out onto the plaza . . . He probably sent letters to all the papers, the freak . . . Right, right, right. And what measures do you intend to take?" he asked, addressing Heiger.

"I've already taken them," said Heiger.

"Right, of course you have!" Izya said impatiently. "You've classified it, put out the official lies, let Ruhmer off the leash—that's not what I meant. What do you think about this in general? Or do you assume that it's an isolated incident?"

"Uh-uh. I don't assume that it's an isolated incident," Heiger said slowly.

"Thank God!" Izya exclaimed.

"And what do you think?" Andrei asked him.

Izya quickly turned to face Andrei. "And you?"

"I think that any orderly society is bound to have its own psychos. And Denny was a psycho, that's for sure. His philosophy had clearly driven him crazy. And of course, he's not the only one in the City."

"And what did he say?" Izya asked avidly.

"He said he was bored. He said we hadn't found our true goal. He said all our work on improving the standard of living was garbage and it solved nothing. He said lots of things, but he couldn't propose anything worthwhile himself. A psycho. Hys-terical."

"But what would he really have wanted to see?" asked Heiger.

Andrei gestured dismissively. "The usual populist nonsense. Like Nekrasov: 'With its broad, radiant chest, the people will bear whatever the Lord may send . . .'"

"I don't understand," said Heiger.

"Well, he believed it was the task of enlightened people to raise up the people to their own enlightened level. But of course, he didn't know how to go about it."

"And why did he kill himself?" Heiger asked doubtfully.

"I told you, he was a psycho."

"And what's your opinion?" Heiger asked Izya.

Izya didn't take even a second to ponder. "If a psycho is what you call a man who wrestles with a problem that has no solution," he said, "then yes, he was a psycho. And you"—Izya jabbed his finger at Heiger—"will never understand him. You're one of those people who only take on problems that have solutions."

"Let's assume," said Andrei, "that Denny was absolutely certain his problem did have a solution."

Izya brushed his opinion aside. "Neither of you understand a damned thing," he declared. "You believe you're the technocratic elite. *Democrat* is a dirty word for you: the cobblers should stick to their lasts. You have appalling contempt for the broad masses and you're appallingly proud of the way you despise them. But in reality, it's you who are the genuine, one hundred percent slaves of those masses! Everything you do, you do it for the masses. Everything you rack your brains over—the whole kit and caboodle, above all else it's what the masses need. You live for the masses. If the masses disappeared, your lives would lose all meaning. You're pathetic, pitiful applications engineers. And that's why you'll never be psychos. After all, rustling up everything the broad masses need is relatively simple, isn't it? So your problems are by definition problems that have solutions. You'll never understand people who kill themselves as a gesture of protest."

"Why won't we?" Andrei asked irritably. "What is there really to understand here? Of course we do what the overwhelming majority wants. And we give, or try to give, that majority everything short of flying pigs—which, by the way, are not actually required by the majority. But there's always an insignificant minority that wants flying pigs and nothing else. Because it's an idée fixe for them, you see. A morbid obsession. They have to have flying pigs! Simply because it's impossible to find flying pigs anywhere. And that's how the social psychos appear. What's so hard to understand about that? Or do you really believe that all this rabble can be raised up to the level of the elite?"

"We're not talking about me," said Izya, baring his teeth in a grin. "I don't consider myself a slave of the majority, a.k.a. a servant of the people. I've never worked for the majority and I don't consider myself under any obligation to it."

"All right, all right," said Heiger. "Everyone knows you're a case apart. Let's get back to our suicides. You believe that suicides will happen, no matter what political line we pursue?"

"They'll happen precisely because you pursue an entirely definite political line!" said Izya. "And the longer it goes on, the more of them there'll be, because you take away from people the onus of providing their own daily bread and you don't give them anything in return. People get sick of it all and start feeling bored. That's why there'll be suicides, drug addiction, sexual revolutions, fatuous revolts over paltry nonsense . . ."

"That's bullshit!" Andrei said furiously. "Think before you spout that kind of drivel, you lousy experimenter! 'Spice his life up a bit, add a little pepper!' Is that it? Are you suggesting we create artificial shortages? Just think where what you're saying leads to!"

"It's not what I'm saying that leads there," said Izya, reaching right across the table with his mutilated arm to take the pan of meat sauce. "It's what you're doing. But it's a fact that you can't give them anything in exchange. Your Great Construction Sites are nonsense. The experiment on the experimenters is hogwash, no one gives a damn about it . . . And stop attacking me, I'm not saying this to condemn you. It's just the way things are. It's the fate of every populist, whether he poses as a technocratic benefactor or vainly attempts to inculcate certain ideals in the people—ideals which, in his opinion, the people can't live without . . . Two sides of the same coin, heads or tails. In the end, you get food riots or affluence riots, take your choice. You've chosen affluence riots, and good luck to you—why attack me over it?"

"Don't pour sauce on the tablecloth," Heiger said angrily.

"Sorry . . ." Izya absentmindedly smeared the puddle across the tablecloth with a napkin. "But the arithmetic's quite clear," he said, "even if the discontents only make up one percent. If there are a million people in a city, that means ten thousand discontents. Even if it's a tenth of a percent—that's a thousand discontents. And when that thousand starts clamoring under your windows! And then, note, there's no such thing as completely contented people. There's something everyone wants that he doesn't have, right? You know, he's quite happy with everything, but then he doesn't have a car. Why not? You know, he got used to having a car on Earth, but here he hasn't got one, and what's even more important, there's no way he can expect to get one . . . Can you imagine how many people like that there are in the City?" Izya broke off and started greedily gobbling down macaroni, drowning it in sauce. "The chow here's delicious," he said. "With my modest level of affluence the Glass House is the only place I can really fill my belly."

Andrei watched him guzzling, snorted, and poured himself some tomato juice. He drank it and lit a cigarette. It's always the apocalypse with him . . . Seven chalices of the wrath of God and the seven last plagues . . . The rabble is the rabble. Of course they'll rebel, that's what we keep Ruhmer for. Affluence riots are something new though, a kind of paradox. There's probably never been anything like that on Earth. At least not in my time. And the classics don't say anything about it. But rebellion is rebellion . . . The Experiment is the Experiment, soccer is soccer . . . Dammit!

He looked at Heiger. Fritz was leaning back in his chair, absentmindedly and yet intently picking his teeth with his finger, and Andrei was suddenly stunned by a simple thought that was terrifying in its simplicity: Fritz was nothing more than a noncommissioned officer of the Wehrmacht, wasn't he? A semi-educated drillmaster who hadn't read ten worthwhile books in his entire life, and yet he was the one who decided things. As a matter of fact, I decide things, too, Andrei thought.

"In our situation," he said to Izya, "any decent man simply had no choice. People were hungry, people were being victimized, they lived with fear and physical torment—children, old people, women . . . It was our duty to create decent living conditions."

"That's right, that's right," said Izya. "I understand all that. You were motivated by pity, compassion, etc., etc. That's not what I'm talking about. It's not hard to feel pity for women and children who are weeping from hunger—anyone can do that. But will you be able to feel pity for a burly hunk of a guy with a sex organ this big"—Izya demonstrated with his hands—"a man pining away from boredom? Denny Lee clearly could, but will you be able to do it? Or will you take the horsewhips to him?"

He paused, because ruddy-cheeked Parker had come into the dining room, accompanied by two pretty girls in white aprons. They cleared the table and served coffee with whipped cream; Izya immediately smeared it across his face and proceeded to lick himself clean, like a cat, all the way out to his ears.

"And anyway, do you know what I think?" he said thoughtfully. "As soon as society has solved some problem that it has, it immediately comes face-to-face with a new problem of the same magnitude . . . no, of even greater magnitude." Then he livened up. "And that, by the way, gives rise to an interesting little point. Eventually society will come face-to-face with problems of such complexity that it will be beyond mankind's power to solve them. And then so-called progress will stop."

"Nonsense," said Andrei. "Mankind doesn't set itself problems that it can't solve."

"But I'm not talking about the problems mankind sets itself," Izya objected. "I'm talking about the problems mankind runs into. They just come up on their own. Mankind never set itself the problem of famine. It simply used to starve."

"Oh, here we go!" said Heiger. "That's enough. You've got carried away with your fancy verbiage. Anyone would think we had nothing to with our time but gab."

"What *do* we have to do with our time?" Izya asked in surprise. "I, for instance, am on my lunch break."

"As you wish," said Heiger. "I wanted to talk about your expedition. But of course, we can always defer that."

Izya froze with a coffee cup in his hand. "Oh, come now," he said dourly. "Why defer it? Let's not defer it—we've deferred it so many times already."

"Well then why are you gabbling like that?" asked Heiger. "It makes me feel sick listening to you."

"What expedition is that?" Andrei asked. "For the archives, or what?"

"The great expedition to the north!" Izya proclaimed, but Heiger stopped him by holding up his large, white, open hand.

"This is a preliminary discussion," he said. "But I've already made the decision to go ahead with the expedition, and funds have been allocated. Transport will be ready in three or four months. But at this point we need to define the general goals and program of action."

"You mean it will be an expedition with multiple goals?" asked Andrei.

"Yes. Izya will get his archives, and you'll get your observations of the sun and whatever else it is you want . . ."

"Thank God!" Andrei said, "At last!"

"But we shall have at least one other goal," said Heiger. "Long-range reconnaissance. The expedition must travel very far to the north. As far as possible. As far as the fuel and water last. And therefore the members of the team must be specially selected, with great discrimination. Only volunteers, and only the very best of the volunteers. No one really knows what might be up there, in the north. It's quite possible that apart from searching for papers and gazing through your tubes, you'll have to shoot, sit out a siege, break out, and so on. So there will be soldiers in the group. We'll specify who and how many of them later."

"Oh, as few as possible!" Andrei said, wincing. "I know your soldiers; working with them would be intolerable." He pushed his cup away in annoyance. "And anyway, I don't understand. I don't understand why we need soldiers. I don't understand what kind of gun battles there can be out there. It's a desert out there, ruins—how could there be any gun battles?"

"There could be anything at all out there, my brother," Izya said merrily.

"What does 'anything' mean? So maybe the place is swarming with devils—do you want us to take priests along with us?"

"Maybe I could be allowed to finish what I was saying?" Heiger asked.

"Say what you have to say," Andrei replied, annoyed. That's always the way, he thought. Like the story about the monkey's paw. If a wish does come true, it always comes with the kind of add-on that means you'd be better off if it hadn't. No, dammit. I won't let the officers and gentlemen have this expedition. The leader of the expedition is Quejada—the head of the scientific section and the entire team. Otherwise you can go to hell, you won't get any cosmography, and your sergeant majors can order Izya around all on his own. It's a scientific expedition, so it has to be led by a scientist . . . At this point he recalled that Quejada was politically unreliable, and recalling it made him so furious that he missed part of what Heiger was saying.

"What was that?" he asked with a start.

"I asked you how far away from the City could the end of the world be?"

"More precisely—the beginning," Izya put in.

Andrei shrugged angrily. "Do you read my reports at all?" he asked Heiger.

"I do," said Heiger. "You say there that as one moves farther to the north, the sun will decline toward the horizon. Obviously, somewhere far to the north it will set behind the horizon and completely disappear from sight. So I'm asking you how far it is to that place—can you tell me?"

"You don't read my reports," said Andrei. "If you did read them, you'd have realized that my whole idea for this expedition is precisely in order to discover where that 'beginning of the world' is."

"I realized that," Heiger said patiently. "I'm asking you for an approximation. Can you tell me that distance, at least approximately? How far is it—a thousand kilometers? A hundred thousand? A million? We're determining the goal of the expedition, do you understand that? If that goal is a million kilometers away, then it's no longer a goal. But if—"

"OK, that's clear," said Andrei. "Why didn't you say so? Well then . . . The difficulty here is that we don't know the curvature of the world or the distance to the sun. If we had numerous observations along the entire line of the City—not the present City, you realize, but from the beginning to the end—then we could determine these magnitudes. We need a large arc, you understand? At least several hundred kilometers. All the material we have so far only covers an arc of fifty kilometers. And that means the accuracy is negligible."

"Give me the absolute minimum and absolute maximum," said Heiger.

"The maximum is infinity," said Andrei. "That's if the world is flat. And the minimum is in the order of a thousand kilometers."

"You lousy spongers," Heiger said in disgust. "All the money I've put into you, and what do I get . . ."

"Ah, come on now," said Andrei. "I've been trying to get this expedition out of you for two years. If you want to know what sort of world you live in, put up the money, the transport, the men. Otherwise, nothing will be done. All we need is an arc of about five hundred kilometers. We'll measure the gravity, variations in brightness, variations in height—"

"All right," Heiger interrupted. "We won't talk about that now. Those are details. You just get it clear that one of the expedition's goals is to reach the beginning of the world. Have you got that clear?"

"We have," said Andrei. "But we don't understand why you need that."

"I want to know what's there," said Heiger. "There is something there. And it might be important for many reasons."

"For instance?" Andrei asked.

"For instance, the Anticity."

Andrei snorted. "The Anticity . . . You mean to say you still believe in it?"

Heiger got up, clasped his hands behind his back, and started striding around the dining room. "Believe in it, don't believe in it," he said. "I have to know for certain whether it exists or not."

"It became clear to me a long time ago," Andrei said, "that the Anticity is merely an invention of the former leadership."

"Like the Red Building," Izya said in a low voice, giggling.

Andrei frowned. "The Red Building has nothing to do with this. Heiger himself stated that the former leadership was preparing a military dictatorship, it needed an external threat—and there you have the Anticity."

Heiger stopped in front of them. "But why exactly are you protesting against an expedition all the way to the very end? Surely you must be at least a little bit curious about what might be there? What kind of counselors has God given me?"

"But there isn't anything there!" said Andrei, feeling disoriented. "There's fierce cold, eternal night, a desert of ice . . . The far side of the moon, do you understand?"

"I am in possession of different information," said Heiger. "The Anticity exists. There isn't any desert of ice, or if there is, it can be crossed. There's a city, exactly like ours, but what goes on there, we don't know, and what they want there—we don't know that either. But they say, for instance, that everything there is the other way round. When things are good for us here, things are bad for them there . . ." He broke off and started walking around the dining room again.

"Oh God," said Andrei. "What is this mumbo jumbo?"

He glanced at Izya and bit his tongue. Izya was sitting there with his arms thrown back behind his chair. His necktie had slipped around under his ear; he was looking triumphantly at Andrei, with a greasy, beaming smile on his face.

"I see," said Andrei. "Might I be informed from which sources you drew this information?" he asked Izya.

"The same ones as ever, my dear man," said Izya. "History is a great science. And in our City it has an especially large number of tricks up its sleeve. After all, in addition to all the other things, what is really great about our City? The archives in it don't get destroyed, do they? There are no wars, no invasions, what is written with the pen is not hacked apart with the ax . . ."

"Those archives of yours . . ." Andrei said in annoyance.

"Yes indeed! Fritz will tell you I'm not lying—who found coal? Three hundred thousand tons of coal in an underground storage facility. Did your geologists find it? No, Katzman found it. Without even leaving his little study, mind you."

"In brief," said Heiger, sitting down on his chair again, "setting aside the science and the archives, I want to know the following. One. What lies in our rear? It is possible to live there? What useful materials can we extract there? Two. Who lives there? Along the entire distance: from this place"—he tapped his fingernail on the table—"all the way to end of the world, or the beginning, or as far as you get . . . What kind of people are they? Are they people? Why are they there? How did they get there? And three. Everything you can manage to find out about the Anticity. This is the *political* goal that I have set myself. And this is the genuine goal of the expedition, Andrei, you have to understand that. You'll take this expedition, explore everything that I've mentioned, and report the results to me here, in this room."

"What did you say?" Andrei asked.

"You'll report. Here. In person."

"You want to send me there?"

"Naturally. What did you think?"

"I'm sorry," said Andrei, flustered. "What on Earth for? I wasn't planning on going anywhere . . . I'm up to my eyes with work here in the City—who can I dump that on? And I don't want to go anywhere!"

"What do you mean by that—you don't want to go? Why have you been pestering me? If not you, then who can I send?"

"My God," said Andrei. "Anyone at all! Appoint Quejada to lead it . . . a highly experienced prospector . . . or Butz, for example . . ."

He fell silent under Heiger's intent stare. "Let's not talk about Quejada or Butz," Heiger said in a quiet voice.

Andrei couldn't think of anything to say to that, and an awkward silence fell.

Then Heiger poured himself some cold coffee. "In this City," he said in the same quiet voice, "there are only two or three men I trust. Out of them, you're the only one who can lead the expedition. Because I'm certain that if I ask you to go all the way to the end, you'll go all the way to the end. You won't turn off halfway down the road and you won't allow anyone else to turn off halfway down the road. And when you present your report to me afterward, I'll be able to believe that report. I could trust Izya's report, for instance, too, but Izya's goddamned worthless as an administrator and a totally useless politician. Do you understand me? Either you lead this expedition or the expedition won't happen."

Silence fell again. Izya said awkwardly, "Oh-ho-ho-ho . . . Maybe I should step outside, administrators?"

"Stay in your seat," Heiger ordered, without even turning toward him. "There, eat the cakes."

Andrei feverishly tried to make sense of things. Abandon everything. Selma. The house. My calm, smooth-running life. Why the hell has this been landed on me? Amalia. Trudging all that way to God knows where. Heat. Filth. Lousy food . . . Have

I gotten old, then? A couple of years ago I'd have been thrilled with an offer like this. But now I don't want it. I just don't want it at all . . . Izya every day—in Homeric doses. Soldiers. And we'll probably travel on foot, won't we, for the whole thousand kilometers, carrying sacks over our shoulders, and not empty sacks either, dammit . . . And guns. Mother of God, we might have to shoot out there! What the hell do I want with that— facing up to bullets? What the hell does a goat want with an accordion? Why the hell would a wolf want a waistcoat—to fray it on the bushes? I'll definitely have to take Uncle Yura— I don't trust those soldiers an inch . . . Heat, and blisters, and stench . . . And then right at the very edge—hellish damned cold, probably . . . At least the sun will be behind us all the time . . . And I have to take Quejada, I won't go without Quejada, and that's that—never mind that you don't trust him, with Quejada at least I can feel confident about the science part . . . And all that time without a woman, enough to drive you crazy, I'm not used to that anymore. But you'll pay me for this. You'll let the chancellery have something, for a start, give me some full-time positions for the Social Psychology department . . . and a few for Geodesy wouldn't do any harm . . . And second, you'll rap Vareikis over the knuckles. And in general, all these ideological restrictions—I won't have them anywhere near my science. In the other departments, by all means, that's no concern of mine . . . There isn't even any water there! That's why the City keeps creeping southward, isn't it—in the north the springs are drying up. So will you order us to carry water with us? For a thousand kilometers? "So am I going to lug the water on my back?" he asked irritably.

Heiger jerked up his eyebrows in amazement. "What water?"

Andrei realized he'd spoken out loud. "Well, all right, then," he said. "Only I'll choose the soldiers myself, since you insist on them so firmly. Or else you'll hand me all sorts of boneheads . . . And there has to be a unified command!" he said threateningly, raising his finger. "I'm the one in charge!"

"You, you," Heiger said reassuringly, and smiled, leaning back in his chair, "You'll select everybody, in fact. The only man I impose on you is Izya. The others are up to you. Make sure to get good mechanics, select a doctor—"

"Yes. By the way, will I have some kind of transport?"

"You will," said Heiger. "And it will be genuine transport. Like we've never had here before. You won't have to lug anything around yourself, except maybe your gun . . . But don't get distracted; these are all details. We'll have a special discussion about them later, when you've selected the heads of the subunits . . . What I want to focus your attention on is this . . . Secrecy! Make sure you give me that, guys. Of course, it's impossible to completely conceal an undertaking like this, so we have to put out disinformation—say you've gone prospecting for oil, for instance. Out on the 240 kilometer line. But the political goals of the expedition must remain known only to you. Agreed?"

"Agreed," Andrei responded.

"Izya, that especially applies to you. Do you hear?"

"*Ughu*," Izya said with his mouth stuffed full.

"But why all the secrecy?" asked Andrei. "What are we going to do that means we have to shroud it in secrecy like this?"

"You don't understand?" Heiger asked, making a wry face.

"No, I don't," said Andrei. "I absolutely cannot see anything about this that is a threat to the system."

"Not to the system, you blockhead!" said Heiger. "To you! It's a threat to you! Surely you can understand that they're just as afraid of us as we are of them?"

"Who are *they*? Your Anticitizens, is it?"

"But of course! If we've finally gotten around to sending out a reconnaissance party, why not assume that they did it ages ago? That the City is simply crawling with their spies? Don't smile, don't, you stupid fool. I'm not joking here! You run into an ambush and they'll slaughter you all like little chicks."

"OK," said Andrei. "You've persuaded me. I say no more."

Heiger contemplated him doubtfully for a moment, then said, "All right, then. So you've grasped the goals. And the need for secrecy too. So, basically, that's all. Today I'll sign the decree appointing you the leader of Operation . . . *mmm* . . . Let's say . . ."

"Murk and Gloom," Izya prompted, opening his eyes innocently wide.

"What? No . . . Too long. Let's say . . . Zigzag. Operation Zigzag. That has a good ring to it, doesn't it?" Heiger took a notepad out of his breast pocket and jotted something down. "Andrei, you can get started on the preparations. I'm only talking about the scientific part for now. Select the people, define your tasks . . . order equipment and tackle . . . I'll make sure your orders get the green light. Who's your deputy?"

"In the chancellery? Butz."

Heiger frowned. "Well, OK," he said. "Let it be Butz. Dump the entire chancellery on him, and you switch over completely to Operation Zigzag . . . And warn that Butz of yours not to shoot his mouth off so much!" he suddenly barked out.

"I tell you what," said Andrei. "Let's agree between the two of us—"

"Dammit, dammit!" said Heiger. "I don't wish to talk about these matters. I know what you want to say to me! But a fish rots from the head, Mr. Counselor, and in your chancellery you've created a gang of . . . ah, dammit!"

"Jacobins," Izya suggested.

"And you keep quiet, Jew!" Heiger roared. "Damn you all to hell, you blabbermouths! You've completely put me off . . . What was I saying?"

"That you don't wish to talk about these matters," said Izya.

Heiger stared at him blankly, and then Andrei said in an emphatically calm voice, "Fritz, I ask you please to protect my staff from all sorts of pompous ideological nonsense. I selected those people myself, I trust them, and if you really want to have any science in the City, leave them in peace."

"Well, all right, all right," Heiger growled, "we won't discuss this today."

"Yes we will," Andrei said meekly, amazed at himself. "You know me—I'm behind you a hundred percent. Please understand that these people can't help grouching. It's just the way they are. The ones who don't grouch aren't worth a damn. Let them grouch! I'll take care of ideological morals in my own chancellery somehow. You don't need to worry. And please tell our dear Ruhmer to remember once and for all—"

"Can we manage without the ultimatums?" Heiger inquired haughtily.

"Yes," Andrei said with absolute meekness now. "We can manage without anything. Without any ultimatums, without any science, without any expedition . . ."

Breathing noisily through flared nostrils, Heiger stared at him point-blank. "I do not wish to talk about this subject now!" he said.

Andrei realized that that was enough for today. Especially since it really was better to talk about these subjects one on one. "If you don't wish to, then we won't," he said in a placatory tone. "It just happened to be an appropriate moment. You see, Vareikis really got under my skin today . . . Listen, here's a question for you. What's the total load I can take with me? At least approximately."

Heiger forced the breath out through his nostrils a few more times, then squinted at Izya and leaned back again in his chair. "Count on five tons, or six . . . maybe even more," he said. "Get in touch with Manjuro . . . Only bear in mind that he might be the fourth figure in the state but he knows nothing about the genuine goals of the expedition. He's responsible for transport. You can find out all the details from him."

Andrei nodded. "All right. And as for the soldiers, you know who I want to take? The colonel."

Heiger started. "The colonel? You've got expensive tastes! Who will that leave me with? The entire general staff revolves around the colonel."

"Well, that's excellent," said Andrei. "Then the colonel can carry out deep reconnaissance at the same time. Make a personal study, so to speak, of the potential theater of operations. And we already get along well together . . . By the way, guys, I'm having a little party this evening. Beef bourguignonne. How are you fixed?"

A preoccupied expression immediately appeared on Heiger's face. "Hmm . . . Today? I don't know, my old friend, I can't say for certain . . . I simply don't know. Maybe I'll drop by for a minute or two."

Andrei sighed. "*Oookay.* Only if you don't come, please don't send Ruhmer to take your place like the last time. I'm not inviting the president to my house, you know, but Fritz Heiger. I don't need any official substitutes."

"Well, we'll see, we'll see . . ." said Heiger. "How about another cup? There's still time. Parker!"

Ruddy-faced Parker appeared in the doorway and listened to the order for coffee, inclining his head with an ideal part in the hair, then said in a deferential voice, "Counselor Ruhmer is waiting on the phone for Mr. President."

"Speak of the devil," Heiger growled, getting up. "Sorry, guys, I'll be right back."

He walked out, and immediately the girls in white aprons appeared. They rapidly and soundlessly organized a second round of coffee and disappeared, together with Parker.

"Well, will *you* come?" Andrei asked Izya.

"Glad to," said Izya, gulping his coffee with whistling and champing sounds. "Who'll be there?"

"The colonel will be there. And the Dolfusses, maybe Chachua . . . Why, who would you like?"

"To be honest, I could do without Madam Dolfuss."

"Never mind, we'll set Chachua on her."

Izya nodded, and then suddenly said, "It's a pretty long time since we got together, eh?"

"Yes, brother, work . . ."

"Lies, lies, what kind of work do you do? You just sit there, polishing your collection . . . make sure you don't accidentally shoot yourself . . . Oh yes, by the way, I got hold of a pistol for you. A genuine Smith & Wesson, from the prairies."

"Honestly?"

"Only it's rusty, completely covered in rust—"

"Don't even think of cleaning it!" Andrei shouted, bouncing up and down on his chair. "Bring it just the way it is—you'll ruin everything, your hands are like grappling hooks . . . And it's not a pistol, it's a revolver. Where did you find it?"

"In the right place to look, that's where," said Izya. "Just wait, on the expedition we'll find so many you won't be able to lug them back home."

Andrei put down his coffee cup. This aspect of the expedition hadn't occurred to him, and he instantly felt his mood lift tremendously as he imagined a unique collection of Colts, Brownings, Mausers, Nagants, Parabellums, Sauers, Walthers . . . and moving further back into the depths of time, Lefaucheux and Lepage dueling pistols . . . immense boarding pistols with bayonets . . . magnificent homemade specials from the Far West . . . all those indescribably valuable items that he hadn't even dared to dream of having as he read and reread the catalog of the private collection of the millionaire Brunner, which had ended up in the City in some miraculous fashion. Cases, crates, warehouses of firearms . . . Maybe he'd get lucky and find a *Česká zbrojovka*, with a silencer . . . or an Astra 900, or maybe even, dammit, a "Number Nine"—the Mauser 08, a real rarity, a dream of his . . . *Yesss* . . .

"Do you collect antitank mines?" Izya asked. "Or culverins, maybe."

"No," Andrei said, smiling joyfully. "I only collect personal firearms."

"Well, there happens to be a bazooka on offer," said Izya. "They don't want much—only two hundred tugriks."

"You'd better offer the bazooka to Ruhmer, brother," said Andrei.

"Thanks. I've been at Ruhmer's place before," Izya said, and his smile froze.

Ah, *dammit*, thought Andrei, feeling awkward, but fortunately just then Heiger came back in. He was pleased.

"Come on then, pour the president a cup," he said. "What were you talking about here?"

"Art and literature," said Izya.

"Literature?" Heiger took a sip of coffee. "Come on then, out with it! What exactly do my counselors say about literature?"

"Oh, he's just babbling," said Andrei. "We were talking about my collection, not literature."

"And what's suddenly got you interested in literature?" asked Izya, giving Heiger a curious look. "You've always been such a practical president."

"That's why I'm interested, because I'm practical," said Heiger. "Look at the figures," he told them, starting to count on his fingers. "In the City we publish two literary journals, four literary supplements to newspapers, at least ten regular series of rubbishy adventure stories . . . and I think that's all. And also about fifteen books a year. And in all that there's nothing that's even halfway decent. I've spoken to people who know about these things. Neither before the Turning Point nor after it has a single even slightly significant work of literature appeared in the City. Nothing but trash. What's wrong?"

Andrei and Izya exchanged glances. Yes, Heiger could always spring a surprise, no denying that.

"I don't quite understand what you're saying here," Izya told Heiger. "What does it matter to you anyway? Are you looking for a writer so he can write your life story?"

"Just drop the jokes, will you?" Heiger said patiently. "There are a million people in the City. More than a thousand are registered as writers. And they're all third-rate hacks. That is, I don't read them, of course."

"Third-rate hacks, third-rate hacks," Izya said, nodding. "The information you've been given is correct. No Tolstoys or Dostoyevskys anywhere in sight. Neither Leos nor Alexeis . . ."

"But seriously, why aren't there?" Andrei asked.

"No outstanding writers," Heiger continued. "No artists. No composers. No . . . what are they called . . . sculptors either."

"No architects," Andrei put in. "No movie directors . . ."

"None of all that," said Heiger. "A million people! At first I was simply surprised, and then, to be honest, I felt alarmed."

"Why?" Izya immediately asked.

Heiger indecisively chewed on his lips. "It's hard to explain," he confessed. "I personally don't know what it's all needed for, but I've been told that every decent society has all this. And if we don't, it means something's out of order . . . That's the way I think about it. All right, then: before the Turning Point life in the City was hard, it was a shambles, and let's assume no one had any time for the fine arts. But now life is basically coming together—"

"No," Andrei interrupted pensively. "That has nothing to do with it. As far as I know, the greatest artists in the world actually worked in incredibly messy circumstances. There isn't any general rule here. An artist could be a beggar, a madman, or a drunk, or he could be a really prosperous man, even rich, like Turgenev for instance . . . I don't know."

"In any case," Izya said to Heiger, "if you're planning, for instance, to abruptly improve the living standards of our writers—"

"Yes! For instance!" said Heiger taking another sip of coffee. He licked his lips and started looking at Izya through narrowed eyes.

"Nothing will come of it," Izya said with some satisfaction. "And there's no point in hoping it will."

"Hang on," said Andrei. "Perhaps artistic and creative people simply don't end up in the City? They don't agree to come here?"

"Or, let's say, they're not invited," said Izya.

"No way," said Heiger. "Fifty percent of the City's population are young people. On Earth they were nobody. How would it be possible to tell if they were creative types?"

"Maybe it is possible to tell," said Izya.

"Even so," said Heiger, "there are tens of thousands of people in the City who were born and grew up here. What about them? Or does talent have to be inherited?"

"Yes, that really is rather strange," said Andrei. "The City has excellent engineers. And pretty good scientists. No Mendeleyevs, maybe, but solid, world class. Take Butz, for instance . . . There are heaps of talented people—inventors, administrators, craftsmen, professionals . . . all sorts of applied specialists, in fact."

"That's just it," said Heiger. "That's what surprises me."

"Listen, Fritz," said Izya. "What do you want with unnecessary hassle? Say talented writers do appear here, and say they start lambasting you in their brilliant works—you, and the way you do things, and your counselors . . . Then you'll have really bad problems. First you'll try to persuade them, then you'll threaten them, then you'll have to jail them."

"And why would they definitely lambaste me?" Heiger asked indignantly. "Maybe just the opposite—they'd sing my praises?"

"No," said Izya. "They won't sing your praises. Andrei already explained to you today about the scientists. Well, great writers are always grouching too. It's their normal condition, because they are society's sick conscience, although society doesn't have the slightest suspicion that they even exist. And since in this case *you* are the symbol of society, you'll be the first one they start throwing tin cans at." Izya giggled. "I can just imagine what a roasting they'll give your Ruhmer!"

Heiger shrugged. "Of course, if Ruhmer has shortcomings, a genuine writer is obliged to depict them. That's what a writer does: he heals the open sores."

"Writers have never, ever healed any open sores," Izya objected. "A sick conscience simply hurts, that's all—"

"But after all, that's not the question," Heiger interrupted. "You give me a straight answer: Do you consider the current situation to be normal or not?"

"Well, what do you take as the norm?" Izya asked. "Can we regard the situation on Earth as normal?"

"Away he goes!" Andrei said, screwing up his face. "You're being asked a simple question: Can a society exist without creative talents? Have I got that right, Fritz?"

"I'll ask even more precisely," said Heiger. "Is it normal for a million people—it doesn't matter if they're here or on Earth—not to produce a single creative talent in decades?"

Izya said nothing, absentmindedly plucking at his wart, and Andrei said, "If we judge by ancient Greece, for example, it's very far from normal."

"Then what's wrong?" asked Heiger.

"The Experiment is the Experiment," said Izya. "But if we judge by the Mongols, for instance, then everything here is in fine shape."

"What do you mean by that?" Heiger asked suspiciously.

"Nothing special," Izya said in surprise. "Just that there are a million of them, or maybe even more. We could also take the example of the Koreans, say . . . and almost any Arab country . . ."

"Why not take the gypsies?" Heiger asked peevishly.

Andrei suddenly brightened up. "Yes, by the way, guys," he said. "Are there any gypsies in the City?"

"You can all go to hell!" Heiger said angrily. "It's absolutely impossible to talk seriously about anything with you . . ."

He was about to add something else, but at that point ruddy-cheeked Parker appeared in the doorway, and Heiger immediately looked at his watch.

"Well, that's it," he said, getting up. "Got to go!" He sighed and started buttoning up his military tunic. "To your posts, Counselors!" he said, "To your posts!"

3

Otto Friese hadn't lied to them: the rug was genuinely luxurious. It was black and crimson, with aristocratic tones, and it occupied the entire wall on the left of the study, opposite the windows. Hanging there, it gave the study an absolutely special look. It was devilishly beautiful, it was elegant, it was significant.

Absolutely delighted, Andrei gave Selma a peck on the cheek, and she went back to the kitchen to give the maid orders while he walked around his study, examining the rug from every possible viewpoint, gazing at it straight on first, then at a steep angle with his peripheral vision. Then he opened his cherished cupboard and took out a massive Mauser—a ten-round monster, born in the special section of the Mauserwerke, which became famous during the Russian Civil War as the beloved weapon of commissars in dusty helmets, and also of Japanese imperial officers in greatcoats with dog-fur collars.

The Mauser was clean and burnished to a high gleam—it looked completely combat ready—but unfortunately the firing pin had been filed down. Andrei held the gun, weighing it in both hands, then took hold of the rounded, fluted handle, lowered the gun, raised it again to eye level, and aimed it at the trunk of an apple tree outside the window, like Heiger at the shooting range.

Then he turned to face the rug and started choosing a spot. It didn't take long to find one. Andrei kicked off his shoes, climbed up onto the couch, and held the Mauser at that spot. Pressing it against the rug with one hand, he leaned back as far as he could and admired it. It was superb. He skipped down onto the floor, impetuously ran out into the hallway in his socks, pulled a toolbox out of the wall cupboard, and went back to the rug.

He hung the Mauser, then a Luger with an optical sight (Tailbone had shot two militiamen dead with that Luger on the last day of the Turning Point), and he was fiddling with a 1906 model Browning—small and almost square—when a familiar voice spoke behind his back:

"Farther to the right, Andrei, a little farther to the right. And a centimeter lower."

"Like that?" Andrei asked, without turning around.

"Yes."

Andrei secured the Browning, jumped down backward off the couch, and backed away as far as the desk, surveying the work of his own hands.

"It's beautiful," the Mentor said approvingly.

"Beautiful, but not enough," Andrei said with a sigh.

Without making a sound, the Mentor walked over to the cupboard, squatted down, rummaged around, and took out a Nagant army revolver. "What about this?" he asked.

"No wooden grips on the handle," Andrei said regretfully. "I keep meaning to order some and I always forget." He found his shoes, sat on the windowsill beside the desk, and lit a cigarette. "I'll put my dueling arsenal at the top. Early nineteenth century. You come across some incredibly beautiful examples, with incised silver work, and the shapes are quite amazing—from tiny little ones like this to huge ones with long barrels . . ."

"Lepages," said the Mentor.

"No, in fact the Lepages are small . . . And at the bottom, just above the couch, I'll hang the seventeenth- and eighteenth-century combat weapons."

He fell silent, picturing to himself how beautiful it would be. The Mentor, squatting on his haunches, rummaged in the cupboard. Somewhere close by outside the window a motorized lawn mower spluttered. Birds twittered and whistled.

"A good idea—to hang the rug here, wasn't it?" Andrei asked.

"An excellent idea," said the Mentor, getting up. He tugged a handkerchief out of his pocket and wiped his hands. "Only I'd put the floor lamp over in that corner, beside the phone. And you need a white phone."

"I'm not entitled to a white phone," Andrei said with a sigh.

"Never mind," said the Mentor. "When you get back from the expedition, you'll have a white one."

"So I did the right thing by agreeing to go?"

"Did you have any doubts about it?"

"Yes," Andrei said, and stubbed out his butt in the ashtray. "In the first place, I didn't want to go. I just didn't want to. And in the second place, to be quite honest, it's a bit frightening."

"Oh, come on," said the Mentor.

"No, really. You—can you tell me what I'll come up against out there? There, you see! Total uncertainty . . . A dozen of Izya's terrifying legends and total uncertainty . . . Plus all the charms of life on the march. I know these expeditions. I've been on archeological expeditions, and all sorts of other kinds . . ."

At this point, just as Andrei was expecting, the Mentor asked curiously, "What is it about these expeditions . . . how can I put it . . . what's the most frightening thing about them, the most unpleasant thing?"

Andrei really loved this question. He'd invented the answer to it a very long time ago, and even written it down in his notebook, subsequently using it repeatedly in conversations with various girls.

"The most frightening thing?" he repeated, to pick up momentum. "The most frightening thing is this. Imagine it: the tent, the night, desert all around, absolutely no one, wolves howling, hailstones falling, a stormy wind . . ." He paused and looked at the Mentor, who was leaning forward, listening. "Hailstones, you understand? The size of a hen's egg . . . And you have to go out to relieve yourself."

The tense anticipation on the Mentor's face was replaced by a rather perplexed smile, and then he burst into laughter. "Very funny," he said. "Did you make that up yourself?"

"Yes, I did," Andrei said proudly.

"Good for you, that's funny . . ." The Mentor laughed again, wagging his head. Then he sat down in the armchair and started looking at the garden. "This is a nice place you have here, in the White Court," he said.

Andrei turned around and also looked at the garden: green foliage drenched in sunlight, butterflies fluttering above flowers, apple trees standing motionless, and about two hundred meters away, behind some lilac bushes, the white walls and red roof of the next cottage . . . And Wang in his long white shirt, striding along, calm and unhurried, behind the spluttering lawn mower, with his youngest toddling along beside him, clutching his trouser leg . . .

"Yes, Wang has found peace," the Mentor said. "Perhaps he really is the happiest man in the City."

"That could very well be," Andrei agreed. "In any case, I wouldn't say that about my other acquaintances."

"Well, that's the circle of acquaintances you have now," the Mentor rejoined. "Wang is the exception among them. I'd even say quite simply that he's a man of a different circle. Not yours."

"Uh-huh," Andrei drawled pensively. "But after all, there was a time when we toted garbage together, sat at the same table, drank from the same mugs . . ."

The Mentor shrugged. "Everyone receives what he deserves."

"What he achieves," Andrei muttered.

"You can put it that way if you like—it's the same thing. After all, Wang always wanted to be right down at the bottom. The East is the East. Beyond our comprehension. And so your paths have parted."

"The most amusing thing," said Andrei, "is that I still enjoy being with him as much as I used to. We always have something to talk about, something to remember . . . When I'm with him, I never feel awkward."

"But does he feel awkward?"

Andrei thought for a moment. "I don't know. But probably yes. Sometimes I get the feeling he makes a great effort to keep well away from me."

The Mentor stretched, cracking his fingers. "But is that really the point?" he asked. "When you and Wang sit down with a bottle of vodka and you recall how things used to be, Wang relaxes, you must agree. But when you and the colonel sit down with a bottle of scotch, do either of you really relax?"

"Relaxation's irrelevant," Andrei mumbled. "What relaxation? I simply need the colonel. And he needs me."

"And when you have lunch with Heiger? And when you drink with Dolfuss? And when Chachua tells you his new jokes over the phone?"

"Yes," said Andrei. "That's the way it all is. Yes."

"Probably Izya's the only one you're still on the same terms with, and even then . . ."

"Precisely," said Andrei. "And even then."

"Uh-uh, there's no question about it!" the Mentor exclaimed emphatically. "Just picture it to yourself: the colonel's sitting right here, the deputy chief of staff of your army, an old English aristocrat from a glorious noble line. Dolfuss is sitting here, the counselor for construction, once a famous engineer in Vienna. And his wife, a baroness, a Prussian Junker. And sitting facing them is Wang. A caretaker."

"Yep, yep," said Andrei. He scratched the back of his head and laughed. "It does seem kind of tactless."

"No, no! Forget about the official tact, that doesn't matter. Just imagine what Wang will feel in this situation—what will it be like for him?"

"I understand, I understand . . ." said Andrei. "I understand . . . It's all a load of hokum anyway! I'll invite him tomorrow, we'll sit down and spend some time together, just the two of us, Mei-lin and Selma will rustle up some kind of *ch'ih-fan* for us, and I'll give the little boy a Bull Dog—I have one without a firing hammer . . ."

"You'll have a drink together!" the Mentor continued. "Tell each other something about your lives—he has plenty that he could tell you, and you're good at telling a story too, and he doesn't know anything about Penjikent, or Kharbas . . . It will be wonderful! I even slightly envy you."

"You come as well," Andrei said, and laughed.

The Mentor laughed too. "I shall be with you in my thoughts," he said.

Just then the front doorbell rang. Andrei looked at his watch— it was precisely 7:00. "That has to be the colonel," he said, and jumped to his feet. "Shall I go?"

"Why, naturally!" said the Mentor. "And I ask you, please, in the future never forget that there are hundreds of thousands of Wangs in the City, but only twenty counselors . . ."

It really was the colonel. He always arrived precisely at the agreed-upon time, and consequently was always first. Andrei met him in the hallway, shook his hand, and invited him into the study. The colonel was in civilian dress. His light gray suit sat on him as dapperly as on a mannequin, his sparse gray hair was neatly combed, his shoes gleamed, and so did his smoothly shaved cheeks. He was short and lean, with good posture, but at the same time slightly relaxed, without the woodenness so typical of the German officers that the army was awash with.

Once inside the study, he stopped in front of the rug, clasped his dry, white hands behind his back, silently surveyed the crimson and black magnificence in general and the weapons hanging on that background in particular. Then he said "Oh!" and gave Andrei an approving look.

"Have a seat, Colonel," said Andrei. "A cigar? Whiskey?"

"Thank you," said the colonel, sitting down. "A little drop of good cheer wouldn't come amiss." He took a pipe out of his pocket. "Today has been a frantic day," he declared. "What happened on the plaza outside your place? I was ordered to put the barracks on alert."

"Some blockhead or other," said Andrei, rummaging in the bar, "collected some dynamite from the depot and couldn't find any better place to stumble than under my window."

"So there wasn't an assassination attempt, then?"

"Good Lord, Colonel!" Andrei said, pouring the whiskey. "This isn't Palestine, after all."

The colonel chuckled and accepted a glass from Andrei. "You're right. In Palestine no one was surprised by incidents of that sort. Or in Yemen either . . ."

"So they put you on alert?" Andrei asked, sitting down with his glass opposite the colonel.

"Oh yes indeed." The colonel took a sip from his glass, thought for a moment with his eyebrows raised, carefully set down the glass on the telephone table beside him, and started filling his pipe. He had old man's hands, covered in silvery fluff, but they didn't tremble.

"And what was the force's combat readiness like?" Andrei inquired, also sipping from his glass.

The colonel laughed again, and Andrei felt a momentary envy—he would really love to know how to laugh in the same way. "It's a military secret," said the colonel. "But I'll tell you. It was terrible. I never saw the like, even in the Yemen. Ah, never mind the Yemen! I never saw the like, even when I was training those black chappies in Uganda! Half the men weren't even in the barracks. Half of the other half turned out for the alert without their weapons. And those who did turn out with their weapons didn't have any ammunition, because the commanding officer of the munitions store had gone off with the keys to work his hour at the Great Construction Site."

"You're joking, I hope," said Andrei.

The colonel puffed on his pipe, flapping away the smoke with his hand, and looked at Andrei with his colorless old man's eyes. His eyes were surrounded by droves of wrinkles, and it looked as if he were laughing. "Perhaps I am exaggerating slightly," he said, "but judge for yourself, Counselor. Our army was created without any definite purpose, simply because a certain individual known to both of us cannot imagine the organization of a state without an army. It is obvious that no army is capable of functioning normally in the absence of a real enemy. Even if only a potential one. From the chief of staff down to the last cook, our army is presently imbued with the conviction that this undertaking is merely a game of little tin soldiers."

"And if we assume that a potential enemy does exist after all?"

The colonel shrouded himself in honeyed smoke once again. "Then tell us who he is, Messrs. Politicians!"

Andrei took another sip from his glass, thought for a moment, and asked, "Tell me, Colonel, does the general staff have any operational plans in case of an invasion from the outside?"

"Well now, I wouldn't call them operational plans as such. Imagine, say, your Russian general staff on Earth. Does it have operational plans in case of an invasion, let's say, from Mars?"

"Well now," said Andrei. "I think it's quite possible that something of the sort does exist . . ."

"We also have 'something of the sort,'" said the colonel. "We're not expecting an invasion from above or below. We don't concede the possibility of a serious threat from the south . . . apart, naturally, from the possibility of a successful revolt by the criminals working in the settlements, but we're ready for that . . . That leaves the north. We know that during the Turning Point and afterward, quite large numbers of supporters of the old regime fled to the north. We accept—in theory—that they could organize themselves and attempt some kind of sabotage or even a restoration of the old regime . . ." He took a pull on his pipe, wheezing hoarsely. "But what is an army needed for here? It's obvious that in the event of all these menaces, Counselor Ruhmer's special police are perfectly adequate, and in tactical terms, the most basic cordon and search tactics will serve."

Andrei waited for moment and then asked, "Should I understand you, Colonel, to mean that the general staff is not prepared for a serious invasion from the north?"

"You mean a Martian invasion?" the colonel asked thoughtfully. "No, it is not. I understand what you mean. But we have no reconnaissance. No one has ever seriously considered the possibility of such an invasion. We simply have no data for that. We don't even know what's going on fifty kilometers away from the Glass House. We have no maps of the northern environs . . ." He laughed, exposing his long, yellow teeth. "The city archivist, Mr. Katzman, provided the general staff with something like a map of those areas . . . As I understand it, he drew it himself. This remarkable document resides in my safe. It gives the quite distinct impression that Mr. Katzman made the map while he was eating and repeatedly dropped his sandwiches and spilled his coffee on it . . ."

"Come now, Colonel," Andrei said reproachfully, "my chancellery has provided you, I think, with some rather good maps."

"Definitely, definitely, Counselor. But for the most part those are maps of the inhabited City and the southern environs. According to the basic setup, the army must be in a state of combat readiness in case of public disorders, and public disorders can only occur in the aforementioned areas. This makes the work you have done absolutely indispensable, and thanks to you we are prepared for disorders. But as for an invasion . . ." The colonel shook his head.

"As far as I'm aware," Andrei said significantly, "my chancellery has never received any requests from the general staff to map the northern areas."

The colonel looked at Andrei for some time, and his pipe went out. "I should tell you," he said slowly, "that we have addressed such requests to the president in person. The answers were, I must admit, entirely indefinite . . ." He paused again. "So you believe, Counselor, that for the good of the cause we should address such requests to you?"

Andrei nodded. "I had lunch with the president today," he said. "We talked a lot about this subject. It has been decided in principle to proceed with mapping the northern regions. However, adequate participation by military specialists is required. An experienced operative . . . Well, no doubt you understand."

"I understand," said the colonel. "By the way, where did you dig up a Mauser like that, Counselor? The last time I saw such monsters, if I'm not mistaken, was in Batumi, in about 1918 . . ."

Andrei started telling the colonel where and how he had obtained the Mauser, but at that point the doorbell rang again in the hallway. Andrei apologized and went to meet his guest.

He was hoping it would be Katzman; however, against all his expectations, it turned out to be Otto Friese, whom Andrei hadn't actually invited at all. Somehow Friese had completely slipped his mind. Otto Friese was constantly slipping Andrei's mind, although as the head of the Glass House's housekeeping unit, Friese was an extremely useful man, even indispensable. But then, Selma never, ever forgot this circumstance. And so now she accepted from Otto a neat little basket, thoughtfully covered with a supremely fine batiste napkin, and a little bouquet of flowers. Otto was graciously permitted to kiss her hand. He clicked his heels, blushed red to his ears, and was quite obviously happy.

"Ah, my old friend," he said to Andrei. "There you are!"

Otto was still the same as ever. It suddenly occurred to Andrei that of all the old-timers, Otto had changed least. In fact, he simply hadn't changed at all. Still with the same scrawny neck and huge, protruding ears, with the same expression of constant uncertainty on his freckled features. And the clicking heels. He was in the pale blue uniform of the special police, wearing his square Medal of Merit.

"Thanks a million for the rug," said Andrei, putting his arm around Otto's shoulders and leading the guest into his study. "Now I'll show you how it looks in here . . . It's the bee's knees, you'll just die of envy . . ."

However, on finding himself in the study, Otto Friese didn't give any signs of dying of envy. He saw the colonel.

Otto Friese, a lance corporal in the Volkssturm, harbored feelings bordering on awe for Colonel St. James. In the colonel's presence he was struck absolutely dumb, fettered his features into a smile with steel bolts, and was ready to click heel against heel at any moment, to click continuously and with constantly increasing force.

Turning his back to the illustrious rug, he stood to attention, thrust out his chest, squeezed his palms against his thighs, stuck out his elbows, and bobbed his head so abruptly in a bow that the crack made by his neck vertebrae rang round the study. Smiling lazily, the colonel got up to meet him and held out his hand. In the other hand he was holding his glass.

"Very pleased to see you . . ." he said. "Welcome, Mr. . . . *mmm* . . ."

"Lance Corporal Otto Friese, Colonel!" Otto squealed ecstatically, then he bent over double and tremulously touched the colonel's fingers. "I have the honor to report!"

"Otto, Otto!" Andrei said reproachfully. "We don't have any ranks here!"

Otto giggled piteously, took out a handkerchief and wiped his forehead, then immediately took fright and started trying to stuff the handkerchief back in the pocket, but kept missing.

"At El Alamein, I recall," the colonel said good-naturedly, "my lads brought me a German lance corporal . . ."

The bell rang in the hallway again; Andrei apologized once more and went out, leaving the unfortunate Otto to be devoured by the British lion.

Izya had shown up. While he was kissing Selma on both cheeks, and wiping his shoes at her insistence, and being subjected to processing by clothes brush, Chachua and Dolfuss, with Madam Dolfuss, all tumbled in together. Chachua was holding Madam Dolfuss by the arm, dragging her along and deluging her with jokes as they walked, while Dolfuss trailed along behind with a wan smile on his face. In contrast with the temperamental head of the Chancellery for Legal Affairs, he seemed especially gray, colorless, and insignificant. He had a warm raincoat over each arm, in case it turned cold at night.

"Everyone to the table, to the table!" Selma chimed like a delicate little bell, clapping her hands.

"My dear," Madam Dolfuss protested in a deep bass voice. "But I must tidy myself up!"

"What for?" Chachua asked, rolling his bulging eyes in astonishment. "Such great beauty—and you want to tidy it up? In accordance with article 218 of the Criminal Procedural Code, the law is resolutely opposed . . ."

The usual hubbub started up. Andrei couldn't smile fast enough at everyone. Izya was seething and bubbling in his left ear, recounting something about a total screwup at the barracks during today's combat alert, and right off the bat Dolfuss was droning in his right ear about lavatories and the main sewer, which was close to being blocked . . . Then they all piled into the dining room. As he invited, seated, cracked gags, and passed compliments, out of the corner of his eye Andrei saw the door of the study open and the smiling colonel emerge from it, stuffing his pipe into his side pocket. Alone. Andrei's heart sank, but then Lance Corporal Otto Friese appeared—evidently he was simply maintaining a distance of five meters behind a senior officer, as prescribed by the drill regulations. A staccato clicking of heels began.

"Now we'll drink and have a good time!" Chachua bellowed in a gravelly voice.

Knives and forks started clattering. After inserting Otto between Selma and Madam Dolfuss with some difficulty, Andrei sat down in his own seat and looked around the table. Everything was fine.

"And just imagine it, my dear, there was a hole this size in the rug! That's a swipe at you, Mr. Friese, you beastly little boy!"

"They say that you shot someone in front of the ranks, Colonel?"

"And mark my words, it's the sewerage system, the sewerage system that will be the ruin of our City some day!"

"So much beauty and such a small glass?"

"Otto, darling, stop worrying that bone . . . Here's a good piece for you!"

"No, Katzman, it's a military secret. I had more than enough bother with the Jews in Palestine."

"Vodka, Counselor?"

"Thank you, Counselor!"

And heels clicked under the table.

Andrei drank two shots of vodka in quick succession—to get up steam—savored the snack that he followed it with, and joined everyone else in listening to a never-ending and fantastically indecent toast proposed by Chachua. When it finally turned out that the counselor of legal affairs was raising this tiny little glass with great big feelings, not in order to commend all the above-mentioned sexual perversions to the present company but merely to honor "my fiercest and most merciless enemies, with whom I have done battle throughout my life, and from whom I have suffered defeats throughout my life, that is—here's to beautiful women!" Andrei burst into relieved laughter along with everyone else and downed a third shot. Madam Dolfuss gurgled and sobbed in absolute prostration, covering her face with a napkin.

Somehow everyone got tanked very quickly. "Yes! Oh, yes!" a familiar voice intoned at the far end of the table. Chachua, with his twitching nose suspended over Madam Dolfuss's dazzling décolleté, kept talking without breaking off for a single second. Madam Dolfuss gurgled in total collapse, playfully shrinking away from him and heavily leaning her immensely broad back against Otto, who had already dropped his fork twice. Right beside Andrei, Dolfuss had finally left the sewerage system in peace, and lapsed into a state of official departmental elation at precisely the wrong time and in precisely the wrong place: he started recklessly giving away state secrets. "Autonomy!" he mumbled menacingly "The key to aun- . . . to aumon- . . . autonomy is chlorella! The Great Construction? Don't make me laugh. What damned airships? It's chlorella!"

"Counselor, Counselor," said Andrei, trying to reason with him. "For goodness' sake! There's absolutely no need for every-one to know that. Why don't you tell me how things are going with the laboratory block?" The maid took away the dirty plates and brought clean ones. The hors d'oeuvres had already been swept away, and the beef bourguignonne was served.

"I raise this tiny little glass!"

"Yes, oh yes!"

"Beastly little boy! It's quite impossible not to love you."

"Izya, stop pestering the colonel! Colonel, would you like me to sit beside you?"

"Fourteen cubic meters of chlorella is zero . . . Autonomy!"

"Whiskey, Counselor?"

"Why, thank you, Counselor!"

At the height of the merriment ruddy-faced Parker suddenly appeared in the dining room. "The president sends his apologies," he reported. "An urgent meeting. He sends his very warmest greetings to Mr. and Mrs. Voronin and likewise to all their guests . . ." They forced Parker to drink a shot of vodka—for that the efforts of all-crushing Chachua were required. A toast was proposed to the president and the success of all his undertakings.

Things got a bit quieter and coffee was served with ice cream and liqueurs. Otto Friese tearfully lamented his failures in love. Madam Dolfuss told Chachua about darling Königsberg, at which Chachua nodded his nose and passionately intoned, "But of course! I remember . . . General Chernyakhovsky . . . They battered it with cannon for five days . . ."

Parker disappeared, and it was dark outside. Dolfuss greedily drank coffee and unfolded to Andrei's gaze phantasmagorical projects for the reconstruction of the northern districts. The colonel was telling Izya a joke: ". . . He was given ten days for disorderly conduct and ten years' hard labor for disclosing a state and military secret." Izya sprayed, gurgled, and replied, "But that's old stuff, St. James. In Russia they used to tell that one about Khrushchev!"

"Politics again!" shouted Selma, offended. She managed somehow to squeeze in between Izya and the colonel, and the old soldier paternally patted her little knee.

Andrei suddenly felt sad. He apologized into empty space, got up on numbed legs, and walked through into his study, where he sat on the windowsill, lit a cigarette, and started looking at the garden.

It was pitch dark in the garden, and the windows of the next cottage shone brightly through the black foliage. It was a warm night, with fireflies stirring in the grass. And what about tomorrow? Andrei thought. So I'll go on the expedition, so I'll reconnoiter . . . I'll bring back a heap of guns, sort them out, hang them up . . . and then what?

In the dining room they were making a din. "Do you know this one, Colonel?" Izya yelled. "The Allied command is offering twenty thousand for Chapaev's head!" And Andrei immediately remembered how it went on: "The Allied command, Your Excellency, could pay more. After all, they have the city of Guriev behind them, and Guriev has oil. Ha-ha-ha."

"Chapaev?" the colonel asked. "Ah, that's your cavalryman. But I think they executed him, didn't they?"

Selma suddenly started singing in a high voice, "And next morning Katya was awoken by her mother . . . Get up, get up, Katya. The ships at anchor ride . . ." But she was immediately interrupted by Chachua's velvety roar: "I brought you flowers . . . Oh, what wonderful flowers . . . You didn't take those flowers from me. Why didn't you take them?"

Andrei closed his eyes and suddenly remembered Uncle Yura with an unusually keen pang of yearning. Wang wasn't here at the table, and Uncle Yura wasn't here . . . And what the hell, I wonder, do I need this Dolfuss for? He was surrounded by ghosts.

Donald was sitting on the couch in his battered cowboy hat. He crossed one leg over the other and firmly clasped his fingers around his pointed knee. *Grieve not in leaving, rejoice not in arriving* . . . And Kensi sat down at the desk in his old police uniform, propping his elbow on the table and setting his chin on his fist. He looked at Andrei without condemnation, but there was no warmth in that glance either. And Uncle Yura kept slapping

Wang on the back and intoning, "Never mind, Wang, don't you grieve now, we'll make you a minister, and you'll ride around in a swanky 'Victory' automobile . . ." There was a familiar, heart-wrenching smell of coarse tobacco, healthy sweat, and moonshine. Andrei managed to catch his breath with an effort, rubbed his numbed cheeks, and looked at the garden again.

The Building was standing in the garden.

It stood there solidly and naturally among the trees, as if it had been there for a very long time, since forever, and it intended to stand there until the end of time: four stories of red brick, and just like the other time, the windows of the first floor were covered over with shutters, the roof was covered with galvanized sheeting, a flight of four stone steps led up to the door, and a strange, cross-shaped aerial stuck out beside the only chimney. But now all the Building's windows were dark, in some places on the ground floor the shutters were missing and the windowpanes were streaked with dirt and cracked, in some places the panes had been replaced with warped sheets of plywood, and in some places they were crisscrossed with strips of paper. And there was no more solemn, somber music—a heavy, stifling silence crept out of the Building like an invisible mist.

Not taking even a second for reflection, Andrei flung his legs over the windowsill and jumped down into the garden, into the soft, thick grass. He walked over to the Building, frightening away the fireflies, burrowing deeper and deeper into the dead silence, keeping his eyes fixed on the familiar brass handle on the oak door, only now that handle was dull and covered in greenish splotches.

He walked up onto the porch and looked back. In the brightly lit windows of the dining room, human shadows merrily leaped about, twisting into fantastic poses, the sounds of dance music reached him faintly, and for some reason there was a clatter of knives and forks again. Dismissing all that, he turned away and took hold of the damp chased brass. The hallway was dimly lit, damp, and musty now; the branching coat stand protruded from the corner, as naked as a withered tree. There was no carpet on the marble stairway; there were no metal rods—all that was left on the steps were the green, tarnished rings, old yellowed cigarette butts, and some indefinite kind of trash. Treading heavily and hearing nothing but his own steps and his own breathing, Andrei slowly walked up to the top landing.

The long-extinct fireplace gave out a smell of old soot and ammonia, and something was stirring about in it with a faint rustling and scurrying. The immense hall was just as cold—he felt a draft on his legs—black, dusty rags hung down from the invisible ceiling, the marble walls were covered with dark, messy, suspicious-looking patches and glinted with dribbles of damp, the gold and purple had sloughed off them, and the haughtily modest busts of plaster, marble, bronze, and gold looked blindly out of their niches through clumps of dirty cobwebs. The parquet under Andrei's feet creaked and yielded at every step, squares of moonlight lay on the littered floor, and ahead of him a gallery he had never been in before stretched onward and inward. And suddenly an entire swarm of rats shot out from beneath his feet, darted along the gallery with a pattering of paws, and disappeared into the darkness.

Where are they all? Andrei thought in confusion as he wandered along the gallery. What has become of them? he thought as he walked down rumbling iron steps into the musty inner depths. How did all this happen? he thought as he walked from room to room, with crumbled plaster crunching, broken glass squeaking, and dirt, covered in fluffy little mounds of mold, squelching under his feet . . . and there was a sweet smell of decomposition, and somewhere water was ticking, falling drop by drop, and on the tattered walls there were huge black pictures in mighty frames, but he couldn't make out anything in them . . .

Now it will always be like this here, Andrei thought. I've done something—we've all done something—that means it will always be like this here. It won't move from this spot again, it will stay here forever, it will rot and decay, like an ordinary dilapidated building, and in the end they'll smash it apart with iron balls, they'll burn the garbage, and take the burnt bricks off to the garbage dump . . . There isn't a single voice. Not even a single sound, apart from rats squealing in despair in the corners . . .

He saw a huge cupboard with shelves and a rolling shutter and suddenly remembered there used to be a cupboard exactly like it standing in his little room—six square meters of floor space, with a single window looking out into an enclosed yard like a well shaft, and with the kitchen beside it. There were lots of old newspapers lying on the cupboard, and rolled-up posters that his father used to collect before the war, and some other old paper trash . . . and when a mousetrap smashed the face of a huge rat, it somehow managed to climb onto that cupboard and rustled and scrabbled up there for a long time, and every night Andrei was afraid that it would fall off onto his head, and one day he took a pair of binoculars and looked from a distance, from the windowsill, to see what was going on there, in among the paper. He saw—or did he imagine that he saw?—two jutting ears, a gray head, and an appalling bubble, gleaming as if it had been varnished, instead of a face. This was so terrifying that he darted out of his room and sat on the trunk in the corridor for a while, feeling the weakness and nausea inside him. He was alone in the apartment, there was no one there to make him feel embarrassed, but he was ashamed of his fear, and eventually he got up, went into the large room and put "Rio-Rita" on the gramophone . . . And a few days later a sweetish, nauseating smell appeared in his little room. The same smell as here . . .

In a vaulted chamber as deep as a well shaft he glimpsed the strange, surprising gleam of the leaden gray pipes of a huge organ, long since dead, cold, and dumb, like some abandoned graveyard of music. And close to the organ, beside the organist's chair, a little man was lying, huddled up tight and shrouded in a ragged carpet, with an empty vodka bottle glinting by his head. Andrei realized that everything really was over, and hurried back to the way out.

He walked down from the porch into his garden and saw Izya, who was exceptionally drunk and somehow especially disheveled and mussed. He was standing there, swaying, holding on to the trunk of an apple tree with one hand and looking at the Building. In the twilight his bared teeth glittered in a frozen smile.

"It's over," Andrei told him. "It's the end."

"The delirium of an agitated conscience!" Izya mumbled indistinctly.

"Nothing but rats running around," said Andrei. "Rotten."

"The delirium of an agitated conscience . . ." Izya repeated, and giggled.

PART V

CONTINUITY
DISRUPTED

1

Andrei suppressed the cramp in his stomach and swallowed the last spoonful of mush, then pushed his mess tin away with a feeling of revulsion and reached for his mug. The tea was still hot. Andrei wrapped his hand around the mug and started taking little sips, staring into the small, hissing flame of the gasoline lamp. The tea was unusually strong after standing for too long; it smelled like a birch-twig broom and it had a strange aftertaste, maybe from the cruddy water they'd collected after 820 kilometers, or maybe because Quejada had slipped his crappy remedy for diarrhea into all the command staff's mugs again. Or maybe the mug simply hadn't been properly washed—it felt especially greasy and sticky today.

In the street below his window he could hear the soldiers clattering their mess tins. The comic wit Tevosyan cracked some kind of gag about Skank and the soldiers started braying with laughter, but at that very moment Sergeant Vogel suddenly bellowed out in his Prussian voice, "Are you on your way to your post or to slip under the blanket with some woman, you low, creeping amphibian? Why are you barefoot? Where's your footwear, you troglodyte?" A sullen voice responded that the troglodyte's feet were chafed raw, and right through to the bone in some places. "Shut your mouth, you pregnant cow! Get those boots on immediately—and get to your post! Move it!"

Andrei wiggled the toes of his bare feet under the table, relishing the sensation. His feet had already recovered a bit on the cool parquet floor. If he just had a basin full of cold water . . . If he could stick his feet in it . . . He glanced into the mug. It was still half full of tea. To hell with it all, he thought, impulsively downing the remainder in three sensuous gulps.

His stomach immediately started gurgling. For a while Andrei apprehensively listened to what was going on in there, then he put down the mug, wiped his mouth with the back of his hand, and looked at the metal documents box. He ought to get out yesterday's reports . . . I'm not in the mood. Right now I could just stretch out, snuggle up under my jacket, and grab an hour's shut-eye . . .

Outside the window a tractor engine suddenly started furiously clattering. The remnants of glass in the window jangled, and a lump of plaster fell off the ceiling, landing beside the lamp. Trembling rapidly, the empty mug crept toward the edge of the table. Screwing up his entire face, Andrei got up, padded across to the window in his bare feet, and looked out.

He felt a breath of heat on his face from the street, which hadn't cooled off yet, along with the caustic odor of exhaust fumes and the nauseating stench of heated oil. In the dusty light of a swiveling headlamp, bearded men were sitting right there in the road, lazily scrabbling in mess tins with spoons. All of them were barefoot, and almost all of them were naked to the waist. Their sweaty bodies gleamed white but their faces looked black, and their hands were black, as if they were all wearing gloves. Andrei suddenly realized that he didn't recognize any of them. A troop of strange, unfamiliar naked monkeys. Sergeant Vogel stepped into the circle of light holding a huge aluminum kettle, and the monkeys immediately started excitedly fidgeting, jostling and holding out their mugs to the kettle. Pushing the mugs aside with his free hand, the sergeant started yelling, but Andrei could barely hear him above the rattling of the engine.

Andrei went back to the table, jerked open the lid of the box, and took out the logbook and yesterday's reports. Another lump of plaster fell on the table from the ceiling. Andrei looked up. The room was immensely high—about four meters, or maybe even five. The molding on the ceiling had come away in places, so that he could see the lathwork, and that immediately aroused sweet memories of homemade jam pies, served with huge amounts of perfectly brewed, transparent tea in transparent, thin-walled glasses. With lemon. Or you could simply take an empty glass and collect as much pure, cold water as you wanted in the kitchen . . .

Andrei jerked his head, got up again, and walked obliquely right across the room to a huge bookcase. There was no glass in the doors, and there were no books either—just empty, dusty shelves. Andrei already knew that, but nonetheless he examined them one more time and even felt in the dark corners with his hand.

There was no denying the room was pretty well preserved. There were two perfectly decent armchairs in it, and another one with a torn seat of tooled leather that had once been luxurious. Several plain chairs stood in a row along the wall opposite the window, there was a little table with short legs in the middle of the room, and standing on the table was a cut-glass vase, with some sort of black, dried-up gunk inside it. The wallpaper had come loose on the walls, and even fallen away completely in some places, and the parquet floor had dried out and warped, but even so the room was in perfectly good condition—someone had lived here recently, no more than ten years ago.

It was the first time Andrei had seen such a well-preserved building since they passed the five-hundred-kilometer mark. After all those kilometers of neighborhoods burned to cinders and transformed into black, charred desert; after all those kilometers of continuous ruins, overgrown by prickly, brownish briars, and doddering, empty multistory boxes with collapsed floors absurdly towering up out of them; and kilometer after kilometer of waste lots, planted with rotten log-built houses with no roofs, where you could see right across the entire terrace from the road—from the Yellow Wall in the east to the edge of the precipice in the west—after all this, neighborhoods that were almost intact had appeared again, and a road paved with cobblestones, and perhaps there were people somewhere here—in any case, the colonel had ordered the sentries to be doubled.

I wonder how the colonel's doing? The old man's health has gone downhill a bit recently. But then, recently everyone's health has gone downhill. It's perfect timing that we'll be spending the night under a roof for the first time in twelve days and not under the open sky. If we could just find water here, we could make this a long halt. Only it looks like there won't be any water here either. At least, Izya says we shouldn't count on finding any. Out of the whole herd of them, Izya and the colonel are the only ones who ever talk any sense.

There was a knock at the door, barely audible above the clatter of the tractor engine. Andrei hurried back to his seat, pulled on his jacket, opened the logbook, and barked, "Yes!"

It was only Duggan—a lean old man and a good match for his colonel: smoothly shaved, neat and tidy, every button fastened. "Permission to tidy up, sir?" he shouted.

Andrei nodded. Good God, he thought. What an effort it must take to keep yourself so smart in this shambles . . . And he isn't even an officer, is he, not even a sergeant—he's nothing but an orderly. A lackey. "How's the colonel?" Andrei asked.

"Beg your pardon, sir?" Duggan froze, holding the dirty tableware in his hands, with one long, gristly ear turned toward Andrei.

"How is the colonel feeling?" Andrei roared, and that very second the engine outside fell silent.

"The colonel is drinking tea!" Duggan roared in the sudden silence, immediately adding in an embarrassed voice, "Beg your pardon, sir. The colonel is feeling passably well. He ate supper and now he is drinking tea."

Andrei nodded absentmindedly and flipped over a few pages of the logbook.

"Will there be any instructions, sir?" Duggan inquired.

"No, thank you," said Andrei.

When Duggan walked out, Andrei finally got started on yesterday's reports. Yesterday he hadn't recorded anything at all; he'd had the runs so bad, he barely managed to sit through to the end of the evening reporting session, and afterward he was in torment half the night—squatting out in the middle of the road with his bare ass pointed toward the camp, tensely peering into the gloom and straining his ears to catch any sounds, with a pistol in one hand and a flashlight in the other.

"Day 28," he inscribed on a clean page, and underscored what he had written with two thick lines. Then he took Quejada's report.

"Distance covered 28 kilometers," he noted down. "Height of sun 63°51'13".2 (at 979 km). Average temperature: in the shade +23°C, in the sun +31°C. Wind 2.5 m/sec, humidity 0.42. Gravity 0.998. Drilling carried out at 979, 981, 986 km. No water. Fuel consumption . . ." he took Ellisauer's report, badly soiled by oil-stained fingers, and spent a long time trying to decipher the chicken-scratch writing.

"Fuel consumption: 1.32 of daily norm. Remaining at end of day 28: 3,200 kg. Condition of engines: No. 1, satisfactory; No. 2, worn wrist pins and problems with the cylinders . . ."

Andrei wasn't able to decipher what exactly had happened to the cylinders, although he held the sheet of paper right up close to the flame of the lamp.

"Condition of personnel: physical condition—almost every-one has abrasions on the feet and the general diarrhea continues, the rash on Permyak's and Palotti's shoulders is getting worse. No wounded, no injuries. No exceptional incidents. Shark wolves appeared twice and were driven away by shooting. Munitions expended 12 cartridges. Water expended 40 L. Remaining at end of day 28—1,100 kg. Foodstuff expended 20 daily rations. Remaining at end of day 28: 730 daily rations."

Outside the window Skank started twittering in a shrill voice, and throats husky from smoking started braying hoarsely. Andrei raised his head and listened. The devil only knows, he thought. Maybe it's not such a bad thing that she tagged along with us. At least it's some kind of amusement for the men . . . Only just recently they've started fighting over her.

There was another knock at the door.

"Come in," Andrei said bad-temperedly.

Sergeant Vogel walked in—huge and red-faced, with wide, blurred patches of black sweat below the arms of his tunic.

"Sergeant Vogel requests permission to address Mr. Counselor!" he barked, pressing his palms against his thighs and thrusting out his elbows.

"Go ahead, Sergeant," said Andrei.

The sergeant squinted sideways at the window. "I request permission to speak in confidence," he said, lowering his voice.

This is something new, Andrei thought with an ominous feeling. "Come on in and sit down," he said.

The sergeant tiptoed up to the table, sat down on the very edge of an armchair, and leaned toward Andrei. "The men don't want to go any farther," he said in a low voice.

Andrei leaned back in his chair. So, he thought. This is what things have come to . . . Wonderful . . . Congratulations, Mr. Counselor . . . "What does that mean—they don't want to. Who's asking them?"

"They're worn out, Mr. Counselor," Vogel said in a confidential tone. "The tobacco's almost finished. The diarrhea has worn them down. But worse than that—they're frightened. It's fear, Mr. Counselor."

Andrei looked at him without speaking. He had to do something. Immediately. But he didn't know exactly what.

"We haven't seen a single human in eleven days of walking, Mr. Counselor," Vogel went on, almost whispering. "Mr. Counselor recalls that we were warned there'd be thirteen days with no people in sight, and then—curtains for everyone. There are only two days left, Mr. Counselor."

Andrei licked his lips. "Sergeant," he said, "shame on you. An old war dog like you, believing old wives' tales. I didn't expect that of you!"

Vogel grinned crookedly, thrusting out his huge lower jaw. "Not at all, Mr. Counselor. You can't frighten me. If only all of them out there . . ." He jabbed a large, gnarled finger at the window. "If only I had just Germans out there, or at least Japs, we wouldn't be having this conversation, Mr. Counselor. But what I've got out there is riffraff. Ities, Armenians or some such—"

"Stop right there, Sergeant!" Andrei said, raising his voice. "Shame on you. You don't know the army regulations! Why are you addressing me unordered? What kind of laxness is this, Sergeant? On your feet!"

Vogel ponderously got up and stood to attention.

"Sit down," Andrei said after a deliberate pause.

Vogel sat down as awkwardly as he had gotten up, and for a while neither of them spoke.

"Why have you come to me and not to the colonel?"

"I beg your pardon, Mr. Counselor. I did go to the colonel. Yesterday."

"And what came of it?"

"The colonel was not inclined to take my report under consideration, Mr. Counselor."

Andrei laughed. "Precisely! What kind of damned sergeant are you, if you can't keep your own men in order?" They're frightened, he tells me! Little children . . . "They should be afraid of *you*, Sergeant!" he bellowed. "Of you! Not the thirteenth day!"

"If only they were Germans . . ." Vogel began again morosely.

"What is all this?" Andrei asked cajolingly. "Do I, the head of the expedition, have to teach you what has to be done when subordinates mutiny, as if you were some snot-nosed kid? For shame, Vogel! If you don't know, read the regulations. As far as I'm aware, this is all provided for there."

Vogel grinned again, shifting his lower jaw. Evidently cases like this were not provided for in the regulations after all.

"I thought more highly of you, Vogel," Andrei said harshly. "Much more highly! Get this into your head once and for all: no one is interested in whether your men want to go on or they don't. We'd all like to be at home right now, not trudging through this scorching heat. Everyone's thirsty, and everyone's exhausted. But nonetheless everyone carries out their duty, Vogel. Is that clear?"

"Yes sir, Mr. Counselor," Vogel growled. "Permission to leave?"

"On your way."

The sergeant withdrew, ferociously stomping across the dried-out parquet in his boots.

Andrei took off his jacket and went over to the window again. The gathering seemed to have calmed down. The impossibly tall Ellisauer towered up in the circle of light, hunching over to examine some document—Andrei thought it was a map—that broad, bulky Quejada was holding up in front of him. A soldier emerged from the darkness, walked past them, and disappeared into a building—barefoot, seminaked, disheveled, carrying his automatic by the strap.

At the spot he had come from, another soldier's voice called out in the darkness: "Beaky! Hey, Tevosyan!"

"What do you want?" a voice answered from an invisible cargo sled, where cigarettes flared up and faded away like fireflies.

"Turn the light this way! I can't see a damned thing."

"What do you need it for? Can't you do it in the dark?"

"They've crapped everywhere here already . . . I don't know where to step . . ."

"The sentry's not supposed to go," a new voice joined in from the throng. "Dump where you're standing!"

"Aw, give me some light, for fuck's sake! Is it too much bother to move your ass?"

Lanky Ellisauer straightened up, and in two strides he was beside the tractor and swiveled the headlamp to shine along the street. Andrei saw the sentry. Holding his lowered trousers with one hand, he was hovering uncertainly on bent knees beside the massive iron statue that some weirdos or other had put up right on the sidewalk at the nearest intersection. The statue represented a stocky character wearing something like a toga, with a shaved head and repugnant, toadish features. In the light of the headlamp the statue looked black. Its left arm pointed up to the heavens, and its right arm was stretched out above the earth, with the fingers of the hand splayed out. Right now an automatic rifle was hanging on that arm.

"Good job, thanks a bunch!" the sentry roared, overjoyed, and squatted down in a firm position. "You can shut it off now!"

"Come on, come on, get on with it!" someone encouraged him from the sled. "We'll give you covering fire, if you need it . . ."

"Aw, shut off the light, guys!" the sentry begged, getting edgy.

"Don't shut it off, Mr. Engineer," a voice from the sled advised. "He's joking. And the regulations don't allow—"

But Ellisauer turned the light away after all. Andrei heard jostling and guffawing on the sled. Then two of the men started whistling a duet—some kind of march.

Everything's just the same as ever, thought Andrei. If anything, they're more cheerful than usual today. I didn't hear any of these jokes yesterday or the day before. Maybe it's the apartment houses? Yes, it could be that. Nothing but desert and more desert, but now there are houses! At least they can catch up on their sleep in peace; the wolves won't bother them. Only Vogel's no alarmist. Uh-uh, he's not that kind . . . Andrei suddenly imagined himself tomorrow, giving the order to move out, but the men bunch up together, with their automatics bristling out, and say, "We won't go!" Maybe that's why they're so cheerful right now—they've settled everything among themselves, already decided to turn back tomorrow (". . . what can he do to us, the gutless jerk, the crummy office clerk?") and now they couldn't give a damn, they don't have a care in the world, they don't give a fuck . . . And Quejada, the bastard, is with them. He's been whining for days now that it's pointless to go any farther . . . he looks daggers at me during the evening reports . . . he'd only be delighted if I went creeping back to Heiger empty handed, with my tail between my legs . . .

Andrei shrugged his shoulders with a shudder. It's your own fault, you wimp—you dropped the reins, you lousy democrat, you damned populist . . . You ought to have put that Hnoipek with the ginger hair up against the wall that first time, the slime-ball, taken the whole gang by the throat in a single stroke—I'd have them all toeing the line now! And it was just the right opportunity! A gang rape, and a brutal one, and the victim was a native girl, an underage native girl . . . And the insolent way that Hnoi-pek grinned—that insolent, sated, loathsome grin—when I yelled at them . . . and the way they all turned green when I pulled out the revolver. Ah, Colonel, Colonel, you're a liberal, not a combat officer! "Oh, why start shooting straightaway, Counselor? After all, there are other means of influence!" Uh-uh, Colonel. It's obvi-ous you can't influence these Hnoipeks any other way . . . And after that everything went askew. The girl attached herself to the squad, I shamefully turned a blind eye (out of amazement, was that it?), and then the squabbling and brawling over her began . . . And again I should have interfered in the first fight, put someone up against the wall, had the girl flogged and slung her out of the camp . . . Only where could we sling her out to? We were already in the burned-out districts, there was no water there, the wolves had appeared . . .

Down in the street someone started furiously growling and swearing, something fell over and started clattering around, and a completely naked monkey came flying backward out of a door-way into the circle of light, landed smack on his ass, raising a cloud of dust, and before it could even pull up its legs, another monkey pounced like a tiger out of the same doorway, and they went at it tooth and claw, rolling around on the cobblestones, howling and snarling, wheezing and spitting, flailing at each other with all their might.

Andrei gripped the windowsill with one hand and dull-wittedly fumbled at his belt with the other, forgetting that his holster was lying in the armchair, but then Sergeant Vogel emerged from the darkness, swooping down like a sweaty black storm cloud driven by a hurricane, and hovering over the miscreants. And then he had grabbed one by the hair and the other by the beard, jerked them up off the ground, slammed them against each other with a dry crunch and tossed them away in opposite directions, like puppies.

"Very good, Sergeant!" the colonel's weak but firm voice declared. "Tie the scoundrels to their beds for the night, and tomorrow put them in the advance guard out of turn for the whole day."

"Yes, sir, Mr. Colonel," the sergeant replied, breathing heavily. He glanced to the right, where a naked monkey was scrabbling at the cobblestones, struggling to get up, and added uncertainly, "If I might make bold to report, Colonel, one isn't ours. The cartographer Roulier."

Andrei shook his head with a jerk, clearing a space in his throat, and roared in an unnatural voice. "Put cartographer Roulier in the advance guard for three days, with full combat gear. If the fight is repeated, shoot both of them on the spot!" Something cracked painfully in his throat. "Shoot all miscreants who dare to fight on the spot!" he croaked.

When he recovered his self-control, he was already seated at the table. Too late, probably, he thought, examining his dirty, trembling fingers. Too late. I should have acted sooner . . . But you'll toe that line for me! You'll do what you're ordered to do! I'll order half of you to be shot . . . I'll shoot you myself . . . but the other half will toe the line for me. No more . . . No more! And Hnoipek gets the first bullet, whatever the circumstances. The first!

He rummaged behind his back, pulled out his holster and belt, and took out the pistol. The barrel was packed with dirt. He pulled back the bolt. It moved sluggishly, pulling back halfway and jamming in that position. Dammit, everything's jammed, everything's filthy . . . Outside the window it was quiet, with only the steel tips of the sentries' boots clicking on the cobblestones in the distance, and someone blowing his nose on the ground floor and droning loudly through his teeth.

Andrei walked to the door and glanced out into the corridor. "Duggan!" he called in a low voice.

Something stirred in the corner. Andrei started and looked that way: it was the Mute. He was sitting in his usual pose, with his legs crossed over each other and interwoven in some highly complex fashion. His eyes glinted moistly in the semidarkness.

"Duggan!" Andrei called more loudly.

"Coming, sir!" a voice answered from somewhere deep inside the building. He heard footsteps.

"Why are you sitting here?" Andrei asked the Mute. "Come into the room."

Without stirring from the spot, the Mute raised his broad face and looked at him.

Andrei went back to the table, and when Duggan knocked and glanced into the room, Andrei told him, "Clean up my pistol, please."

"Yes, sir," Duggan said respectfully, and took the pistol. At the door he moved aside to let Izya into the room.

"Aha, a lamp!" said Izya, heading straight for the table. "Listen, Andrei, have you got another lamp like that? I'm sick of using a flashlight—my eyes hurt . . ."

Izya had lost a load of weight over the last few days. All his clothes hung loose; everything on him was torn. And he stank like an old goat. But then, everyone stank that way. Apart from the colonel.

Andrei watched as Izya, taking no notice of anything, pulled over a chair, sat down, and moved the lamp across toward himself. Then he started taking old, crumpled papers out from under his jacket and laying them out in front of him. As he did this, he bobbed up and down on his chair in his habitual fashion, peering at the papers as if he were rifling through them, as if he were trying to read them all at once, and every now and then plucking at his wart. It was hard for him to get to the wart now, because his cheeks and neck and even, seemingly, his ears, were covered with an immensely thick coating of hair.

"Listen, why don't you get a shave, really?" said Andrei.

"What for?" Izya asked absentmindedly.

"The whole command staff shaves," Andrei said angrily. "You're the only one walking around like a scarecrow."

Izya raised his head and looked at Andrei for a while, exposing yellowish, long-unbrushed teeth among the hair. "Yes?" he said.

"Well, you know, I'm not big on prestige. Look at the jacket I'm wearing."

Andrei looked. "You could darn that too, by the way. If you don't know how—let Duggan have it."

"I think Duggan has enough to do without me . . . And by the way, who are you intending to shoot?"

"Whoever I need to," Andrei said darkly.

"Well, well," Izya said, and immersed himself in reading.

Andrei glanced at his watch. There were ten minutes to go. Andrei sighed and reached under the table, groped to find his shoes, pulled out the stiff socks and surreptitiously sniffed at them, then lifted up his right foot toward the light and examined the skinned heel. The abrasion had started healing over slightly, but it was still painful. Wincing in anticipation, he cautiously pulled on his rigid sock and moved his foot a bit. Wincing really hard now, he reached for his shoe. When he had his shoes on, he put on the belt with the empty holster, straightened his jacket, and buttoned it.

"Here," said Izya, pushing a pile of papers covered in writing across the table to him.

"What's that?" Andrei asked, totally uninterested.

"Paper."

"Aah . . ." Andrei picked up the sheets of paper and put them in the pocket of his jacket. "Thank you."

Izya was already reading again. Fast, like a machine.

Andrei remembered how much he hadn't wanted to bring Izya on this expedition—with his absurd vegetable-plot-scarecrow appearance, with his provocatively Jewish features, with his insolent giggling, with his self-evident inability to handle heavy physical demands. It had been absolutely clear that Izya would cause him a heap of trouble, and the archivist would be pretty useless in field conditions verging on combat conditions. But things hadn't turned out that way at all.

That's to say, things had turned out that way as well. Izya was the first to skin his feet. Both of them at once. Izya was insufferable at the evening report sessions, with his idiotic, inappropriate little jokes and gratuitous informality. On the third day of the journey he managed to fall through into some kind of cellar, and the entire team had to help drag him out of there. On the sixth day he got lost and delayed their departure by several hours. During the skirmish at 340 kilometers he behaved like a total cretin and only survived by a miracle. The soldiers mocked him and Quejada constantly quarreled with him. Ellisauer turned out to hate all Jews on principle, and Andrei had to read him the riot act about Izya . . . It happened. It all happened.

And despite all this, pretty soon Izya turned out to be the most popular figure on the expedition, with the possible exception of the colonel. And even more popular in some ways. First, he found water. The geologists spent a long time vainly searching for springs, drilling rocks, sweating, and making exhausting forays during the general rest halts. Izya simply sat in a cargo sled under a grotesque improvised parasol and rummaged through old documents, of which he had accumulated several crates. And four times he predicted where to look for underground cisterns. True, one cistern was dried out, and the water in another was rank and fetid, but the expedition had twice discovered excellent water, thanks to Izya and only Izya.

Second, he found a cache of diesel oil, after which Ellisauer's antisemitism had become largely abstract. "I hate yids," he explained to his lead mechanic. "There's nothing on Earth worse than a yid. But I've never had anything against Jews! Take Katzman, for instance . . ."

And what was more, Izya supplied everyone with paper. Their supplies of bathroom tissue had run out after the first outbreak of gastrointestinal disorders, and Izya's popularity—as the only owner and custodian of paper wealth in country where you couldn't find so much as a burdock leaf or a clump of grass—had risen to astronomical levels.

Less than two weeks went by before Andrei realized, with a certain degree of envy, that they all loved Izya. Everyone. Even the soldiers, which was absolutely incredible. During the halts, they jostled around him and listened openmouthed to his prattle. Without being asked, they lugged his metal crates of documents from place to place, taking pleasure in it. They complained to him and showed off to him like schoolboys with their favorite teacher. They hated Vogel, they were in awe of the colonel, they fought with the scientific staff, but with Izya, they laughed. And not at him but with him! "You know, Katzman," the colonel said one day, "I never understood what commissars were needed for in an army, but I think I'd take you on for that job."

Izya finished sorting out one batch of documents and extracted another one from under his jacket. "Is there anything interesting?" Andrei asked. He didn't ask because he was really curious but simply because he wanted somehow to express the affection he suddenly felt at this moment for this clumsy, absurd man with his sleazy appearance.

Izya barely had time to give a brief nod. Before he could reply, the door swung open and St. James stepped into the room.

"With your permission, Counselor?" he said.

"Please come in, Colonel," said Andrei, getting up. "Good evening."

Izya jumped to his feet and moved up an armchair for the colonel.

"Most kind of you, Commissar," the colonel said, and sat down slowly, in two stages. He looked the same as usual—trim and fresh, with a fragrance of eau de cologne and good tobacco—only his cheeks had become a little hollower just recently and his eyes had sunk in quite startlingly. And he didn't walk around with his distinctive swagger stick any longer but with a long black cane, on which he noticeably leaned when he had to remain standing.

"That disgraceful fight under the windows . . ." said the colonel. "I apologize for my soldier, Counselor."

"Let's hope that was the last fight," Andrei said morosely. "I don't intend to tolerate this any longer."

The colonel nodded absentmindedly. "Soldiers always fight," he remarked casually. "In the British Army it's actually encouraged. Fighting spirit, healthy aggression, and so on . . . But you are right, of course. In such arduous field conditions it's quite intolerable." He leaned back in his chair, took out his pipe, and started filling it. "But the potential enemy is still nowhere to be seen, is he, Counselor?" he said humorously. "In this connection, I foresee great complications for my poor general staff. And also for the Messrs. Politicians, to be frank."

"On the contrary!" Izya exclaimed. "The hectic times are just about to start for all of us! Since no genuine enemy exists, he has to be invented. And as universal experience demonstrates, the most terrible enemy is an invented one. I assure you, it will be an incredibly gruesome monster. The army will have to be doubled in size."

"So that's how it is?" said the colonel, still in humorous vein. "I wonder who will invent him? Could it possibly be you, my commissar?"

"You!" Izya said triumphantly. "You, first and foremost." He started counting on his fingers. "First, you will have to set up a department of political propaganda attached to the general staff—"

There was a knock at the door, and before Andrei could answer, Quejada and Ellisauer walked in. Quejada was sullen and Ellisauer was smiling down vaguely from somewhere right up under the ceiling.

"Please be seated, gentlemen." Andrei greeted them coolly. He rapped his knuckles on the table and told Izya, "Katzman, we're starting."

Izya broke off in midword and eagerly turned his face toward Andrei, flinging one arm over the back of his chair. The colonel drew himself erect again and folded his hands on the knob of his cane.

"You have the floor, Quejada," Andrei said.

The head of the science section was sitting right in front of him, with his fat weightlifter's legs set wide apart to avoid getting damp in the crotch, and Ellisauer, as always, had installed himself behind Quejada's back, hunching right over there so he wouldn't stick out too much.

"Nothing new on the geology," Quejada said sullenly. "The same clay and sand as before. No signs of water. The local water main here dried out a long time ago. Maybe that's the reason why they left, I don't know . . . The data on the sun, the wind, and so on . . ." He took a sheet of paper out of his breast pocket and tossed it across to Andrei. "That's all I have for now."

Andrei didn't like that "for now" at all, but he just nodded and started looking at Ellisauer.

"And on transport?"

Ellisauer straightened up and started talking over Quejada's head. "Today we covered thirty-eight kilometers. The motor of tractor number two needs to be laid up for a major overhaul. I very much regret, Mr. Counselor, but—unfortunately . . ."

"I see," said Andrei. "What does that mean, a major overhaul?"

"Two or three days," said Ellisauer. "Some elements will have to be replaced and others will need to be fixed. Maybe even four days. Or five."

"Or ten," said Andrei. "Give me your report."

"Or ten," Ellisauer agreed, still with the same vague smile. "I'm afraid to say exactly. We're not in a garage here, and then my Permyak . . . he has some kind of rash, and he's been vomiting all day long. He's my lead mechanic, Mr. Counselor . . ."

"What about you?" asked Andrei.

"I'll do everything I can . . . But the problem is, in our conditions . . . I mean, in field conditions . . ."

For a while he carried on babbling something about motor mechanics, about a crane that they hadn't brought with them, although he had warned them, hadn't he . . . about a bench drill that they didn't have here and, unfortunately, couldn't possibly have had here, about the motor mechanic again, and something else about wrist pins and pistons . . . With every minute that passed he spoke more and more quietly, less and less distinctly, and finally fell completely silent, and all this time Andrei stared him in the eye without looking away, and it was absolutely clear that this lanky, cowardly con artist had lied his way into a tight corner, and he'd already realized this, and he could see everyone else had realized it too, and he was trying to squirm out of it somehow, only he didn't know how, but even so, he firmly intended to stick to his lies until the victory was won.

After that Andrei lowered his eyes and stared at Ellisauer's report, at the slovenly lines scratched out in chicken-claw scribble, but he didn't see or understand anything. They've conspired, the bastards, he thought in quiet despair. These men are in the conspiracy too. So now what do I do with them? A pity my pistol's not here . . . Wallop Ellisauer . . . or frighten him so badly that he shits himself . . . No, it's Quejada. Quejada's the one in charge of them all. He wants to dump all the responsibility on me . . . He wants to dump this entire rotten, stinking lost cause on me, and only me . . . the scumbag, the fat pig . . . Andrei wanted to yell out loud and slam his fist down on the table with all his might.

The silence was becoming unbearable. Izya suddenly started nervously squirming on his chair and mumbling. "What actually is the problem here? After all, we're not in any particular hurry to get anywhere. Let's make a halt . . . There could be manuscripts in the buildings. There's no water here, it's true, but we can send a separate team on ahead for water . . ."

And at that point Quejada interrupted him. "Rubbish," he said harshly. "No more idle talk, gentlemen. Let's dot the i's and cross the t's. The expedition has failed. We haven't found water. Or oil. And there's no way we could have found them with the geological prospecting organized like this. We tear along like lunatics; we've run the men into the ground and totally wrecked our transport. Discipline in the crew is shot to hell, we feed stray girls and ferry rumormongers around with us . . . All sense of perspective was lost a long time ago; no one gives a damn for anything. The men don't want to go on, they can't see why we need to go on, and there's nothing we can tell them. The cosmographic data have simply turned out to be absolutely damned useless: we prepared for freezing polar conditions but we drove into a red-hot desert. The personnel for the expedition were badly selected, completely at random; the medical arrangements are appalling. And the result is that we get what we were bound to get: a slump in morale, a collapse of discipline, veiled insubordination, and today or tomorrow—mutiny. That's all."

Quejada stopped talking, took out a cigarette case, and lit up. "What are you actually suggesting, Mr. Quejada?" Andrei said in a stale, flat voice. That loathsome face with the fat mustache hovered in front of him, suspended in a web of blurred, indistinct lines. He really wanted to smash it good and hard. With the lamp. Right on that mustache . . .

"In my opinion, it's absolutely obvious," Quejada said contemptuously. "We have to pack it in and go back where we came from. Immediately. While we're still in one piece."

Keep calm, Andrei told himself. Right now, calm, nothing but calm. As few words as possible. No arguing, no matter what. Listen calmly and say nothing. Ah, how I'd love to whop him!

"Yes, really," Ellisauer spoke up. "How long can we keep going? My men ask me, What's going on here, Mr. Engineer? We agreed to keep going until the sun sank behind the horizon. But instead of sinking, it gets higher. And then we agreed to keep going until it reaches its zenith . . . But it doesn't rise toward any zenith, it just keeps skipping up and down . . ."

Just don't argue, Andrei kept telling himself. Let them babble. In fact it's quite interesting to see what they'll come up with . . . The colonel won't betray me. The army decides everything. The army! Could they really have talked Vogel onto joining them, the bastards?

"And what do you say?" Izya asked Ellisauer. "You?"

"What about me?"

"Your men ask you, that's clear enough . . . But how do you answer them?"

Ellisauer started shrugging his shoulders and wiggling his sparse eyebrows. "A strange question . . ." he mumbled as he did it. "What answer can I give them, I ask you? I'd like to know what answer I'm supposed to give them. How do I know?"

"That is, you don't give them any answer?"

"But what answer can I give them? What? I tell them the boss knows best."

"What an answer!" said Izya, glaring horrendously. "With answers like that you can demoralize an entire army, never mind the poor drivers . . . 'Well guys, I'm ready to go back right now, only the big bad boss won't let me . . .' Do you even understand why we're making this journey? You're a volunteer, aren't you— no one forced you to come!"

"Listen, Katzman . . ." Quejada tried to interrupt. "Let's get down to brass tacks!"

"You knew it was going to be hard, didn't you, Ellisauer? You did. You knew we weren't going for a walk in the park, didn't you? You did. You knew the City needed this expedition, didn't you? You did—you're an educated man, an engineer . . . You knew what the orders were, didn't you: keep going as long as the fuel and water last? You knew that perfectly well, Elli- sauer!"

"I'm not objecting, am I!" Ellisauer gabbled hastily, absolutely terrified. "I'm only trying to explain to you that my explana- tions . . . That is, I mean it's not clear to me how I should answer them, because after all, they ask me—"

"Will you stop waffling, Ellisauer!" Izya said, closing in for the kill. "Everything's perfectly clear: you're afraid to go on, you're conducting moral sabotage, you've demoralized your own sub- ordinates, and now you've come running here to complain . . . And you, by the way, don't even have to walk. You ride all the time . . ."

Go on, Izya, give it to him, buddy, Andrei thought lovingly. Whop him, the motherfucker, whop him! He's already shit him- self, now he'll ask to go to the john . . .

"And I don't understand at all what all this panic is about," Izya continued without easing up. "So the geology's come up short. To hell with the geology—we'll get by without any geology. And we'll get by even more easily without any cosmography . . . Surely it's clear that our main job is reconnaissance, collecting information. I personally can vouch that to date the expedition has already achieved a great deal, and it can do even more. The tractor's broken down? So fine, let them repair it here, two days or ten, I don't know—let's leave the sickest and most exhausted men and move ahead gently on the other tractor. If we find water, we'll stop and wait for the others. It's all very simple, you know; it's no big deal . . ."

"Sure, it's all very simple, Katzman," Quejada said acidly. "How would you like a bullet in the back, Katzman? Or in the forehead? You've gotten too carried away with your archives, you don't notice anything going on around you. The soldiers won't go any farther. I know it. I heard them deciding for themselves . . ."

Ellisauer suddenly sprang up from behind him and dashed out of the room, mumbling incoherent apologies and demonstratively clutching his stomach. The rat, Andrei thought savagely. The cowardly swine. The gutless shit . . .

Quejada seemed not to have noticed anything. "Out of all my geologists, there's only one man I can rely on," he continued. "The soldiers and the drivers can't be relied on at all. Of course, you can shoot one or two of them to frighten the rest . . . maybe that would help. I don't know. I doubt it. And I'm not sure you have the moral right to do that. They don't want to go on because they feel cheated. Because they've gotten nothing out of this expedition, and now they have no hope of getting anything. The wonderful legend that Mr. Katzman so opportunely invented—the legend of the Crystal Palace—doesn't work anymore. Different legends have overshadowed it now, you know, Mr. Katzman . . ."

"What the hell do you mean?" said Izya, stammering from indignation. "I didn't invent anything!"

Quejada brushed that off almost affably: "All right, all right, that's immaterial now. It's already clear that there's not going to be any palace, so there's nothing to talk about. You know perfectly well, gentlemen, that three-quarters of your volunteers came on this expedition for booty, and only for booty. And what have they received instead of booty? Bloody diarrhea and a vermin-ridden idiot for their nocturnal frolics . . . But even that's not the point. As if the disappointment wasn't enough, they're scared too. Let's thank Mr. Katzman. Let's thank Mr. Pak, to whom we have so graciously offered bed and board with our expedition. Thanks to the efforts of these gentlemen, we have learned a vast amount about what lies in store for us if we continue our advance. The men are afraid of the thirteenth day. The men are afraid of talking wolves. The shark wolves weren't enough for us, so we've been promised talking ones! The men are afraid of Ironheads. And together with what they've already seen—all these mutes with their tongues cut out, abandoned concentration camps, all these cretins who have reverted to savagery and pray to springs, and the well-armed cretins who fire at you out of the blue, without rhyme or reason . . . together with what they've seen today, here, in these houses—those bones in the barricaded apartments . . . it all makes a delightful and impressive combination! And if yesterday what the men were most afraid of in the entire world was Sergeant Vogel, today they couldn't give a rotten damn for Vogel—they have more terrifying things to fear."

Quejada finally stopped talking, caught his breath, and wiped away the sweat that had sprung out on his fat face. And then the colonel lifted one eyebrow ironically and said, "I have the impression that you are thoroughly frightened yourself, Mr. Quejada. Or am I mistaken?"

Quejada squinted at him with a red eye. "Don't you worry about me, Colonel," he growled. "If I'm afraid of anything, it's a bullet between the shoulder blades. Out the blue. From men I sympathize with, by the way."

"So that's it?" said the colonel. "Well now . . . I don't presume to judge the importance of the present expedition, and I don't presume to tell the leader of the expedition how he ought to act. My job is to carry out orders. However, I feel obliged to state that I consider all this discussion of mutiny and insubordination to be idle prattle. Leave my soldiers to me, Mr. Quejada! If you like you can also leave to me those of your geologists that you don't trust. I'll be glad to deal with them . . . I must point out to you, Counselor," he continued with the same devastating politeness, "that today too much is being said about the soldiers by precisely those individuals who have no official connection with the soldiers—"

"The individuals talking about the soldiers," Quejada interrupted angrily, "work round the clock with them, and eat and sleep beside them."

In the silence that followed, a leather armchair quietly creaked as the colonel sat completely upright. He said nothing for a while. The door opened quietly and Ellisauer snuck back to his place with a sour smile, bowing slightly as he walked.

Come on, Andrei mentally urged the colonel, staring at him with all his might. Come on, whop him! Right on the mustache! Whop his ugly mug, whop it!

The colonel finally spoke: "I am obliged to draw to your attention, Counselor, that today a certain section of the command staff has evinced sympathy for and, even worse, connivance at perfectly understandable and ordinary but entirely unacceptable sentiments among the lower ranks of the army. As the senior officer, I have the following declaration to make: If the aforementioned connivance and sympathy should assume any practical forms, I shall deal with the connivers and sympathizers as is appropriate to deal with such individuals in field conditions. Other than that, Mr. Counselor, I have the honor to assure you that the army remains ready henceforth to carry out any commands you may give."

Andrei quietly caught his breath and gave Quejada a jubilant look. Quejada was smiling crookedly as he lit a new cigarette from the butt of the old one. Andrei couldn't see Ellisauer at all.

"And exactly how *are* connivers and sympathizers dealt with in field conditions?" Izya inquired with tremendous curiosity; he was jubilant too.

"They are usually hanged," the colonel replied drily.

Silence fell again. So there now, thought Andrei. I hope that's all clear. Mr. Quejada? Or perhaps you have questions? You don't have any questions, no way! It's the army! The army decides everything, my friends . . . But even so, I don't understand anything, he thought. Why is he so confident? Or maybe it's only a mask, Colonel? I look very confident right now too, don't I? At least, that's the way I'm supposed to look . . . I'm obliged to.

He squinted warily at the colonel, who was still sitting up very straight, with his extinct pipe firmly clutched in his teeth. And he was very pale. Perhaps it's merely anger. Let's hope it's just down to anger . . . To hell with it, to hell with it, Andrei thought frantically. A long halt! Right now! And Katzman can find me water. Lots of water. For the colonel. Just for the colonel. And starting tonight the colonel gets a double ration of water!

Ellisauer, all twisted out of shape, leaned out from behind Quejada's fat shoulder and squeaked pitifully. "Please . . . I've got to go . . . Again . . ."

"Sit down," Andrei told him. "We're just finishing up." He leaned back in the armchair and grasped the armrests. "Orders for tomorrow. I'm declaring a long halt. Ellisauer! Put all your men on the faulty tractor. I give you three days; kindly get it done in that time. Quejada. All day tomorrow, attend to the sick. The day after tomorrow, be prepared to accompany me on deep reconnaissance. Katzman, you will go with us . . . Water!" He tapped his finger on the table. "I need water, Katzman! Colonel! Tomorrow I order you to rest. The day after tomorrow you will take command of the camp. That's all, gentlemen. Dismissed."

2

Shining the flashlight down at his feet, Andrei hurried upstairs to the next floor—he thought it was the fifth at this point. *Dammit, I'm not going to make it* . . . He stopped for a moment, tensing every muscle as he waited for an acute urge to pass. Something in his belly churned with a muted glug and he felt a bit better. *The fiends, they've fouled every level—there's nowhere left to step* . . . He reached the landing and pushed on the very first door. The door half-opened with a squeak, and Andrei squeezed in through the opening and sniffed. *It didn't seem too bad* . . . He shone his flashlight around . . . Right beside the door, on the dried-out parquet, white bones lay in a tangle of stiffened rags, and a skull with clumps of hair caked on it grinned toothily. Clear enough: they looked inside and took fright. Moving his legs unnaturally, Andrei almost ran along the passage. *The parlor* . . . *Dammit, something like a bedroom* . . . *Where's their john? Ah, there it is* . . .

Afterward, feeling calm, although the griping in his gut still hadn't completely subsided and he was covered in cold, sticky sweat, he walked back out into the corridor and took the flashlight out of his pocket again. The Mute was right on cue, standing there, leaning his shoulder against some kind of endlessly tall, polished cupboard, with his large hands thrust in under his broad belt.

"Standing guard?" Andrei asked him with casual affability. "You do that, stand guard, or someone might sneak round a corner and stick a knife in my back—then what will you do?"

Andrei suddenly realized he'd gotten into the habit of talking to this strange man as if he were a huge dog, and he felt embarrassed. Giving the Mute a friendly pat on his cool, naked shoulder, he set off along the corridor, no longer hurrying, shining the flashlight right and left. Behind him he could hear the Mute's soft footsteps following, neither moving closer nor falling back.

This apartment was more luxurious. Lots of rooms packed with heavy antique furniture, massive chandeliers, huge, blackened paintings in museum-style frames. But almost all the furniture was smashed: armrests had been torn off armchairs, chairs without legs were scattered around the floor, doors had been ripped off wardrobes. Did they use the furniture to heat the place, then? Andrei thought. In this heat? Strange . . .

To be honest, the entire house was a bit strange—he could completely understand the soldiers. Some apartments were standing wide open, and they were simply empty, absolutely nothing but the bare walls. Others were locked from the inside, sometimes even barricaded with furniture, and if you managed to break in, there were human bones lying on the floor. It was the same in the other houses nearby, and they could assume the picture would be the same in the other houses of this district.

None of this seemed to make any sense at all, and so far even Izya Katzman hadn't come up with any sensible way to explain why some of the residents of these houses fled, taking with them everything they could carry, even books, and others had barricaded themselves in their homes, only to die there, apparently from hunger and thirst. And maybe from cold, too—in some of the apartments they had discovered wretched little iron stoves, and in others fires had clearly been lit directly on the floor, or on sheets of rusty iron that most likely had been torn off the roof.

"Do you understand what happened here?" Andrei asked the Mute.

The Mute slowly shook his head.

"Have you ever been here before?"

The Mute nodded.

"Did anyone live here then?"

No, the Mute signaled.

"I see," Andrei muttered, trying to make out what was represented in a blackened painting. He thought it was some kind of portrait. Apparently of a woman . . .

"Is this place dangerous?" he asked.

The Mute looked at him with absolutely still eyes.

"Do you understand the question?"

Yes.

"Can you answer it?"

No.

"Well, thanks for that at least," Andrei said thoughtfully. "So maybe things aren't too bad after all. OK, let's go home."

They went back to the second floor. The Mute stayed in his corner, and Andrei went through into his room. Pak the Korean was already waiting for him, talking to Izya about something. When he saw Andrei, he stopped speaking and got up to greet him.

"Sit down, Mr. Pak," Andrei said, and sat down himself.

After a very slight pause, Pak cautiously sank down onto the seat of his chair and put his hands on his knees. His yellowish face was calm, and his sleepy eyes glinted through the cracks between his puffy eyelids. Andrei had always liked him—in some subtle way Pak reminded him of Kensi, or maybe it was simply that he was always neat and clean, always good-natured and amiable with everyone, but without any familiarity; he was laconic, but polite and respectful—always a little apart, always keeping a subtle distance . . . Or maybe because it was Pak who put a stop to that absurd skirmish at 340 kilometers: when the shooting was at its height, he walked out of the ruins, holding up his open hand and slowly advancing toward the shots . . .

"Did they wake you up, Mr. Pak?" Andrei asked.

"No, Mr. Counselor. I hadn't gone to bed yet."

"Is your stomach bothering you a lot?"

"No more than everyone else's."

"But probably no less," Andrei remarked. "And how are your feet?"

"Better than everyone else's."

"That's good," said Andrei. "And how are you feeling in general? Are you completely worn out?"

"I'm fine, thank you, Mr. Counselor."

"That's good," Andrei repeated. "The reason why I bothered you, Mr. Pak, is that I've declared a long halt tomorrow. But the day after tomorrow I intend to make a short reconnaissance sortie with a special group. Fifty to seventy kilometers ahead. We have to find water, Mr. Pak. We'll probably travel light but move fast."

"I understand you, Mr. Counselor," said Pak. "I request permission to join you."

"Thank you. I was going to ask you to do that. So we leave the day after tomorrow, promptly at six in the morning. You'll be issued field rations by the sergeant. Agreed? Now let me ask you this: What do you think, will we succeed in finding water here?"

"I think so," said Pak. "I've heard a thing or two about these parts. There ought to be a spring here somewhere. According to the rumors, there was a very abundant spring here. It has probably been depleted now. But it might possibly be enough for our team. We need to check it out."

"But maybe it has completely dried up?"

Pak shook his head. "It's possible, but highly unlikely. I've never heard of springs completely drying up. The flow of water can be reduced, even greatly reduced, but apparently springs don't dry up completely."

"I haven't found anything helpful in the documents yet," said Izya. "Water was supplied to the town via an aqueduct, and now that aqueduct is as dry as . . . as I don't know what."

Pak said nothing to that.

"And what else have you heard about these city blocks?" Andrei asked him.

"Various more or less terrible things," said Pak. "Some are clearly tall tales. And as for the rest . . ." He shrugged.

"Well, for instance?" Andrei asked amiably.

"Well, basically I've already told you all this before, Mr. Counselor. For instance, according to the rumors, the so-called City of the Ironheads is somewhere not far from here. But I haven't been able to understand just who these Ironheads are . . . The Bloody Waterfall—but it seems that is still a long way off. Probably what we're talking about is a stream of water that erodes some red-colored kind of rock. At least there'll be plenty of water there. There are legends about talking animals—that's already pushing the bounds of probability. And it clearly makes no sense to talk about what lies beyond those bounds . . . But then, the Experiment is the Experiment."

"You're probably sick and tired of all these questions," Andrei said with a smile. "I can imagine how weary you are of repeating the same thing to everyone for the twentieth time. But please excuse us, Mr. Pak. After all, you are better informed than any of us."

Pak shrugged again. "Unfortunately, the value of my knowledge is not very high," he said drily. "Most of the rumors are not borne out. And vice versa—we come across many things that I have never heard anything about . . . And as far as the questions are concerned, does it not seem to you, Mr. Counselor, that the common soldiers in the team are too well informed when it comes to rumors? I personally only answer questions when I'm talking with someone from the command staff. I don't consider it right, Mr. Counselor, for the privates and other rank-and-file members of the expedition to be aware of all these rumors. It's bad for morale."

"I entirely agree with you," said Andrei, trying not to look away. "And in any case, I would prefer a few more rumors about a land flowing with milk and honey."

"Yes," said Pak. "And that's why, when the soldiers ask me questions, I try to avoid unpleasant subjects and mostly dwell on the legend of the Crystal Palace . . . Although just recently they don't want to hear about that anymore. They're all seriously afraid and want to go home."

"And you too?" Andrei asked sympathetically.

"I don't have a home," Pak said calmly. His face was inscrutable; his eyes turned absolutely somnolent.

"*Mmm*, yes," Andrei said, and drummed his fingers on the table. "Well then, Mr. Pak. Thank you once again. Do please get some rest. Good night."

He watched as Pak's blue-twill-clad back receded, waited until the door closed, and said, "I'd really like to know why he tagged along with us."

"What do you mean, why?" Izya asked with a start. "They couldn't organize their own reconnaissance, so they asked to join up with you."

"And what exactly do they need reconnaissance for?"

"Well, my dear friend, not everyone finds Heiger's kingdom as congenial as you do! They didn't want to live under Mr. Mayor before—that doesn't surprise you, now does it? And now they don't want to live under Mr. President. They want to live by themselves, you understand?"

"I understand," said Andrei. "Only, in my opinion, no one intends to prevent them living by themselves."

"That's your opinion," said Izya. "You're not the president, are you?"

Andrei reached into a metal box, took out a flat flask of neat alcohol, and started unscrewing the cap.

"Surely you don't imagine," said Izya, "that Heiger will tolerate a strong, well-armed colony right there beside him? Two hundred men, seasoned in battle after battle, just three hundred kilometers from the Glass House! Of course he won't leave them in peace. So they have to move farther north. But where to?"

Andrei splashed alcohol on his hands and rubbed his palms together as vigorously as he could. "I'm so damned sick of all this filth," he muttered with revulsion. "You have absolutely no idea . . ."

"Yessiree, filth . . ." Izya said absentmindedly. "Filth sure ain't sugar . . . Tell me, why are you always hassling Pak? What has he done to annoy you? I've known him for a long time, almost from the very first day. He's an absolutely honest, highly cultured individual. So why do you hassle him? Only your feral hatred of the intelligentsia can explain these interminable, jesuitical interrogations. If you're really that desperate to find out who's spreading the rumors, interrogate your own informers, but Pak's got nothing to do with it."

"I don't have any informers," Andrei said icily.

Neither of them spoke for a few moments.

Then on a sudden impulse, Andrei asked, "Do you want an honest answer?"

"Well?" Izya said avidly.

"Well then, my friend, recently I've started getting the feeling that someone very much wants to call a halt to our expedition. A complete halt, do you understand? Not just get us to turn tail and go home, but finish us off. Wipe us out. So we disappear without a trace, do you understand?"

"Oh brother, come on!" said Izya. His fingers rummaged in his beard with a squeaky sound, searching for the wart.

"Yes, yes! And I keep trying to figure out who stands to gain from that. And it turns out that your Pak stands to gain. Quiet! Let me finish! If we disappear without a trace, Heiger won't find out anything—not about the colony or anything else . . . And it will be a long time before he decides to organize another expedition like this one. Then they won't have to move farther north and pull up their roots. That's the conclusion I come to, do you understand?"

"I think you're out of your mind," said Izya. "Where do these feelings of yours come from? If they're about turning tail and going home, you don't need any feelings. Everyone wants to turn back . . . But where do you get the idea that someone wants to wipe us out?"

"I don't know!" said Andrei. "I told you, it's a feeling . . ." He paused for a moment. "In any case, it was the right decision to take Pak with me the day after tomorrow. I'm not leaving him hanging around in this camp when I'm not here."

"But what has he got to do with all this?" Izya snapped. "Just take that addled brain of yours and think about it! So he wipes us out, and then what? Eight hundred kilometers on foot? Across arid desert?"

"How should I know?" Andrei snapped back. "Maybe he can drive a tractor."

"Why not suspect Skank while you're at it?" said Izya. "Like that . . . like in the fairy tale about Tsar Dadon. The Queen of Shamakha."

"*Mmm*, yes . . . Skank," Andrei said pensively. "Another blasted dark horse . . . And that Mute . . . Who is he? Where's he from? Why does he follow me everywhere, like a dog? Even to the john . . . And by the way, it turns out that he's been in these parts before."

"What a discovery!" Izya said scornfully. "I realized that ages and ages ago. Those tongueless people arrived here from the north . . ."

"Maybe someone cut their tongues out here?" Andrei said in a low voice.

Izya looked at him. "Listen, let's have a drink," he said.

"There's nothing to dilute it with."

"Then would you like me to bring Skank to you?"

"You go to hell . . ." Andrei got up, wincing as he moved his sore foot about in his shoe. "OK, I'll go check out what's going on." He slapped his empty holster. "Have you got a pistol?"

"I've got one somewhere. Why?"

"Never mind, I'll go as I am," said Andrei.

He walked into the corridor, taking out his flashlight on the way. The Mute got up to meet him. On the right, from inside the apartment behind a half-open door, Andrei heard low voices. He stopped.

"In Cairo, Duggan, in Cairo!" the colonel insisted grandly. "I see now that you've forgotten everything, Duggan. The Twenty-First Yorkshire Fusiliers, and their commander at the time was old Bill, the fifth Baronet Stratford."

"I beg your pardon, Colonel," Duggan protested respectfully. "We could consult the colonel's diaries . . ."

"Don't bother, no diaries needed, Duggan! Attend to your pistol. You promised to read to me tonight as well."

Andrei walked out onto the landing and ran into Ellisauer, standing there like a telegraph pole. Ellisauer was smoking, hunched over with his backside propped against the iron banister.

"Last one before bed?" Andrei asked.

"Precisely, Mr. Counselor. I'm just on my way."

"Off to bed, off to bed," Andrei said he walked on past. "You know the saying: the more you sleep, the less you sin."

Ellisauer giggled respectfully as Andrei walked away. You half-witted beanpole, Andrei thought. You just try not getting that done in three days—I'll harness *you* to the sled . . .

The lower ranks had installed themselves on the ground-floor level (although they'd gotten into the habit of crapping on the upper floors). He couldn't hear any conversations here—apparently all of them, or almost all, were already sleeping. The apartment doors leading into the lobby were wide open—left that way to create a draft—and through them emerged a discordant medley of snoring, sleepy smacking of lips, muttering, and hoarse heavy-smoker coughing.

Andrei first of all glanced into the apartment on his left. The soldiers had occupied this one. He saw light coming from a little room with no windows. Sergeant Vogel was sitting at a small table in just his shorts, with his peaked cap tilted to the back of his head, diligently filling out some kind of record sheet. There was good order in the army; the door of the little room was standing wide open so that no one could come in or go out unnoticed. At the sound of steps, the sergeant quickly raised his head and peered, shielding his face from the light of the lamp.

"It's me, Vogel," Andrei said in a quiet voice, and walked in.

In a flash the sergeant had moved up a chair for him. Andrei sat down and looked around. So there was good order in the army. All three cans of disbursable water were here. The boxes of canned goods and hardtack for tomorrow's breakfast were here too. And a box of cigarettes. The sergeant's superbly cleaned pistol was lying on the table. The room had an oppressive, male, field-campaign odor. Andrei set one hand on the back of the chair.

"What's for breakfast, Sergeant?" he asked.

"The usual, Mr. Counselor," Vogel replied in surprise.

"See if you can think up something different from the usual," said Andrei. "Rice porridge with sugar, maybe . . . Is there any canned fruit left?"

"It could be rice porridge with prunes," the sergeant suggested.

"Make it with prunes, then. Issue a double ration of water in the morning. And a half bar of chocolate for every man . . . We do still have chocolate?"

"We have a little bit," the sergeant said reluctantly.

"Then issue it . . . What about cigarettes—the last box?"

"Yes, sir!"

"Well, nothing can be done there. Tomorrow as usual, and starting the next day reduce the ration . . . Ah yes, and another thing. From now on, starting today, a double water ration for the colonel."

"I beg to report, sir—" the sergeant began.

"I know," Andrei interrupted. "Tell him it's an order from me."

"Yes, sir . . . Would the counselor care to . . . Anastasis? Where are you going?"

Andrei looked around. A soldier, also wearing only his shorts and boots, was standing, swaying unsteadily, in the passage, totally addled with sleep.

"Sorry, Sergeant . . ." he muttered. He was obviously completely out of it. Then his arms straightened out against his sides. "Permission to absent myself to visit the latrine, Sergeant?"

"Do you need paper?"

The soldier smacked his lips and wiggled his face.

"Negative. I have some." He held out a scrap of paper clutched in his fist, obviously from Izya's archives. "Permission to go?"

"Granted . . . I beg your pardon, Mr. Counselor. They've been running all night. And sometimes they just go right where they are. The manganese crystals used to help, but now nothing does any good . . . Would you care to check the sentries, Mr. Counselor?"

"No," Andrei said, getting up.

"Will you order me to accompany you?"

"No. Stay here."

Andrei went back out into the lobby. It was just as hot here, but at least the stink wasn't quite so bad. The Mute soundlessly appeared beside him. He heard Private Anastasis stumble and hiss through his teeth on the steps one floor higher. He'll never get to the john; he'll dump it on the floor, Andrei thought with queasy sympathy.

"Right, then," he said to the Mute in an undertone. "Shall we check out how the civilians have settled in?"

He walked across the lobby and in through the door of the apartment opposite. The field-campaign odor hung in the air here too, but the good order of the army was lacking. A dimmed lamp in the passage faintly illuminated an untidy, jumbled heap of instruments in tarpaulin covers and guns, a dirty rucksack with its contents chaotically dragged out, and canteens and mess tins dumped by the wall. Andrei took the lamp and stepped into the nearest room, and immediately stumbled over someone's shoe.

The drivers were sleeping here, naked and sweaty, stretched out on crumpled sheets of tarpaulin. They hadn't even laid out any bedsheets . . . But then, he supposed, the bedsheets were probably dirtier than the tarpaulin. One of the drivers suddenly raised himself and sat upright, without opening his eyes, fiercely scratched at his shoulders, and mumbled indistinctly, "We're going hunting, not to the bathhouse. Hunting, got that? The water's yellow . . . under the snow it's yellow, got that?" Without finishing what he was saying, he went limp again and slumped over onto his side.

After checking that all four drivers were there, Andrei moved on to the next apartment. This was the residence of the intelligentsia. They were sleeping on folding camp beds, covered with gray sheets, and they, too, were sleeping restlessly, snoring unhealthily, groaning, and gritting their teeth. Two cartographers in one room and two geologists in the next one. In the geologists' room Andrei caught an unfamiliar, sweetish smell, and immediately remembered the rumors going around that the geologists smoked hash. The day before yesterday Sergeant Vogel had confiscated a reefer from Private Tevosyan, thumped him in the face, and threatened to put him in the advance guard and leave him there to rot. And although the colonel had taken a rather humorous view of the incident, Andrei had found it all very disturbing.

The other rooms in the huge apartment were empty, except for the kitchen, where Skank was sleeping, completely swaddled in rags—they had obviously worn her out this evening. Her skinny, naked legs, sticking out from under the rags, were covered in raw grazes and some kind of blotches. Yet another disaster visited on us, Andrei thought. The Queen of Shamakha. Damn the rotten bitch to hell. The filthy whore . . . Where is she from? Who is she? Babbling her gibberish in an incomprehensible language . . . Why is there an incomprehensible language in the City? How is that possible? Izya was totally floored when he heard it . . . Skank. That's the name Izya gave her. A good name. It really suits her. Skank.

Andrei went back to the drivers' room, lifted the lamp up over his head, and pointed out Permyak to the Mute. Silently slipping through between the sleeping men, the Mute leaned down over Permyak and took hold of the man's ears in his hands. Then he straightened up. Permyak sat there, propping himself up with one hand and using the other to wipe away the spittle that had overflowed onto his lips in his sleep.

Catching his eye, Andrei nodded in the direction of the corridor, and Permyak immediately got to his feet, lightly and soundlessly. They went through into an empty room deeper inside the apartment, and the Mute closed the door firmly and leaned back against it. Andrei looked for a place to sit. The room was empty, and he sat down on the floor. Permyak squatted down in front of him. His pockmarked face had a dirty look in the lamplight, and his tangled hair tumbled down over his forehead, with a crooked tattoo—KHRUSHCHEV's SLAVE—showing through it.

"Thirsty?" Andrei asked in a low voice.

Permyak nodded. The familiar roguish smile appeared on his face. Andrei took a hip flask out of his back pocket and held it out to him—there was water splashing about in the bottom of it. He watched as Permyak drank in miserly little sips, with his bristly Adam's apple moving up and down. The water immediately sprang out on his body as sweat.

"Warm . . ." Permyak said hoarsely, handing back the empty flask. "Cold would be good . . . straight out of the faucet . . . *Agh!*"

"What's wrong with that motor of yours?" Andrei asked, stuffing the flask back in his pocket.

Permyak gathered the sweat off his face with his splayed fingers. "The motor's shit," he said. "We built it after the first one, racing against the deadline . . . It's a miracle it held out for this long."

"Can it be fixed?"

"Yes, it can be fixed. We'll fiddle with it for a day or two and get it fixed. Only it won't last long. We'll slog on for maybe another two hundred kilometers, and then we'll be back sunbathing. The motor's shit."

"I see," said Andrei. "Did you happen to notice the Korean Pak hanging around the soldiers?"

Permyak peevishly disregarded that question. "At today's lunch break the soldiers got together and agreed not to go any farther."

"I already know that," Andrei said, clenching his teeth. "You just tell me who's running things on their side, will you?"

"I can't make that out, boss," Permyak wheezed in a whisper. "Tevosyan shoots his mouth off more than anyone else, but he's always full of crap, and every morning lately he's been wigged out."

"What?"

"Wigged out . . . You know, stoned, tripping . . . No one listens to him. But who the real ringleader is, I can't tell."

"Hnoipek?"

"Damned if I know. Maybe it's him. He's a big man, all right . . . Seems like the drivers are for it—I mean, not going any farther. Nothing Mr. Ellisauer says makes any sense; he just giggles like a creep and tries to please everyone . . . which means he's afraid. But what can I do? I just keep laying it on the line that the soldiers can't be trusted, they hate us drivers. We ride and they walk, that's what they say. They get private's rations, and we get the same as the gentlemen scientists . . . Why should they like us, they say. It used to work all right, but not any longer. But you know the most important thing? The day after tomorrow is the thirteenth day—"

"And what about the science team?" Andrei interrupted.

"Damned if I know. They cuss a blue streak, but I can't make out who they're for. They brawl with the soldiers every damned day over that Skank . . . And you know what Mr. Quejada said? He said the colonel won't hold out much longer."

"Who did he say it to?"

"Well, what I think is, he says it to everyone. I heard him myself, telling his geologists never to part with their weapons. In case they're needed. Got a cigarette about you, Andrei Mikhailovich?"

"No," said Andrei. "And what about the sergeant?"

"There's no getting close to the sergeant. With him you get off at the same stop you got on at. Hard as flint. They'll kill him first. They really hate him."

"All right," said Andrei. "But what about the Korean, after all? Is he working on the soldiers or not?"

"I haven't seen him doing that. He always keeps himself to himself. If you like, I can keep a special eye on him, but I reckon it's a waste of time . . ."

"Right, here's the story," said Andrei. "Starting tomorrow there's a long halt. Basically, there's no work to be done. Except on the tractor. And the soldiers will just be loitering about and shooting the bull. So what you have to do, Permyak, is figure out for me who's running this show. That's your top priority. Think of some way; you know better than I do how it can be done . . ." He got up, and Permyak jumped to his feet too. "Did you really vomit today?"

"Yeah, I got it real bad . . . Seems like it's eased off a bit now."

"Do you need anything?"

"Nah, it's not worth the bother. But I could use some smokes."

"OK. You get the tractor fixed and I'll give you a bonus. Off you go."

Permyak slipped out through the door past the Mute, who moved aside for him. Andrei walked across to the window and leaned on the windowsill, waiting the regulation five minutes. The beam of the swiveling headlamp picked out the black, bulky forms of the cargo sleds and the second tractor and set the remaining shards of glass glittering in the windows of the house opposite. To the right the metal heel plates on the boots of an invisible sentry clinked as he wandered back and forth across the street, quietly whistling some mournful tune or other.

Never mind, Andrei thought. We'll survive. If I could just find the ringleader . . . He pictured it to himself again—the sergeant lines up the unarmed men in a single rank on Andrei's order and he, the leader of the expedition, slowly walks along the rank, holding a pistol in his lowered hand and glancing into the stony faces overgrown with stubble, and he stops at Hnoipek, right in front of that red-haired scumbag's face, and shoots him in the stomach—first one shot, and then another . . . without charge or trial. "And that's what will happen to every cowardly rat who dares to . . ."

And it seems that Mr. Pak really doesn't have anything to do with this business, he thought. That's something, at least. Nothing will happen tomorrow. Nothing will happen for another three days, and three days is long enough to come up with all sorts of things . . . For instance, we could find a good spring a hundred kilometers farther on. No doubt they'll gallop on like horses to get to water. This sweltering heat is unbearable . . . We've only been here one night and the whole place already stinks of shit . . . And anyway, time is always on the side of the bosses against the troublemakers. It's always been that way, everywhere . . . Where did I get that from? Izya. No, I probably made it up myself. It's a good thought, a correct thought. Attaboy . . . So today they conspired and decided they won't move on tomorrow. They'll get up sizzling in the morning and we'll hand them a long halt. No need to go anywhere after all, guys, it was a waste of time showing your teeth . . . And here's some rice porridge with prunes for you, a second mug of tea, and chocolate . . . So take that, Mr. Hnoipek! But I'll get around to you, just give me time . . . *Dammit*, I'm so sleepy . . . You just forget about drinking anything, Mr. Counselor, you need to sleep. Tomorrow at first light . . . Damn you to hell, Fritz, you and your expansion plans. The emperor of all shit, that's you . . .

"Let's go," he said to the Mute.

Izya was still thumbing through his papers. He'd developed a new bad habit now—biting his beard. He collected a handful of the matted hair, stuck it in between his teeth, and gnawed on it. What a booby, honestly . . . Andrei walked over to his camp bed and started spreading out the sheet. It stuck to his hands like oilcloth.

Izya suddenly turned right around toward him and said, "So, the story is that they lived here under the rule of the Kindest and Simplest. Both words with capital letters, note. They had a good life, plenty of everything. Then the climate started changing and temperatures fell sharply. And then something else happened and they all died. I found a diary here. The man who wrote it barricaded himself in his apartment and starved to death. Or rather, he hanged himself—after he went insane . . . It all started when this sort of shimmering appeared outside . . ."

"When what appeared?" Andrei asked, and stopped tugging off his shoe.

"Some kind of shimmering appeared. Shimmering! And if anyone got caught in that shimmering, they disappeared. Sometimes they managed to shout out, but sometimes they didn't even have time for that; they simply dissolved into thin air—and that was it."

"Crazy bullshit . . ." Andrei growled. "Well?"

"Anyone who went out of the house died in that shimmering. But at first the ones who got frightened and realized they were in really deep shit stayed alive. At first they talked to each other on the phone, and then they gradually started dying off. After all, they had nothing to eat, it was freezing outside, and they hadn't laid in any firewood, the heating wasn't working . . ."

"And where did the shimmering go to?"

"He doesn't write anything about that. I told you, he lost his mind at the end. The last entry he made is this . . ." Izya rustled the papers. "Here, listen: 'I can't go on. There's no point anyway. It's time. This morning the Kindest and Simplest walked along the street and glanced in at my window. It's the smile. It's time.' That's all. And note that his apartment is on the fifth floor. The poor wretch hung a noose from the ceiling lamp . . . It's still hanging there, by the way."

"Yes, sounds like he really did go insane," said Andrei, getting into bed. "That's the starvation, for sure. Listen, what about water, is there anything?"

"Nothing so far. Tomorrow, I think, we ought to walk to the end of the aqueduct . . . What's this, going to bed already?"

"Yes, and I recommend you do the same," said Andrei. "Turn down the lamp and clear out."

"Ah, listen," Izya said plaintively. "I wanted to read for a bit longer. You've got a good lamp here."

"And where's yours? You've got one just like it."

"You know, it got broken. In the sled . . . I stood a crate on it. By accident . . ."

"You cretin," said Andrei. "All right, take the lamp and leave."

Izya hastily rustled his papers and moved out his chair, then he said, "Ah yes! Duggan brought your pistol back. And he passed on a message from the colonel for you, but I've forgotten . . ."

"OK, let me have the pistol," Andrei said. He stuck the pistol under his pillow and turned over onto his side, with his back toward Izya.

"How about I read you a letter?" Izya asked in a cajoling voice.

"Get out," Andrei said calmly.

Izya giggled. Lying with his eyes closed, Andrei heard the rustling as he bustled about, gathering up his papers, and the creaking of the dried-out parquet. Then the door squeaked, and when Andrei opened his eyes, it was already dark.

Some kind of shimmering . . . *Mmm*, yes. Well, we'll have to see how it goes. There's nothing we can do about that. We have to think about the things we can control . . . There wasn't any shimmering in Leningrad, there was bitter, atrocious, hideous, freezing cold, and people who were freezing to death cried out in the icy entranceways—hour after hour, getting weaker all the time . . . He used to fall asleep listening to someone calling out, and wake up to the same hopeless call, and he couldn't have said it was frightening; it was more sickening, and in the morning, when he walked down the stairs that were flooded with frozen shit, muffled right up to his eyes, to get water, holding his mother's hand, the one that was pulling the little sled with a bucket lashed to it, that person who had been calling out was lying down at the bottom, beside the elevator shaft, probably still where he fell the day before, it had to be the same spot—he couldn't get up or even crawl, and absolutely no one had come out to him . . . And no shimmering was needed. We only survived because my mother was in the habit of ordering firewood in the early spring instead of in summer. The firewood saved us. Twelve adult cats and a little kitten that was so hungry, when I tried to stroke it, it pounced on my hand and started greedily chewing and biting my fingers. I'd like to send you there, you bastards, Andrei thought about the soldiers with sudden malice. That was no Experiment . . . And that city was more terrible than this one. I would definitely have gone insane. What saved me was being so young. The little children simply died . . .

And they didn't surrender the city after all, he thought. Those who stayed gradually died off. They stacked them in the wood-sheds and tried to get the living out—the authorities were still in control and life carried on—a strange, delirious life. Some people just died quietly, some committed acts of heroism, and then they died too . . . Some slaved in a factory to the bitter end, and when the time came, they died too . . . Some grew fat on all this, buy-ing valuables, gold, pearls, and earrings for scraps of bread, and then they died too—they took them down to the Neva and shot them, then walked back up, not looking at anyone, slinging their rifles on their flat backs . . . Some hunted with axes in the side streets and ate human flesh and even tried to trade in it, but they died too anyway . . . In that city nothing was more ordinary than death. But the authorities still functioned, and while the authori-ties functioned, the city stood.

I wonder, did they feel sorry for us at all? Or did they simply not think about us? Did they just carry out orders, and the orders were about the city, with nothing about us? That is, there was something about us, of course, but only under point "P for Popu-lation" . . . At the Finland Station, trains of suburban-line railroad cars stood under a clear sky that was white from the cold. In our car there were lots of kids just like me, about twelve years old—some sort of orphanage. I remember almost nothing. I remember the sun in the windows, and the steam of people's breath, and a child's voice that kept repeating the same phrase over and over, with the same helpless, squealing intonation: "You fuck off out of here!" And then again: "You fuck off out of here!" And again . . .

Wait, that's not what I was thinking about. Orders and com-passion—that was it. Take me, for instance: I feel sorry for the soldiers. I understand them very well and even sympathize with them. We selected volunteers, and above all else, of course, the volunteers were adventurers, hotheads itching for action, who were bored to tears in our well-run City and fancied the idea of seeing somewhere completely new, getting to play with an automatic rifle when they got the chance, looting ruins, and then when they came home, stuffing their pockets with bonus money, tacking new stripes on their uniforms, and strutting their stuff with the girls . . . And instead of that . . . they get diarrhea, bloody blisters, and spooky crap . . . Anyone would mutiny!

But what about me? Is it any easier for me? Did I come here for the diarrhea? I don't want to go on either, I don't see anything good up ahead either, and I had hopes of my own, too, dammit! My very own Crystal Palace just over the horizon! Maybe I'd only be too glad right now to give the order: *That's it, guys, pack up and turn back!* I'm sick and tired of all this filth too, aren't I? I'm afraid too, dammit—of that shimmering, or those people with iron heads. Maybe the sight of those people with no tongues froze my insides solid: there it is, a warning—don't go that way, you fool, go back . . . And the wolves? When I was alone in the rear guard—because you were all so afraid you crapped your pants— do you think I enjoyed walking back there? They can just come darting out of the dust, rip off half your ass, and disappear . . . So there you have it, my dear friends, my dear bastards: you're not the only ones having it tough; I'm all dried out and cracked inside from thirst too.

So OK, he told himself. Then what the hell are you going on for? Just give the order tomorrow, we'll flap our wings and fly, and in a month we'll be home, and we'll dump the high authority delegated to us at Heiger's feet: right, fuck you, brother, go and do it yourself, if you're so eager to press on with this expansion, if you've got an itch up the you-know-where . . . Ah, no, why necessarily make a big scandal out of it? After all, we've covered nine hundred kilometers, made a map, collected ten crates of archives—isn't that enough? There isn't anything up ahead! How much longer can we go on grinding down our feet? This isn't

Earth, it's not a sphere . . . There isn't any oil here, there isn't any water, there aren't any large settlements . . . And there isn't any Anticity—of course not, that's absolutely clear now; no one here has ever even heard of it . . . Anyway, the excuses can be found. Excuses . . . That's just it. They're excuses!

Exactly how do things stand here? The agreement was to go all the way, and you were ordered to go all the way. Right? Right. And now: Can you go on? I can. We have chow. We have fuel, the guns are in good order . . . Of course, the men are bushed, but they're all unscathed, none of them are hurt . . . And when all's said and done, they're not so badly exhausted, if they can monkey around with Skank all evening. No, brother, your argument doesn't hold water. *You're a crappy boss*, that's what Heiger will tell you. *I was mistaken about you*, he'll say. And he's got Quejada whispering in one ear and Permyak in the other, and Ellisauer standing by in reserve . . .

Andrei tried to drive this last thought out of his head as quickly as possible, but it was already too late. He realized with a shudder that his status as "Mr. Counselor" was in fact very important to him, and he found it very painful to think that this status might suddenly change.

Well, let it change, he thought defensively. Am I going to starve to death without that position? By all means, let Mr. Quejada take my place, and I'll take his. What harm will that do to the cause? My God, he suddenly thought. What cause is that, anyway? What are you driveling about, friend? You're not a little kid any longer, taking responsibility for the fate of the world. You know, the fate of the world will get by without you, and without Heiger . . . Everyone must do his own duty at his own post? By all means, I don't object to that. I'm willing to do my own duty at my own post. At my own. At this one. Wielding power. And there you have it, Mr. Counselor! What the hell! What gives a former noncommissioned office of a defeated army the right to rule a city of a million people, and here I am, within spitting distance of a doctorate, a man with a university education, a Komsomol member, and I don't have the right to run a science department? What's wrong here? Do I get worse results than he does? What's the problem?

This is all garbage—*I have the right*; *I don't have the right* . . . The right to power belongs to whoever holds the power. Or more precisely, if you like, the right to power is held by whoever exercises power. If you know how to bend people to your will, you have the right to power. And if you don't—sorry!

And you will go on when I tell you to, you motherfuckers! he thought, addressing the sleeping expedition. And you'll go on when I tell you to not because I'm desperate to push on into uncharted territory like that bearded baboon; you'll go on when I tell you to because I order you to go on. And I'll order you to go on, you sons of bitches, you slobs, you shit-assed soldiers of fortune, not out of any sense of duty to Heiger—perish the thought—but because I have power, and I have to constantly affirm that power—affirm it to you, you dumb assholes, and affirm it to myself. And to Heiger . . . To you—because otherwise you'll devour me. To Heiger—because otherwise he'll sack me, and he'll be right. And to myself . . . You know, the kings and all the monarch types used to have this hocus-pocus formula: their power was given to them by God in person; they couldn't even imagine themselves without power, and neither could their subjects. And even so, they still had to keep their wits about them. But we little people don't believe in God. No one has anointed us to the throne. We have to take care of ourselves. Fortune favors the brave—that's the way it is with us. We don't need any imposters; I'm the one who's going to command. Not you, not him, not those guys, and not those dames. Me. The army will support me . . .

What a heap of baloney, he thought, even feeling a bit embarrassed. He turned over onto his other side, pushing his hand in under the pillow, where it was a bit cooler, to make himself more comfortable. His fingers ran into the pistol . . .

So how do you intend to implement your program of action, Mr. Counselor? You'll have to shoot! Not just imagine yourself shooting ("Private Hnoipek, step out of the ranks!"), not just engage in mental masturbation, but do it—go ahead and shoot a live human being, a man who might be unarmed, not even suspecting anything, maybe not even guilty when all's said and done . . . but to hell with all that! A *live* human being—shoot him in the stomach, the soft belly, the guts . . . No, I don't know how do that, I've never done that, and God help me, I can't even imagine it . . . Of course, in the skirmish at 340 kilometers, I fired like everyone else, simply out of fright, I didn't understand anything . . . But I couldn't see anyone there, and they were firing at me too, dammit!

OK, he thought. All right, then—so I'm some kind of humanist, and then again, I'm not accustomed to it . . . But then, what if they won't go on? I order them to and they answer, you can fuck off, brother, go yourself, if you've got an itch up the you-know-where . . .

Now there's an idea! he thought. Issue the slobs a small amount of water, allocate them some of the food for the journey back, and let them fix the broken tractor . . . Off you go, we'll get by without you. Now, wouldn't that be great, to just dump all that shit in a single stroke! But then he immediately imagined the colonel's face if he heard a proposal like that. *Mmm*, yes, the colonel won't understand. He's the wrong breed. He's precisely one of those . . . those monarchs. The idea of possible insubordination doesn't even enter his head. And in any case, he won't agonize over all these problems . . . Aristocratic, military blood. It's fine for him—his father was a colonel, and his grandfather was a colonel, and his great-grandfather was a colonel; just look what an empire they built up, and no doubt they killed plenty of people in the process . . . So let him shoot them, if need be. After all, they're his men, and I've got no intention of interfering in his business . . . *Dammit*, I'm sick of all this. Gutless intelligentsia whining, it's turned my brains to mush! They must go—and that's the end of it! I'm carrying out my orders, so you carry out yours, all right? I won't get any thanks for disobeying, and it won't be good for your health either, damn and blast you! That's all. To hell with it. I'd be better off thinking about women than this hogwash. Some philosophy of power this is . . .

He turned over again, twisting up the sheet under him, and strained to picture Selma in that lilac negligee of hers, bending over in front of the bed and putting down the tray of coffee on the little table . . . He imagined all the details of how it would be with Selma, then suddenly—without any strain this time—he was in his office, where he found Amalia in the big armchair, with her little skirt rolled right up to her armpits . . . Then he realized things had gone too far.

He flung off the sheet and deliberately sat in an uncomfortable position, with the edge of the camp bed cutting into his backside, staring at the rectangle of the window, filled with a diffuse light. Then he looked at his watch. It was already after midnight. If I get up now, he thought, and I go down to the ground-floor level . . . Where is she sacked out down there—in the kitchen? This idea always used to provoke a response of healthy disgust, but this time that didn't happen. He imagined Skank's naked, dirty legs, but he didn't dwell on them, he moved higher . . . He suddenly felt curious about what she was like naked. After all, a woman's a woman.

"My God!" he said in a loud voice.

The door immediately creaked and the Mute appeared. A black shadow in the darkness, with only the whites of his eyes gleaming.

"Well, what are you doing here?" Andrei asked dejectedly. "Go and sleep."

The Mute disappeared. Andrei yawned uneasily and slumped sideways onto the camp bed.

He woke in horror, soaking wet.

"Halt, who goes there?" the sentry howled again under his window. His voice was high-pitched and desperate, as if he were calling for help.

And immediately Andrei heard heavy, crunching blows, as if someone huge were regularly and repeatedly hammering on crumbling stone with a huge sledgehammer.

"I'll fire!" the sentry squealed in a voice that didn't even sound human, and started shooting.

Andrei couldn't remember how he got to the window. In the darkness to his right he saw the fitful orange flashes of shots. The fiery flickering outlined the form of something black, massive, and unmoving farther up the street, with showers of green sparks flying out of it. Andrei didn't have time to understand anything. The sentry's ammunition clip ran out, and for a brief moment there was silence, then he squealed again out there in the darkness—exactly like a horse—and his boots started thudding, and suddenly he was there, in the circle of light under the window, waving his empty automatic and still squealing. He dashed to a tractor and cowered in the black shadow behind the caterpillar track, repeatedly tugging on his spare ammunition clip, trying to jerk it out from behind his belt, but he couldn't . . . And then those crunching blows of a sledgehammer on stone started up again: *boooom, boooom* . . .

When Andrei darted out into the street without his trousers, with his shoelaces dangling free and his pistol in his hand, a lot of men were already there. Sergeant Vogel was roaring like a bull: "Tevosyan, Hnoipek! To the right! Prepare to fire! Anastasis! Onto the tractor, behind the cabin! Observe, prepare to fire! Move it! You lily-livered pigs . . . Vasilenko! To the left! Lie down, and—To the left, you Slavic bonehead! Get down and observe! Palotti! Where are you going, you greasy wop!"

He grabbed the aimlessly running Italian by the collar, gave him a ferocious kick on the backside, and flung him in the direction of the tractor.

"Behind the cabin, you animal! Anastasis, shine the light along the street!"

Men were jostling Andrei in the back and from the sides. He gritted his teeth and tried to stay on his feet, not understanding anything, fighting an overpowering urge to yell out something nonsensical. He pressed himself up against the wall, holding his pistol out in front of him and looking around like an animal at bay. Why are they all running that way? What if there's an attack from the rear? Or from the roof? Or from the houses across the street?

"Drivers!" Vogel roared. "Drivers, onto the tractors. Who's that firing there, you bastards? Cease fire!"

Gradually Andrei's head cleared. Things turned out not to be so bad after all. The men had taken cover where they were ordered to, the scurrying about was over, and at last someone on the tractor turned the searchlight to light up the street.

"There he is!" a strangled voice shouted.

Automatic rifles barked briefly and then fell silent. Andrei only had time to spot something huge, almost higher than the houses, something ugly, with stumps and spikes jutting out in different directions. It cast an endless shadow along the street and immediately turned the corner two blocks away. It disappeared from sight, and the heavy blows of a sledgehammer on crunching stone became quieter, then even quieter, and soon completely faded away.

"What happened there, Sergeant?" the colonel's calm voice asked above Andrei's head.

The colonel, with all his buttons fastened, was standing at his window, leaning his hands on the windowsill. "The sentry raised the alarm, Colonel," Sergeant Vogel replied. "Private Terman."

"Private Terman, report to me!" said the colonel.

The soldiers started turning their heads, looking around.

"Private Terman!" the sergeant barked. "Report to the colonel!"

In the diffused light of the headlamp, they saw Private Terman frantically scrambling out from behind the caterpillar track. Some piece of the poor devil's gear got snagged again. He yanked on it with all his might, got to his feet, and shouted in a squeaky voice: "Private Terman reporting on the colonel's orders!"

"What a scarecrow!" the colonel said fastidiously. "Fasten yourself up, man."

And at that moment the sun came on. It was so sudden that a chorus of muffled, incoherent exclamations ran through the camp. Many of the men put their hands over their eyes. Andrei squeezed his eyes shut.

"Why did you raise the alarm, Private Terman?"

"An intruder, Colonel," Terman blurted out with a note of despair in his voice. "He failed to respond when challenged. He was coming directly at me. The ground was shaking! In accordance with regulations, I challenged him twice, then opened fire."

"Well now," said the colonel. "I commend you."

In the bright light everything seemed completely different from five minutes ago. The camp looked like a camp now—weary, worn-out sleds, dirty metal barrels of fuel, tractors covered in dust. Against this ordinary, drearily familiar background, the half-dressed armed men, lying and squatting down with their machine guns and automatic rifles, with mussed hair, creased faces, and disheveled beards, looked absurd and ludicrous. Andrei remembered that he wasn't wearing any trousers and his shoelaces were dangling loose, and he suddenly felt embarrassed. He cautiously backed away toward the door, but a crowd of drivers, cartographers, and geologists was standing there.

"I beg to report," Terman was saying in the meantime, having perked up a bit, "that it was not human, Colonel."

"Then what was it?"

Private Terman was lost for words.

"It was more like an elephant, Colonel," Vogel said authoritatively. "Or some kind of antediluvian monster."

"It was like a stegosaurus more than anything," Tevosyan put in.

The colonel immediately turned his gaze on Tevosyan and examined him curiously for a few seconds. "Sergeant," he said at last. "Why do your men open their mouths without permission?"

Someone giggled spitefully.

"Silence in the ranks! Permission to punish him, Colonel?"

"I consider—" the colonel began, and at that point he was interrupted.

"*Aaaaaaaaaaaa . . .*" someone started whimpering quietly at first, then wailing louder and louder, and Andrei started rapidly glancing around the camp, trying to see who was making that noise and why.

Everyone began shifting about in alarm, turning their heads to and fro, and then Andrei saw Anastasis, whiter than a sheet, almost green, jabbing his hand at something up ahead of him, unable to say a single intelligible word. Gathering his nerve, ready for anything at all, Andrei looked where the man was pointing, but couldn't see anything there. The street was empty and the heat haze was already shimmering at the far end of it. Then the sergeant suddenly cleared his throat with a hollow sound and tugged his cap down over his forehead, and someone swore in a quiet, desperate voice, but Andrei still didn't understand, and it was only when an unfamiliar voice wheezed "God save us!" right in his ear that he finally understood. The hairs on the back of his neck started rising and his legs went weak.

The statue on the corner was gone. The huge man of iron with the face like a toad and the theatrically outstretched arms had disappeared. There was nothing left at the intersection but the heaps of dried-out crap that the soldiers had dumped around the statue the day before.

3

"I'll be going, then, Colonel," Andrei said, getting up.

The colonel also got up, and immediately leaned heavily on his cane. Today he was even paler, his face was drawn, and he seemed like a genuinely old man. Nothing left, not even his bearing, you could say . . . "A safe journey to you, Mr. Counselor," said the colonel. His faded eyes had an almost guilty look. "Damn it all, commander's reconnaissance is basically my job . . ."

Andrei picked up his automatic off the table and hooked the strap over his shoulder. "I don't know about that," he said. "For instance, I have the feeling I'm running off and dumping everything on you. And you're not well, Colonel."

"Yes, just imagine, today I . . ." the colonel began and then stopped short. "I suppose you'll be back before dark?"

"I'll be back quite a bit earlier than that," said Andrei. "I don't even regard this sortie as reconnaissance. I simply want to show these cowardly bastards that there's nothing terrible up ahead. Walking statues, my eye!" Then he realized what he'd said. "That wasn't intended as a reproach to your men, Colonel . . ."

"Think nothing of it," said the colonel, gesturing feebly with his gaunt hand. "You're perfectly right. Soldiers are always cowardly. I've never seen any brave soldiers in my life. And why on Earth should they be brave?"

"Well," Andrei said with a smile, "if there were merely enemy tanks waiting for us up ahead . . ."

"Tanks!" said the colonel. "Tanks are a different matter. But I remember very clearly one incident when a squadron of paratroopers refused to advance into a village that was home to a sorcerer famous for miles around."

Andrei laughed and held out his hand to the colonel. "I'll see you later," he said.

"Just a moment," said the colonel, stopping him. "Duggan!"

Duggan was instantly there in the room, holding a flask sheathed in silver grillwork. A little silver tray appeared on the table, with little silver shot glasses on it.

"Be my guest," said the colonel.

They drank and shook hands. "I'll see you later," Andrei repeated.

He walked down the stinking stairway into the lobby, nodded coolly to Quejada, who was fiddling with some theodolite-like instrument right there on the floor, and went out into the red-hot street. When his short shadow fell across the cracked slabs of the sidewalk, a second shadow immediately sprang up beside it, and then Andrei remembered about the Mute. He looked around. The Mute was standing in his usual pose, with his open hands stuck into the belt on which his terrifying machete hung. His thick black hair was standing up on end, his bare feet were planted wide apart, and his brown skin gleamed as if it had been smeared with grease.

"Maybe you'll take an automatic after all?" Andrei asked.

No.

"Well, please yourself."

Andrei looked around. Izya and Pak were sitting in the shade of a trailer with a map spread out in front of them, studying the layout of the City. Two soldiers were craning their necks and glancing over their heads. One of the soldiers caught Andrei's eye, hastily looked away, and nudged the other in the side. They both immediately walked off, disappearing behind the sled.

The drivers were jostling around the second tractor under Ellisauer's supervision. They were dressed in various odds and ends, and Ellisauer was sporting a gigantic, wide-brimmed hat. Two soldiers were hanging about close beside them, giving advice and frequently spitting off to the side.

Andrei looked up along the line of the street. Nothing there. Scorching hot air shimmering above the cobblestones. Heat haze.

A hundred meters away it was impossible to make out anything—like being underwater.

"Izya!" he called.

Izya and Pak looked around and got to their feet. The Korean picked up his small, handmade automatic rifle off the road and tucked it under his arm. "Already time, is it?" Izya asked briskly.

Andrei nodded and walked on.

Everyone looked at him: Permyak, screwing his eyes up against the sun; feeble-minded Ungern, with his permanently slack mouth rounded into a circle of alarm; the morose gorilla Jackson, slowly wiping his hands on a piece of fiber packing . . . Ellisauer, looking just like a ragged, dirty wooden-mushroom shelter from a children's play area in Leningrad, set two fingers to the brim of his hat with a supremely solemn air of commiseration, and the spitting soldiers stopped spitting, exchanged inaudible remarks through their teeth, and drifted off together through the dust. Run scared, you yellow bastards, Andrei thought vindictively. If I called you now, just as a joke, you'd crap in your pants . . .

They walked past the sentry, who performed a hasty "present arms," and then they strode off across the cobblestones—Andrei in front with his automatic over his shoulder, and the Mute hard on his heels with a rucksack containing four cans of food, a pack of hardtack, and two flasks of water, while Izya plodded along about ten steps behind in his battered shoes, carrying an empty rucksack over his shoulder; he was holding the map in one hand and feverishly patting at his pockets with the other, as if checking to see to if he had forgotten anything. At the back, striding along easily with the slightly waddling gait of a man used to long-distance marches, came Pak, his short-barreled automatic under his arm.

The street was scorching hot and the ferocious sun roasted their shoulder blades and the tops of their shoulders. They were deluged by surges of heat from the walls of the houses. There was no wind at all today.

In the camp behind them the wrecked motor was started up—Andrei didn't even look back. He was suddenly engulfed by a sense of liberation. For a few glorious hours the soldiers, with their stink and their inscrutably simplistic minds, were disappearing from his life. And Quejada was disappearing too, that schemer who was so totally transparent, which made Andrei loathe him all the more; all those loathsome problems with other people's sore feet were disappearing too, all the problems with someone else's squabbles and fights, with someone else's puking (could it be poisoning?) and someone else's blood-saturated diarrhea (could it be dysentery?). To hell with all of you, Andrei euphorically repeated over and over. I never want to see you again. It feels so good without you!

Of course, he immediately recalled the dubious Korean Pak, and for a moment it felt as if the bright joy of liberation had been clouded with new anxieties and suspicions, but he instantly dismissed the idea without a second thought. Just a Korean. Calm and impassive, he never complains about anything. A Far East version of Izya Katzman, that's all. He suddenly recalled something his brother once told him—that all the peoples of the Far East, especially the Japanese, felt exactly the same way about the Koreans as all the peoples of Europe, especially the Russians and Germans, felt about the Jews. Just at this moment he found that amusing, and for some reason he suddenly remembered Kensi . . . Yes, if only Kensi were here, and Uncle Yura, and Donald . . . *Agh* . . . If only he had managed to persuade Uncle Yura to join this expedition, everything would be very different now.

He recalled how, a week before he left, he had carved out a few hours, taken Heiger's limousine with the bulletproof windows, and hit the road to Uncle Yura's place. And what a time they had, drinking together in the large village house that was clean and bright, with a delicious scent of mint, smoke from the hearth, and freshly baked bread. They drank moonshine, snacked on piglet in aspic and crunchy home pickles of a kind that Andrei hadn't eaten in God only knew how long, they gnawed on lamb ribs, dipping the pieces in a sauce suffused with the scent of garlic, and then Uncle Yura's wife, Marthe, a buxom Dutch woman, who was pregnant for the third time already, brought in a whistling samovar that Uncle Yura had bought for a cartload of grain and a cartload of potatoes, and they spent a long time staunchly and substantially drinking tea with some amazing kind of jam— they sweated and panted, wiped their wet faces with embroidered towels, and Uncle Yura kept mumbling, "Things are fine, guys, life's pretty tolerable now. Every day they march five parasites from the camp over here to me, I reeducate them with labor, and I don't spare the effort, you know . . . If need be, I just poke them in the teeth, but they stuff their bellies full here, they eat the same as I do, I'm not some kind of blood-sucking exploiter . . ." And when they were saying good-bye, as Andrei was already getting into the car, Uncle Yura squeezed Andrei's hand in his huge paws that seemed to have turned into two great callouses and tried to catch Andrei's eyes as he said, "You'll forgive me, Andrei, I know you will . . . I'd abandon everything, I'd abandon my woman . . . But I can't abandon those guys—that's something I can't allow myself to do," and he pointed over his shoulder with his thumb in the direction of two white-haired little boys with no more than a year between them, who were pummeling away at each other behind the porch—but quietly, so that no one would hear . . .

Andrei looked back. He couldn't see the camp anymore; the heat haze had hidden it. The stuttering of the motor only faintly reached him—as if it were coming through cotton wool. Izya was walking alongside Pak, waving the map under his nose and shouting something about scale. Pak wasn't actually arguing. He just smiled, and when Izya tried to stop, in order to unfold the map and demonstrate what he was thinking, Pak delicately took him by the elbow and led him on. A serious man, no doubt about it. Other things being equal, he could definitely be relied on. I wonder what his beef is with Heiger? They're completely different people, that much at least is clear . . .

Pak had studied at Cambridge and he had a PhD. On returning to South Korea, he took part in some kind of student protests against the regime, and Syngman Rhee clapped him in jail. He was released by the Korean army in 1950, and the newspapers wrote about him as a genuine son of the Korean people, who hated Syngman Rhee's clique and the American imperialists. He became a deputy president of the university, and a month later he was clapped in jail again, where he was held without any charges being brought until the landing at Chemulpo, when the jail came under fire from the First Cavalry Division, which was pushing hard toward the northeast. Seoul was sheer hell on Earth, and Pak didn't expect to survive—and then he was offered the chance to participate in the Experiment.

He had arrived in the City a long time before Andrei, run through twenty different professions, and of course found himself in conflict with the mayor and joined an underground organization of intellectuals that supported Heiger at the time. Something happened between him and Heiger. For some reason or other, the large group of underground oppositionists left the City two years before the Turning Point and moved away to the north. They were lucky: 350 kilometers from the City they discovered a "time capsule" in the ruins—a huge metal tank, packed to overflowing with all sorts of cultural artifacts and examples of technology. It was a good spot, with water and fertile soil, right beside the Wall—so they settled there.

They knew nothing about what had happened in the City, and when the expedition's armor-plated tractors arrived, they thought they had come for them. Fortunately only one man was killed in the furious, brief, and absurd skirmish. Pak recognized Izya, an old friend of his, and realized the fighting was a mistake . . . And afterward he asked to join up with Andrei. He said that his motivation was curiosity, that he had been planning a trek to the north for a long time but the emigrants didn't have the resources for it. Andrei didn't entirely trust him, but he took him along. He thought Pak's knowledge would come in handy, and Pak really had been useful to him. He had assisted the expedition in every way he could and had always been friendly and obliging with Andrei—and even more so with Izya, his old friend—but it was impossible to get him to speak frankly. Not even Izya, let alone Andrei, could discover where Pak had obtained so much mythical and real-world information about the road ahead, why he had tagged along with the expedition, and what he thought in general—about Heiger, about the City, about the Experiment . . . Pak never made conversation on abstract subjects.

Andrei stopped, waited for his rear guard to catch up, and asked, "Well, have you agreed what exactly we're interested in?"

"What exactly?" said Izya, finally unfolding his map. "Look . . ." and he started pointing with his black-edged fingernail. "Right now, we're here. That means . . . one, two . . . in six city blocks there should be a square. There's a big building of some kind there, probably something to do with government. We definitely have to get in there. Well, and if something interesting turns up along the way . . . Ah yes! It would be interesting to get here too. It's quite a long way, but the scale here's not worth a damn, so we can't tell—maybe it's all pretty close . . . See, it says 'Pantheon.' I just love pantheons."

"Well now . . ." said Andrei, adjusting his automatic. "We can do it like that, of course . . . So we're not going to look for water today, then?"

"It's a long way to water," Pak said in a low voice.

"Yes, brother," Izya put in. "The water's a long way off . . . See what they show here—a water tower . . . Is it here?" he asked Pak.

Pak shrugged. "I don't know, but if there is any water left in this neighborhood, it can only be there."

"Uh-huh," Izya drawled. "It's a pretty long way, about thirty kilometers; we can't get there and back in one day . . . Of course, there's the scale . . . Listen, why do you want water right now? We can go for the water tomorrow, the way we agreed . . . we'll drive there, right?"

"All right," said Andrei. "Let's go."

They walked side by side now, and no one said anything for a while. Izya kept twisting his head around and seemed to be sniffing at the air, but nothing of any interest turned up, either on the left or the right. Three- or four-story houses, sometimes rather beautiful. Broken-out window panes. Some windows boarded up with warped sheets of plywood, and half-ruined flower boxes on balconies. Lots of houses entwined in coarse, dusty ivy. A large store, with huge display windows that had somehow survived, too dusty to see through, although the doors had been smashed in . . . Izya darted away at a jog, glanced inside, and came back again.

"Empty," he announced. "All smashed to hell."

Some kind of public building—maybe a playhouse, maybe a concert hall, or maybe a movie theater. Then another store—with the display window cracked right across—and yet another store across the street . . . Izya suddenly stopped, drew his breath in noisily through his nose, and raised a dirty finger.

"Oh!" he said. "Here's something!"

"What?" asked Andrei, looking around.

"Paper," Izya replied tersely.

Without looking at either of them, he made a confident beeline for a building on the right side of the street. It was an ordinary-looking building, not distinguished in any way from the others nearby, except perhaps by a slightly more sumptuous entrance and a certain Gothic accent detectable in its general style. Izya disappeared through the entrance, and before they could even get across the street, he stuck his head back out and called excitedly, "Come in here, Pak! A library!"

Andrei merely shook his head in admiration. Attaboy, Izya.

"A library?" said Pak, lengthening his stride. "Impossible!"

The vestibule was cool and dark after the searing yellow heat of the street. Tall Gothic windows, filled with stained glass, obviously overlooking an internal courtyard. A floor paved with decorative tiles. A double staircase of white stone leading upward to the left and the right . . . Izya was already running up to the left; Pak easily overtook him and they disappeared, striding up three steps at a time

"Why the hell do we want to trudge all the way up there?" Andrei asked the Mute.

The Mute agreed with him. Andrei looked for a place to sit down, and lowered himself onto the cool, white steps. He took off his automatic and put it down beside him. The Mute was already squatting down by the wall with his eyes closed and his long, powerful arms wrapped around his knees. It was quiet, with only an indistinct murmur of voices coming from upstairs.

I'm sick of this, Andrei thought impatiently. I'm sick of the dead city blocks. Of this silence. Of these riddles . . . If only we could find people, stay with them for a while, ask them a few questions . . . and if only they would feed us something . . . Anything at all, just not that gruesome oatmeal . . . and give us cool wine! Lots of it, as much as we want . . . or beer. His stomach started gurgling and he tensed up in fright, listening. No, it's OK. Today I haven't had to run even once—knock on wood, so far, so good! And it seems like my heel's grown new skin . . .

Upstairs something tumbled over with a heavy, rumbling crash, and Izya yelled, articulating in a clear voice, "Hey, what do you think you're doing, God almighty!" There was a laugh and the voices started murmuring again.

Rummage away, rummage away, Andrei thought to himself. You're our only hope. You're the only ones we can expect to come up with anything . . . And all that will come out of this wild goose chase will be my report and Izya's twenty-four crates of documents!

He stretched out his legs and leaned back onto the steps, propping himself on his elbows. The Mute suddenly sneezed, and an echo replied clearly and brightly. Andrei threw back his head and started looking at the distant vaulted ceiling. They built well here, with style, better than us. And they obviously had a pretty good life too. But they still vanished anyway . . . Fritz won't like all this at all—of course, he'd prefer a potential enemy. Or else what do we get? They lived here, they built here, they glorified some Heiger of their own . . . the Kindest and Simplest . . . And what's the result? An empty void. As if no one had ever been here. Nothing but bones, and not very many of those for a population this

large . . . So there you have it, Mr. President! Man proposes, but
God sends down some mysterious shimmering. End of story.

He sneezed too and sniffed. It's kind of cool in here . . . And
it would be a good idea to have Quejada indicted when we get
back . . . Andrei readily slipped into his habitual line of thought:
how to pen Quejada into a corner so that he wouldn't dare to
open his mouth, how to make sure all the documentation was
as clear as day and Heiger would immediately understand everything . . . But he put these thoughts aside—this was the wrong
place and the wrong time. Right now he should only be thinking
about tomorrow. And a bit of thinking about today wouldn't do
any harm. For instance, where did that statue go to, after all?
Someone with horns on his head, some kind of stegosaur, came
along, tucked it under his arm, and carried it away. What for?
And it happens to weigh about fifty tons, by the way. If a beast
like that wanted to, it could carry off a tractor under its arm.
We've got to get away from here, that's the point. If not for the
colonel, we'd have pulled up stakes and moved out today . . . He
started thinking about the colonel, and suddenly realized he was
listening to something.

Some kind of vague, distant sound had appeared—not voices;
the voices upstairs were still droning in the same way. No, out
there in the street, outside the tall entrance doors standing ajar.
The colored glass in the windows started audibly clinking and
the stone steps under his elbows and backside started palpably
vibrating, as if there were a railroad somewhere nearby and a
train were rolling along it right now—a heavy freight train. The
Mute suddenly opened his eyes wide and turned his head, listening warily.

Andrei cautiously pulled in his legs and got up, holding his
automatic by the strap. The Mute immediately got up too, still
listening and squinting sideways at Andrei with one eye.

Holding his weapon at the ready, Andrei silently ran to the
doors and warily glanced out. The hot, dusty air scorched his face.
The street was as yellow, scorching hot, and empty as before.

Only the cotton-wool silence had disappeared. A huge, distant hammer was pounding on the road with dreary regularity, and the blows were clearly moving closer—heavy, crisp blows, crushing the cobblestones of the road into small fragments.

In the building across the street the cracked store window collapsed in a jangling shower of glass. Andrei started back in surprise, but immediately pulled himself together and drew back the bolt of his automatic, biting on his lip. Why the hell did I ever come here? some corner of his mind thought.

The hammer kept moving closer. It was absolutely impossible to tell which direction it was approaching from, but the blows grew heavier and heavier, crisper and crisper, and they had a strange, relentless ring to them, ineluctable and triumphal. The footsteps of fate, Andrei thought fleetingly. He looked around in confusion at the Mute.

He got a shock. The Mute was standing there, leaning his shoulder against the wall, focusing intently on trimming the nail on the little finger of his right hand with his machete. And he looked absolutely indifferent, even bored.

"What?" Andrei asked hoarsely. "What are you doing?"

The Mute looked at him, nodded, and went back to working on his fingernail. *Boooom, boooom, boooom*—the hammer blows were really close now; the ground under their feet was shaking. Then suddenly there was silence. Andrei glanced outside again. And he saw it: a dark figure standing at the nearest intersection, with its head towering up to third-floor level. A statue. An archaic metal statue. The same character he already knew, with the toadish face—only now he was standing there rigidly erect, with his heavy chin uplifted and one hand held behind his back, while the other was raised, with the index finger extended, either to threaten or to point to the sky . . .

Numb with fear, Andrei watched this monster as if he were having a bad dream. But he knew it was no nightmare. It was just a statue—an idiotic, mediocre contrivance of metal, covered in calx, or maybe ferriferous oxide, positioned grotesquely out of place. In the hot air rising from the road surface, its outlines trembled and wavered exactly like the outlines of the buildings along the street.

Andrei felt a hand on his shoulder and looked around— the Mute was smiling and nodding reassuringly at him. The *boooom, boooom, boooom* started up again outside. The Mute kept hold of his shoulder—fondling and caressing, kneading the muscles with affectionate fingers. Andrei pulled away sharply and glanced out again. The statue was gone. And once again there was silence.

Then Andrei pushed the Mute aside and ran up the stairs on numb legs, to where the voices were still droning in the same way, as if nothing at all had happened.

"That's enough!" he barked as he tore into the library hall. "Let's get out of here!"

His voice had turned completely hoarse, and they didn't hear him, or maybe they heard him but took no notice because they were too absorbed. It was a huge space, receding into an unbe- lievable distance, and the shelves stacked with books muffled all sounds. One set of shelves had been knocked over and the books from it were lying in a heap. Izya and Pak were rummaging in this heap—both of them flushed and sweaty, excited and delighted . . . Andrei walked across to them, striding straight over the books, grabbed them both by the collar, and jerked them up onto their feet.

"We're getting out of here," he said. "That's enough. Let's go."

Izya cast a bleary glance at him, jerked himself free, and immediately came to his senses. He ran a rapid glance over Andrei from head to foot.

"What's wrong with you?" he asked. "Has something hap- pened?"

"Nothing's happened," Andrei said angrily. "That's enough digging around in here. Where did you want to go? The Pan- theon? So let's go to the Pantheon."

Pak, whom Andrei was still clutching by the collar, delicately wriggled his shoulders and cleared his throat. Andrei let go of him.

"Do you know what we found here?" Izya began excitedly, then suddenly broke off. "Listen, what *has* happened?"

Andrei had already pulled himself together. Everything that occurred down below seemed absolutely ludicrous and impossible up here—in this austere, airless hall, under Izya's searching gaze, and in the presence of the imperturbably correct Pak.

"We can't waste so much time on every site," he said with a frown. "We've only got one day. Let's go."

"A library isn't just any other site!" Izya immediately objected. "This is the first library on our entire route . . . Listen, you look terrible. Come on, what really has happened?"

Andrei still couldn't bring himself to tell them. He didn't know how. "Let's go," he growled, turning away and striding back across the books toward the way out.

Izya overhauled him, took him by the arm, and walked along beside him. The Mute in the doorway stepped aside to let them pass. Andrei still didn't know how to begin. All the possible beginnings and all the possible words were idiotic. Then he remembered about the diary.

"You were reading me a diary yesterday . . ." he said as they walked down the stairs. "You know, written by that guy who hanged himself . . ."

"Yes?"

"Yes, yes . . ."

Izya stopped. "The shimmering?"

"Did you really not hear anything?" Andrei asked despairingly.

Izya shook his beard from side to side, and Pak replied in a quiet voice. "We probably got carried away. We were arguing."

"You maniacs . . ." said Andrei. He convulsively caught his breath, glanced around at the Mute, and finally said it. "The statue. It came and went . . . It seems they wander around the City, like they were alive . . ."

He lapsed into silence. "Well?" Izya asked impatiently.

"Well what? That's it."

Izya's expression of intent interest changed to immense disappointment. "Well, so what?" he said. "So it's a statue . . . another one walked last night, so what?"

Andrei opened his mouth and closed it again.

"The Ironheads," Pak put in. "This is obviously where the legend came from."

Unable to utter a word, Andrei glanced from Izya to Pak and back again. Izya rounded his lips in an sympathetic expression—the penny had finally dropped—and kept trying to pat Andrei on the arm, but Pak clearly didn't think any further explanations were needed and furtively glanced back over his shoulder into the library.

"W-Well now . . ." Andrei finally managed to force out. "That's just great. So you believed it straight off?"

"Listen, calm down, will you," said Izya, grabbing hold of his sleeve. "Of course we believed it, why wouldn't we? The Experiment is the Experiment, isn't it? We lost sight of that, thanks to rampant diarrhea and our constant bickering, but the fact of the matter . . . Lord Almighty, what's the big deal? So they're statues, so they walk . . . But we've got a library here! And you know what a fascinating picture it paints? The people who lived here were our contemporaries—from the twentieth century . . ."

"I get it," said Andrei. "Let go of my sleeve."

It was obvious to him now that he'd made a total fool of himself. But then, these two still haven't seen the statue for real. I reckon they'll change their tune when they do. But then, the Mute acted kind of strange too . . . "Don't even try to persuade me," he said. "We haven't got time for this library right now. When we drive by with the tractors, you can load up an entire sledful. But right now we're leaving. I promised to get back in time for taps."

"All right, then," Izya said soothingly. "Right, let's go. Let's go."

Shit, Andrei thought uneasily as he hurried down the stairs. How could I act that way? he asked himself as he opened the entrance door and walked out into the street first, so no one could see his face. And I'm not some common soldier or crude, ignorant driver, he thought, striding over the sizzling-hot cobblestones. It's all down to Fritz, he thought furiously. He proclaimed that there was no Experiment anymore, and I believed it . . . that is, I didn't really believe it, of course, I just accepted the new ideology—out of a sense of loyalty and sworn duty . . . Ah, no, guys, all these new ideologies are for fools, for the masses . . . But we lived for four years and never even spared a thought for the Experiment, didn't we; we were up to our eyes in other business . . . Making our little career . . . he thought scathingly. Acquiring carpets and items for our private collections . . .

At the intersection he slowed down for a moment and cast an oblique glance into the side street. The statue was there, gesturing menacingly with a finger fifty centimeters long, repulsively grinning with its toadish mouth. As if to say, *I'll get you, you sons of bitches!*

"Is this the one?" Izya casually asked.

Andrei nodded and moved on.

They walked on and on, gradually sinking into a stupor in the heat and the blinding light, stepping on their own short, ugly shadows, with the sweat drying into a salty crust on their foreheads and temples, and even Izya had stopped yakking about how some elegant hypotheses he had constructed had been demolished, and even the tireless Pak was already dragging one foot—the sole of his boot had torn off—and from time to time even the Mute opened his black, gaping mouth, stuck out his gruesome stump of his tongue, and started panting in double-quick time, like a dog . . . And nothing else happened, except that once Andrei lost his grip and shuddered when he happened to look up and saw a huge, green-stained face in a wide-open window on the fourth floor, staring at him with blind, bulging eyes. Well, after all, it was a ghastly sight—an ugly face with green blotches, filling the entire window up on the fourth floor.

400 THE DOOMED CITY

Then they walked out into the square.

They hadn't come across any squares like this before. It looked like some weird kind of forest had been felled here. The square was studded all over with plinths—round, square, hexagonal, stelliform, shaped like weird abstract hedgehogs, artillery towers, and mythical beasts, made of stone, cast iron, sandstone, marble, stainless steel, and even, apparently, gold . . . And all these plinths were empty, except for one fifty meters ahead of them, on which a leg as tall as a man, with an exceptionally muscly calf, had been snapped off above the knee, leaving the naked foot trampling the head of a winged lion.

The square was huge—they couldn't see the far side of it through the murky heat haze—but on the right, at the very foot of the Yellow Wall, they could make out the form of a long, low building with a facade of closely spaced columns, distorted by the currents of hot air.

"Well, I'll be damned," Andrei blurted out.

But Izya quoted something that Andrei didn't recognize: "Sometimes he is bronze, and sometimes he is marble, sometimes he has a pipe, and sometimes he has no pipe . . ." and then he asked, "But where have they all gone to?"

No one answered. They all just gazed at this sight, as if they couldn't get enough of it—even the Mute. Then Pak said, "Apparently we need to go over there . . ."

"Is that your Pantheon?" Andrei asked, for the sake of saying something, and Izya exclaimed in an indignant-sounding voice, "I don't understand! What are they all doing, gadding about town? Then why didn't we see then? There must be thousands of them here, thousands!"

"The City of a Thousand Statues," said Pak.

Izya promptly swung around to face him. "You mean there's a legend about that too?"

"No. But that's what I would call it."

"Hallelujah!" Andrei declared, struck by a sudden thought. "How are we going to get through here with our sleds? No explosives could possibly clear all these tank traps . . ."

"I think there must be a road around the square," said Pak. "Along the Cliff."

"Let's go, shall we?" said Izya, already impatient to move on.

They set off directly toward the Pantheon, walking between the podia, over cobblestones that were smashed and crushed to small fragments, walking into the white dust that glittered brightly in the sunlight. Every now and then they stopped for a moment and either bent down or went up on tiptoe to read the inscriptions on the pediments, and the strangeness of the inscriptions was startling and confusing.

ON THE NINTH DAY A SMILE MAKES. THE BLESSING OF YOUR MUSCULUS GLUTEUS SAVED THESE LITTLE ONES. THE SUN SOARED UP AND THE DAWN OF LOVE WAS EXTINGUISHED. Or even simply, WHEN! Izya laughed and gurgled, slamming his fist into his palm. Pak smiled and swayed his head, but Andrei was embarrassed; he felt that this merriment was inappropriate, even indecent somehow, but his feelings were hard to pin down, and he just patiently tried to hurry them along. "Come on, that's enough, that's enough," he repeated. "Let's go. Come on, what the hell! We're running late, it'll be embarrassing . . ."

The sight of these idiots made him furious—what a time and place to choose to have fun and games! And they just kept on loitering and loitering, tediously wasting time, running their dirty fingers over the incised letters, cackling and clowning around, and he gave up on them and felt nothing but tremendous relief when he realized their voices had been left far behind and he couldn't make out what they were saying.

It's better like this, he thought delightedly. Without this retinue of fools. After all, they weren't invited along, were they—I don't remember that. They were mentioned, all right, but exactly what was it that was said? They were either asked to come in dress uniform, or on the contrary, they were asked not to come at all. Agh, what difference does it make now? Well, if it comes to that, they can wait down here for a while. Pak's more or less OK, but Izya might suddenly start finding fault with my style and then, God forbid, he'll get pushy and want to speak himself . . . No, no, it's better without them, really. And the Mute? You stick behind me, here on the right, and keep your eyes peeled! You definitely can't afford to daydream here. Don't forget: we're in the camp of serious adversaries here, nothing like Quejada or Hnoipek. Here, brother, take the automatic, I've got to have freedom of movement, and climbing up on the rostrum with an automatic—I'm not Heiger, thank God . . . And pardon me, but where's my synopsis? A fine how d'you do this is! How can I manage without a synopsis?

The Pantheon towered up over him, a panoply of columns and broken, chipped steps, displaying their rusty reinforcing rods. He felt a cold draft from the columns—it was dark in there, where it smelled of anticipation and putrefaction, and the gigantic golden doors had already been flung open, and all he had to do was walk in. He strode from step to step, taking great care to make sure that he didn't stumble—heaven forbid!—and end up sprawled out here, where everyone could see, and he kept groping at his pockets, but of course the synopsis wasn't there, because of course, it had been left behind in the metal box . . . no, in the new suit, I was going to wear the new suit, wasn't I, then I decided this would make a more dramatic impact . . .

Damn it all, how am I going to manage without a synopsis? he thought as he stepped into the dark vestibule. But just what did it say in the synopsis? he thought, cautiously placing his feet as he walked across a slippery floor of black marble. Greatness came first, he recalled with an intense effort, feeling the icy cold creeping in under his shirt. It was very cold in here, in this vestibule, they could have warned him, after all, it was summer outside, and by the way, they could have sprinkled some sand around, it wouldn't have killed them, this way he could slip at any moment and smash in the back of his head.

Well, which way do I go in here? To the right, to the left? Ah yes, sorry . . . All right, then. First, about greatness, he thought, heading for a completely dark corridor. Now this is more like it—a carpet. They got that right! Only they didn't think to put in torches. That's always the way with them: they might put in torches, or even floodlights, but then there won't be any carpet. Or the other way around, like now . . . So—greatness . . .

In speaking of greatness, we recall the so-called great names. Archimedes. Very good! Syracuse, "Eureka," the bathhouse . . . bathtubs, that is. Naked. Next. Attila! The doge of Venice. I beg your pardon, Othello was the doge of Venice. Attila was the king of the Huns. Riding along. As silent and somber as the grave . . . But we don't need to look so for examples! Peter! Greatness. Peter the Great, the First. Peter the Second and Peter the Third weren't great. And very possibly that's because they weren't the first. It's extraordinary how often "great" and "first" are effectively synonyms. *Althooough*. Catherine the Second, the Great. The second, but nevertheless the great. It is important to note this exception. We shall often encounter exceptions of this kind, which merely serve, as it were, to confirm the rule . . .

He firmly clasped his hands together behind his back, tucked his chin into his chest, and strode to and fro several times, each time elegantly skirting around his stool. Then he pulled his stool out with his foot, braced his fingers on the table, knitted his brows together, and looked over the heads of his audience.

The table, clad in gray zinc, was completely bare, and it stretched out in front of him like a major highway. He couldn't see the far end of it. Down there little candle flames blinked though a yellow mist as they fluttered in the draft, and Andrei thought with fleeting annoyance that damn it all, it was indecent, at least he ought to be able to see who was down there, at the far end of the table. It was far more important to see *him* than these . . . But then, that's none of my concern . . .

He examined the rows of "these" with indifferent condescension. Meekly seated along both sides of the table, with their attentive faces turned toward him—faces of stone, cast iron, copper, gold, bronze, plaster, jasper . . . and whatever other kinds of faces they could have. Silver, for instance. Or jade, say . . . Their unseeing eyes were repellent, and anyway, what could possibly be attractive about those ponderous carcasses, with their knees jutting up a meter, or even two, above the tabletop? At least they were keeping quiet and sitting still. At this moment any movement would have been unbearable. Andrei listened in delight, with a pleasure that was almost sensual, as the final drops of his brilliantly executed pause drained away.

"But what is the rule? Of what does it consist? What is the nature of its intrinsic essence, intrinsic exclusively to this and not to any other substantive predication? In this regard I'm afraid I shall have to talk about things that you are not accustomed to hearing about, things you will not find pleasant to hear . . . Greatness. Ah, how much has been said, painted, danced, and sung about it! What would the human race be without the category of greatness? A gang of naked monkeys that would make even Hnoipek look like the apex of civilization, would it not? After all, no specific, individual Hnoipek knows the proper measure of things—'modus in rebus.' Nature has taught him only how to digest and reproduce. Any other action performed by the aforesaid Hnoipek cannot be independently evaluated by him as being either good or bad or useful, nor as being either futile or harmful—and precisely as a consequence of this very situation, other things being equal, sooner or later each specific, individual Hnoipek finds himself facing a field court martial, and this court decides how to deal with him . . . Thus, the absence of any internal court that passes judgement is naturally compensated, I would even say *fated* to be compensated, by the presence of an external court, for instance a field court martial . . . However, gentlemen, a society consisting of Hnoipeks and also, without a doubt, of Skanks, is simply not capable of devoting such a huge amount of attention to the external court—it matters not if it be a military court martial or a jury court, a secret inquisition court or a lynching court, a Vehmic court or a so-called honor court. Not to mention comrades' courts and other such instances . . . It became necessary to find a form for organizing the chaos consisting of the sexual and digestive organs of both Hnoipeks and Skanks, a form for this shambolic universal bedlam, such that at least some of the functions of the aforementioned external courts could be transferred to an internal court. And *that* was when the category of greatness became both necessary and serviceable! The point being, gentlemen, that in the vast and entirely amorphous horde of Hnoipeks, in the vast and even more amorphous horde of Skanks, from time to time individuals appear for whom the meaning of life is by no means primarily or entirely limited to the digestive and sexual functions. There is, if you will, a third need! This individual is not content merely to digest something and derive pleasure from the physical charms of others. In addition to this, you see, he wants to create something remarkable and out of the ordinary, something that never existed before. For example, some multileveled or, let's say, hierarchical structure. Or some kind of wild mountain goat on a wall. With balls. Or he wants to write a myth about Aphrodite . . . What the hell he needs all this for, he himself doesn't really understand. And indeed, what would Hnoipek want with Aphrodite born of the sea foam, or that wild mountain goat on a wall. With balls. Hypotheses do exist, of course—there are quite a few of them! After all, a wild mountain goat is a great deal of meat, isn't it? I won't even go into the subject of Aphrodite. However, if we are to be entirely honest and frank, the origin of this third need remains a mystery for our materialistic science as yet. But at the present moment this should not be of any interest to us. What *is* important to us at the present moment, my friends? The sudden appearance in the gray common herd of an individual who is not content with crud like oatmeal porridge or a filthy Skank whose legs are a mass of red blotches; he's not content with the universally accessible realism but starts idealizing and abstracting, the lousy pest; he starts mentally transforming oatmeal porridge into a juicy wild mountain goat covered in garlic sauce and transforming a Skank into a voluptuous, well-washed creature with hips—she came out of the ocean, he says. Out of the water . . . Why, heavens above!

A man like that is invaluable! A man like that should be set upon a high place and the Hnoipeks and Skanks should be led out to him by the battalion, in order to teach the parasites to know their place. Hey there, you crummy bastards, can you do what he can? Hey there, you lousy redheaded jerk, can you paint a burger that looks so juicy, it makes you want to gobble it down on the spot? Or make up a little joke at least? You can't? Then what makes you think you can set yourself on the same level as him? Go and work, work, work your asses off. Catch fish, gather mussels!"

Andrei pushed himself back from the table and walked to and fro again, exultantly rubbing his hands together. It had all turned out just great. Magnificent! Without any synopses. And all these tedious old fogies had listened with bated breath. Not a single one had moved. Oh yeah, that's me! Of course, I'm not Katzman, I keep quiet most of the time, but if they wind me up, if they ask me, dammit . . .

Uh oh, looks like someone else has started up down there at the invisible end of the table. Some Jew or other. Maybe Katzman crept in after all? Well, we'll see who comes off best.

"And so, greatness as a category arose out of creativity, for only he who creates is great, only he who creates something new, previously unheard of. But let us ask ourselves, dear sirs: In that case who's going to stick their noses in the shit? Who's going to say to them, where are you going, scumbag, who do you think you are? Who will be, so to speak, the creative individual's high priest?—I'm not afraid to use that term. The one who will be his priest, dearest gentlemen, is the individual who can't paint the aforementioned burger or Aphrodite, say, but no way does he want to gather mussels—the creative organizer, the creative liner-up in ranks, the creative extorter of gifts and likewise distributor thereof! And this brings us face-to-face with the question of the role of God and the Devil in history. A question that is, quite frankly, a highly complex, knotty tangle, a question concerning which everyone has piled lie upon lie . . . After all, even a babe in arms with no religion knows that God is a good person, and the

Devil, conversely, is a bad person. But this is driveling gibberish, gentlemen! What do we really know about them? That God set about chaos and organized it, while the Devil, on the contrary, strives every day and every hour to demolish this organization, this structure, and return it to chaos. This is true, is it not? But on the other hand, the whole of history teaches us that man as an individual aspires precisely to chaos. He wants to exist on his own terms. He wants to do what he feels like doing. He constantly clamors about how he is free from nature. And we don't have to look far for examples—take our notorious Hnoipek yet again! You understand, I hope, what I'm driving at? What, let me ask you, has been the stock-in-trade of the most savage tyrants throughout history? They have all, without exception, striven to take the aforementioned chaos, intrinsic to man, that selfsame chaotic, amorphous hnoipekoskankness, and arrange it in decorous order, organize it, institutionalize it, neatly line it up—preferably in a single column—aim it at a single point, and generally clamp down on it. Or, to put it more simply, to do it in. And by the way, as a general rule, they have succeeded! Although, it's true, not for very long, and only at the cost of spilling a lot of blood. So I ask you: Who is really the good person here? The one who aspires to allow the free play of chaos—a.k.a. freedom, equality, and brotherhood—or the one who aspires to reduce this hnoipekoskankness (read as 'social entropy'!) to the minimum? Who? And that's the whole point!"

Now that was a fine passage . . . Lean and precise, but at the same time not without a certain passion . . . Just what is he droning about, down there at the other end? Son of a bitch, what a rude bastard! Interfering with my work, and basically—

Andrei suddenly noticed with an ominous feeling that several heads in the neat rows of listeners were turned with their backs toward him. He looked more closely. There was no doubt about it—the backs of several heads. One, two . . . six of them! He cleared his throat as forcefully as he could and gravely rapped his knuckles on the zinc-clad tabletop. It didn't do any good. Well, just you wait, he thought menacingly. I'll get you now! What would that be in Latin?

"*Quos ego!*" he barked. "It seems like you've gotten it into your heads that you mean something? *We're made of stone, and you're just putrefying flesh? We're from everlasting to everlasting, and you're ephemeral trash?* Here, take that!" He gave them the fig sign. "Who remembers you anyway? You were all erected in memory of some jerks or other who were forgotten long ago . . . Archimedes—big deal! Sure, I know there was someone called that who ran naked through the streets—absolutely shameless . . . And so what? At the appropriate level of civilization they would have ripped his balls off for that. To teach him not to run around that way. 'Eureka'—know what I mean? Or that Peter the Great. So, OK, he was the czar, the Emperor of All Russia . . . We've seen plenty of his kind. But what was his surname? Eh? You don't know? All those monuments that have been erected! All those works that have been written! But just ask a student at his examination—you'll be lucky if one out of ten remembers what his surname was. That's 'great' for you! And it's the same with all of you, isn't it? Either no one remembers you at all, they just gape and bat their eyelids, or, let's say, they do remember the first name but not the surname. And vice versa too: they remember the surname—the Kalinga Prize—but as for the first name . . . Who gives a damn about the first name? Who was he anyway? Maybe he was some kind of writer, or maybe he speculated in wool . . . Who wants to know, anyway, judge for yourself. Remembering all of you would make a man forget the price of vodka."

Now he could see the backs of more than ten heads in front of him. It was offensive. And down at the other end Katzman was getting louder and louder, pushier and pushier, but his droning was still as unintelligible as ever.

"A lure!" Andrei yelled with all his might. "That's what your much-vaunted greatness is! A lure! Hnoipek looks at you and thinks, well, would you ever, what tremendous people have lived in the world. Right, I'll give up drinking, I'll give up smoking, I'll stop tumbling my Skank around in the bushes, I'll go and join a library, and I'll achieve all this too . . . That is, that's what he's supposed to think! But that's not what he really thinks when he looks at you, no way! And if they don't post sentries around you and fence you in, he'll crap great big heaps all around you, write words on you with chalk, and go back to his Skank, feeling very pleased with himself. So much for your educational function! So much for the memory of mankind! And what the hell would Hnoipek want with memory anyway? Why the hell should he remember you, pray tell? Admittedly, there have been times when remembering all of you was considered good form. So what could people do—they committed you to memory. Alexander the Great, the king of Macedonia, that is, born on this date, died on that date. A conqueror. Bucephalus. 'Countess, your Bucephalus is rather tired, and by the way, how would you like to sleep with me?' Polite, eloquent, genteel . . . You have to cram stuff at school now too, of course. Born on this date, died on that date, member of the ruling oligarchical clique. Exploiter. And it's absolutely impossible to understand who needs all that. We just used to pass the exam then wash our hands of the whole business. 'Alexander the Great was a great general too, but why go smashing stools?' That was this film. *Chapaev*. Have you seen it? 'My brother Mika's dying, he's asking for fish broth . . .' And that's all your Alexander the Great is good for."

Andrei stopped talking. All this talk was pointless. No one was listening to him. Now the backs of all the heads were turned toward him—cast iron, stone, iron, jade . . . shaved, bald, curly, with little braids, chipped and dented, or else completely concealed under chain mail, helmets, three-cornered hats. They don't like it, he thought. The truth is hard to swallow. They're used to anthems and odes. *Exegi monumentum* . . . But what did I say that was so upsetting? Well, of course, I didn't lie, I didn't grovel to you—I just said what I thought. I've got nothing against greatness. Pushkin. Lenin. Einstein . . . I don't like idolatry. Deeds should be worshipped, not statues. And maybe not even deeds should be worshipped. Because everyone only does what he's capable of doing. One makes a revolution, another makes a tin whistle. Maybe I only have enough strength for a tin whistle—so now does that mean I'm shit?

But the voice from behind the yellow fog kept droning on, and now he could hear separate words: ". . . unprecedented and exceptional . . . from a catastrophic situation . . . only you . . . merits eternal gratitude and eternal glory . . ." Now that's what I really can't stand, thought Andrei. I absolutely hate it when someone juggles with eternalities. Brothers for all eternity. Eternal friendship. Together for eternity. Eternal glory . . . Where do they get all that from? What can they see that's eternal?

"Stop lying!" he shouted down the table. "Have you no shame?"

No one took any notice of him. He turned around and plodded back the way he came, feeling the draft chilling him to the bone—the stinking draft, saturated with the fetid vapors of the crypt, rust and tarnished copper . . . It wasn't Izya jabbering there, was it, he listlessly thought. Izya has never spoken words like that in his entire life. I shouldn't have blamed him . . . I shouldn't have come here. Why the hell did I come here anyway? Probably I thought I'd understood something. After all, I'm over thirty now, it's time to be figuring out what's what. What sort of crazy idea is that—trying to persuade monuments that no one needs them? You might as well try to persuade people that no one needs them . . . Maybe that's the way it is, but who's going to believe it?

Something's happened to me in the last few years, he thought. I've lost something . . . I've lost my sense of a goal, that's what. About five years ago, I knew for certain why I had to take one course of action or another. But now—I don't know. I know that Hnoipek should be put up against the wall, but I don't understand what for. I mean, I understand that it would make my job a whole lot easier, but is that all it's needed for—to make my job easier? I'm the only one who needs that. For myself. That's probably right. No one else is going to live my life for me, I'll have to take care of that for myself. But it's boring, depressing, I don't have the strength . . . And I don't have any choice either, he thought. That's what I've understood. A man can't do anything; he doesn't know how to do anything. The only thing he can do and knows how to do is live for himself. He even gritted his teeth at the hopeless clarity and certitude of this thought.

Walking out of the crypt into the shade of the columns, he screwed up his eyes. The yellow, sweltering square, studded with empty pediments, lay stretched out before him. The heat from it surged over him, like a blast from a furnace. Heat, thirst, exhaustion . . . This was the world in which he had to live and also, therefore, to act.

Izya was sleeping, stretched out on the stone slabs in the shade, with his forehead nestling in an open book. A jagged tear gaped open in the back of his trousers and his feet in down-at-heel shoes were unnaturally turned out. And in addition he stank from a mile away. The Mute was right there—squatting on his haunches with his eyes closed, leaning back against a column, with the automatic lying on his knees.

"Reveille," Andrei said wearily.

The Mute opened his eyes and got up. Izya raised his head and looked at Andrei through swollen eyebrows.

"Where's Pak?" Andrei asked, looking around.

Izya sat up, sank his hooked fingers into his mop of hair, and started scratching furiously. "*Daaamn* . . ." he mumbled in a thick voice. "Listen, I'm desperately hungry . . . How long can this last?"

"We'll leave straightaway," Andrei told him, still looking around. "Where's Pak?"

"*Gontolibry*," Izya replied, yawning fervently. "Ah, yuck, I'm totally wasted, dammit . . ."

"Where did he go?"

"He went to the library." Izya jumped to his feet, picked up his small volume, and started stuffing it into his rucksack. "We decided that he'd go and select some books in the meantime. What time is it now? Seems like my watch has stopped . . ."

Andrei glanced at his own watch. "Three," he said. "Let's go."

"Maybe we could eat first?" Izya tentatively suggested.

"As we walk," said Andrei. He had a vaguely uneasy feeling. Something was bothering him. Something was wrong. He took the automatic from the Mute, narrowed his eyes, and strode out onto the incandescent steps.

"That's just great . . ." Izya grumbled behind him. "Now we eat on the move. I waited for him, like an honest man, and he won't even let me eat right . . . Hey, Mute, hand me that rucksack . . ."

Andrei walked quickly between the pediments, without looking back. He was hungry too, his insides felt sore, but something urged him to keep moving, and move fast. He arranged the strap of his automatic more comfortably on his shoulder and glanced rapidly at his watch again. It was still one minute to three. His watch had stopped.

"Hey, Mr. Counselor!" Izya called to him. "Take this."

Andrei stopped for a moment and accepted two hard biscuits with a filling of fatty canned pork. Izya was already zestfully crunching and chomping. Andrei examined his sandwich as he walked along, trying to see which side would be most convenient to bite on, and asked, "When did Pak leave?"

"Well, he went almost immediately," Izya said with his mouth full. "The two of us looked over the Pantheon, and we didn't find anything interesting, so he set off."

"That was wrong," said Andrei. He'd realized what was worrying him.

"What was wrong?"

Andrei didn't answer.

Ц

There was no sign of Pak in the library. Of course; he was never intending to come in here. The books were still lying in a heap, exactly like before.

"Strange," said Izya, turning his head this way and that in bewilderment. "He said he was going to pick out everything on sociology."

"He said, he said," Andrei growled through his teeth. He kicked the nearest plump volume with the toe of his shoe, turned around, and ran down the stairs. "So he outfoxed us after all. Cunning old slant-eye outfoxed us. The Jew of the Far East . . ." Andrei didn't really understand what the Jew of the Far East had done that was so cunning, but every fiber of his being cried out that he had been outfoxed.

Now they stuck close to the walls as they walked along— Andrei on the right side of the street and the Mute, who had also realized things were looking ugly, on the left. Izya tried to set out straight down the middle, but Andrei yelled at him so fiercely that the archivist immediately dashed back and fell in behind him, walking with him step for step, sniffing in indignation and scornfully snorting. The visibility was about fifty meters; beyond that the street looked as if it were submerged in an aquarium, with everything blurred and trembling, shimmering and glimmering— waterweed even seemed to be rippling above the surface of the road.

When they drew level with the movie theater, the Mute suddenly stopped. Andrei, who was watching him out of the corner of his eye, stopped too. The Mute stood there motionless, as if he were listening to something, clutching his naked machete in his lowered hand.

413

"I smell burning," Izya in a low voice behind Andrei.

And Andrei immediately caught the smell of burning too. That's it, he thought, gritting his teeth.

The Mute raised the hand holding the machete, gestured along the street, and moved on. They covered another two hundred meters or so, taking every possible precaution. The burning smell grew stronger—a cocktail of hot metal, smoldering rags, diesel oil, and some other sweetish, almost appetizing odors. What happened back there? Andrei thought, gritting his teeth so hard he heard his temples crack. What have they gone and done? he repeated over and over in his anguish. What's burning back there? Because that's where the burning is, no doubt about it . . . And at that moment he saw Pak.

He immediately thought it was Pak because the body was wearing the familiar jacket of faded blue denim twill. No one else in the camp had a jacket like that. The Korean was lying on the corner of the street, with his legs sprawled out and his head lowered onto his short-barreled, handmade automatic. The short barrel was pointing along the street in the direction of the camp. Pak looked unusually fat, as if he'd been inflated, and his hands were a glossy bluish-black.

Before Andrei could even grasp what he was really seeing, Izya shoved him aside with a strange croaking sound and trampled on Andrei's feet as he darted across the intersection and went down on his knees beside the dead body.

Andrei gulped and looked toward the Mute, who was nodding emphatically and pointing to something up ahead with his machete. Andrei spotted another body up there, at the very limit of visibility—someone else fat and black was lying there. And now through the haze Andrei caught sight of an image, distorted by refraction—a column of gray smoke rising up over the roofs.

Lowering his automatic, Andrei cut across the intersection. Izya had already gotten up off his knees, and when Andrei got close, he realized why: the body in the light blue denim twill exuded an unbearable, sickly sweet odor.

"My God . . ." said Izya, turning his dead face, streaming with sweat, toward Andrei. "They killed him, the scum . . . All of them together aren't worth even his little finger . . ."

Andrei glanced down briefly at the ghastly, bloated puppet with a black, gaping wound where the back of its head ought to be. The sun glinted dully on a scattering of copper cartridge cases. Andrei walked around Izya and cut slantwise across the street, no longer hiding or stooping over, toward the next bloated puppet and the Mute, who was already squatting down beside it.

This one was lying on his back, and although his face was appallingly swollen and black, Andrei recognized him: it was one of the geologists, Quejada's deputy for surveying work, Ted Kaminski. It seemed especially horrible that he was dressed in nothing but his shorts and, for some strange reason, a wadded jacket like the drivers wore. He had obviously been shot from behind, and the burst of gunfire had passed right through him—on his chest the jacket was peppered with holes, with clumps of gray wadding sticking out of them. An automatic rifle with no ammunition clip was lying about five steps away.

The Mute touched Andrei on the shoulder and pointed ahead, to where there was another body, doubled up and huddled against the wall on the right side of the street. It turned out to be Permyak. He had obviously been shot in the middle of the street—there was still a dried-out black patch on the cobblestones there—but in his agony he had crept over to the wall, leaving a thick black trail behind him, and died with his head tucked down, clutching his bullet-shredded stomach in his arms with every last ounce of strength.

They had killed each other here in a fit of demented fury, like enraged predators, like frenzied tarantulas, like rats deranged by hunger. Like men.

Tevosyan was in the unpaved side street nearest to the camp, lying slantwise across the road on the dried-up excrement. He had been chasing the tractor, which turned into this alley and moved off toward the precipice, ripping up the hard-baked earth with its impatient caterpillar treads. Tevosyan chased it all the way from the camp, shooting as he ran, and they shot at him from the tractor, and here, at the intersection where the statue with the toadish face had stood that night, they got him, and he had been left lying here, grinning with his yellow teeth, in his army tunic, smeared with dust, excrement, and blood. But before he died, or maybe after he died, he hit the target too: halfway to the cliff edge, Sergeant Vogel was lying in a bloated heap, clutching with his gnarled fingers at the earth crushed to powder by the caterpillar tracks. From there the tractor had gone on without him—all the way to the cliff edge and down into the Abyss.

In the camp a burnt-out sled was smoldering. Little tongues of smoky orange flame were still flicking over the metal barrels, warped and battered by the bullets shot through them and turned bluish-black by the heat, and clouds of greasy smoke were rising up into the pale sky. Someone's burnt legs protruded from a caked heap of slag on a trailer, and the appetizing odor that made Andrei feel nauseous hung in the air.

Roulier's naked body was hanging out the window of the cartographers' room—his long, hairy arms reached almost down to the sidewalk, where an automatic rifle was lying. The wall all around the window was gouged and chipped by bullets, and on the opposite side of the street Vasilenko and Palotti were lying together in a heap, cut down by a single burst of gunfire. There were no weapons anywhere near them, and Vasilenko's shrunken face still wore an expression of boundless amazement and fear.

The other geologist, the other cartographer, and Ellisauer, the deputy expedition leader for technical matters, had all been stood up against that same wall and shot. They were lying there in row in front of a door riddled with bullet holes—Ellisauer in his shorts, and the other two naked.

And at the very center of this stinking hecatomb, right in the middle of the street, Colonel St. James, draped in the British flag, was calmly lying on a table with aluminum legs, with his hands folded on his chest. He was in full dress uniform, with all his medals. Still as prim and imperturbable as ever, and even smiling ironically. Beside him, with his gray-haired head nestling against the road, lay Duggan—also in full dress uniform, and clutching the colonel's broken cane in his hands.

And that was all. Six soldiers, including Hnoipek, plus the engineer Quejada and the debauched girl Skank, and the tractor with its sled, had disappeared, leaving behind corpses, geological equipment dumped in a heap, and a few automatic rifles stacked in a pyramid. And a vile stench. And greasy soot. And a suffocating odor of roasted flesh from the sled that was still smoldering. Andrei stumbled into his room, collapsed into a chair, and lowered his head onto his hands with a groan. It was all over. Forever. And there was no salvation from the pain, no salvation from the shame, and no salvation from death.

I brought them here. I did it. I left them here on their own, like a stinking coward. I wanted to take a break. From their ugly faces—what a skunk, what a namby-pamby jerk, what a lousy wuss . . . Colonel, ah, Colonel! You shouldn't have died, you shouldn't have done that! If I hadn't gone he wouldn't have died. If he hadn't died, no one here would have dared to lift a finger. Animals, animals . . . Hyenas! I ought to have shot them, shot them!

He gave another long, drawn-out groan and dragged his wet cheek across his sleeve. We've been idling away the time in libraries . . . making speeches to statues . . . You lousy bungler, you bag of wind, you screwed everything up, let everything unravel . . . So now croak, you bastard! No one will cry. What damned use are you to anyone anyway? But I'm afraid, aren't I, afraid. But it's so horrible, so horrible . . . They hunted each other down, they shot each other—they shot men lying on the ground, they shot dead men, they put them up against the wall, swearing and reviling them, punching and kicking them . . . How did it come to this, guys? What have I reduced you to? And for what? For what?

He slammed his fists down onto the tabletop, then straightened up and wiped his face with his open palm. Through the window he could hear Izya screeching inarticulately and the Mute cooing soothingly, like a pigeon. I don't want to live, Andrei thought. I don't want to. To hell with all this. He got up from the table to go out there, to Izya, to the men—and suddenly he saw the expedition log lying open in front of him. He pushed it away from him in disgust, but immediately noticed that the last page wasn't written in his handwriting. He sat down again and started reading.

Quejada wrote:

> Day 31. Yesterday, in the morning of day 30 of the expedition, Counselor Voronin, the archivist Katzman, and the emigrant Pak set off on a reconnaissance sortie, intending to return to the camp before taps, but did not come back. Today at 1430 Colonel St. James, the acting leader of the expedition, died of a sudden heart attack. Since Counselor Voronin has still not returned from the reconnaissance sortie, I am assuming command of the expedition. Signed: deputy expedition leader for scientific matters, D. Quejada, 1545.

Then came the usual gobbledygook about provisions and water expended, about the temperature and the wind, and also an order appointing Sergeant Vogel commander of the military unit, a reprimand to deputy expedition leader for technical matters Ellisauer for procrastination, and an order, also to Ellisauer, to expedite the repair of the second tractor. After that Quejada wrote:

> Tomorrow I intend to hold a funeral with full military honors for the untimely deceased Colonel St. James and immediately after the ceremony dispatch a well-armed group of men to search for Counselor Voronin's reconnaissance party. Should the missing party not be found, I intend to give the order to turn back, since I consider continuing our advance to be even more pointless that it was before.

Day 32. The reconnaissance party has not returned. For a shameful brawl that broke out last night, I am giving the cartographer Roulier and privates Hnoipek and Tevosyan a final warning and withdrawing their water ration for one day . . .

After that the page was streaked with black zigzags and spatters of ink, and the entries came to an end. Evidently shooting had broken out in the street, and Quejada had jumped up and never come back.

Andrei reread the entries twice. Yes, Quejada, this is what you wanted. You got what you wanted. And I blamed it all on Pak, may he rest in peace . . . He bit his lip and squeezed his eyes shut when the bloated puppet in a faded blue jacket appeared in front of him again, and suddenly he realized. Day thirty-two? Thirty! Yesterday I wrote the entry for day twenty-eight . . . He flipped the page back hurriedly. Yes. Twenty-eight . . . And these bloated corpses—they've been lying here for days . . . My God, what is all this? One, two . . . What date is it today? We only left this morning!

And he remembered the hot square studded with empty pediments, and the icy darkness of the Pantheon, and the blind statues at the infinitely long table . . . That was a long time ago. It was a very long time ago. Yep, yep. Some unholy power must have swept me up and swirled me around, set my head spinning and addled my brains . . . I could have come back the same day. I would have found the colonel still alive, I wouldn't have let it happen . . .

The door swung open and Izya walked in, looking like a different person—all dried out, somehow, with a bony, tight-drawn face, sullen and bitter, as if it wasn't he who had just been shrieking under the windows like a woman. He flung his half-empty rucksack into the corner, sat in an armchair facing Andrei, and said, "The bodies have been lying here for at least three days. What's happening? Do you understand?"

Without saying anything, Andrei pushed the logbook across the table to him. Izya avidly grabbed it, devoured the entries in a single gulp, and looked up at Andrei with red eyes.

"The Experiment is the Experiment," Andrei said with a crooked grin.

"Lousy, devious crap . . ." Izya said with hatred and disgust. He glanced through the log entries again and dropped the logbook on the table.

"I think they tampered with us at the square," said Andrei. "Where the pediments are."

Izya nodded, leaned back in the armchair, jerked up his beard, and closed his eyes. "Well, what are we going to do, Counselor?" he asked.

Andrei didn't answer.

"Just don't you even think of shooting yourself!" said Izya. "I know you . . . the Komsomol member . . . the young eagle . . ."

Andrei gave another crooked grin and tugged on his collar. "Listen," he said, "let's go somewhere else . . ."

Izya opened his eyes and stared at him.

"The stink from the window . . ." Andrei said with an effort. "I can't . . ."

"Let's go to my room," said Izya.

In the corridor the Mute got up to greet them. Andrei took hold of his bare, muscular arm and drew him along. They all walked into Izya's room together. The windows here looked out onto a different street. Beyond the low roofs behind the windows, the Yellow Wall soared upward. There was no stink at all here, and for some reason it was even cool. Only there was nowhere to sit—the floor was completely covered with heaps of paper and books.

"On the floor, sit on the floor," Izya said, and collapsed onto the tangled, dirty sheets on his bed. "Let's think," he said. "I don't intend to croak here. I've still got a whole heap of work to do."

"What's there to think about?" Andrei said morosely. "It all comes down to one thing . . . There's no water, they took it. And all the food's been burned. There's no way back—we'd never make it across the desert . . . If we overtook those scumbags . . . But then, we can't, it's been days . . ." He paused for a moment. "If we could find water—is it far to that pumping station of yours?"

"About twenty kilometers," said Izya. "Or thirty."

"If we travel by night, in the cool . . ."

"We can't travel by night," said Izya. "It's too dark. And the wolves . . ."

"There aren't any wolves here," Andrei objected.

"How do you know that?"

"Well, then let's just shoot ourselves and to hell with it," said Andrei. He already knew he wasn't going to shoot himself. He wanted to live. He'd never realized before how much he could want to live.

"Ah, come on," said Izya. "But seriously?"

"Seriously, I want to live. And I will survive. I don't give a rotten damn for anything now. It's just the two of us now, got it? The two of us have got to survive, and that's all. And they can all damn well go to hell. We'll just find water and live beside it."

"That's right," said Izya. He sat up on the bed, pushed his hand under his shirt, and started scratching. "We'll spend the day drinking water, and I'll spend the night screwing you."

Andrei looked at him, bewildered. "Have you got any other suggestions?" he asked.

"Not yet. That's right—we have to find water. Without water we're done for. Then we'll see what comes after that. What I'm thinking right now is this: they obviously took off out of here in a big hurry, straight after the bloodbath. They were afraid. They climbed into the sled and stepped on the gas! We ought to ferret around in the house a bit—we're bound to find water and food here . . ." He was about to say something else, but he stopped with his mouth hanging open and his eyes bulging. "Look, look!" he said in a frightened whisper.

Andrei rapidly swung around to face the window. He didn't notice anything unusual at first; he only heard something—a kind of distant rumbling, like a landslide, as if rocks were showering down somewhere . . . Then his eyes spotted movement on the vertical yellow cliff face above the roofs.

From out of the bluish-whitish haze up high above, a strange triangular cloud was hurtling downward, with its pointed angle first. It was moving down from an unbelievable height, and was still a very long way from the foot of the Wall, but he could already make out a bulky form with painfully familiar outlines spinning furiously at the leading point, crashing into invisible projections and bouncing off them. At every blow, parts flew off the hulk and carried on falling beside it. Crushed rock hurtled down, fanning out as it fell, puffs of bright dust swirled up, and they drew together to form a cloud that widened out farther and farther, like the wake behind the stern of a speedboat, and the distant, rumbling roar grew louder, breaking up into separate blows, a drumroll of fragments crashing against the monolithic Cliff, the menacing rustling of a gigantic landslide . . .

"The tractor!" Izya exclaimed in a strangled voice.

Andrei only understood what Izya had said at the last moment, when the mangled and twisted vehicle smashed into the roofs, the floor under his feet shuddered from the appalling impact, a column of brick dust swirled upward, and fragments of stone and metal sheeting were sent flying through the air—an instant later all this was hidden under the tidal wave of the yellow avalanche.

For a long time they sat there without speaking, listening as the rumbling, crunching, and snapping tumbled on, and the floor under their feet kept shaking, and they couldn't see anything over the roofs any longer through the motionless yellow cloud.

"Holy shit!" said Izya. "How the hell did they get up there?"

"Who?" Andrei asked obtusely.

"That's our tractor, you blockhead!"

"What do you mean, our tractor? The one that took off?"

Izya massaged his nose as vigorously as he could with his dirty fingers before answering. "I don't know," he said. "I don't understand a thing. . . Do you understand it?" he suddenly asked, turning to the Mute. "I don't understand a thing."

The Mute nodded indifferently. Izya slammed his fist down on his knees in annoyance, but just then the Mute made a strange gesture: he stretched his index finger out in front of him, rapidly lowered it to the floor, then lifted it up over his head, tracing out an elongated circle in the air.

"Well?" Izya asked avidly. "Well?"

The Mute shrugged and repeated the same gesture. Andrei suddenly remembered something, and when he remembered, he immediately understood everything.

"Falling Stars!" he exclaimed. "Well, would you believe it!" he laughed bitterly. "And I've only understood it now!"

"What have you understood?" Izya yelled. "What stars?"

Still laughing, Andrei just waved his hand. "Forget it," he said. "Forget it, the whole damned thing! What does it matter to us now? No more blathering, Katzman! We have to survive, got that? Survive! In this abominable, impossible world! We need water, Katzman!"

"Hang on, hang on . . ." Izya muttered.

"There's nothing else I want!" Andrei roared, shaking his clenched fists. "I don't want to understand anything anymore! I don't want to find out anything! Those are dead bodies lying out there, Katzman! Dead bodies! They wanted to live too, didn't they, Katzman? And now they're bloated and they're rotting!"

Thrusting out his beard, Izya got up off the bed, grabbed hold of Andrei's jacket, and forced him to sit down on the floor.

"Shut up!" he said with terrible wheezing hiss. "Want me to smack you in the face right now? I will. You whining old woman!"

Andrei grated his teeth and said nothing.

Puffing and panting, Izya went back to his bed and started scratching again. "He's never seen dead bodies before . . ." he growled. "Never seen this world before. Stop griping, you wimp!"

Burying his face in his hands, Andrei fought to trample down and crush the senseless, hideous wailing inside him. But some small corner of his mind understood what was happening to him, and that helped. It was terrifying to be here, surrounded by dead men, supposedly still alive yourself but actually already dead too . . . Izya was saying something, but Andrei couldn't hear it. Then it passed. "What were you saying?" he asked, taking his hands away from his face.

"I was saying that I'll go and ferret around in the soldiers' quarters, and you ferret around in the intelligentsia's room. And don't forget Quejada's room—he must have kept some kind of geologists' emergency supplies in there somewhere. And don't panic, we'll pull through this."

At that moment the sun went out.

"Damnation! The worst possible moment!" said Izya. "Now we have to look for a lamp . . . Hang on, your lamp ought to be here somewhere, right?"

"Our watches," Andrei said with an effort. "We have to set our watches . . ."

He raised his wrist to his eyes, focused on the phosphorescent hands, and set them to 1200 hours. Izya was scrabbling around in the darkness, swearing through his teeth, moving his bed around for some reason, and rustling papers. Then a match scraped and lit. Izya stood on his knees in the middle of the room, waving the match from side to side.

"Don't just sit there, damn you," he yelled. "Look for the lamp! Move it, I've only got three matches!"

Andrei got up reluctantly, but the Mute had already found the lamp, raised the glass, and handed it to Izya. The room got brighter. Izya wiggled his beard intently as he tried to adjust the burner. But he fumbled too clumsily and the burner refused to be adjusted. The Mute, gleaming all over with sweat, went back into the corner, squatted down on his haunches, and stared out at Andrei from there with plaintive devotion, his eyes wide open like a child's. The troops. The rump of a routed army . . .

"Let me have the lamp," said Andrei.

He took the lamp from Izya and adjusted the burner.

"Let's go," he ordered.

He pushed open the door of the colonel's room. The windows here were firmly closed and the glass in them was unbroken, so he couldn't smell the stench at all. The air smelled of tobacco and eau de cologne. Of the colonel.

Everything was neat and tidy: the high-quality leather of two packed suitcases glimmered in the lamplight; the folding camp bed was made up without a single wrinkle. At the head of the bed a shoulder belt with a holster and military cap with an immense visor hung on a nail. A gas lantern stood on a circle of felt on a bulky chest of drawers in the corner, with a box of matches, a pile of books, and a pair of binoculars in a case lying beside it.

Andrei put down his lamp on the table and looked around again. The tray with the flask and inverted shot glasses was standing on one shelf of an empty bookcase.

"Hand me that," Andrei said to the Mute.

The Mute darted across, grabbed the tray, and set it on the table, beside the lamp. Andrei poured cognac into the shot glasses. There were only two of them, so he filled the cap of the flask for himself.

"Take it," he said. "Here's to life."

Izya gave him an approving look, took a shot glass, and sniffed at it with the air of a connoisseur.

"That's good stuff! Here's to life, you say? Is this really life?" He giggled, clinked glasses with the Mute, and drained his glass. His eyes turned moist. "*Goo-ood*," he said in a slightly hoarse voice.

The Mute drained his glass, too—as if it were water, without the slightest interest. But Andrei carried on standing there, holding the full flask-cap, in no hurry to down his drink. He wanted to say something, but he didn't really know what it was. Yet another major stage was ending and a new one was beginning. And although he couldn't possibly expect anything good from tomorrow, at least tomorrow was a reality—an exceptionally tangible reality, because it could well be one of a very, very small number of days still remaining. This was a feeling entirely new to Andrei, a very poignant feeling.

But he couldn't think of anything else to say, so he just repeated the same words—"Here's to life!"—and drank.

Then he lit the colonel's gas lantern and handed it to Izya, with a promise: "You smash that one, you cack-handed hairy ape, and I'll box your ears for you."

Izya left, muttering resentfully, but Andrei lingered on, absentmindedly glancing around the room. Of course, he ought to ferret around in here—Duggan must have kept some kind of stash for the colonel—but the idea of ferreting around in this place somehow felt . . . shameful, was that it?

"Don't be shy, Andrei, don't be shy," he suddenly heard a familiar voice say. "The dead don't need anything."

The Mute was sitting on the edge of the table, dangling his legs, and he wasn't the Mute any longer—or, rather, not entirely the Mute. He was still wearing only his trousers, with the machete on the broad belt, but now his skin was dry, a matte ivory color, his face had rounded out, and his cheeks had acquired a healthy bloom, like two peaches. It was the Mentor, as large as life—and the sight of him brought Andrei neither joy nor hope; it didn't lift his spirits. He felt annoyed and uneasy.

"You again . . ." he growled, turning his back to the Mentor. "Long time no see."

He walked over to the window, pressed his forehead against the warm glass, and started looking out into the darkness that was faintly illuminated by little flames on the still-smoldering sled. "Well, as you can see, we're all set to die here . . ."

"Why die?" the Mentor said cheerfully. "You have to live! You know, it's never too late and always too early to die, isn't that right?"

"And what if we don't find water?"

"You'll find it. You always have and you will now."

"Good. We'll find it. Do we live beside it for the rest of our lives? Then what's the point of living?"

"What's the point of living anyway?"

"That's what I keep thinking too: what's the point of living? I've lived a stupid life, Mentor. An idiotic kind of life. Bobbing about aimlessly like a turd that won't flush. At first I fought for some kind of ideas, then for rugs that were in short supply, and then I totally flipped . . . and I destroyed those men."

"Come on, come on, you're not being serious," said the Mentor. "People always end up dead. You're not to blame for that, are you? You're starting a new stage, Andrei, and, in my opinion, a decisive one. In a certain sense it's actually good that things have turned out exactly this way. Sooner or later all this would inevitably have happened anyway. The expedition was doomed, wasn't it? But you could have perished with it, without ever crossing this important borderline . . ."

"I wonder exactly what borderline that is," Andrei said with a chuckle. He turned to face the Mentor. "I've already had ideas—all sorts of hooey about the good of society and other mumbo jumbo for kids still wet behind the ears . . . I've already made a career, thanks—I've had enough of being a big boss . . . So what else is there that can happen to me?"

"Understanding!" said the Mentor, slightly raising his voice.

"What—understanding? Understanding of what?"

"Understanding," the Mentor repeated. "That's what you've never had before—understanding!"

"I've got this understanding of yours right up to here now!" said Andrei, tapping the edge of his open hand against his Adam's apple. "I understand everything in the world now. It took thirty years to reach this understanding, and now I've got there at last. Nobody needs me, and nobody needs anyone. Whether I exist or I don't, whether I fight the fight or kick back and lounge on the sofa—it makes no difference. Nothing can be changed, nothing can be put right. All I can do is find myself a more or less comfortable niche. Everything moves along on its own; I don't make any difference. There it is, that's your understanding—and there's nothing else left for me to understand. But you tell me what I'm supposed to do with this understanding! Pickle it for winter or eat it right now?"

The Mentor nodded. "Precisely," he said. "That *is* the final borderline: What do you do with your understanding? How do you live with it? You have to live anyway, don't you?"

"The right time to live is when you don't have any understanding!" Andrei said with quiet fury. "With this understanding the right thing to do is die! And if I weren't such a coward, if the damned protoplasm didn't scream so loud inside me, I'd know what to do. I'd choose a good, strong rope . . ."

He stopped speaking.

The Mentor took the flask, carefully filled one shot glass, then the other, and pensively screwed the cap back on. "Well, let's start from the fact that you're not a coward," he said. "And the reason you haven't used that rope has nothing to do with you being afraid . . . Somewhere in your subconscious, and not so very deep, I assure you, lies the conviction that it is possible to live, even with understanding. And live pretty well. Interesting, that." He started pushing one of the shot glasses over to Andrei with his fingernail. "Remember how your father tried to force you to read *The War of the Worlds*, and you didn't want to? How furious you were—you stuck that cursed book under the sofa so you could get back to your illustrated *Baron Munchausen* . . . Wells bored you, he made you feel sick, you didn't understand why the hell you had to read him, you didn't want to know about him . . . But later you read that book twelve times, until you knew it by heart, you drew illustrations for it, and you even tried to write a sequel."

"So what?" Andrei said morosely.

"And that kind of thing happened to you time and again!" said the Mentor. "And it will happen again, more than once. You've just had understanding hammered into you, and it makes you feel sick, you don't understand what the hell you need it for, you don't want to know about it . . ." He picked up his shot glass. "Here's to the sequel!" he said.

Andrei stepped up to the table, and he took his shot glass, and he raised it to his lips, feeling the usual sense of relief as all his dismal doubts were dispersed yet again, and a new glimmer of light appeared somewhere up ahead in the darkness that had seemed impenetrable, and now he was supposed to drink up, and briskly slam the empty glass down onto the table, and say something bright and cheerful, and spring into action, but just at that moment some third character, who previously had always remained silent—he must have been sleeping, or lying around drunk, or he simply couldn't give a damn—suddenly snickered and babbled, *"Doo de doo de doo de doo!"*

Andrei splashed the cognac onto the floor, put the shot glass down on the tray, stuck his hands in his pockets, and said, "But there's something I still don't understand, Mentor . . . Drink, drink, enjoy it, I'm not in the mood." He couldn't look at that ruddy face anymore. He turned away and went over to the window again. "You're too much of a yes-man, Mr. Mentor. You're Voronin number two, my yellow, rubbery conscience, a used condom . . . *Everything's fine with you, Voronin, everything's just great, my dear friend.* The important thing is that we're safe and sound, and all the others can go croak. If there isn't enough food, I'll just shoot Katzman, eh? All fine and dandy!"

The door creaked behind him. He looked around. The room was empty. And the shot glasses were empty, and the flask was empty, and his chest felt empty, as if something large that was always there had been cut out of it. Maybe a tumor. Maybe his heart . . .

Already growing accustomed to this new sensation, Andrei walked over to the colonel's bed, took the belt down off the nail, girded it on real good and tight, and shifted the holster around onto his stomach.

"A keepsake," he told the snow-white pillow in a loud voice.

PART VI

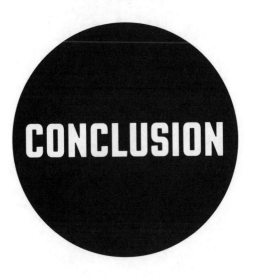

CONCLUSION

The sun was at its zenith. Its disk, copper colored through the dust, hung at the center of a dirty white sky, and his misshapen shadow writhed and bristled right under the soles of his shoes, sometimes gray and blurred, sometimes suddenly seeming to come alive, acquiring sharply defined outlines and flooding with blackness—and then it was especially ugly. There wasn't even a hint of any road here—there was bumpy, yellow-gray clay, cracked and dead, as hard as stone, so naked it was quite impossible to understand how there could be so much dust everywhere.

The wind, thank God, was blowing at his back. Somewhere far behind him it had sucked up countless tons of this abominable, incandescent powder and was dragging it with obtuse stubbornness along this sunbaked ledge squeezed in between the Abyss and the Yellow Wall, sometimes flinging it in swirling protuberances right up to the sky, sometimes spinning it into lithe, flirtatious, swan-necked dust devils, or sometimes simply tumbling it along in a billowing wave, and then, suddenly enraged, it would fling this fine, prickly flour against his back and into his hair, hurling it furiously at the sweat-soaked nape of his neck, lashing his hands and ears with it, filling his pockets with it, pouring it in behind his collar . . .

There was nothing here; there hadn't been anything here for a long time. Maybe never. Sun, clay, wind. Only occasionally, swirling and skipping like some antic jester, the prickly skeleton of a bush would go hurtling by, torn out by the roots at some spot lying God only knew how far behind him. Not a drop of water, not a single sign of life. Nothing but dust, dust, dust, dust . . .

Every now and again the clay under his feet disappeared and a covering of crumbled stone began. Everything here was as scorching hot as in hell. Sometimes on the right, sometimes on the left, gigantic, craggy fragments of cliffs peered out of the clouds of swirling dust—looking as gray as if they had been sprinkled with flour. The wind and heat had given them incredibly strange and astonishing forms, and the way they appeared and then disappeared again, like ghosts, was frightening, as if they were playing a crags' game of hide-and-go-seek. And the crumbled stone he walked over kept getting coarser and coarser, until suddenly the deposit ended and the clay rang under his feet again.

The stones behaved very badly. They squirmed out from under his feet or did their damnedest to pierce as deeply as possible into the soles of his shoes, to pierce through them into his living body. The clay behaved a bit more decently. But it still tried every trick it knew. It suddenly bulged up into bald mounds, or out of the blue produced idiotic inclines; it parted to form deep, steep-sided ravines, on the bottom of which the stagnant heat of millennia made it impossible to breathe . . . It played its own game too, its own clay version of "statues," inventing tricky metamorphoses within the limits of its own clayey imagination. Everything here played its own game. But everything played on the same side . . .

"Hey, Andrei!" Izya called hoarsely. *"Andriukhaaa!"*

"What do you want?" Andrei asked over his shoulder, and stopped. Wobbling about on its loose little wheels, the cart ran on by inertia and hit him on the back of his knees.

"Look!" Izya was standing about ten paces behind Andrei, holding out his hand to show him something.

"What is it?" asked Andrei, not particularly interested.

Izya laid into his harness and trundled his cart toward Andrei, without lowering his hand. Andrei watched him as he approached—a terrible sight, with his beard hanging down over his chest and his hair, gray with dust, standing up on end, in an unbelievably ragged jacket, with his wet, hairy body showing through the holes. The fringe of his trousers barely covered his knees, and his right shoe was gaping wide open, as if it were begging to be fed, exposing a set of dirty toes with broken, black nails . . . A luminary of the spirit. A priest and apostle of the eternal temple of culture . . .

"A comb!" Izya proclaimed triumphantly when he got close.

It was the very cheapest kind of comb—plastic, with broken teeth—not even a comb, really, more a fragment of a comb, and at the point where it was broken off, it was still possible to make out some kind of Soviet Industrial Standard number, but the plastic had been bleached by many decades of the sun's heat and ferociously corroded by a scab of dust.

"There now," said Andrei, "and you keep harping on: no one before us, no one before us."

"That's not what I harp on about at all," Izya said amicably. "Why don't we sit down for a while, eh?"

"OK then, let's sit," Andrei agreed without any enthusiasm, and Izya instantly plumped his backside down on the ground, without even taking off his harness, and started stuffing the fragment of comb into his breast pocket.

Andrei set his cart crosswind, took off his harness, and sat down, leaning his back and his head against the hot canisters. Immediately there was noticeably less wind, but now the naked clay burned his buttocks cruelly through the old, worn fabric.

"Where's this reservoir of yours?" he said derisively. "Windbag."

"Keep on looking!" Izya replied. "It's got to be there!"

"What's that supposed to mean?"

"It's this joke, about a merchant," Izya gladly explained. "A certain merchant went to a bawdy house—"

"Here we go again!" said Andrei. "Still yammering on about that? There's no way to cool you off, Katzman, I swear to God . . ."

"I can't afford to cool off," Izya explained. "I've got to be ready at the very first opportunity."

"The two of us are going to croak here," said Andrei.

"God forbid! Don't even think about it, don't even imagine it."

"I don't think about it," said Andrei.

It was true. The thought of death—which was inevitable, of course—entered his head only very rarely now. Either the cutting edge of this sense of doom had already been completely blunted, or his flesh was so desiccated and exhausted that it had given up yelling and howling, and now only croaked faintly somewhere on the threshold of audibility . . . Or perhaps quantity had finally been transformed into quality, and he had begun to be affected by the presence of Izya, with his almost unnatural indifference to death, which constantly circled around them, sometimes moving in right up close, then suddenly moving away again, but never letting them out of its sight . . . Whatever way it was, for many days now, if Andrei did start talking about the inevitable end, it was only to convince himself again and again of his growing indifference to it.

"What did you say?" Andrei asked.

"I said: the important thing is, don't you be afraid of croaking here."

"Ah, you've told me that a hundred times already. I haven't been afraid for ages, and you just keep yammering on."

"Well, that's good," Izya said peaceably. He stretched out his legs. "What could I tie this sole up with?" he inquired profoundly. "It's about to fall off in the very next increment of time."

"Cut off the end of the harness there and tie it up with that . . . Shall I give you a knife?"

Izya contemplated his protruding toes for a while. "Never mind," he said eventually. "Later, when it completely comes off . . . Maybe we could take a little nip?"

"Hands and feet too cold to jig," Andrei said, and immediately remembered Uncle Yura. It was hard to remember Uncle Yura now. He was from another life.

"Maybe we should take a swig?" Izya joined in exuberantly, glancing searchingly into Andrei's eyes.

"Screw you!" Andrei said with relish. "Know what water you can swig? That water you read about somewhere. You lied to me about the reservoir, right?"

Just as he expected, Izya immediately blew his top. "Go to hell! Who do you think I am—your nanny?"

"Well, your manuscript lied, then."

"Fool," Izya said contemptuously. "Manuscripts don't lie. They're not books. You just have to know how to read them."

"Well, you don't know how to read them, then."

Izya merely glanced at him and instantly started fidgeting about, getting up. "There'll be all sorts of shit here . . ." he muttered. "Come on, get up! You want a reservoir? Then stop sitting around here . . . get up, I tell you!"

The wind exulted, lashing Andrei's ears with prickles, and joyfully started swirling dust around in circles above the bald clay, like a playful dog, but the clay moved sluggishly toward him, behaving docilely for a while, as if it were gathering its strength, and then started tilting up into an incline.

If I could just finally figure out where the hell I'm rushing so fast, thought Andrei. All my life I've been rushing somewhere— like a stupid fool, I just can't stay still . . . And the worst thing is, there's no meaning to it any longer. There always used to be some kind of meaning. Even if it was absolutely paltry, maybe even totally screwy, but even so, whenever I was getting beaten, let's say on the face, I could always tell myself: it's OK, it's in the name of . . . it's the struggle . . .

"Everything in the world is worth no more than shit," Izya had said. (It was in the Crystal Palace; they'd just eaten chicken, pressure-roasted, and they were lying on mattresses of bright synthetic material on the edge of a pool with transparent, backlit water.) "Everything in the world is worth no more than shit," said Izya, picking his teeth with a well-washed finger. "All those plowmen of yours, all those lathe operators, all those blooming mills, cracking plants, branched varieties of wheat, lasers and masers. All that is shit, manure. It all passes away. Either it simply passes away without a trace, forever, or it passes away because it changes. All this only seems important because the majority believes it's important. And the majority only believes it's important because its goal is to stuff its belly and gratify its flesh with absolutely as little effort as possible. But if you think about it, who gives a damn about the majority? I personally have nothing against it—to some extent I am the majority. But I'm not interested in the majority. The history of the majority has a beginning and an end. At the beginning the majority eats what it's given. And at the end it spends its entire life trying to solve the problem of choice. What special, tasty sort of item can I choose to eat? Something I haven't eaten before?"

"Well, that's still a pretty long way off," Andrei said.

"Not as far off as you imagine," Izya objected. "And even if it is a long way off, that's not the point. The main thing is, there's a beginning and there's an end . . ."

"Everything that has a beginning has an end too," Andrei said.

"Right, right," Izya said impatiently. "But I'm talking about the magnitudes of history, not the magnitudes of the universe. The history of the majority has an end, but the history of the minority will only come to an end together with the universe."

"You're a lousy elitist," Andrei told him lazily, before getting up off his mat and plunking into the pool. He swam for a long time, snorting in the cool water and diving right down to the bottom, where the water was icy cold, greedily gulping it there, like a fish . . .

No, of course I didn't gulp it. Now I'd gulp it. My God, how I'd gulp it! I'd gulp down the entire pool, I wouldn't leave any for Izya—he can go search for his reservoir . . .

Over on the right, some kind of ruins peeped out from behind the swirling yellowish-gray clouds—a blank, half-collapsed wall, spiky with dust-covered plants, the remains of a clumsy quadrangular tower.

"There now, see," Andrei said, stopping. "And you say: no one before us . . ."

"Ah, I never said that, you great lunkhead!" Izya wheezed. "I said—"

"Listen, maybe the reservoir's here?"

"It very easily could be," said Izya.

"Let's go and take a look."

They both slipped out of their harnesses and trudged over to the ruins.

"Ha!" said Izya. "A Norman fortress! Ninth century . . ."

"Water, look for water," said Andrei.

"Ah, to hell with your water!" Izya said angrily. His eyes opened wide and started bulging, and with a long-forgotten gesture he reached under his beard to search for his wart. "Normans . . ." he muttered. "Well, well . . . I wonder how they lured them here?"

Catching their tattered rags on prickles, they forced their way through a gap in the wall and found themselves in a calm spot. Standing there in the smooth, quadrangular space was a low building with a collapsed roof.

"The union of the sword and wrath . . ." Izya muttered, hurrying toward the doorway. "Or maybe I don't understand a damn thing about what that union is . . . Where would a sword come from here? How can you make sense of something like that?"

Inside the building the devastation was total, total and ancient. Centuries old. The collapsed roof timbers had mingled with fragments of rotted boards—the remains of a long table that ran the full length of the building. Everything was dusty, crumbling, and decayed, and the wall on the left was lined with equally dusty and decayed benches. Still muttering, Izya waded in to rummage through this heap of decay, and Andrei went out and walked around the building. He very soon came across what had once been a reservoir—an immense round pit lined with stone slabs. The slabs were as dry as the desert now, but there was no doubt that there had been water here at one time: the clay at the edge of the pit was as hard as cement, and it preserved the deep imprints of booted feet and dogs' paws. Things are looking bad, thought Andrei. The old terror clutched his heart and then immediately released its grip: at the far end of the pit the broad, shaggy leaves of a "ginseng" plant were flattened out on the clay in a star shape. Andrei jogged around the pit toward them, feeling for the knife in his pocket on the way.

For several minutes, panting and streaming with sweat, he scrabbled furiously at the rock-hard clay with his knife and his nails, raked out the crumbs and scrabbled again, and then, grabbing hold of the thick stock of the root with both hands, he pulled hard, but cautiously—God forbid that the root should break off somewhere in the middle.

The root was a big one, about seventy centimeters long and as thick as a fist—white, clean, and glossy. Pressing it against his cheek with both hands, Andrei set off back to Izya, but along the way he gave in, sank his teeth into the succulent, crunchy flesh, and started chewing delightedly, relishing it, trying not to hurry, trying to chew as thoroughly as possible, so as not to lose even a single drop of this delightful minty bitterness that made his mouth and his entire body feel as fresh and cool as a forest in the morning, and cleared his head, so that he no longer feared anything, and he could move mountains . . .

Then they sat in the doorway of the building, joyfully gnawing and crunching and champing, merrily winking at each other with their mouths full, and the wind howled disappointedly over their heads and couldn't reach them. They'd deceived it again; they hadn't allowed it to toy with their bones on the bald clay. Now they could match their strength against it one more time.

They drank two swallows each from a hot canister, harnessed themselves into their carts, and strode on. And it was easy to walk now; Izya didn't drop behind anymore but stepped out beside Andrei, with the half-detached sole of his shoe slapping.

"By the way, I spotted another little plant there," Andrei said. "A small one. On the way back . . ."

"That's a mistake," said Izya. "We should have eaten it."

"Didn't you get enough?"

"Why let good stuff go to waste?"

"It won't go to waste," said Andrei. "It'll come in useful for the return journey."

"There's not going to be any return journey."

"That's something no one knows, brother," said Andrei. "Why don't you just tell me this: Is there still going to be water?"

Izya threw his head back and looked up at the sun. "At the zenith," he announced. "Or almost at the zenith. What do you think, Mr. Astronomer?"

"Looks like it."

"The most interesting part will start soon," said Izya.

"What could be so interesting about it? So, we pass through the zero point. Then we start walking toward the Anticity . . ."

"How do you know that?"

"About the Anticity?"

"No. Why do you think we'll just simply pass through and walk on?"

"I'm not thinking a damned thing about it," said Andrei. "I'm thinking about water."

"Oh Lord, give me strength! The zero point is the beginning of the world, do you understand? And he talks about water!"

Andrei didn't reply. The ascent of yet another hillock had begun; walking had become hard, and the harness was cutting into his shoulders. That "ginseng" is great, he thought. How come we know about it? Did Pak tell us? I think that was it—Ah, no! Skank brought a few roots into camp one day and started eating them, and the soldiers took them away from her and tried them themselves. Yes. They were all strutting and swaggering afterward, and they tumbled Skank all night long . . . And later Pak said that this "ginseng," like the real ginseng, is only found very rarely. It grows in places where there used to be water, and it's really good when your energy's low. Only it's impossible to store it—you have to eat it immediately. Because after an hour or even less, the root withers and becomes almost poisonous . . . There was a lot of this "ginseng" near the Pavilion, a whole truck farm of it . . . That was where we stuffed ourselves with it, and all Izya's sores disappeared overnight. It was good at the Pavilion. And all the time there Izya kept pontificating about the edifice of culture . . .

"All the rest is just the scaffolding around the wall of the temple," he had said. "All the best things that humankind has invented in a hundred thousand years, all the important things it has understood and achieved through the power of thought, go into that temple. Through all the millennia of its history, howling, starving, lapsing into slavery and rebelling, guzzling and copulating, humanity carries this temple along on the turbid crest of its wave, without even suspecting it. Sometimes it suddenly notices this temple on its back and stumbles, and then it starts either taking the temple apart brick by brick or frenziedly worshipping it, or building a different temple next to it in order to vilify it, but humankind never really understands what it's dealing with, and after it despairs of making use of the temple in some way or other, it's soon distracted by its own so-called vital needs. It starts dividing up all over again something that has already been divided up thirty-three times, crucifying somebody, glorifying somebody—but the temple just carries on growing and growing from century to century, from millennium to millennium, and it's impossible either to destroy it or to ultimately abase it.

"The most amusing thing," said Izya, "is that every little brick of this temple, every eternal book, every eternal melody, every unique architectural silhouette, bears within itself the compressed experience of this humankind, its thoughts and thoughts about it, ideas about the goals and contradictions of its existence; that no matter how separate it might seem from all the vital interests of this herd of swine, at the same time it is always inseparable from this herd and inconceivable without it . . .

"And another amusing thing," Izya said, "is that no one actually builds this temple consciously . . . It can't be planned out in advance on paper or in the brain of some genius; it grows of its own accord, unerringly absorbing all the best that human history produces.

"Maybe you think," Izya asked acidly, "that the most exceptional builders of this temple aren't swine? Lord Almighty, what hideous swine they are sometimes! The thief and scoundrel Benvenuto Cellini, the hopeless drunk Hemingway, the pederast Tchaikovsky, the schizophrenic and black reactionary Dostoyevsky, the thief and gallows bird François Villon . . . My God, the decent people among them are the rare ones! But like the coral polyps, they know not what they do. And neither does the whole of humankind. Generation after generation they guzzle, wallow in pleasure, ravage, kill, turn up their toes—and before you know it an entire coral atoll has sprung up, and how beautiful it is! And how enduring!"

"Well OK then," Andrei said to him. "So it's a temple. The only imperishable embodiment of value. OK. But then, what have we all got to do with this? What have I got to do with this?"

"Stop!" said Izya, grabbing his harness. "Wait. The stones."

Yes, the stones here were certainly convenient—rounded and flat, like solidified cowpats.

"Are we going to build yet another temple?" Andrei asked with a chuckle. He took off his harness, stepped to one side, and picked up the nearest stone. The stone was exactly the kind required for a foundation—lumpy and prickly underneath, and smooth on the top, worn down by the dust and the wind. Andrei set it on a fairly level deposit of small pieces of crumbled stone, ground it in with movements of his shoulders as deeply and firmly as he could, and went to get another one.

While he was laying out the foundation he felt something like satisfaction: after all, this was work, wasn't it, not meaningless movements of the legs but actions performed with a definite goal in mind? The goal could be contested; Izya could be declared a psycho and a crank (which, of course, he was) . . . But working like this, stone after stone, Andrei could lay out, as evenly as possible, the platform for a foundation.

Izya panted and grunted beside him, rolling the largest stones, stumbled, and tore the sole completely off his shoe, and when the foundation was ready, he galloped to his cart and extracted another copy of his *Guidebook* from under the rags.

When, at the Crystal Palace, they had finally realized and almost believed that they would never meet anyone again on the journey north, Izya had sat down at a typewriter and dashed off at supernatural speed *A Guidebook to the Crazy World.* Then he had personally reproduced this *Guidebook* on a bizarre copying machine (in the Crystal Palace they had all sorts of different amazing machines); he had personally sealed all fifty copies in envelopes of a strange, transparent, and very strong material that was called "polyethylene film" and loaded up his cart right to the top, leaving only just enough room for a sack of rusks . . . And now he only had about ten, or maybe even fewer, of these envelopes left.

"How many of them do you still have?" asked Andrei.

Setting an envelope at the center of the foundation, Izya replied absentmindedly, "Damned if I know . . . Not many. Give me some stones."

Again they started dragging stones, and soon a pyramid a meter and a half tall had sprung up over the envelope. It looked rather strange in this desolate landscape, but to make it look even stranger still, Izya poured poisonous red paint over the stones from a huge tube that he had found in the storeroom under the Tower. Then he moved away to his cart, sat down, and started binding the detached sole of his shoe with a piece of string. While he was doing it, he kept glancing at his pyramid, and the doubt and uncertainty in his face were gradually replaced by a look of satisfaction and burgeoning pride.

"Eh?" he said to Andrei, completely puffed up with conceit at this stage. "Not even an absolute fool would walk past it—he'd realize it had a purpose."

"Uh-huh," said Andrei, squatting down beside Izya. "And a fat lot of good it'll do you when this pyramid is excavated by some absolute fool."

"Never mind, never mind," Izya growled. "A fool is a rational creature too. If he doesn't understand, he'll tell others about it . . ." He suddenly brightened up. "Take myths, for instance! As we know, fools are the overwhelming majority, which means that the witness to any interesting event has generally been a fool. Ergo: a myth is a description of a real event as perceived by a fool and refined by a poet. Eh?"

Andrei didn't answer. He was looking at the pyramid. The wind cautiously crept up to it, uncertainly stirred the dust around it, whistled feebly between the stones, and Andrei suddenly

pictured very clearly to himself the countless numbers of kilometers left behind them, and the thin dotted line of pyramids
like this, stretching across those kilometers, abandoned to the
wind and to time . . . And he also pictured a traveler, almost a
desiccated mummy, crawling up to this pyramid on his hands
and knees, dying of hunger and thirst . . . how frantically, straining every last ounce of strength, he tugs out these stones and
thrusts them aside, breaking his nails, and his inflamed imagination is already painting him a picture of a secret cache of food
and water, there under the stones . . . Andrei let out a hysterical
snigger. At that moment I'd definitely shoot myself. It's not possible to survive something like that . . .

"What's wrong with you?" Izya asked suspiciously.

"Nothing, nothing, everything's fine," Andrei said, and got up.

Izya got up too, and looked at the pyramid critically for a
while. "There's nothing funny about it!" he declared, and stamped
the foot that was bound with shaggy string. "It will do for a start,"
he declared. "Shall we go?"

"Yes, let's go."

Andrei harnessed himself to his cart, but Izya couldn't resist
the temptation and walked around his pyramid once again. He
was obviously imagining something, pictures of some kind, and
these pictures were flattering to his inner spirit; he smiled stealthily, rubbing his hands together and panting noisily into his beard.

"Well, you're a real sight!" Andrei said, unable to stop himself. "Just like a toad. You've dumped a load of eggs, and now
you're totally stupefied with pride. Or like a keta salmon."

"You watch your mouth!" said Izya, threading his arms into
the harness. "The keta dies after that business."

"Precisely," said Andrei.

"So watch your mouth!" Izya said menacingly, and they
moved on.

Then Izya suddenly asked, "Have you ever eaten keta?"

"Tons of it," said Andrei. "D'you know how great it is with
vodka? Or on a sandwich with tea . . . Why?"

"I just wondered," said Izya. "But my daughters have never tried it."

"Daughters?" Andrei exclaimed in surprise. "You have daughters?"

"Three of them," said Izya. "And not one of them knows what a keta salmon is. I explained to them that keta and sturgeon are extinct fish. Like the ichthyosaurs. And they'll tell their children the same thing about herring . . ."

He said something else, but Andrei was too stunned to listen. Would you ever believe it! Three daughters. Izya has three daughters! I've known him for six years and nothing like that ever even occurred to me. So then how come he took the plunge and decided to come here? Way to go, Izya . . . What damned crazy people there are in the world . . . But no, guys, he thought. It's all right, it all fits: no normal person will ever reach this pyramid. Once any normal person has reached the Crystal Palace, he'll just stay there for the rest of his life. I saw them there, those normal people . . . You can't tell their faces from their asses . . . No, guys, if anyone does reach this pyramid, it can only be some kind of Izya number two . . . And how eagerly he'll dig up this pyramid and rip open the envelope, and then immediately forget about everything—he'll die here, still reading . . . But then, on the other hand, I ended up here, didn't I? For what? It was good in the Tower. It was even better in the Pavilion. And in the Crystal Palace . . . I've never lived like I did in the Crystal Palace and I never will again . . . So all right . . . It's Izya. He's got an awl up his ass and he can't sit still anywhere. But if Izya hadn't been with me, would I have left that place or stayed? That's the question!

"Why do we have to go forward?" Izya asked at the Plantation, and the little blackface girls, with smooth skin and big tits, sat nearby and meekly listened to us. "Why, after all, do we have to go forward, regardless of everything?" Izya pontificated, absentmindedly stroking the nearest one on her satin-smooth knee. "Why, because behind us there is either death, or boredom, which is also death. That simple observation must be enough for you, surely? After all, we're the first, do you understand that? After all, not a single person has yet passed right through this world from one end to the other: from the jungles and the swamps all the way to the zero point . . . And maybe this whole bag of tricks was only set up in order to find a man like that? So that he would go the whole way?"

"What for?" Andrei asked morosely.

"How should I know?" Izya exclaimed indignantly. "But what is the temple being built for? It's obvious that the temple is the only goal in sight, but asking what it's for isn't the correct question. Man has to have a goal, he can't manage without a goal, that's what he was given reason for. If he doesn't have a goal, he invents one."

"And you've invented yours," said Andrei. "You have to go all the way. What sort of goal is that?"

"I didn't invent it," said Izya. "It's my unique one and only. I've got nothing to choose from. It's either the goal or aimlessness—that's the way things are for you and me."

"But why do you keep hammering that temple of yours into my head?" Andrei asked. "What has your temple got to do with all this?"

"It has a lot to do with it," Izya parried keenly, as if this was exactly what he'd been waiting for. "The temple, my dear Andriushka, is not only eternal books, not only eternal music. Otherwise they would only have started building the temple after Gutenberg or, as you were taught, after Ivan Fyodorov. No, my dear man, the temple is also built out of deeds. If you like, the temple is cemented together by deeds; it is held up by them, it rests on them. It all began with deeds. First the deed, then the legend, and all the rest only comes afterward. Naturally, what is meant here is the exceptional deed, one that exceeds the normal bounds, inexplicable, if you like. That's what the temple began with—the significant deed!"

"The heroic deed, in short," Andrei observed, chuckling derisively.

"Well, so be it, let's call it heroic," Izya agreed condescendingly."

"In other words, you turn out to be a hero," said Andrei. "In other words, you long to be a hero. Sinbad the Sailor and the mighty Ulysses . . ."

"And you're a stupid fool," said Izya. He said it affectionately, without the slightest offense intended. "I assure you, my friend, that Ulysses didn't long to be a hero. He simply *was* a hero. That was his nature. He couldn't be any other way. You can't eat shit—it makes you puke, and it made him feel sick being a little king in his seedy little Ithaca. I can see that you pity me, you know: what a crank, a total screwball . . . I can see that. But there's no need for you to pity me. Because I know with absolute certainty that the temple is being built, that nothing else serious is happening in history apart from this, and there's only one purpose in my life—to protect that temple and increase its wealth. Of course, I'm not Homer and I'm not Pushkin; I won't get to put a brick in the wall. But I am Katzman. And that temple is in me, and that means I'm a part of the temple, it means that with my recognition of myself the temple has expanded by one more human soul. And that's already wonderful. Even if I don't add a single scrap to the wall . . . Although I'll try to add one, you can be quite sure of that. It will definitely be a very small speck—and, even worse, in time that speck might simply fall off, it won't be any use to the temple, but in any case I know that the temple was in me, and I also lent it strength . . ."

"I don't understand any of this," said Andrei. "Your explanation is too confused. Some kind of religion: temple, spirit . . ."

"Well, of course," said Izya, "since it's not a bottle of vodka and it's not a twin mattress, it's got to be religion. What are you getting bristly about? You're the one who's been nagging me about how you've lost the ground under your feet and you're suspended in empty space . . . And that's right, you are. That's what had to happen to you. It happens to any man who thinks even the tiniest little bit . . . Well, I'm giving you some ground.

The most solid ground there can ever be. Plant both feet on it and stand there, if you want, and if you don't, then bug off! But don't bellyache afterward!"

"You're not presenting me with ground to stand on," said Andrei, "you're fobbing me off with some kind of amorphous cloud! Well, OK. Let's say I've understood all about this temple of yours. Only what good is that to me? I'm not good enough to be one of the builders of your temple—I'm no Homer, either, to put it mildly . . . But you at least have the temple in your soul, you can't live without it—I can see the way you run around the world like a little puppy, avidly sniffing at everything, and whatever you come across, you lick it or take a bite to see how it tastes! I see the way you read. You can read twenty-four hours a day . . . and you actually remember everything too . . . But I can't do any of that. I like to read, but in moderation, after all. I love listening to music. But not twenty-four hours a day either! And my memory's absolutely ordinary—I can't possibly enrich it with all the treasures that mankind has accumulated . . . Even if I never did anything else—I still couldn't. With me it flies in one ear and out the other. So now what good is your temple to me?"

"Well that's true, that's right," said Izya. "I won't argue. The temple's not for everyone . . . I won't deny that it's the heritage of the minority, a matter of human nature . . . But you listen, and I'll tell you the way I see it. The temple has"—Izya started counting on his fingers—"builders. Those are the ones who construct it. And then, let's say . . . goddammit, I can't find the right word, religious terminology keeps coming to mind . . . Well, all right. Let's call them priests. They're the ones who bear it within themselves. The ones through whose souls it grows and in whose souls it exists . . . And there are consumers—those who, so to speak, partake of it . . . So then Pushkin is a builder. I'm a priest. And you're a consumer . . . Don't pull that face, you fool! That's really great! After all, without a consumer, the temple wouldn't have any human meaning. Just think how lucky you are, you blockhead! After all, it takes years and years of special processing, brainwashing, and supremely cunning systems of deception to provoke you, the consumer, into attempting to destroy the temple . . . And there's no way the kind of consumer you've become now can be pushed into that sort of thing, except maybe under threat of death! Just think, you rattlebrain: the ones like you are an extremely small minority too! Give the majority the wink, give them permission, and off they'll go, whooping and hollering to smash everything with crowbars, burn everything to the ground with blazing torches . . . that has already happened, many times over! And it will probably happen again, time after time . . . And you complain! But if it is possible at all to ask, what is the temple for? there can only be one answer: for you!"

"Andriukha!" Izya called in that familiar, obnoxious voice. "Maybe we should grab a drink?"

They were standing right on the very top of a massive hillock. On the left, the side where the Cliff was, everything was concealed behind a murky veil of dust hurtling along at furious speed, but on the right the air had cleared for some reason, and they could see the Yellow Wall—not smooth and even, the way it was within the limits of the City, but completely covered in mighty folds and wrinkles, like the root of some monstrous tree. Ahead of them at the bottom of the Wall, a field of white stone began—not loose chips but solid stone, a single, monolithic mass—and this field of stone extended as far as the eye could see, and swaying above it half a kilometer away from the hillock were two tall, scrawny dust devils—one yellow and the other black . . .

"This is something new," Andrei said, screwing up his eyes. "Look, solid stone."

"Eh? Yes, I suppose so . . . Listen, let's have a glass of water— it's been four hours already."

"Yes," Andrei agreed. "Only let's go down first."

They walked down from the hillock and slipped out of their harnesses, and Andrei lugged a red-hot canister out of his cart. The canister caught on the belt of his automatic, then on the sack with the broken remains of the rusks, but Andrei dragged it out anyway, squeezed it between his knees, and opened it. Izya skipped around beside him, holding two plastic mugs at the ready.

"Get the salt," said Andrei.

Izya instantly stopped skipping. "Oh, come on . . ." he whined. "Why? Let's just down it . . ."

"You're not getting any without salt," Andrei said wearily.

"Then let's do it like this," said Izya, struck by an inspired idea. He had already put down the mugs on a rock and was rummaging in his cart. "Let's say I eat my salt and then wash it down with the water."

"Oh God," said Andrei, astounded. "OK then, do it that way." He half-filled the two mugs with hot water that had a metallic smell, took the pack of salt from Izya, and said, "Give me your tongue."

He sprinkled a pinch of salt on Izya's thick, furry tongue and watched Izya wince and choke, reaching out greedily for his mug, then he salted his own water and started drinking it in miserly little sips, without taking any pleasure in it, as if it were medicine.

"Good!" Izya said with a croak. "Only not enough. Eh?"

Andrei nodded. The water he had drunk immediately emerged as sweat, and everything in his mouth remained the same as it had been, without even the slightest feeling of relief. He lifted up the canister, figuring something out. There'd probably be enough for a couple of days, and then . . . And then something else will turn up, he told himself fiercely. The Experiment is the Experiment. They won't let you live, but they won't let you croak either . . . He cast a glance at the white plateau that stretched out ahead of them, radiating heat, bit on his dry lip, and started setting the canister back in the cart. Izya had squatted down and was binding up the sole of his shoe again.

"You know," Izya panted, "this really is a strange kind of place. Actually I can't recall anything like it at all." He glanced at the sun, shading his eyes with his hand. "At the zenith," he said. "I swear to God, at the zenith. Something's going to happen . . .

Oh, dump that damned lump of iron, will you, what are you fumbling with that for?"

Andrei carefully arranged the automatic beside the canister. "Without that lump of iron the two of us would have left our bones behind the Pavilion," he reminded Izya.

"That was behind the Pavilion!" Izya retorted. "Since then we've been walking for more than four weeks and we haven't even seen a fly."

"All right," said Andrei. "You don't have to carry it . . . Let's go."

The stone plateau turned out to be amazingly smooth. The carts rolled over it as if it were asphalt, with the wheels squeaking. But the heat became even more terrible. The white stone flung the sun's rays back up, and now there was no escape for their eyes. Their feet burned as if they weren't wearing any shoes at all, and strangely enough, there was as much dust as ever. If we don't snuff it here, Andrei thought, then we'll live forever. He walked with his eyes screwed almost closed, and then closed them completely. That made it a bit easier. This is the way I'm going to walk, he thought. And I'll open my eyes, let's say, every twenty steps. Or thirty . . . Take a quick look and move on . . .

The basement of the Tower had been floored with very similar white stone. Only there it had been cool and dark, and there were lots of thick cardboard boxes standing along the walls, mysteriously full of various hardware items. There were nails, screws, bolts of every possible size, cans of different kinds of glue and paint, bottles of different-colored varnishes, carpentry and machine-work tools, ball bearings wrapped in oilpaper . . . They hadn't found anything edible, but in the corner a short, rusty pipe protruded from the wall, with a thin trickle of cold, incredibly delicious water flowing out of it and disappearing under the ground . . .

"Everything in your system is good," Andrei had said, setting his mug under the trickle for the twentieth time. "There's just one thing I don't like. I don't like it when people are divided into the important and the unimportant. It's not right. It's abhorrent. There's the temple, and there's the inane rabble swarming around it. 'Man is a poor soul, burdened with a corpse.' Even if that really is true, it's still not right. The whole damn system should be changed."

"And am I saying it shouldn't?" said Izya. "Of course it would be a good thing to change that order of things. Only how? So far all attempts to change the situation and level out the human playing field and set everyone on the same level, in order to make everything right and just—all these attempts have ended in the demolition of the temple so that it wouldn't tower over everyone, and the severing of any heads that jutted up above the general level. And that's all. And then the foul-smelling pyramid of the new political elite started growing over the leveled field, expanding as rapidly as a cancerous tumor, even more repulsive than the old one. And so far, you know, no other ways have been invented. Of course, all these excesses haven't altered the course of history and they haven't been able to completely destroy the temple, but plenty of brilliant heads have been chopped off."

"I know," said Andrei. "But even so. Even so, it's vile. Any elite is odious."

"Oh, I beg your pardon!" Izya exclaimed. "Now, if you said, 'Any elite that controls the lives and fates of other people is odious,' then I'd agree with you. But an elite in itself, an elite for itself—who does that interfere with? It irritates people; it makes them furious, it drives them wild!—that's a different matter, but then, after all, irritating people is one of its functions . . . And complete equality is a stagnant swamp. We should thank old Mother Nature that such a thing as complete equality is impossible . . . Don't get me wrong, Andrei, I'm not proposing a system for rearranging the world. I don't know any system like that, and I don't believe it exists. Too many different kinds of systems have been tried, and basically everything has remained the way it was . . . All I'm offering you is a goal for existence . . . dammit, I'm not even offering it, you've confused me. I've discovered this goal in myself and for myself—the goal of my existence, do you understand me? Of my existence and the existence of others like me . . . After all, I'm only talking to you about it and talking to you at this time because I felt sorry for you—I can see a man who is ready, who has burned everything that he used to worship, and now he doesn't know what to worship. And you can't live without worshipping; you imbibed that with your mother's milk: the need to worship something or someone. They beat it into your head once and for all that if there's no idea that's worth dying for, then it's not even worth living. And people like you, who've reached a final understanding, are capable of terrible things. A man can blow his brains out, or turn into a supernatural villain—a convinced villain, a principled, disinterested villain, do you understand? Or else even worse: he'll start taking revenge on the world because the world is the way it really is, and doesn't conform to some predetermined ideal or other. And another good thing about the idea of the temple, by the way, is that dying for it is positively counterindicated. You have to live for it. Live every day, with all your strength, at full throttle."

"Yes, I suppose so," said Andrei. "Probably that's the way it all is. But even so, this idea still isn't mine!"

Andrei stopped and took a tight grip on Izya's sleeve. Izya immediately opened his eyes and asked in a frightened voice, "What? What is it?"

"Shut up," Andrei said through his teeth.

There was something up ahead of them. Something was moving, not spinning around in a column, not trailing about just above the stone, but moving through all of that. Toward them.

"People," Izya said delightedly. "Listen, Andriukha, people!"

"Quiet, you jerk," Andrei said in a whisper.

He'd already realized that they were people. Or one person . . . No, it looked like two. Standing there. They'd probably noticed him and Izya too . . . Now he couldn't see a damned thing through the cursed dust again.

"There, you see!" Izya said in a triumphant whisper. "And you kept moaning: we're going to croak . . ."

Andrei cautiously took off his harness and backed toward his cart, keeping his eyes fixed on the indecipherable shadows ahead of them. *Dammit,* how many of them are there, after all? And how far is it to them from here? About a hundred meters, maybe? Or less? He found the automatic in the cart by touch, slid back the bolt, and said to Izya, "Move the carts together, lie down behind them. You can cover me if anything . . ."

He stuck the automatic in Izya's hands and slowly set off forward, without looking back, holding his hand on his holster. The visibility was abominable. He'll shoot me he thought, meaning Izya. Plant a bullet right in the back of my head . . .

Now he could make out that one of the others was also walking toward him—an indeterminate, lanky silhouette in the swirling dust. Does he have a gun or not? Here's the Anticity for you. Who could ever have thought it? Oh, I don't like the way he's holding his hand! Andrei cautiously unbuttoned his holster and took hold of the ribbed handle. His thumb automatically set itself on the safety catch. It's OK, everything will work out fine. It has to. The main thing is not to make any abrupt movements.

He pulled the pistol out of the holster. The pistol got caught on something. Suddenly he felt afraid. He tugged harder, then even harder, and then with all his strength. He clearly saw an abrupt movement by the man who was walking toward him (tall, tattered, exhausted, with a dirty beard right up to his eyes) . . . It's stupid, he thought, squeezing the trigger. There was a shot, there was the flash of a return shot, he thought there was a shout from Izya . . . and there was a blow to his chest that instantly extinguished the sun.

✦✦✦

"Well now, Andrei," the Mentor's voice said with a note of solemnity. "You have passed through the first circle."

The bulb under the green glass shade was lit, and in the circle of light a fresh copy of *Leningrad Pravda* was lying on the desk, with a large leading article entitled "The Love of Leningraders for Comrade Stalin Is Boundless." A radio was buzzing and muttering on a set of shelves behind him. Mom was rattling dishes in the kitchen and talking to the woman who shared the apartment. There was a smell of fried fish. In the enclosed yard outside the window little kids were squealing and kicking up a racket in a game of hide-and-go-seek. The damp autumn air came in through the small transom at the top of the window, which was wide open. Only a minute ago, all this had been completely different from the way it was now—far more ordinary and familiar. It had been without a future. Or rather, separate from the future.

Andrei aimlessly smoothed out the newspaper before he spoke. "The first? Why the first?"

"Because there are many more still to come," the Mentor's voice said.

Then Andrei got up, trying not to look in the direction the voice came from, and leaned his shoulder against the cupboard by the window. The black well shaft of the yard, weakly illuminated by the yellow rectangles of the windows, was below him and above him, and somewhere far above, in a sky that had already turned dark, Vega was shining. It was absolutely impossible to leave all this again and absolutely—even more!—impossible to stay here among all this. Now. After everything.

"Izya! Izya!" a woman's voice called stridently in the yard. "Izya, come home for supper already! Children, have you seen Izya?"

And the children's voices down below started shouting, "Izka! Katzman! Go on, your mom's calling you."

Tense in every muscle, Andrei stuck his face right up against the glass, peering into the darkness. But all he could see were indecipherable shadows darting between the banked-up stacks of wood on the wet, black bottom of the shaft.

AFTERWORD

BY BORIS STRUGATSKY

The idea for *The Doomed City* first came to us in March 1967, when the work on *Tale of the Troika* was going full steam ahead. It was at the Artists' and Writers' House in Golitsyno—in the evenings there we regularly took a stroll through the village before bed, lazily discussing our work, both current and forthcoming, and during one of these strolls we hit on a subject, which at the time we called *The New Apocalypse*. It is very difficult, probably even impossible at this stage, to reconstruct the image of the *City* that we painted for ourselves back then, in those bygone days. I suspect it was something drastically different from the final version of the world of the Experiment. Suffice it to say that another provisional title for the same novel turns up in our letters from the late 1960s: *My Brother and I*. Seemingly this novel was originally conceived as autobiographical to a significant degree.

We never worked so long and so painstakingly on any of our other works, either before or after. Three years was spent amassing, scrap by scrap, the episodes, the characters'

biographies, individual phrases and turns of speech; we invented
the City, its peculiarities, and the laws governing its existence,
as well as a cosmography, as authentic as we could possibly
make it, for this artificial world, and its history. It was genuinely delightful and fascinating work, but everything in this
world ends sometime, and in June 1969 we drew up the first
detailed plan and adopted the definitive title—*The Doomed City*.
This is the title of a famous painting by Roerich that had once
astounded us with its somber beauty and the sense of hopelessness emanating from it.

The draft of the novel was completed in six sessions (in all,
about seventy full working days) over a period of two and a quarter years. On May 27, 1972, we wrote in the final period, heaved
a sigh of relief, and stuffed the unusually thick file into the bookcase. Into the archive. For a long time. Forever. It was perfectly
obvious to us that the novel had absolutely no prospects.

I can't really say we had cherished any serious hopes earlier
either, when we were just beginning to work on it. Already in the
late 1960s, and even more so in the early '70s, it was clear that we
would not be able to publish this novel. Very probably never, but
certainly not during our lifetime. However, at the very beginning
we still had a rather optimistic idea of how future events would
develop. We imagined that after finishing the manuscript, we
would type up a clean copy and tote it (with an air of absolute
innocence) around to publishers. To lots of publishers. To lots of
various different publishers. It would be rejected, naturally, at all
these publishers, but first they would be certain to read it. And
at each publisher's office not just one person would read it but
several, in the usual way. And they would make copies, in the
usual way. And then give them to people whom they knew to
read. And then the novel would start to exist. The same way as
had happened more than once before—with *The Snail on the Slope*,
and with *Tale of the Troika*, and with *The Ugly Swans*. It would
be an illegal, silent, almost transparent existence, but existence
nonetheless—interaction between the work of literature and the

reader, the interaction without which there is no work of literature, and no literature in general.

But by mid-1972 this modest plan already looked impracti-
cal and even rather dangerous. The story of Vasily Grossman's
remarkable epic novel *Life and Fate*, the manuscript of which was
sent directly from the offices of the literary journal *Znamya* of
those days to the "organs," where it sank without a trace (after
all the searches and confiscations, only a single, solitary copy survived by a miracle; just a little longer and the novel would have
completely ceased to exist, as if it had never even existed at all!)—
we knew this story very well, and it served as a somber warning
to us. In times like that it was absolutely unwise even to take the
manuscript out of the house. Even giving it to people we knew
had become dangerous. And the very best thing to do, of course,
was to never even mention the book's existence—to play it safe.
And so we read the draft (out loud, in our home) only to our
very closest friends, and for many years everyone else who took
an interest remained convinced that "the Strugatskys *are* writing
a new novel, they've been writing it for ages, but they just can't
pull themselves together and finish it."

And after the summer of 1974, after the "Heifetz-Etkind case,"
after the predatory gaze of the "competent authorities" stopped
merely browsing through the general neighborhood and focused
right in on one of the coauthors, the situation became even more
threatening. A new Leningrad Case was clearly being put together
in Petersburg, which meant that in theory they could *come* at
any moment for anyone whose cover had been blown, and that
would have meant (apart from everything else) the end of the
novel, since it existed only as a single, solitary copy, and that
was lying in the bookcase, "in plain sight," so to speak. And so
in late 1974 the manuscript was hastily typed out in three copies
by this author (with an indispensable proofreading being carried
out at the same time) and then two copies were delivered, with
every possible precaution being observed, to reliable individuals—one Muscovite and one Leningrader. And in addition, these

individuals were selected as being, on the one hand, absolutely and unimpeachably honest, above even the very slightest suspicion, and, on the other hand, not obviously numbered among our closest friends, so that if things took a turn for the worse, no one ought to *come* to them. Thank God, everything turned out well and nothing untoward happened, but those two copies lay there, in their "special archives," until the end of the 1980s, when we finally managed to get *City* published.

And even then, the very first publication (in the Leningrad journal *Neva*) was no simple matter; it involved a number of neurotic compulsive maneuvers: the novel was divided into two books, and it was implied that the first book had been written a long time earlier, while the second had supposedly only just been completed. Somehow it was felt that this was important and helped (in some entirely incomprehensible manner) to pull the wool over the eyes of the Leningrad Regional Committee, which in those days no longer kept a tight stranglehold on publishers' throats but was still clutching their coattails in its sharp claws. The "first" book was published in late 1988, and the "second" in early 1989, and entirely preposterous dates of composition were given at the end of the novel. The flames of perestroika were just taking hold; new times were beginning, filled with prodigious promise but still as uncertain, unstable, and insubstantial as the light of an icon lamp fluttering in the wind.

I strongly suspect that the present-day reader is entirely incapable of understanding, let alone re-creating in his imagination, all these fears and precautionary ruses. "What's the problem?" he will ask in justified incomprehension. "What's all this fuss and bother about? Just what's so almighty shocking about this novel of yours, that you had to weave this high-tension, Frederick Forsyth–style political thriller around it?" I admit that it's not easy for me to dispel misunderstandings of this kind. The times have changed so much, and so have ideas about what is admissible and what is not in literature.

For instance, in our novel Alexander Galich is cited ("They sent the prophet up the river a short while later . . .") and naturally he is cited without any references, but in those days even a disguised allusion like this was absolutely unacceptable, in fact downright dangerous. It was a bomb planted under the editor, the editor-in-chief, the publishing house. Even from a distance, it's terrifying to imagine what the authorities could have done to a publisher if a quotation like that slipped through into print.

And what about our Izya Katzman—a unequivocal Jew, and worse still, an ostentatiously provocative Jew, one of the main characters, and moreover one who constantly lectures the central character, a Russian, like some greenhorn kid, and not only lectures him but regularly defeats him in all their ideological clashes?

And the central character himself, Andrei Voronin, a Komsomol Leninist-Stalinist, a thoroughgoing communist true believer, a champion of the happiness of the common people, who evolves with such spontaneous ease into a top-ranking bureaucrat, a smooth, lordly, self-indulgent, petty chieftain and arbiter of human destiny?

And what about the instinctive ease with which this Komsomol Stalinist becomes first the good friend and then the comrade-in-arms of an inveterate Hitlerite Nazi—and how much these apparent ideological antagonists turn out to have in common?

And the characters' seditious speculation about a possible connection between the Experiment and the problem of building communism? And the absolute ideological aberration of the scene with the Great Strategist? And the central character's utterly cynical line of reasoning about monuments and greatness? And the entire *spirit* of the novel, its atmosphere, permeated with doubts, disbelief, and a stubborn reluctance to glorify and acclaim anything?

Nowadays no reader or publisher is going to be astounded, let alone frightened, by all these themes, but back then, twenty-five years ago, when the authors were working on the novel, we constantly repeated to each other, like an incantation, "You have to write for the desk drawer in a way that makes it impossible to publish, but also makes it seem like there's nothing they can put you away for." At the same time, the authors realized that you could be put away for absolutely anything at any moment, even for improperly crossing the street, but nonetheless we were counting on the context of a "nonprejudicial approach," in which the order to put someone away has not yet been handed down from the top but is still only maturing, so to speak, down below.

The primary goal of our novel was not clear from the very beginning, but gradually assumed the following form: to demonstrate how, under the pressure of the circumstances of life, a young man's worldview radically changes, how he shifts from the position of an unshakable fanatic to the condition of a man suspended, as it were, in an airless ideological void, without even the slightest purchase for his feet. A life trajectory very familiar to the authors, and one which we consider not merely dramatic but also instructive. After all, an entire generation traveled this path over the period from 1940 to 1985.

How to live in conditions of ideological vacuum? How and what for? In my opinion this question remains highly relevant even today—which is why *City*, despite being so vehemently politicized and so categorically of its own time, potentially remains of interest to the present-day reader—provided that this reader has any interest at all in problems of this kind.